Brenda Jackson is a *New York Times* bestselling author of more than one hundred romance titles. Brenda lives in Jacksonville, Florida, and divides her time between family, writing and travelling.

Email Brenda at authorbrendajackson@gmail.com or visit her on her website at brendajackson.net

Joanne Rock credits her decision to write romance to when a book she picked up during a flight delay engrossed her so thoroughly that she didn't mind at all when her flight was delayed two more times. Giving her readers the chance to escape into another world has motivated her to write over eighty books for a variety of Mills & Boon series.

Also by Brenda Jackson

The Real Thing
The Secret Affair
Breaking Bailey's Rules
Bane
The Rancher Returns
His Secret Son
An Honourable Seduction

Also by Joanne Rock

The Magnate's Mail-Order Bride
The Magnate's Marriage Merger
His Accidental Heir
Little Secrets: His Pregnant Secretary
Claiming His Secret Heir
For the Sake of His Heir
The Forbidden Brother
Wild Wyoming Nights
One Night Scandal

Discover more at millsandboon.co.uk

HIS TO CLAIM

BRENDA JACKSON

RANCHER
IN HER BED

JOANNE ROCK

MILLS & BOON

First Published in Great Britain 2019
by Mills & Boon, an imprint of HarperCollinsPublishers,
1 London Bridge Street, London, SE1 9GF

His to Claim © 2019 Brenda Streater Jackson
Rancher in Her Bed © 2019 Harlequin Books S.A.

Special thanks and acknowledgement are given to Joanne Rock
for her contribution to the Texas Cattleman's Club: Houston series.

ISBN: 978-0-263-27182-9

0619

HIS TO CLAIM

BRENDA JACKSON

Acknowledgements

To the man who will always and forever be
the love of my life and the wind beneath my wings:
Gerald Jackson, Sr.

Special thanks to my readers who are attending
the Brenda Jackson Readers Reunion 2019 as we
cruise to Aruba. Fun! Fun! Fun! I always enjoy
spending time with you!

To all my readers who requested Mac's story.
This book is for you.

Sending congratulations to my goddaughter,
Ty'ra Malloy, who is celebrating her graduation
from Florida State University.
Your Goddy is very proud of you!

Though thy beginning was small,
yet thy latter end should greatly increase.
—Job 8:7

One

Thurston McRoy, called Mac by all who knew him, got out of his rental vehicle and slid the keys into the pocket of his jeans. There was a dark blue sedan parked in his driveway.

At two in the morning.

It looked like a brand-new luxury Lexus and had a Georgia license plate. The only people he knew who lived in Georgia were his parents. Was this their vehicle?

They would often visit Virginia to check on his wife, Teri, and the kids whenever he was away for long periods of time. With his work as a navy SEAL, he often took part in missions where he was out of communication with his family. He appreciated his parents for all they did to make his work easier on his family. However, he was surprised to see their car here, tonight. Over the last year or so, they'd begun staying at a nearby hotel whenever they came to town. Unfortunately, there were no longer any spare rooms at the McRoy house.

The last time Mac had come home, he'd discovered Teri had given Tia, their oldest daughter of nine, her own room—namely the spare room. According to Teri, Tia was at the age where she now wanted privacy from her three younger sisters, Tatum, Tempest and Tasha. But did she have to take the only spare room in the house? The one that doubled as his man cave whenever he came home?

He and Teri had always talked about buying a bigger place. Frankly, he had more than enough means to make it happen thanks to the investments he'd made on the advice of his friend and teammate, Bane Westmoreland. However, over the past several years, he'd been gone a lot, sent on several missions, and he was too hands-on to even think of letting her make such a major purchase like that without him. He knew exactly what he wanted in a home and Teri knew what she wanted. And their wants were on the opposite ends of the spectrum. She wanted a two-story home and he wanted ranch style. The fewer stairs he had to climb, the better.

Tonight, he was returning home from an eight-month-long, highly classified covert operation near Libya. During that time, he hadn't been able to let anyone, not even Teri, know of his whereabouts. He had left home in the wee hours of the morning after making passionate love to his wife, without being able to tell her where he was going or when he would return.

As a toddler he recalled sitting on his maternal grandfather's knee and listening to stories of his military days, specifically as a SEAL. His paternal grandfather had been a military man, as well, an army ranger. Although Mac's father hadn't been in the military Mac had decided early in life protecting his country was something he wanted to do. Being a SEAL had always been his dream and he'd worked hard to make that particular dream come true. Now after almost twenty years whenever he thought it was time to retire, a part of him was convinced there was one more mission, one more opportunity to defend the country he loved.

The last operation had been brutal, but all the members of his team were alive and accounted for. Now he was glad to be back home with his wife and kids, and as much as he loved his parents, he hadn't counted on having any company. He needed a cold beer and his wife. Not necessarily in that order.

He figured everyone was in bed, yet an uneasy feeling crept over him as he entered his home. He paused in the foyer. Was that the television he heard coming from the living room? Typically, Teri would be in bed before ten because she got up around six to jump-start her day.

Tatum was seven and attended a different school than Tia. Tempest was five and attended kindergarten at the same school as Tatum. Tasha, their baby, who was barely three, attended day care. He hadn't liked the idea of Tasha in day care, but Teri claimed Tasha needed to be around kids her age at least a few days a week to start developing her social skills.

Mac hadn't wanted Teri to work outside the home, either, but she'd insisted that she needed to get out of the house for a while during the day. So now she was working part-time at one of the libraries in town.

Mindful of not waking the kids, while at the same time intent on not scaring his parents, he took out his phone and texted Teri. She practically slept with the phone beside her. When the message didn't immediately show as delivered, he frowned, wondering what was wrong with her phone. He'd tried calling her earlier, twice in fact, when his plane had landed in DC. He hadn't gotten an answer either time.

What was going on?

He placed his gear down and was headed toward his bedroom when his father rounded the corner. Carlton McRoy nearly jumped out of his skin when he saw his son.

"Damn it, Mac, you trying to give me heart failure?" his father asked. "I didn't hear you come in."

Mac crossed the floor to give his father a bear hug. "You weren't supposed to hear me. I'm a SEAL, Dad."

"Why didn't you ring the doorbell?"

Mac thought that was a crazy question. "I live here. I don't need to ring the doorbell. Besides, I didn't want to wake anyone. By the way, I like your new set of wheels."

His father beamed. "Thanks. It's your mom's car. I surprised her with it as an early anniversary gift. It's been almost forty years, you know."

Yes, Mac knew. He was the oldest of two and Carlton and Alexis Youngblood-McRoy hadn't wasted any time after their wedding to start a family. He'd been born a week shy of their first anniversary. He figured he was supposed to be one and done, but his sister Kylie had been born on his parents' tenth anniversary. "That's a nice gift."

"I thought so, and Lex was more than deserving," his father said.

Mac smiled. His parents were special. There weren't two adults he admired more and they had always been great role models for him and his sister. Their interracial marriage had worked for them because they'd always said love got them together and it would be love that kept them together.

"Thurston!"

Mac glanced around and chuckled when his mother practically threw herself into his arms. "Hey, Mom," he said, placing a kiss on her cheek.

"I heard voices and thought one of the girls had awakened."

"No, it's just me and Dad. He saw me when I was headed down the hall to my bedroom to let Teri know I was home."

He still had his arms around his mother's shoulders when he felt her tense up. "Mom? You okay?" he asked, looking down at her.

He thought the same thing now that he'd thought while growing up. His mother was a beautiful woman with eyes a unique shade of blue and ash-blond hair. His father had a dark chocolate complexion, which accounted for Mac and his younger sister's skin tone being a combination of the two.

When his mother still hadn't answered his question, he turned his eyes to his father, who had the same wary expression on his face that Mac's mother wore. Releasing his arm from around his mother's shoulder, Mac straightened to his full height of six feet three inches. "Okay, what's going on?"

When his parents glanced at each other, that uneasy feeling from earlier crept over him again. Not liking it, he turned to go down the hall toward his bedroom when his father reached out to stop him.

"Teri isn't here, Mac."

Mac turned back to his father. His mother had moved to stand beside his dad. "It's after two in the morning and tomorrow is a school day for the girls. So where is she?"

His mother reached out and touched his arm. "She needed to get away and she asked if we would come keep the girls."

Mac frowned. He knew his wife. She would not have gone anywhere without their daughters. "What do you mean she needed to get away? Why?"

"She's the one who has to tell you that, Thurston. It's not for us to say."

His mother looked up at him with an uncomfortable expression on her face. His gaze left his mother and moved over to his father, who was wearing the same look.

"What's going on, Dad? Mom? Why can't you tell me the reason Teri felt she had to get away?"

"Because it's not our place to do so, son."

Mac drew in a deep breath, not understanding any of this. Because his parents were acting so secretive, he felt his confusion and anger escalating. "Fine. Where is she?"

It was his father who spoke. "She left three days ago for the Torchlight Dude Ranch."

Mac's frown deepened. "The Torchlight Dude Ranch? In Wyoming?"

"Yes."

"What the hell did she go there for?"

His father didn't say anything for a minute and then gave Mac an answer. "She said she always wanted to go back there."

Mac rubbed his hand across his face. Yes, Teri had always wanted to go back there, the place he'd taken her on their honeymoon a little over ten years ago. And he'd always promised to take her back. But between his covert missions and their growing family, there had never been enough time. Teri, who'd been raised on a ranch in Texas, was a cowgirl at heart and for a short while had competed on the rodeo circuit due to her roping and riding skills. She'd even represented the state of Texas as a rodeo queen before they'd met.

When they'd married, she had given it all up to travel around the world with her naval husband. She'd said she'd done so gladly. Why in the world would Teri leave their kids and go to a dude ranch by herself?

He knew the only person who could answer that question was Teri.

"I tried calling her twice from the airport and she's not answering her phone," he finally said, his tone truly filled with anger now.

"She probably couldn't. We talk to her every day when she calls to check on the girls. The reception at the dude ranch is not good and she has to drive into town to call out. Teri usually phones us around five every evening. I'm sure she'll be calling today as usual, so you'll get a chance to talk to her," his mother said, smiling.

He stared at his parents. Did they honestly think he intended to hang around and wait for Teri's call?

"I want to see the girls. I won't wake them, but I need to see them before I leave."

"Leave?" his father asked, looking at him strangely.

"Yes, leave."

"Where are you going?" his mother asked.

He met their gazes. "I'm going to the Torchlight Dude Ranch."

"Now?"

"Yes. Now."

Moments later, he slid open the door to his oldest daughter's room. Tia was asleep but he needed to look at her for himself to see that she was all right. He smiled as he studied her in sleep. She had her mother's mouth, but that was about it. Everything else was his. Her eyes didn't need to be open for him to know they were the exact color of his. A color so rich they looked like dark chocolate.

He'd been the one who'd chosen the name Tia for their first child and it had been Teri's decision to name all the other girls with the starting letter of *T* like his and Teri's names. Tia was determined to follow in her mother's footsteps and become a cowgirl, which was why she'd been taking horse-riding lessons since she turned five. He still didn't like the idea of her competing, though, not even in her age group, which was another thing he and Teri couldn't agree on.

Leaning down, he placed a kiss on Tia's cheek before leaving the room to check on Tatum and Tempest. Both had honey-brown eyes like Teri and favored their mother a lot. There was barely a two-year difference in Tatum's and Tempest's ages and the two were extremely close. They looked out for each other. He liked that about them. He figured that unlike Tia, they would never grow up and ask for separate rooms. They would enjoy being in each other's pockets for as long as they could. Placing kisses on their cheeks, as well, he moved to the room that was closest to his bedroom. The one where three-year-old Tasha slept.

Although he tiptoed into the room, he wasn't surprised when Tasha's eyes flew open and she stared at him a minute before a huge smile touched her lips. "Daddy!"

She threw himself into his arms and he held her. After three girls, he and Teri had been hoping for a boy, but when the nurse had placed Tasha in his arms, it hadn't mattered that he had gotten a fourth girl. Tasha looked more like him than any of the others. She was his Mini-Me.

Picking her up into his arms, he went over to the rocking chair he'd gotten for Tia, the one that had been passed down from daughter to daughter. He gazed down at his daughter and saw dark brown eyes staring back up at him.

"Tasha loves Daddy."

He smiled. "And Daddy loves Tasha."

Cradling her against his chest, he began rocking her back to sleep. Having come back from such a dangerous mission, he needed peace in his life at that moment, but he knew true peace wouldn't come until he went after Teri and found out what was going on with her. Why she'd called his parents to keep the girls so she could get away.

Other than him, his sister and his parents, Teri had no family. Her parents had died when she was young and her grandparents had raised her on their ranch in Terrell, Texas, which was a stone's throw from Dallas. When Mac had met her, the grandparents she'd adored had died and at twenty three Teri was trying to run the ranch alone. After their whirlwind romance she'd made the decision—one that he knew had been hard for her, even though she'd never complained about it—to sell the ranch and accept his marriage proposal. She'd turned in her spurs to become a SEAL wife.

It had been her suggestion that they go to a dude ranch for their honeymoon, which would be her last hurrah as a cowgirl. That had been two weeks he'd totally enjoyed, and he'd gotten to show her how well he could handle a horse, thanks to his mother's family, who'd owned a horse ranch in Ocala, Florida.

The timing of their meeting had been perfect. He'd just graduated from the naval academy three years before and was enjoying being a SEAL. It had been his intention to remain a bachelor for quite a while, but all that had changed after he met Teri.

As he continued to rock his daughter back to sleep, Mac closed his eyes, recalling the day Teri Cantor walked into his life…

Ten years ago

"Damn, Lawton, will you slow down?"

Mac glanced over at the man walking beside him. Lawton was walking so fast you'd think he was rushing to put out a fire. Against his better judgment, Mac had let Lawton talk him into coming here of all places—a rodeo—just to see a woman.

"You shouldn't walk so slow," Lawton said, grinning, not breaking his stride.

"Whatever. Now, how did you and this woman meet again?"

"We met online three months ago and officially met last month when I flew to Atlanta for the weekend. She's a photographer for the Bill Pickett Rodeo circuit. LaDorria mentioned they would be in the DC area, so I figured this would be my chance to see her again."

As they neared the entrance to the arena Lawton slowed down and so did Mac. "Is there a particular spot where the two of you plan to meet once we're inside?" Mac asked, looking around.

"Yes. She said to meet her at the booth that sells the commemorative booklets."

Ten minutes later they were there, and Lawton introduced Mac to LaDorria Clark. Mac had to admit she was an attractive woman, and just for the hell of it, he asked if she had a single friend. She quickly replied, "It just so happens I do. Her name is Teri and she's competing tonight."

LaDorria grabbed one of the commemorative booklets and flipped through to a certain page, pointed and said, "This here is Teri."

Mac figured if a man could fall in love with a photograph, then he had done so in that moment. The very beautiful woman in a cowgirl outfit was smiling for the camera and she captured his heart then and there.

"What event is she competing in?"

"Roping and barrel racing. She's the current champ in the women's division. She was also rodeo queen last year."

Mac looked at the photo again. He could definitely believe that. He figured her age was around twenty-two or twenty-three and she had the most gorgeous pair of honey-brown eyes. They were perfect for her high cheekbones and full, shapely lips. Her skin was the color of rich mocha and he loved the way the mass of curly hair fell around her shoulders.

He looked over at LaDorria. "And you'll introduce us?"

She laughed. "Yes, just as soon as the rodeo is over, and only if you cheer for Teri tonight. Like I said, she's competing."

As far as Mac was concerned, Teri Cantor didn't need him cheering for her because she had her own fan section in the stands. And she was good. So good that she won both competitive events easily. He couldn't help admiring how well she handled a horse, how skillfully she rode the animal. Nor could he fight his attraction to her—she was a beautiful woman in person and in action in the ring. And he definitely liked the way she looked in her cowgirl outfits. She had changed into a couple of different ones and each one he would claim as a favorite.

He liked the way she handled a rope and how easily her lasso fell over the cow's head. He knew that sort of aptitude came from hours of practice. That meant she was well disciplined.

Mac had heard the comments from the men around him. Men who'd made it obvious they had the hots for Teri. Some had even admitted to hitting on her and striking out. He hoped he wouldn't be one of those men.

He thought about other women he'd dated in the past. Most liked the idea of dating a military man, but none ever fancied marrying one. They'd all heard the life of a SEAL's wife was too demanding. The thought of not knowing where their husband was and when he'd be returning was just something they couldn't tolerate.

Their attitude was something he hadn't been able to tolerate, either. Although he had no intention of acquiring a wife for years to come, it still bothered him how some women thought a relationship was all about them. They had no idea that a navy SEAL wife was, in a way, serving her country, as well.

"I just got a text from LaDorria," Lawton said at the end of the rodeo. "They asked us to give them thirty minutes and then they'll meet us by that souvenir table again."

"Okay, and it looks like you're kind of serious about LaDorria," he said to Lawton.

"I am. I just hope she's serious about me."

Mac hoped she was, as well, since Lawton was a pretty decent guy.

It was almost forty-five minutes later, but Mac was convinced it was worth every minute of waiting for LaDorria and Teri to arrive. When he saw Teri Cantor walking toward them, he thought she looked even better up close and in person.

She had changed out of her riding outfit into a pair

of slacks and a blouse that made her look feminine as hell. Her hair was no longer tied back away from her face but hung in loose curls around her shoulders. He could tell the moment their gazes connected that there was interest between them and he didn't intend to let that interest go to waste.

"So, what do you think?" Lawton leaned over to ask before the two women had approached them.

Mac's response was quick and honest. "I think I'm in love."

Lawton laughed but Mac was totally serious. That was how his father claimed it had been for him when he'd seen Mac's mother for the first time, when the two had been attending classes together at Ohio State University.

Mac drew in a deep breath and didn't release it until the women had reached them. Introductions were being made by LaDorria. "Teri, I'd like you to meet a friend of Lawton's. Thurston McRoy."

Teri offered him her hand and the moment he took it, he felt…something flow through him. From the look in her eyes, he knew she'd felt it, as well.

"Nice meeting you, Thurston."

He smiled down at her. "My friends call me Mac."

She nodded. "Okay. It's nice meeting you, Mac."

"Same here." And he truly meant it.

That night they went to one of the bar-and-grills that stayed open late. He got to know her better but not as well as he wanted to. They exchanged phone numbers and stayed in touch, sometimes talking on the phone at night for hours.

They had their first official date a month later, when he'd flown to Montana to watch her perform in another rodeo. That was when he was about to be stationed in

Spain and he'd wanted to see her again before leaving the country.

They exchanged texts and phone calls whenever they could, and it was two months later that she'd told him she was thinking about selling her ranch and moving to New York. She felt that maybe it was time to put her college degree in business to good use. He'd known it would be a tough decision for her to make. From their talks, he knew how much she'd enjoyed living on the ranch.

Once she made the decision to sell the ranch it had sold quickly, and before she could pack up and move to New York, he had persuaded her to visit him in Barcelona. When she said she would, he'd made all the arrangements and had sent her an airline ticket within twenty-four hours. He had been there to pick her up from the airport and the moment he saw her again he'd known he wanted to make her a permanent part of his life.

Teri had spent two wonderful weeks with him in Spain and it was during that time that they'd shared a bed for the first time. Making love to her had been just like he'd known it would be.

She'd literally rocked his world.

The intensity of their sexual joining was powerful. It was as if her body was made for him and his for her.

Before leaving to return to the States, he'd asked her to marry him, and she'd accepted.

A month later they were married.

Bringing his thoughts back to the present, Mac opened his eyes and glanced down at Tasha. She had gone back to sleep. Standing, he placed his daughter back in her bed and then he walked out of the room.

It was time to go find his wife.

Two

Teri McRoy sipped her coffee as she stood at the window and looked out.

For miles all she could see were beautiful plains, valleys and mountains. The Torchlight Dude Ranch, located in Torchlight, Wyoming, was a luxury guest ranch on over a thousand acres just west of Cheyenne. Mac had first brought her here for their honeymoon ten years ago and had promised that one day he would bring her back.

He never had.

Knowing she needed time alone to deal with a few issues, this was the first place she'd thought of coming due to the wonderful and lasting memories she had of the time spent here with Mac. Now she was glad she had come. She missed her girls more than anything and appreciated her in-laws for their quick response in coming to look after them. Her daughters couldn't ask for better grandparents. Mac's parents were the best. She couldn't

imagine leaving the girls with anyone else right now.
But still, she was compelled to check on them every
day. She needed to hear their voices. As expected, they
would tell her they missed her—and tell her how much
fun they were having with Pop and Nana.

One of the things Teri liked most about this dude
ranch was that you didn't have to stay in the main house.
If you opted for more privacy, there were several small
cabins spread out over the thousand acres. It was beautiful. Part of the package was that you got your very
own horse to use daily and it was delivered to you each
morning. Hers was a beautiful white stallion named
Amsterdam. Over the past three days, she and Amsterdam had gotten to know each other well. She wasn't
even put off by his spirited side. Being the horse expert
that she was, she loved the challenge.

As she stood there thinking about just how idyllic
this cabin was, she knew in her heart the one thing
missing was her husband's presence. She missed Mac
and always did whenever he was gone for long periods
of time, although she tried hard not to let him know it.
He had a dangerous job and she'd known that when she
had married him. She'd also known he could be sum-
moned away at a moment's notice without being able to
inform her of where he was going or how long he'd be
gone. The longest time he'd ever been gone was seven
months. This time it had been almost nine and she was
beginning to worry. What if…

Teri shook her head, refusing to go there. Mac expected her to be strong and handle things while he was
gone. Unfortunately, this time around it was hard for
her to do that. Things had happened that she hadn't
counted on and her heart broke more and more each day.

Mac was a good man. A wonderful father and loving husband. He provided for his family, whatever their needs were. Financially, Mac's girls didn't want for anything. However, she was discovering that there were some things that money couldn't buy. Peace of mind. More good days than bad. And a marriage that was more blissful than stressful.

A part of her wanted Mac to not only be on the ranch with her to share in the beauty again, but to also just hold her and tell her everything was going to be all right. She needed him to not blame her for what had gone wrong. Even if it was the news of losing the very thing he would have wanted.

A son.

When she felt her tears fall again she drew in a deep breath. Her grief counselor had talked to her, told her that miscarriages were more common than most people even knew. She'd done nothing wrong.

The counselor didn't know the half of it.

She was not supposed to get pregnant. Mac had said that although he would have loved to have a son, when it didn't happen with Tasha that was it. He felt four kids were enough for her to handle on her own while he worked as a SEAL.

They'd talked to her doctor about getting her tubes tied, which could be done as an outpatient procedure. They'd scheduled the surgery, but he'd gotten called away. She was to keep the appointment for the procedure regardless. Then she'd gotten the call from the doctor saying results from presurgical blood work revealed she was already pregnant. There had been no way to reach out to Mac to let him know, but she figured he would eventually be happy about the news. Everything was going fine, but then four months later she'd miscarried.

She fought back the sob rattling her chest. When she was told she was having a boy she'd started thinking of names and in private moments called him TT. Tiny Thurston. She had wanted to share the news with Mac and had worried that by the time he returned, she would have had their son without him.

Wiping the tears from her eyes, she finished the rest of the coffee before forcing her mind to remember something else…namely that phone call she had received from the man who'd been her grandparents' attorney and the news he'd given her. The couple she'd sold her ranch to, close to twelve years ago now, were putting it on the market. According to the terms of the contract, they had to give her the first opportunity to buy it back. At the time she'd made that stipulation, she didn't think they would go for it, but the Jacobins had wanted to buy the ranch badly enough to agree with her terms. And of course, she'd thought they would never sell the ranch, but according to her grandparents' former attorney, because of Mr. Jacobin's failing health, they had no choice.

For her, that offer was a dream come true. She'd only been given ten days to take it and it had to be done in person. Unlike when she'd sold the ranch, she and Mac now had the means to buy it back. But the time frame meant the decision had to be made without Mac's input. So, she had.

She had weighed the advantages against the disadvantages and, in the end, she'd decided that buying the ranch would be good for her family. A bigger house. More land for their kids to spread out and enjoy. Getting back to nature. A way to supplement their income after Mac retired, if they decided to raise cattle for market.

Remembering her days spent on the ranch while

growing up, she wanted the same kind of memories for her girls. There were good schools in the area and although most of the neighbors who'd been her grandparents' friends had passed on, their heirs were people Teri had grown up with and whom she looked forward to sharing friendships with again.

Teri had figured she wouldn't be gone but for a day and appreciated her neighbor and friend Carla for agreeing to watch the kids while Teri flew to Terrell, Texas, to finalize the sale. The day after she returned to Virginia was when she began having stomach pains. Within twenty-four hours, she'd lost the baby. Although the doctor claimed her traveling had nothing to do with it, she couldn't help wondering if it had.

She'd gained the ranch she'd thought lost to her for good, but lost the baby she'd never expected to have.

Losing the baby had been hard and she appreciated her in-laws for their love and support during a very difficult time for her. She'd tried pulling herself out of the slump she'd felt herself slowly sinking into, and when she'd been nearly at her wit's end, she'd called her in-laws after her grief counselor suggested she get away for a while.

Had the home she'd repurchased been empty she would have gone there, but the sellers had asked to remain in the house three months before they were required to move out. She had no problem with that since Mac was gone on a mission and she didn't want to move their family to the ranch without letting him know what she'd done. She could just imagine Mac returning home to find a for sale sign on their home in Virginia without knowing all the details of why.

So here she was trying to deal with a number of things and wishing her husband was here with her. But then, maybe it was a good thing he wasn't. She believed he would understand how she felt about losing the baby and give her all the support and love she needed, but there was also the issue of the ranch she'd purchased. Would he understand that she'd done what she felt she had to do in the time limit she'd been given? They'd talked about getting a new house, but how would he feel about moving from Virginia to Texas? To the house that used to be her childhood home?

The other piece was that she'd paid a lot for the purchase, deciding to pay cash instead of getting a mortgage. How would Mac react when he found out she'd used their money to do so, without consulting him?

All those questions with no answers were issues that had kept her up at night.

She had endured long weeks of foreboding and her senses were filled with unease and worry about both situations. The surgery to have her tubes tied had been rescheduled and she was having apprehensions about that, and although a part of her wanted to believe that buying the ranch had been for the best, she wasn't sure how Mac would feel about it.

Being here at *this* ranch had helped soothe her mind and she didn't regret coming here, although she did miss the girls. There were so many activities to enjoy, and yesterday she'd even helped with the branding of the cattle and participated in a roundup. After today, she would only have four days left here and then she would return to Virginia, to her daughters and to wait for Mac to come home.

Mac.

Lately things hadn't been so great between them.

They seemed to argue more when he returned after being away. She didn't think it was related to PTSD; it

was just a case of two strong-willed individuals not always agreeing on certain things. It was so hard for him
to understand that while he was away, she was both mom
and dad, and when he returned it wasn't easy for her to
relinquish one of them. Usually by the time she did, he
was gone again. Why was it becoming a vicious cycle
that seemed to threaten their marriage to the point where
she'd begun feeling that she was taken for granted?

There it was again.

Questions with no answers. Problems that needed
solving.

She wanted, for the time being, to clear her mind of
all of it and to recall a time when she didn't have any
worries. Or at least not too many—for even back then
she had been trying to decide how she would run a
ranch without her grandparents. But all those years ago
she had been a young girl who'd met a man she knew
was meant to be a part of her life and she a part of his.

As she stood there sipping her coffee, her mind
drifted back to that time…

Ten years ago

Less than an hour after her friend LaDorria had introduced them, Teri had known Thurston McRoy was
a take-charge kind of man who was military through
and through.

In addition to being breathtakingly handsome, he
was also incredibly charming and outrageously kind.
She'd discovered just how kind when they'd left the
rodeo and they'd gone, along with LaDorria and Lawton, to this bar-and-grill for food and beer. He'd opened
doors for her, pulled out chairs and hadn't tried taking
control of their conversations.

He hadn't come on too strong, yet he'd managed to overwhelm her just the same. She had discovered he was someone easy to talk to, someone who had the ability to make her feel comfortable around him. It seemed LaDorria and Lawton had intentionally left them alone by staying on the dance floor. But she hadn't minded. It was during that time that she'd gotten to size him up. To see how he treated people, from the waiter who took their order to the busboy who'd come to clear off their table. He'd treated everyone with respect and gone out of his way to make their servers feel appreciated.

Although she had enjoyed that night with Mac, she hadn't been certain he would want to see her again. He'd asked for her phone number at the end of the night, but that didn't particularly mean anything. She'd long discovered that some men didn't care about dating a girl who not only loved horses but who was an ace on the back of one. Then there was her skill with a rope and her expertise with barrel racing. They preferred women who were all class and sophistication. Ones who wore expensive gowns rather than jeans and a Western shirt.

It didn't take long for her to see Mac wasn't that type of man. He had followed up their date with a number of phone calls. Her ability to rope a calf didn't bother him and he'd even said he liked how she looked in a pair of jeans. He'd told her that although he wasn't an expert on a horse like she was, he could ride and enjoyed riding because his grandparents owned a horse ranch.

Then there was the night he'd surprised her and shown up at one of her rodeos in Montana. She had won her competition that night and had felt good about it. After the rodeo she had seen him waiting on her, dressed as a cowboy with a Stetson on his head. She had found herself even more attracted to him and had offered no resistance when he'd taken her hand to lead her over to the SUV he'd rented.

"Where are we going?" she asked him when he opened the vehicle's door.

"I'm taking you somewhere to celebrate your win. You looked fantastic out there and you did an awesome job."

His words had made her feel good. Pretty darn special and she felt even more special in his company.

They'd had a lively discussion on their way to the restaurant for dinner. He'd told her more about both his grandfathers and how their time in the military had made him desire a military life of his own. She knew when his maternal grandfather had retired he and Mac's grandmother had purchased a ranch in Florida.

"I've never been to Florida."

He glanced over at her strangely when he brought the car to a stop in the restaurant's parking lot. "You haven't?"

"No. I heard the beaches there are beautiful."

He nodded. "They are, but then, Texas has beautiful beaches. I remember spending the weekend in Galveston one year."

She'd been tempted to inquire who he'd spent the weekend with but hadn't. Instead she said, "I bet you had a lot of fun."

"I did," he said, grinning over at her.

During the walk to the restaurant's door he told her more about himself and the more she got to know about him, the more she liked him. That night had pretty much established how things would be between them. She had accepted that he'd opted for a career as a navy SEAL and she knew any woman in his life would have to live with that choice. Since she'd been seriously considering selling her ranch, the idea of having a life with him, which would include traveling around the world, intrigued her.

When he invited her to Barcelona, she'd said yes right away, and those two weeks had been a game changer. She'd seen just what life with Mac would be like. As he showed her around Spain, she'd fallen in love with him. She had been a virgin and the night they'd made love for the first time was something she would never forget. He had made it special for her.

They had talked a lot, as well. Mac had told about his parents' interracial marriage and how dedicated they'd been to making it successful, remaining partners in all things. That was the kind of marriage he wanted for himself. One filled with love and commitment. She'd known that was the kind of marriage she wanted for herself, too, one where divorce would never be an option. The kind she was raised to believe her own parents had found, and the kind she knew her grandparents had shared.

Those had been the best two weeks of her life and before she left to return to the United States, he'd asked her to marry him.

Not seeing any reason to have a long engagement, they'd gotten married a month later and she had no regrets.

Teri brought her thoughts back to the present. Lawton and LaDorria had gotten married a year after Mac and Teri and they were still together, living in New Mexico with their two kids. Lawton had gotten out of the military and had gone to work for the FBI. LaDorria had expanded her love of photography and opened her own shop. Teri and Mac heard from them from time to time, and she always looked forward to the Christmas photo card they sent each year. They always looked so happy. So perfect. She didn't want to think about how things weren't so photo perfect with her and Mac.

Placing the coffee cup aside, she moved toward the bedroom. It was time to get dressed for her daily morning ride on Amsterdam.

"I'm sorry, Mr. McRoy, but your name is not on the registration. Until Mrs. McRoy gives her permission for you to be added, we can't give you a key to her cabin."

Mac forced back his anger, trying to understand the man's position. He knew the rules were due to security measures, which he should appreciate. After all, for all the staff knew, he could very well be an ex-husband intent on doing bodily harm to his wife. That wasn't the case, although he would admit his anger had only grown on the flight here. It had been his fifth flight in less than twenty-four hours. His fifth flight since his commanding officer had told the team they were free to go home and, unless there was some type of international crisis that required their SEAL team to go into action, they had the next six months on leave.

It was six months all of them needed after their last operation. Because of the success of their mission, Americans would be able to sleep safe at night, and to him and his teammates, that was what truly mattered. But for him the battle wasn't over whenever he returned home. Those were the times he had to fight to reconnect with Teri. "That's fine," he finally said, seeing the man's features relax. He knew the clerk had expected an argument and a part of Mac was raring to give him one, but what would have been the use? "Do you have any idea where she is so she can give me permission?"

"We tried calling the cabin and she's not answering, so we can only assume she's out riding. I believe she does that every morning."

"Does she come here for breakfast?"

"No. She's in one of the cabins farthest away, one with a stocked kitchen." And then, as if realizing he might have provided too much information, he added, "That's all I can tell you. I left Ms. McRoy a voice-mail message. If you'd like to sit over there and wait, I'm sure she will be returning my call shortly."

"I'd rather wait outside. That way I can walk around a bit to stretch my legs. Can I leave my gear here while I do?"

"Yes, sir, you can."

Mac handed his duffel bag to the man before turning to walk out the door. He stepped out on the porch and drew in a deep breath, appreciating the moment of breathing in good American air. He'd been in Libya too long and was glad to be home. Only thing, he wasn't home. It wasn't even close enough to home to suit him. Getting on another plane within a few hours after getting off one hadn't made his day or his night, which he was yet to have. He hadn't slept in over thirty hours.

Glancing around, he saw the changes that had been made since the last time he'd been here on his honeymoon. There was a spanking new barn that was a lot bigger than the last one had been. Even the main ranch house had gotten a face-lift. It was three times the size it was before. He'd noticed the sign that read Under New Management the moment he'd walked into the place.

He was about to step off the porch when his cell

phone rang. Recognizing the ringtone, he pulled the phone out of the back pocket of his jeans and clicked on. "Yeah, Bane?"

"You know the routine, Mac. You didn't touch base with any of us to let us know you'd gotten home."

He released a frustrated breath before saying, "I'm not home."

"Why the hell not?" That question came from another team member, Gavin Blake, whose code name was Viper. That meant in addition to Viper and Bane, Mac was on a call with the other two team members he was close friends with, as well: David Holloway, whose code name was Flipper, and Laramie Cooper, whose code name was Coop.

"Because when I got home, I discovered Teri was missing."

"Missing? What do you mean Teri was missing?" Flipper wanted to know.

"And your answer better be good, Mac. I hope she hasn't finally taken enough of your BS and left your ass," Coop added.

Mac rubbed his hand down his face. He didn't need his teammates to remind him that at times he wasn't the easiest man to get along with. "Will the four of you calm down?" Leaning against the porch post, he then told them what he knew. At least what his parents had told him. Which hadn't been much.

"And you haven't seen her yet?" Bane asked.

"No. I haven't been here but a few minutes. She's out riding and since my name isn't on her registration, they won't tell me which cabin she's staying in or give me a key."

"That's understandable," Viper said.

"Yes, but that doesn't mean I have to like it."

"Calm down, Mac," Bane warned.

Now they were the ones telling him to calm down. "I am calm. I haven't hit anything yet."

"And you won't. Listen to what Teri has to say. She must have had a good reason for taking off and leaving the kids with your folks," Coop was saying.

"Yes, and try to be understanding, no matter the reason," Viper suggested.

"And another thing," Flipper, the most recently married one of the team, spoke up to say, but Mac stopped him.

"Hold up. I don't need you guys giving me marital advice. I've been married a lot longer than any of you."

"That might be true, but you have a tendency to act like an ass at times, like you know everything," Coop said. "We've been gone awhile. Eight months, twelve days and fifteen hours to be exact. Show your woman how much you miss her, love her and appreciate her."

Mac shook his head. "Like I said, guys, I don't need your advice. I know how to handle my business."

"Your way of handling things doesn't work all the time, Mac," Viper said. "That's all we're saying."

Mac rubbed the back of his neck and felt a tension headache coming on. He never got headaches. "Duly noted. Now, goodbye."

"Hey, call us later to let us know things are okay," Bane said.

Mac rolled his eyes. "I'll think about it." He then clicked off the phone.

Teri had returned to the cabin after her morning ride and was about to go into the kitchen to prepare something to eat for breakfast when she noticed the blinking light on the cabin's telephone. She thought about ignoring it, thinking it was probably the resort manager giving her a rundown of that day's activities. However, she felt compelled to answer it anyway. Her cell phone was out of range and wasn't working. What if it was her in-laws trying to reach her?

Moving quickly to the phone, she picked it up to retrieve the message. "Ms. McRoy, this is Harold at the front desk. Please call me as soon as you get this message."

Teri pressed the number seven and Harold picked up immediately. "Harold, you called. Is something wrong?"

"No, ma'am. There's a man here who says he's your husband and has asked for a key to your cabin. Company policy restricts us from doing that. Said his name is Thurston McRoy."

Teri's heart suddenly began pounding hard in her chest. Mac was here? She drew in a deep breath. He must have returned and found she'd left and her in-laws had told him where she was? Had they also told him why she'd taken off? Did he know—

"Ms. McRoy? Is it okay to give him a key with directions on how to get to your cabin?"

She swallowed. "Is he there? If so, please let me talk with him."

"No, he's not here inside. He stepped outside."

Probably to cool off, she thought. Coming home and finding her gone had probably pissed him off. Coming after her would have made him angrier. Then being denied access to her cabin would have made the situation even worse.

"I can go outside and get him if you need to talk to him."

She drew in a deep breath. Knowing Mac, she figured that would agitate him even more. "No, that's not necessary. Please give him a key and directions on how to get here."

"Okay, I will."

When Teri hung up the phone, she drew in a deep breath.

She wouldn't have those additional three days alone here after all.

Three

Mac saw Teri the moment the SUV rounded a corner off a battered road lined with oak trees. It was in a secluded area and he wasn't sure he liked knowing she'd gotten a cabin so far from the main house. He didn't care one iota that the front desk guy had said someone from the office checked on her and all the other cabins every morning when they brought the horses.

She was dressed in Western attire and leaning against a post on a small porch. She looked good in a pair of jeans that fit perfectly over her curves, a long-sleeved shirt that, to his way of thinking, looked a little too snug over what he knew were beautiful breasts. A pair of riding boots were on her feet and a hat was covering that mass of gorgeous hair on her head.

It had been eight months since he'd seen her and at that moment his eyes couldn't help but drink in the sight of her. Damn. He'd missed her. She looked good but he couldn't let her looks and how deeply she'd been missed sway how upset he was with her right now. She owed him an explanation.

But still…

He couldn't help the flutter he felt in his heart or the yearning he felt in his soul. They might have their disagreements, some worse than others, but he knew he loved her. Always had and always would. He then thought about those disagreements. Lately there had been a lot of them. Too many. His teammates were right about him and his attitude. He tried working on it every time he returned home but Teri had a knack for making wild decisions about too many things at a time. He always looked at the whole picture. She didn't. If it was something she wanted, then she would find a way to justify them getting it. Then she would go on the defensive when he questioned her about it.

Mac didn't have a problem with her spending money—he just needed her to do so wisely. He remembered his parents' struggles over money and had sworn when he became an adult that wouldn't be him. Of course later he learned most of their struggles had been about sacrifices they'd made for him and Kylie.

Although his parents were pretty close to their own parents, during the earlier years of their marriage, neither liked hitting them up for loans when they'd encountered financial challenges. That wasn't the McRoy way. They had taught him early in life that if you make the bills, then you were responsible for paying them. That's one of the reasons he'd learned early to invest his money and had a nice bank account when he'd married Teri. He'd been intent on making sure she got all the things she needed, but not necessarily those things she wanted just for the sake of having them. There should always be money for rainy days, and then he was also focused on generational wealth to pass on to his daughters. Something his parents hadn't been able to do for him or his sister. So far the stock market had been good and those investments were better than he'd ever imagined.

Bringing the SUV to a stop in front of the cabin, he cut the ignition. She hadn't moved. She was still standing there, leaning against the post with one of those "I need to decipher your mood before I approach" looks on her face. Whether she knew it or not, usually that look told him more than what he wanted to know. Now he couldn't help wondering just what had gone on while he'd been away. He was also curious about how she had handled it and whether or not he would agree with the outcome.

He got out of the vehicle and closed the door behind him. "Teri." He suddenly felt his gut clench from the effect her honey-brown eyes had on him.

"Hi, Mac."

He tried not to focus on her lips but was powerless to do anything less. He loved her lips. The shape. The taste. And then because neither of them could help themselves after being separated for over eight months, they began moving toward each other as sexual tension sizzled between them. The moment she was there, standing directly in front of him, he pulled her into his arms. Explanations would come later. Right now, this was what he needed. The feel of her warm, feminine body pressed against his and the taste of her mouth.

He kissed her, long and deep, the woman he'd loved for over ten years. The woman who had rocked his world the first time he'd seen her. The woman who still managed to remind him what a damn lucky bastard he

was even on those days when he felt like nothing was
going right with her. She was the mother of his children
and the reason he fought hard during every covert operation. He wanted to come back to her.

To this.

He deepened the kiss and she reciprocated in kind.
He loved her taste. Always had and he figured he always would. She moaned into his mouth and he loved
the sound. It had been a while since the last time he'd
heard it. And he wanted more. More moans. More of
her body pressed against his. He wanted her naked.

She could explain the reason she'd felt the need to
come here later. He needed her now.

Sweeping her off her feet, he carried her into the
house.

Teri felt them moving and knew they were headed
for the bedroom. She had to stop him. More important,
she had to stop herself from once again being totally
overwhelmed by Mac. She wanted him and he wanted
her and, in the past, knowing that had been enough.

But not this time.

She was tired of the off-the-chart-lovemaking followed by the questions and arguments. They needed
to talk first.

When she yanked her mouth from his, he placed
her on her feet, and she scrambled out of his arms. She
looked up at him. Mac was tall, way over six feet. He
had skin the color of café au lait, dark brown eyes, solid
cheekbones, a sturdy neck and a pair of the sexiest lips
any man had a right to own. And whether he was clean-
shaven or sporting a beard on his masculine jaw like
he was doing now, Mac was a hunk. A very sensuous
and handsome hunk. He stood there, his focus entirely

on her, and the desire she saw in his eyes wasn't helping the situation.

"What's wrong, Teri?"

If only he knew.

"We need to talk first, Mac." She needed to tell him
everything. About the baby and about the purchase of
her ranch. Not to mention all the doubts she'd been
having.

He reached back out for her. "We can talk later."

That was his answer for almost everything. Whenever sexual need took over his mind on his return from a
mission, the lovemaking would come first, followed by
a good whole day of sleep. After that he'd spend quality
time with the girls. Only then would he turn his well-
rested, all-too-critical attention to her. He would ask
how things had gone while he'd been away. She would
tell him. Then the arguments would start. He would tell
her how he would have handled the situation differently
had he been there.

That "I know what's best" attitude would rattle her. It
was what had driven them to seek marriage counseling
when they'd reached the five-year mark in their marriage. He'd disliked Mr. Blum, the counselor. He hadn't
like airing their dirty laundry to a total stranger, nor
had he liked having that same person remind him that
marriage was a partnership.

"No, Mac, we need to talk now."

He eyed her warily. "Why can't it hold, baby? I
missed you. I love you and I need you, Teri. I need
you bad."

She drew in a deep breath, knowing that was that.
Those sentences got to her as much as the sight of him
standing there.

Her Mac.

Because she knew from the look in his eyes that he did need her. She never knew what happened during those covert operations, the hell he went through, or how close he came to losing his life. Any information was highly classified and he couldn't tell her, so he held it inside. But she would know how hard it had been from the intensity of their lovemaking whenever he returned. And his words were always the key. The words he'd just spoken pretty much let her know that before they talked, he felt an urgency to let himself go. To reclaim his soul and hold on to his sanity. He wanted to forget all the anguish of the last eight months. Forget it and release it in her arms.

But what about her anguish? Wanting to reclaim her soul and hold on to her sanity? What about how she'd suffered in losing the baby she'd wanted and how she inwardly blamed herself...no matter what the doctor said. She would always wonder if traveling to Texas had been the cause.

"Teri?"

Mac saying her name made her realize that she'd just been standing there, staring at him. He had extended his hand out to her. Should she take it and find peace in his arms for a little while? Could they put off talking for later like he'd suggested?

Knowing no matter how much she wanted to, probably should, she couldn't deny Mac anything.

At that moment he was as crucial to her as she believed she was to him.

She took the couple of steps to him and placed her hand in his. He pulled her closer and swept her back into his arms to carry her into the bedroom.

When he placed her on the bed, at that moment everything felt good, right, so totally perfect. For now, she would put out of her mind any thoughts of those things that had driven her here. Instead she would give her full concentration to the man whose eyes were connected to hers. The man who was looking at her with intense, deep passion and desire.

And she was returning that gaze with the same need and longing. She knew her eyes were filled with the desire of a woman who loved and appreciated the man standing beside the bed, staring down at her. He'd removed his shirt and she thought the same thing now that she had when they'd met over ten years ago. Thurston McRoy was a very good-looking man. The six-foot-three-inch hulk of a navy SEAL could be one tough-as-nails badass but also a total pushover when it came to his girls. Although she might not know the details of the covert operation he'd just left, there was no doubt he and his teammates had been through hell and back and that they had left their mark on anyone who dared to threaten the country they loved.

"Like what you see, Teri Anne?"

He always asked her that question and her response would always be the same. Yes, she loved what she saw, especially his well-built body. He exercised often, and it showed. He was slightly older than most of his teammates and claimed he had to make sure he stayed in shape to keep up with them. Whatever the reason, he wore his age of thirty-nine well. She wondered if he was still thinking of retiring from military service at forty-one. He hadn't talked about retirement much lately. Her husband was a SEAL through and through and she couldn't imagine him being anything else. A lot of people assumed SEALs were paid a huge salary for the risks they took with their lives for their country, but they weren't. Most made under sixty thousand a year. She knew for most military men it wasn't about the salary but the service. She could say the same for Mac. The only reason they had everything they needed was because of his initiative in investing alongside his friend Bane Westmoreland.

Knowing he was still waiting on her response, she said, "Yes, I definitely like what I see, Thurston McRoy."

She mostly referred to him by his given name in the bedroom. She called him Thurston and he called her Teri Anne. They felt doing so created an even more intimate bond between them. Like they were using that time to not only deepen their connection but to get to know each other all over again. Something they felt they needed to do whenever he returned from his long excursions.

Smiling, he leaned down and captured her lips and she suddenly became drenched in passion of the most provocative kind. Eight months was a long time to be without each other and their bodies were letting them know it. The starvation and greed were evident.

Their tongues tangled and swirled, feasting on each other. For a minute it was hard to decipher which one was his and which was hers. Didn't matter. They shared the hunger, the persistence, the ravenousness. Everything about Mac was delectable—his taste, the way she fit in his arms, the way their bodies meshed together like that was the way they were supposed to be.

Finally, he snatched his mouth back and began undressing her with the urgency of a man who knew what he wanted but thought he might just die before getting it. When she was totally naked, he paused a moment and stared at her with the keen eyes of a husband. A lover. A man who knew her body in and out. Could he detect that something had been there that he hadn't known about? But was there no more?

"You're beautiful as ever. I am one hell of a lucky man."

His words made a knot in her throat thicken. He could say some of the most touching things. "And I'm a lucky woman."

Her head began whirling as he lowered his mouth to hers again and captured her mouth like he had before. Like he had every right to do so and intended to take full advantage of that fact.

Breaking off the kiss he moved back to remove the rest of his clothes and she got turned on just watching him. Jeans so tight they seemed imprinted on his flesh were slid down tight, masculine thighs. Then he stood there in sexy black briefs that clearly defined how well-endowed her man was.

Her man.

Yes, he was that and he would continue to be her man. Whatever issues they were dealing with were merely hiccups along the way. They would just have to deal with them later. She just hoped that when they did, they would remember this time when they pushed all thoughts, except for each other, aside, and put their love front and center.

She watched him ease his briefs down his legs and then he moved toward her with blazing hot desire burning in his eyes. "I want you," she whispered.

"I want you, too," he whispered back, placing a knee on the bed and then drawing her to him. He kissed her again, long and deep, before releasing her and moving back from the bed to stare at her nakedness.

She felt her stomach tighten and her navel tingle. Seeing him without clothes was making heat consume her from top to bottom. "I love undressing you. I've thought of doing it every single day I was gone."

His words sparked every cell within her. Mac had the ability to use words to take her to another level. That, combined with her physical attraction to him and the sexual chemistry that always seemed to radiate between them, made what they were sharing mind-blowingly extraordinary. The thought that he could desire her so deeply always did something to her.

He moved back to the bed and whispered erotic words in several different languages as he lowered her back against the pillows. And when he towered over her, she felt overwhelmed by the look she saw in his eyes.

She felt his hard shaft sliding inside her and she cried out his name, loving the feel of him stretching her. He kept going deep until he couldn't go any more. He began moving, slow at first, then faster, thrusting in and out, and she couldn't help crying out his name again and again. Then a climax struck her, ripping through her with an impact that nearly stopped her breathing.

She heard Mac's deep growl, the prologue to his orgasmic release. His thrusts kept coming, deeper and harder, and then she felt the instant his body began trembling above her, exploding inside of her.

"Teri…" He whispered her name seconds before leaning in and taking her mouth in his, kissing her as if to make up for the eight months they'd been apart.

She returned his kiss with just as much hunger and need. When he finally released her mouth she whispered, "Welcome back, Mac."

Then he reclaimed her mouth as if to start their lovemaking process all over again.

Four

Teri raced Amsterdam across the grassy plains with her hair blowing in the wind.

She loved this and hadn't realized how much she'd missed racing until this trip. With Tia taking riding classes, Teri had saddled up to ride, as well. But racing her horse was what she liked best. She needed this and she needed it now.

She had awakened that morning feeling somewhat dazed after making love to her husband most of yesterday and last night. Her pulse pounded every time she thought of all the things they'd done. At one point she'd thought he had fallen asleep from exhaustion and she had moved to ease out of bed.

Mac had awakened quickly and looked over at her. His eyes, laden with sleep, still managed to simmer with desire, and he had then proceeded to show her once again just how badly he wanted her.

She didn't have to go into town to call to check on

the kids. Although her cell phone didn't work, Mac's special government issue security phone worked just fine. They'd talked to Mac's parents and the girls.

Late yesterday evening they had left the cabin to drive to Cheyenne for dinner and to shop at one of the Western outfitters. Mac had told her he would be staying with her for the rest of the week, which she'd figured he would. He had purchased several pieces of Western wear and he looked sexy as hell wearing a Stetson on his head.

She figured they would get the chance to have their talk during dinner but instead he steered the conversation, deliberately or otherwise, to other things. Such as the monstrosity of a house his teammate Bane Westmoreland and his wife, Crystal, were having built. They would be hosting a housewarming party when the house was completed and Mac and Teri were invited to attend.

She'd followed his line of conversation and brought him up to date on the girls, telling him how well Tia was doing with her horse-riding lessons and how Tatum had expressed an interest in gymnastics. And of course that meant Tempest was interested, too. She'd mentioned how she'd called in a plumber for the kitchen sink and about their yardman's illness. He'd listened as he always did and asked questions when he'd needed to do so.

She slowed Amsterdam down and headed back toward the cabin. This was the second time she'd ridden him today. As Mac usually did after returning from a long operation, he had slept through breakfast and lunch and there was no reason not to think he wouldn't sleep through dinner. He always said it was only when he was back on American soil he could let his guard down and sleep peacefully. Usually the girls, upon hearing their father had returned home, would camp outside the bedroom door waiting for him to wake up. He had a close relationship with their daughters and was a good dad.

As she trotted the horse back toward the cabin, she saw Mac. He was standing in the same spot on the porch where she'd been standing yesterday when he had arrived. He was leaning against the post, jeans riding low on his hips, shirtless and with a Stetson on his head.

She tightened her hands on the horse's reins. Her libido should be exhausted after the sexual activities she and Mac had participated in during the past twenty-four hours. Instead, however, it was flaring back to life. Why did he have to look so sexy standing there while sipping his coffee with his full attention on her?

She brought the horse to a stop and eased down, tying Amsterdam to the hitching post. "You're up, I see."

"Yes, and the first thing I noticed was that you were gone."

She came up the steps to him. "Did you honestly expect me to stay in bed and sleep as long as you did?"

"You used to."

She nodded, remembering. Yes, she had. That was before their first child. Whenever he came back from being gone on one of his operations, she'd been more than happy to spend her time lying in bed beside him for hours, days and nights.

She tilted her head back to look up at him. "That was the pre-babies days."

He chuckled. "You're right about that. In fact, I do believe it was during one of those sleep-ins that Tia was conceived."

It had been and him bringing that up reminded her of the reason she'd come to the dude ranch in the first place. "Yes, that's when Tia was conceived."

Neither one of them said anything for a minute and then Mac said, "I think it's time for us to talk, Teri. I need to know what drove you to come here."

As far as she was concerned it was past time. "Okay, let's talk."

She walked past him to go inside and he followed.

Mac watched his wife dust herself off before sitting down on the sofa. "Let me put this away," he said, before going into the kitchen to place the empty coffee cup in the sink.

She had wanted to tell him yesterday about whatever had driven her here and he should have been ready to hear it then. After all, he'd come home to find her gone, with his parents suddenly developing lockjaw about why she'd taken off. During the flight here, he'd been antsy about hearing what she had to say.

Then he'd seen her and the only thing he'd wanted was her. That had been pretty damn understandable since she was his wife and he hadn't seen or touched her in eight months. Teri would always be a desirable woman to him. In reality, she was a lot more. Whether she knew it or not, she was his life. He loved her so damn much. His teammates thought if she didn't know her value to him it was his damn fault for not telling her and saying it often.

Mac always felt he shouldn't have to tell her because she should know that she and the girls meant everything to him. He didn't take any chances with his life because of them. His goal for every covert operation was to come home alive and in one piece to Teri and the girls. He loved being a husband and father.

Returning to the living room, he took the seat across

from her. It didn't take a rocket scientist to see that she was nervous. Why?

"So what is it, Teri? What big-ticket item did you buy while I was gone that was over-the-top enough to send you here?"

He could tell by the surprised look on her face that he'd been right. She had bought something and whatever it was, she knew it would be something he wouldn't like. Last year it had been a new bedroom set when they'd given Tia their old one. That didn't bother him as much as the price she'd paid for it. As far as he was concerned, a bed that cost that much should have the ability to sing them to sleep. They didn't have to worry about making ends meet, but it was the principle!

"That's not the reason I came here, Mac."

He nodded. "Okay, then, what's the reason?"

For a long moment, she didn't say anything and he watched her intently. When he saw the first sign of the tears that appeared in her eyes, he was out of his chair in a flash. He went over to the sofa and pulled her into his arms. His wife wasn't a crier unless she was truly upset about something.

"What is it, Teri? What's wrong?"

She looked up at him and took a deep breath, as if trying to find the courage to tell him whatever she had to say. He tensed, not knowing what would come next, and hoped he was prepared for whatever it was.

"We agreed that we wouldn't have any more children, and I was to have that surgery."

He watched her closely. "Yes, we did agree to that. I wanted to be here with you for the surgery, but then I got that call from my commanding officer to leave immediately. You said you would have the surgery as scheduled and get the folks to come help out with the kids."

Mac watched her features and had an idea where this conversation was headed. "Are you trying to tell me that you didn't have the surgery after all, Teri?" He'd known that although they'd agreed the surgery was necessary, having another child would not have bothered her in the least.

"I couldn't."

He stared at her. "What do you mean you couldn't? We agreed that you would."

"I know, but—"

"Let me guess," he interrupted to say. "You changed your mind about having it done, right? It wouldn't be the first time you reneged on something we agreed to do, Teri. You had no right to take it upon yourself to do that. That was a decision we'd made together."

She pushed out of his arms, her features furious. "Damn you, Mac, don't you think I know what we agreed to do. I was going to have the procedure done, but like I said, I couldn't," she said, almost screaming at him, clearly getting emotional.

"Why?" he asked, crossing his arms over his chest.

"Because when I had my presurgical workup done, the doctor discovered I was pregnant."

Mac's head began spinning. He dropped his arms to his side. "Pregnant?"

"Yes, pregnant! Although a baby was something we hadn't planned, I figured you would want him."

"Him?"

"Yes, him. I carried our son for four months and then I lost him. I lost my baby. Our baby." She then rushed from the house.

He stood there in shock. Teri had been pregnant? She'd gotten as far as four months and then miscarried? Their son? Oh, my God, what had happened? Snapping out of his shock, he quickly went to the door after her. He opened it in time to see Teri galloping off on that horse.

Teri kept riding, refusing to look back when Mac called after her and rebuffing the idea of going back to finish her conversation with him. At the moment she needed to get as far away as she could in order to pull herself together. Then she would go back. But not now.

She needed to be alone.

She knew Mac and truly believed that although they hadn't planned for a baby, he would have wanted their son. It would not have mattered if it had been a boy or girl. Mac would have wanted their baby. He loved kids. They both did. They had wanted three but had decided to try a fourth time for a boy. When it turned out to be a girl, they'd decided to have no more tries and had agreed four was enough.

Teri knew the only reason Mac had gone off like he had just now was because they were still at odds with each other. He believed she would defy him at every turn, and unfortunately, over the years, she had given him reason to think so. She never did anything deliberately, but it always seemed that way to him.

What he had to understand and what she'd tried explaining to him countless times was that when he was gone, she became the head of the household. That meant she had to make decisions without him. He claimed he didn't have a problem with that, yet he never agreed with any of the choices she made.

He would return home and begin questioning her decisions. On top of that he tried to control everything, as if he could just reappear after being gone for months and disrupt their lives. While he was gone, everything ran like a finely tuned machine. When he returned, that machine would break down. He would be so glad to see the girls that he would let them get away with murder. Then when he left it was up to her to implement martial law all over again and become what the girls thought of as the mean parent. She was sick and tired of him questioning what she did and why she did it. She wanted a marriage where she felt any decision she made wouldn't be questioned and ridiculed.

She slowed Amsterdam down to a trot and noticed she was in a different area from where she'd ridden before. Ahead she saw a large windmill and remembered that when they'd come here for their honeymoon this had been a coal miners' camp. Several mines were in the area and were now deserted, their openings boarded up.

Teri had been a history major in college and recalled that years ago several settlements in Wyoming had been considered mining towns. Even now Wyoming was the largest producer of coal in the country. She wondered when these particular mines had shut down since she recalled them being in operation when she'd been here on her honeymoon.

She nudged Amsterdam toward an area where she'd seen a huge lake the first day she'd ridden out this far. That particular area had reminded her of a section of her grandparents' property, which was now legally hers again. She wished she could be happy about that but knew she couldn't until she told Mac what she'd done.

It didn't take her long to reach the lake. Getting off Amsterdam, she tied him to a tree and decided to walk around awhile to calm her nerves before heading back. Before knowing all the facts, Mac had reacted pretty angrily to her not having that procedure done. If his reaction was an example of his mood, she wasn't in any hurry to tell him about her ranch. But she would tell him. It was best to tell him everything, let him get mad and then get over it.

And he would get over it, eventually.

She just hated this pattern they had to go through whenever he returned home. Should they seek marriage counseling again? She knew that was out of the question since he'd hated it the last time. Still, Teri couldn't discount the potential of another issue being added to the mix. Like she'd told him, she hadn't gotten that surgical procedure done. What she hadn't told him was that she hadn't been taking any type of birth control since. His arrival had been unexpected and when they'd made love, he hadn't used protection. What if she was pregnant again? Had he considered that possibility yet? Would he understand why she still hadn't gotten the procedure done three months later?

No, he wouldn't understand.

The more she thought about it, the more she felt she still needed time to herself. She'd told him what had happened with the baby and for now that was enough. At a later time she would go more into details, but for now she needed her time here to deal with things without him. The best way to handle Mac was to ask him to leave.

She wasn't sure how long she'd walked around the lake, deep in her thoughts, when suddenly she heard the sound of a horse approaching. When she glanced around, she saw it was Mac. He was racing his horse toward her. Unsurprisingly, he had a fierce frown on his face.

He barely brought the horse to a stop and was off the animal's back, looking every bit the cowboy in his jeans, Western shirt, boots and the Stetson on his head. Her husband was a gorgeous man, regardless of whether he was wearing navy attire or dressed as he was now. She could see him riding the range of the forty-acre ranch they now owned.

A ranch she had yet to tell him about.

He rushed over to her. "Why did you leave like that, Teri?"

She lifted her chin. "Honestly? What else was I to say, Mac?"

He reached out and pulled her into his arms. "I'm sorry, baby," he murmured brokenly. "I'm sorry you went through that alone. I'm sorry I wasn't there for you. And I would have wanted our baby, please know that."

She fought back tears when she lifted her head to look up at him. "I know that, Mac. I never doubted that you would. But what hurts more than anything is that I lost the son we wanted." And then she buried her face in his chest and sobbed.

Mac held his wife while she cried. The sound nearly broke his heart. He felt like an ass for saying what he had earlier without knowing all the facts. And now that he did know, he hurt right along with her.

He'd always wanted a big family and so had Teri. Using sound judgment, they'd decided to stop at four. It was hard enough for Teri to handle everything alone when he was gone on his missions, without adding another child to their family. But that hadn't meant they would not have welcomed a fifth. She was a wonderful mother to his kids. He knew that. He also knew that after having four girls they'd entertained the idea of trying again for a son but had decided not to. There was no guarantee their fifth child would be a boy.

But it had been.

He gently stroked her back, wondering what had

caused the miscarriage. He was about to ask when she pushed herself out of his arms. "I need time alone, Mac. Please leave."

He shook his head. "There's no way I'm going back to the cabin and leave you out here."

"No, I don't want you to do that. I want you to leave and go back to Virginia. I'll be home in a few days and we'll talk some more then."

Mac knew he had to be looking at her like she'd lost her mind. "I'm not going anywhere and leaving you here, Teri. Whatever happens in our marriage we're in this together. We—"

"No, Mac. With you it's never really 'we.' Not really. It's what you want and what you think, and like the good wife, I fall in line. But you know what, Mac? I didn't know how much I wanted another baby until I found out I was pregnant. Then I wanted it with everything within me. I didn't care about how difficult it would be, or how you and I can't seem to agree, because I knew we would make it work."

"Teri—"

"No, you always want me to do what you want, Mac. You never ask what I want. Like how I want to work."

"That's not fair. You knew how I felt about things before we married. Is it wrong for a man to want to take care of what's his?" he asked, not liking the way their conversation was going.

"Only when you start taking our marriage for granted."

He didn't say anything for a minute and then he asked her, "And you honestly think I've done that?"

"All I know is that I woke up yesterday morning feeling sad and depressed, and a part of me wished you were here with me."

"I am here with you now, Teri. I want to spend the rest of the week here with you. We can consider it a second honeymoon. We can—"

"No, I don't need a second honeymoon, Mac. I need a marriage with a husband who won't question everything I do when he returns home. If you stay here, we will only argue…especially when I tell you about the other thing."

Mac lifted a brow. Did that mean there was more? "What other thing?"

She shook her head. "I don't want to talk about it now. I need time alone, Mac. Please go home and stay with the girls until I return. When I get back on Sunday, I'll tell you everything."

"I am not leaving."

At that moment the sound of the horses caught their attention. Both animals were fidgeting, acting anxious and prancing about as if they were trying to get away.

"I wonder what's wrong with them," she said.

"I don't know," he replied, and they moved toward the animals to find out for themselves.

Mac glanced around. Had they picked up the scent of a wolf, coyote or some other wild animal? The closer he and Teri got to the horses, the more agitated the animals seemed to get.

"Oh, my God, Mac. Look!"

The frantic sound of Teri's voice had him looking over at her. She was pointing toward the sky. He saw it. Damn.

In the distance was a gigantic tornado. It had already touched down and was swirling right in their direction.

Five

"We need to get the hell out of here!" Mac said, pulling Teri toward the horses.

"And go where? We're not going to be able to outrun that, Mac."

"I know. I recall passing several abandoned mineshafts coming here," he said, untying her horse and handing her the reins.

"But we'll be headed toward the twister," Teri said, climbing on Amsterdam's back.

"We have no choice. If we stay here, we'll be out in the open. Our chances would be better trying to get to a mine before that damn tornado does. That means we'll need to ride like hell to get there."

Teri had no problem doing that and knew Mac didn't, either. "Then let's go."

She took off and Mac kept up with her. They had to tighten their hold on the reins to control the horses.

Animals had an instinct to avoid danger and they were forcing their steeds head-on toward it.

"It's okay, boy." She leaned in to whisper to Amsterdam. "It's okay."

As if the horse believed her, he picked up speed. And even through the sense of impending doom, Teri couldn't help smiling. From the moment Amsterdam had been selected as the horse for her during her stay, she believed they had bonded.

She glanced over at Mac and knew he had gone into SEAL mode, intent on keeping them alive, regardless of the danger. She doubted he'd talked to his horse, yet the animal seemed to accept the man on his back was master and wherever he led the horse had to go, regardless of whether he wanted to or not.

"We're almost there. I can see the windmill," Mac shouted over to her. She nodded against the wind that had picked up and she refused to look toward the sky. She just refused to do so.

They reached the area and quickly got off the horses. While Teri removed the saddlebags from the animals' backs, Mac grabbed a huge, thick limb off the ground and used it to knock some of the boards from one of the mineshaft openings. She released the horses, knowing their instinct for survival would have them running away to find refuge from the storm.

After the horses raced off, Teri rushed over to Mac. "Why did you decide on this particular mineshaft?" she asked him as she began helping to move the boards aside.

"The wider opening will afford more air to circulate. It also looks sturdier than the others and the ground around here is damp. That means there's water somewhere in this shaft."

Teri glanced down at the ground. She hadn't noticed that. At that moment she looked up to see several limbs from a huge tree blown down near their feet.

"Get in. I'll take the saddlebags."

"I'll help."

Mac looked at her, opened his mouth as if he was about to protest but then changed his mind, and said, "Come on. We need to hurry."

Teri had never been in a mineshaft before and glanced around. The area inside was dark. She could barely see in front of her. When suddenly a light appeared, she saw it was the flashlight from Mac's cell phone. It shone brighter than the one on hers.

"We need to get as far away from the opening as possible."

Heeding Mac's advice, she followed him deeper and deeper into the mineshaft, recalling horror stories of miners who got trapped underground and died for lack of air. "Let's place the saddles here," he said, placing his on the ground, and she followed, placing hers there.

They walked farther into the mineshaft when suddenly the ground beneath their feet began to shake. At the same time sediment began falling from the ceiling. Mac grabbed for her and she clutched him tight while he covered her body with his. Teri knew without being told that the twister was practically above them.

Although they were midway in the mineshaft, they could see debris flying around outside the mine's wide opening. They actually saw a tree, the same one she'd been standing under earlier, ripped from its roots to tumble down to the ground. Appliances, from no telling where, had gotten caught up in the twister and were tossed effortlessly to the ground.

Mac tried to press her face into his chest so she

wouldn't see the devastation happening around them, but she looked anyway. Suddenly, the opening was covered in tree limbs, boards and other flying debris. She glanced up at Mac, and he didn't have to tell her they were trapped inside.

As if he sensed her thoughts, he leaned in close and said, "We'll be fine, Teri. Once it passes, we'll get out of here." She wanted to believe him. She *had* to believe him. They had four little ones at home who needed them.

Five minutes later, when everything went still, they knew the twister had moved on and everything was calm again. "I'm going to remove whatever is blocking the entrance so we can get out of here," Mac said.

"And I'll help you."

Mac and Teri worked together a good twenty minutes before finally accepting the inevitable. Unblocking the entrance wasn't going to be as easy as they'd hoped. In addition to the flying debris, there seemed to be something large blocking the entry. Teri had a feeling that huge windmill had collapsed.

"What do we do now?" she asked Mac. "Can you use your phone to call for help?"

Mac shook his head, obviously frustrated. "No, but the flashlight has at least eight hours of battery life. Let's use it to see if there's another way out of here."

Teri wondered if Mac actually thought there was, or if he was saying that to calm her fears. "Okay."

He didn't say anything more as they walked farther and farther into the mineshaft. Mac would pause every so often to study the walls around them, reaching out to touch a rocky surface or a wooded wall covered with thick dust. He looked around for a long moment before turning to her. "Not certain how sturdy some of these planks are we're walking on, so watch your step."

"I'll be careful, Mac."

As if he assumed she wouldn't, he took her hand in his. She started to pull it back but figured doing such a thing would be childish. He was only making sure she was okay and wasn't going to take any chances. A part of her couldn't help appreciating his protectiveness; she knew that was an ingrained part of Mac and who he was.

When she'd met him, he'd been a SEAL and she had married him knowing what that kind of life meant for her. It hadn't mattered. She had loved him. They'd been different as day and night in how they dealt with life in general but they had always managed to work through it. As their marriage had grown, so had they. But lately it seemed they were encountering more and more roadblocks. He seemed to have less faith in her ability to handle things without his input. Was this what it meant for couples to grow apart?

She glanced over at him and saw how he was walking slowly and with purpose as he continued to take in their surroundings. There was a question she had to ask him. "Mac?"

He turned to her. "Yes?"

"Is our air supply limited in here?"

He held her gaze as if he was trying to decide how much to tell her. He then said, "Yes, somewhat, but not as much as I figured it would be."

"Why do you say that?"

"Because vegetation is covering some of the rocks."

She'd noticed it, too, but hadn't thought much about it. "And?"

"And in order for anything to grow in here it would need a sufficient amount of air, water and sunshine. I figure there is water coming from somewhere, probably some underground canal. But I'm not sure about the sunshine. This mineshaft shouldn't be anything more than a black hole in the earth's surface, and I haven't figured out the atmospheric piece yet."

She nodded. "I wonder how long it's been boarded up."

He shrugged massive shoulders that she had to admit looked good in his Western shirt. "There's no telling."

They continued walking and he held tight to her hand. When was the last time they'd held hands? Honestly, she shouldn't be wondering about that now, but she couldn't help doing so. When was the last time they'd taken time to just spend together? Just the two of them, away from the kids? Whenever he returned home, he slept the first day off. After that he had to readjust to the role of husband and father and would immediately want to become king of the castle. When that happened, his attitude would clash with hers.

Then there were always the numerous activities the kids were involved with, too many for them to set aside "daddy and mommy" time. All four girls were active in something. Even Tasha had started taking piano lessons at an early age. Several people had told them they thought their youngest daughter would grow up to be a gifted pianist one day. While Mac was home it was important to him to be there and share in their training, progress and achievements. Their daily schedules were full and to take off in search of time for each other seemed like a selfish act. Now more than ever she saw how such togetherness was needed for couples.

Dr. Blum had tried to encourage them during their counseling sessions to carve out periods for themselves. They'd said they would and it was then that Mac had promised to take her on a second honeymoon to Torchlight. But they had never found the opportunity and at some point had stopped making the effort to try. Now they were here, a couple still in the same predicament they'd been when they sought Dr. Blum's services.

"Well, what do we have here?"

Skirting around boards and makeshift walls, they came upon what had once been a storage room. Shelves were stocked with several kinds of canned goods. Teri moved closer to see tuna, peaches and dry milk. There were also several huge water barrels.

Mac checked out the barrels, smiled and gave a thumbs-up. "They are full, but I suspect there's an additional water channel somewhere in here, which is even better."

Teri nodded. "What type of place do you think this was?"

He glanced over at her. "I would guess it's what they thought of as their shelter where food, water and supplies were kept. Usually, it's where they would bed down for the night when they weren't in the productive mines. I wouldn't be surprised if there are sleeping quarters somewhere in here."

Teri studied Mac. "You seem knowledgeable about mines."

He nodded. "Not as much mines as caves. Part of my duties as a SEAL is to scout and find the best place for us to hunker down whenever we're in hostile territory. A cave is where we were holed up most of the time while in Syria. Being out in the open in a camp is too risky."

He glanced around before saying, "SEALs have a knack of making caves appear inhabitable. You wouldn't believe how many times our enemies were right there, outside the entrance of the cave, and we were able to listen to their every word. Once we overheard them strategize their entire plan of attack against us."

Teri wondered if Mac realized this was the first time he'd ever talked about his work as a navy SEAL and the danger he faced. Whenever he returned home it was as if he needed to put out of his mind whatever mission he'd gone through. Like that time a couple of years ago, when he'd assumed his teammate Laramie "Coop" Cooper had gotten killed, and Mac had shut up his emotions. No matter how she'd tried, she hadn't been able to tear through the grieving wall he'd erected.

"Ready to move on?"

She looked up at him. "Ready whenever you are."

Teri didn't want to think about how differently things might have turned out if he'd left when she'd asked him to leave earlier. Or if he hadn't come after her at all. She would have tried to outrun the twister and would probably have died doing so. She had begun resenting Mac's presence, but now she appreciated it.

She tightened her hold on his hand and they moved forward, going deeper and deeper toward the back of the mine.

Teri had stopped asking questions and Mac thought that was a good thing. He hadn't given her a straight answer when she asked about how much air they had. In addition to his concern regarding lack of oxygen, he was worried about the possibility of poisonous gases in the air.

Knowing this particular mineshaft had been used as a shelter facility was a good thing. He couldn't tell for sure just how good until they checked out the place more. At least they had water and food for a while. But the uncertainty about the air component bothered him.

Nowadays most mineshafts were equipped with emergency kits that included portable devices providing a supply of breathable oxygen in case anyone got trapped underground, or should any type of poisonous gases leak into the air. Other kits contained small tanks filled with oxygen to which a miner had immediate access. He would love having either about now.

He figured this particular mine had undergone its share of digging and blasting, which accounted for the worn-looking internal structure. Typically mines, especially those used as shelters, had escape tunnels. If this one had such a thing, he was determined to find it.

He suddenly stopped when he heard a sound and immediately placed Teri behind him.

"Mac? What is it?" she asked, whispering close to his ear.

"I thought I heard something."

It wasn't uncommon for wild animals to take refuge in deserted mines. With that thought in mind, he eased his hunting knife from his pocket and immediately his stance went into an attack mode. He waited and when he didn't hear the sound again, he relaxed somewhat.

"False alarm."

"What do you think the sound was?" Teri asked him.

"Probably the shifting of the foundation. There's no telling what all has fallen in on top of us." He glanced up and wondered if there was a chance the ceiling might collapse down on them. It didn't look too solid.

Checking his watch, Mac saw it was late afternoon. Chances were the authorities were out trying to assess damage in the region. Because of the magnitude of that tornado he figured there had been extensive destruction over a wide area. He hoped everyone had time to take shelter and that there weren't any casualties. But he'd seen that tornado, had witnessed its power and knew a number of places were flattened to the ground by now.

Because the cabin Teri had reserved was so far from the main house, there was no telling how long it would take before they were missed. Would the authorities assume they were in the house and look for them there? If the horses returned without riders would that clue them in? He knew that wouldn't necessarily be the case since they'd removed the saddles from the horses' backs.

Mac knew that meant they had to assume no one would be looking for them. Not totally true. He knew a certain group would come looking for him eventually. Namely his SEAL teammates. They would know he was alive and wouldn't give up until they found him.

When he heard Teri's stomach growl he remembered how late it was and realized they'd missed a meal. They wouldn't be eating by candlelight but at least they would be sharing a meal together.

Tightening his hand on hers, he said, "Come on, let's go back to where those canned goods were and get something to eat."

Bane Westmoreland heard the beeping of his phone and recognized it for what it was. It was an alert from one of his teammates. He eased away from his wife's side, hoping not to wake her, but he wasn't surprised when her eyes flew open. He should have known that with three-year-old triplets she didn't know the meaning of sound sleep, especially since it was four in the afternoon. Early on they had learned to take a nap whenever the triplets took theirs.

"That's my SEAL phone," he said, leaning over to kiss her on the lips.

"Do you think they're calling you back for another assignment this soon? You haven't been home but two days," Crystal said, pulling up beside him in bed.

"No, that's not it. That ringtone is from one of the guys. I'll be back in a minute."

He left his bedroom to go into the kitchen, walking over several toys to do so. Glancing out the window, he could see the structure of his home that was still under construction in the distance. He and Crystal had met with the builders that day and had been told their home would be ready in a few months. They were looking forward to moving in. There would definitely be more room for their three-year-old triplets. His cousin Gemma, the interior designer in the family, would be coming all the way from Australia to decorate.

He sat down at the kitchen table and called Coop when he saw the alert had come from him. "What's up, man? I know you aren't calling again for tips on how to get your daughter to sleep." Coop and his wife, Bristol, had a four-year-old son named Laramie and a one-and-a-half-year-old daughter named Paris.

"No, that's not it. Teri and Mac are missing."

Bane sat up straight. "What do you mean they are missing?"

"I take it you haven't been watching the news."

Bane rubbed a hand down his face. "No. Crystal and I decided to grab a nap while the kids took theirs."

"Then you wouldn't know about that tornado that ripped through the outskirts of Cheyenne, namely the town of Torchlight, a little more than an hour ago. And it was a bad one. Already the death toll has reached double digits."

Bane released a whistle, as he stood to his feet. "Mac is still alive," he said with certainty.

"Yes, our tracker says he is, but they're listed as missing for now. Mac's parents called our commanding officer after they were notified Mac and Teri are among

those unaccounted for. I'm letting the others know we
need to head out for Wyoming."

Bane nodded. "I'll see you in Torchlight."

David Holloway, known by family and friends as
Flipper, glanced around the table. He was with his family, dining at their favorite restaurant in Dallas as they
celebrated his brother's announcement that he would be
remarrying in a few months. The woman his brother
was marrying was none other than a cousin of Swan,
Flipper's wife. His brother Liam had met Jamila Fair-
child at his and Swan's wedding a year and a half ago.

Everyone was happy for the couple, especially his
parents, Colin and Lenora Holloway. He knew they'd
been worried about Liam, especially after his split with
Bonnie over five years ago. He hadn't dated anyone seriously since then. He'd concentrated on being the perfect dad to his little girl.

Flipper noted the size of the Holloway family was
growing. Now it included his parents, their five sons and
four of those sons' wives, their grandkids, and Jamila,
soon to be the newest addition to the family. Flipper
and his brothers were close to his parents. Their loving
and tight-knit relationships had been the reason none of
their sons had had any qualms about settling down and
marrying. Unfortunately, the woman his brother Liam
had married the first time around had been bad news.
The only good thing that had come from the union was
their little girl.

Something else others found unique about his family
was that his father had retired as a SEAL commander-
in-chief. All five of his sons had followed in his footsteps to become SEALs, as well.

After congratulations were said by all, his father
made a toast to welcome Jamila to the family. Flipper

could tell from the huge smile on Swan's face that she was happy for the cousin with whom she shared a very close relationship. Although he and Swan made their home in Key West, they visited the family in Dallas every chance they got.

His cell phone went off and he recognized the ringtone. Excusing himself from the table, he moved to a different area to take Coop's call. He returned a few minutes later with a grim look on his face.

"What's wrong, Flipper?" his father asked him.

When all eyes went to him, he said, "That was Coop. A tornado went through Wyoming a few hours ago, not far from Cheyenne. The media is saying it's one of the deadliest to hit the area. Coop got a call from our commander-in-chief. Mac and Teri were there and now they're missing."

"Missing?" It seemed everyone at the table asked all at once.

"Yes, he and Teri were on a dude ranch there. The entire ranch was destroyed, and Mac and Teri can't be found. So they're listed as missing."

He turned to Swan. "I'm leaving tonight to go help find Mac."

"I'm joining you. I can leave tomorrow," Liam said.

"Don't leave us out." His other three brothers agreed to join them.

Flipper wasn't surprised. Because Mac had been a part of his life since his first day as a SEAL—as a teammate, another older brother and a mentor—he had won a special place in the hearts of Flipper's family members.

"Great. We'll need all the help we can get."

"What do you mean Mac is missing?" Viper asked Coop, struggling to prop his cell phone on his shoulder close to his ear, while handing their two-year-old son to his wife, Layla. His words, he noticed, had given her pause, as well.

He'd been out teaching his son, Gavin Blake IV, how to ride a pony. Gavin was at the same age Viper had been when he'd been taught to ride. He listened as Coop gave him the details about the tornado that had touched down near Wyoming, destroying the dude ranch where Mac and Teri had been staying.

"I'm calling everyone so we can get together and find Mac," Coop informed him.

"That's good. I'm leaving tonight."

"Okay. I'll see you then." Coop clicked off the phone knowing they never ceased being a team whether they were on duty or off. That was the SEAL way and for them, the only way.

Six

Mac used his knife to open the cans of tuna and thought the tin mugs from the saddlebags came in handy for water. They had turned over empty water barrels to sit on. Being the ever-efficient mom that she was, Teri never left home without a travel-size bottle of hand sanitizer and pulled it out of her saddlebag.

"This is all we have to eat for now. At least until I scope out the place to find what else might be here."

Teri glanced over at her husband. "No problem. Tuna and water are okay. Besides, I need to lose a few pounds."

"No, you don't. You look good. You always look good."

Teri smiled at her husband's compliment. He would tell her that often enough, but always when they were naked and about to make love. Never when she'd been fully dressed. "Thanks, but losing a few pounds won't hurt."

"If you say so."

She glanced over at him to see what changes she could notice since he'd left eight months ago. There were always invisible changes she wouldn't know about, so for now she would concentrate on the visible ones. He looked more built than ever. Even more alluring. She thought the same thing now that she'd thought when she'd first seen him that night at the rodeo: Thurston McRoy was a handsome man with rakish good looks.

Ten and a half years of marriage hadn't lessened her desire for him, not when he took such good care of himself. But then, he really didn't have a choice. Being a SEAL, especially a member of Team Six, the most highly trained elite forces in the US military, meant being physically fit at all times, and he was certainly that.

Facial hair used to annoy him, but because of the covert operations he'd been involved in lately, a beard had become the norm. However, as soon as he returned home, he would shave. Evidently, coming directly after her had robbed him of the time to do so.

"Is something wrong, Teri? You're staring at me."

She met his gaze. "No. I didn't mean to stare. Just trying to see any changes."

He shrugged. "Why do you expect there will be any?"

Now it was her time to shrug, although she could tell him of a few reasons. Like the time he'd gotten stabbed and hadn't told her until she'd seen the wound for herself. Or that time a bullet had grazed his ear. However, she wouldn't bring any of that up. "No reason."

Things got quiet between them as they ate and she was determined not to let him catch her staring again. But then she could feel him staring at her and she was tempted to glance over at him and ask why he was staring, just like he'd asked her.

It was hard, nearly impossible, not to remember all those sexual fantasies she had about him whenever he was gone. Fantasies he was usually accommodating to play out when he returned and she told him about them. So why was she not telling him about those fantasies now when she'd definitely had a few? Actually, there had been more than a few.

"What happened, Teri? How did you lose the baby? Please tell me what happened."

His words intruded into her thoughts. A part of her didn't want to talk about it, especially not now. But then, she knew he deserved to know and that now was probably the best time to tell him. They had this time alone, where neither of them could walk out. They needed to use it to talk, and she meant really talk about issues that concerned them and their marriage.

Teri wasn't sure what to say. She could tell him just what the doctor said, or she could talk about what she suspected, which the doctor claimed was just guilt and not fact. She had not been restricted from flying. And she'd given birth to four kids with no problem. The only difference between those pregnancies and her recent fifth was that she'd gotten on a plane to travel somewhere during her first four months.

She glanced over at Mac. "The doctor said it was just one of those things, that up to one in five pregnancies end in miscarriage before twenty weeks."

"And you didn't do anything different?"

Was that accusation she heard in his voice? She didn't want to believe that it was and knew she was allowing her feelings of guilt to make her defensive. "I hadn't done anything that Dr. Gleason felt would have had a bearing on the pregnancy. I told him everything I'd been doing, and according to him none of it mattered. Like I told you, he said it was just one of those things and nothing I did contributed to it."

What she'd told him was the truth. He didn't have to know about the inner turmoil within her.

"Did you see the girls while you were home?" she asked, hoping to change the subject.

Mac knew his wife well enough to know when she wasn't being totally forthcoming about something. What was it that she wasn't telling him? And why? He intended to find out in due time. He wouldn't press her about it now.

"Yes, I saw the girls. Everyone was asleep except for Tasha. I think her eyes opened the moment I walked into the room. It was as if she knew I was home."

Teri chuckled. "Figures. I think she has a built-in radar where you're concerned."

"Just like her mama has a built-in radar whenever I'm home?"

Teri didn't say anything because that much was true. Whenever Mac was home it was as if her senses needed to know where he was every second. She tried not to worry about him while he was away on an assignment, instead depending on Bane, Viper, Coop and Flipper, the four SEAL teammates he was close to, to keep him safe. She wouldn't even discount Nick Stover. Although Nick was no longer a SEAL and now worked for Homeland Security, Mac still spoke of him often and included him in the mix even now.

As far as she was concerned, those five looked up to Mac and considered him an older brother since Mac had been a SEAL a few years before them. To hear Mac tell it, he looked out for them, but she was sure it worked the other way around, as well. She was counting on it because she knew her husband could be a hothead at times, although he claimed he wasn't. But still, as much as she tried not to worry, as much as she assured herself she really didn't have to, she always did anyway.

"Yes, just like her mama has her radar," she finally said.

"So, tell me about your radar, Teri McRoy. Why are you so tuned in to me whenever I'm home?"

Teri thought that in all the years of their marriage, he'd never asked her to explain her actions whenever it came to him. Now she could speak freely and share her inner feelings about this particular topic. "I worry about you when you're home, Mac."

She knew it was silly because if anyone could take care of themselves, it was Mac. But because of her deep, unyielding need to protect him, she was very much tuned in to him. She could sense his movements. She knew it used to drive him crazy but now he'd gotten accustomed to it.

"You don't have to worry about me, Teri."

"Easier said than done. I worry about you not getting enough rest before you have to be gone again. As your wife I want to make your life better, less stressful when you come home, but it seems all I do is make it more taxing. You always concentrate on what you think I've done wrong while you were gone and not anything I might have done right."

Did he?

Mac didn't say anything as he thought about what she had said. Were her feelings of being taken for granted justified? He rubbed his hands down his face. When was the last time he'd told her how proud he was of the way she was raising their kids? Or how he appreciated how she made their house into the home he looked forward to returning to? Or better yet, how much he loved her?

Instead, he would come home and start finding fault in the changes or additions she'd made without his input, knowing there were some decisions she had no choice but to make without him.

He looked over at her. "I see what you've done right every time I return home and walk into the house, Teri. The girls are beautiful, well behaved, respectful and doing great in school. My home is my castle and you make it so. I teased you about your radar but I love your attentiveness to me."

Mac paused a moment and then added, "Even with all we have, I worry a lot about our finances. It's something I can't help doing."

She lifted her chin. "I can understand that due to your background, but do you have to be so critical? So obsessive about my decisions, Mac? Do Bane, Viper, Coop and Flipper question every single penny their wives spend?"

In a way her question irritated him because she knew the answer. "No, but then, they don't have to. Bane and Coop were born to wealth and Viper's and Flipper's families aren't exactly poor, Teri. My parents were still paying for student loans when me and my sister were born. There was no money for my parents to inherit or to pass on to their offspring. They worked hard, provided for me and my sister, but there was never any extra money to invest in generational wealth. I'm not complaining, and I don't resent my friends, trust me.

They've helped me make more out of the little I started with. I have no problem making my own way."

As a SEAL he got bonuses, and for years he'd used a portion of those bonuses toward investments that were paying off. His daughters' college funds looked pretty damn good and he was proud of that. In truth, they had more than they needed. But he couldn't escape the feeling that it was never enough to feel secure. Though now he was feeling comfortable about getting that new house they wanted. He'd intended for that to be his surprise to her on his trip back home this time around.

"Trust me, I know, Mac." Then, as if she was ready to change the conversation to something else, she asked, "Are we ever going to get out of here? For all anyone knows we're at that cabin and may not have been missed."

He could hear the worry in her voice. "When they find out we aren't there, they'll come looking for us."

"Yes, but will they know to look for us here?"

If she meant the authorities, then no, they wouldn't know. But he knew of four men, with the help of a fifth, who would. And he felt certain they would find them. He could arrest her fears about them being found but then he would have to explain why he was so certain of it, and he couldn't do that. It was a pact the six of them had made after that time when they'd thought they had lost Coop, whose captors led everyone to believe they had killed him. Instead he'd been held as prisoner in the Syrian mountains for nearly a year. That had been the hardest year of their lives, believing Coop was dead. When they'd gotten word he was alive, their SEAL team had gone in and rescued him. Their enemies had tried breaking his body but they couldn't break his spirit. Coop had said that what had kept him going was his belief that his teammates would eventually come and rescue him. And they had.

After that, Mac and his teammates had decided they never wanted to experience again what they'd gone through with Coop. So, when Nick had told them of this microchip tracking device that was more technologically advanced than any on the consumer market, they'd signed up to be the first to try it. The microchip was inserted under the skin of their right hands and no one knew of the implant other than their commanding officer, who had to approve the procedure. With the microchip, if any of the six of them went missing, they could be tracked to their precise location by latitude, longitude and altitude. Not only that, their body movement could be detected and studied to determine pain level due to the possibilities of injuries. The chip could also sense any other life-threatening symptoms emitted through brain waves. He knew his teammates would be testing the tracker's abilities for the first time with him.

He and Teri were fine for now with enough food and water to last a couple of days. His biggest concern was oxygen—how long would they be able to breathe, shut up underground like this? He wouldn't talk to Teri about it for fear she would worry.

"Mac, will they know to look here?"

His thoughts were pulled back to Teri when she repeated what she'd asked him earlier. A question he hadn't answered. "Not sure, but it doesn't matter."

She frowned. "Why doesn't it matter?"

"Because once Bane, Coop and the others get wind that I'm missing, they'll come looking for us."

She nodded. "You're certain of that?"

"Yes."

"But will they be able to find us, or will they assume we're somewhere in the vicinity of the cabin?"

He smiled over at her. "They are SEALs, Teri. They will figure things out."

"But will they do it in time?"

"They will find us in time."

He saw uncertainty in her eyes. Reaching out, he slid her hand into his and entwined their fingers. "Trust me, baby. I won't let anything happen to you."

She lifted her chin. "And I won't let anything happen to you, either."

He wanted to laugh at that, knowing he could do a better job of protecting her than she could of him. However, if thinking that way made her feel better and worry less he would give her that moment.

Smiling over at her, he said, "Okay, that's a deal. We won't let anything happen to each other. Now let's get rid of this trash and then figure out how and where we need to bunker down for the night."

"Mac's alive and his brain waves aren't showing any signs of distress," Nick said, reading Mac's tracking data off his computer. The tracking devices the six of them wore were manned by Nick since he was the most computer savvy of the group. Any of the others could step in to be Nick's backup if it came to that, but Nick knew they were all hoping it never did.

"That's good to hear. I talked to Bane, Flipper and Viper earlier. We're all heading to Wyoming," Coop said.

"And I'm joining all of you. I'll be able to pinpoint his exact location once I get to the area and study maps of the surroundings."

"How soon do you think you'll get there?" Coop asked.

"Sometime tomorrow. I'll let Natalie know I'll be leaving and that she'll be on her own with the triplets for a while. In the meantime, I'll get periodic readings on Mac to relay to everyone."

"Thanks, Nick, and we'll see you in Wyoming."

Mac had taken her hand again and Teri didn't mind.

He did seem more capable of handling this sort of thing than she, but that didn't mean she wouldn't protect him if it came to that. She'd meant what she'd said about not letting anything happen to him, just like she knew he had meant what he'd said regarding protecting her.

"What if we don't find anything, Mac?"

He looked down at her. "There are blankets in the saddlebags."

She lifted a brow. "How do you know?"

"I checked."

When had he done that? "If we have blankets, then what are we looking for?"

"Something that could possibly serve as a cushion on the floor."

"Oh." He stopped walking and she glanced around. "This place is kind of messy, isn't it?"

He chuckled. "It's a mineshaft, Teri. Not a luxury condo."

"I know that but still you would think it could look better. A lot neater."

Mac checked the time on his watch. She'd noticed him doing that a lot. "What time is it now?" she asked him.

"Eighteen o eight."

She knew that meant 6:08 p.m. You couldn't be married to a military man without adjusting to their time, as well. Even the girls knew to convert to military time whenever he came home. It was dinnertime for most folks. She had a feeling dinner wouldn't be the same for a lot of people tonight.

"I was hoping to come across something like this sooner or later."

They had stumbled upon several horse troughs filled with hay. She was a cowgirl at heart so she understood the excitement that she heard in his voice. "Now I don't have to worry about sleeping on the hard ground tonight."

He glanced over at her. The intensity in his gaze nearly made her knees buckle. "There was never a time you would have had to sleep on the ground tonight or any night."

She lifted a brow. "So where would I have slept?"

He gave her that crooked smile she'd always thought was irresistible when he said, "I would have taken the floor and you would have slept on top of me. Granted we would have gotten little sleep."

The serious look on his face made her heart pound because she believed what he said to be true. If their bodies touched in that way, fire would consume them and they would end up making love all over the place. Finding this hay was a good thing because the thought of sleeping on top of him gave her body sensuous shivers. Had she been tempted to sleep on him, she would be pregnant by the time they woke up tomorrow.

In the back of her mind, and slowly coming to the front, were memories of past lovemaking sessions with him. They would start off mating like rabbits because of the length of time they'd been apart. Then, after getting an hour or two of exhausted sleep, they would start another bout of lovemaking, proving how obsessed they were with each other and just how much they had missed each other.

It was during that second, slower time that they would try the positions their creative minds came up with. Just thinking of a few of those positions now actually brought color to her cheeks.

Mac thought it was rather cute that he could make his wife blush after ten years and four kids. No…five kids, he thought, feeling the loss of the one he hadn't known. His son. She had carried him inside her for four months, which meant she had gotten to spend time with him, develop a bond. Mac regretted he hadn't even been there to give her a tummy rub or to place his ear to her belly to hear his child moving inside her.

He had missed out on all those things.

"Well, now that won't be necessary."

He glanced back over at her and forced a wry smile to his lips. "You can still lie on top of me, though."

She met his gaze. "Like I said, that won't be necessary."

"Maybe not necessary but better."

Although the flashlight from his cell phone was holding its own, there wasn't a lot of light. But it was enough to see her. He thought now what he'd thought the first time he'd seen Teri. His wife was a stunner.

Not only that, she was a pretty damn intelligent woman to boot. And he couldn't forget what a great body she had. Slim waist, luscious hips, mouthwatering breasts and one hell of an ass. Whether she knew it or not, thoughts of her kept him going. Made him appreciate being a man.

A man who always returned home to her.

Then why did they argue so much when he got there?

He remembered what that marriage counselor had told him. He was a man who seemed programmed to sweat the small stuff. He knew that was true. He'd tried to change and for a little while he had. Just until his next assignment. When he'd returned home, he'd slowly slipped back into his old ways.

"Better for what, Mac?"

It was hard to stay focused around her. "Better when we make love again." He couldn't think of any better way to pass the time. He glanced over at all that hay. It would certainly serve a good purpose.

"We won't be making love again."

His head snapped around to look at her. "Excuse me?"

She drew in a deep breath and those luscious breasts moved in a tantalizing way when she did so. "I said we won't be making love again. We can't."

Hmm, maybe he needed to refresh her memory.

"We did. Yesterday. Last night. Before daylight this morning."

She nervously nibbled on her bottom lip. That delicious bottom lip. Intrigued, he studied her. He hadn't seen her do that in a while. She was uptight about something. What?

"I know but we can't do it again."

He lifted a brow. "Why? Last time I looked we were married, which means we can do just about anything, Teri."

"But we shouldn't have."

He heard the agitation in her brusque tone. What the hell was going on here? An awkward silence ensued between them as he looked at her. He was tempted to check her forehead for a possible fever. He'd never, ever recalled a time when they had to put the brakes on making love. They both enjoyed it.

"There must be a reason you think that, Teri," he said in what he hoped was his calmest voice. "You want to explain it to me?"

She didn't say anything for a minute. "There are two reasons, Mac. First, making love only serves as a Band-Aid on a festering wound between us. It's time to stop resorting to temporary solutions and try to heal the wound."

She made it sound like what was going on between them was something they couldn't work out. She had committed herself to his way of life when they married. It had been her choice to agree to move around the world whenever he got a new assignment, her choice to forgo her career to advance his. She'd always seemed understanding of those times he hadn't been there for special occasions and holidays and had done a great job of holding it together for him and their family.

"We'll get through this, Teri."

"How? By making love? I'm tired of you thinking that's all it will take. What about my feelings, Mac? I need more from you than sex. I need for you to understand my feelings, trust my decisions, respect my role not only when you're gone but also when you return home. I need to feel appreciated and like I'm not being taken for granted."

He took in everything she'd said. "Okay, now what's the other reason?"

She nibbled on her bottom lip again before saying, "The reason is something I should have told you yesterday…before we made love."

"Then tell me now," he said, trying to keep the frustration out of his voice.

"It's me."

His gaze roamed all over her, and in his mind, she was still the sexiest woman on a pair of gorgeous legs. "What about you?"

She began nibbling on those lips once again. "Teri," he said in an impatient voice. "What about you?"

She met his gaze and held it. "I'm not on any type of birth control."

Seven

Teri watched Mac go still, as if he'd been frozen in place. He was probably standing there remembering how many orgasms they'd shared within the last twenty-four hours. Enough to make a lot of babies if science worked that way. It didn't. But it had been more than enough times to make one.

"Any reason you didn't tell me before now?"

She could give him plenty of reasons, but they would all come back to one. The main one. "I had missed you and at the time I desperately needed to connect with you."

"Okay, I can understand that."

She knew he could understand because that was the reason they would make love often whenever he came home. Time apart always made them miss each other and want each other more. They couldn't wait to connect intimately. But then when their mating frenzies were over, they would be at odds with each other over one thing or another…like they were now.

"So why didn't you restart the pill after your pregnancy? You knew I was coming home sooner or later."

Whether he realized it or not, he was questioning her actions. Again. It bothered her whenever he did that. "I had rescheduled the surgery and figured I would have it done before you returned."

"You rescheduled the surgery?"

"Yes, it's scheduled for next week. That's one of the reasons I came here. I needed to come to terms with losing the baby and to stay focused on what we'd agreed to do and what it would mean to me."

He didn't say anything for the longest time and then he said, "Did it ever occur to you after losing the baby that proceeding with the surgery was something we needed to talk about?"

She raised an eyebrow. "No, that never occurred to me, Mac. The decision had already been made by us, and I honestly didn't think it would be back up for discussion, regardless of my pregnancy. I know how you can act when I go back on any decisions we've made together."

He stared at her for a long moment without saying anything. Then he turned and grabbed a huge armful of hay before walking off.

I know how you can act when I go back on any decisions we've made together.

Teri's words hit him hard in the gut. As he made several trips back to the trough for hay, he couldn't say anything but he did dwell on what she'd said. She had done a good job of reminding him just what an ass he could be at times. An inflexible ass.

Why was it so hard for him to loosen his grip on control? Mainly because he didn't see it as control but as looking out for someone. In this case, Teri and the girls.

He'd never intended for Teri to work outside the home once they started having kids. She'd known it and had seemed fine with the thought of being a stay-at-home mom. She'd loved children as much as he did, and they wanted a houseful. Only, things were hard with a household. He didn't want to add to Teri's burden while he was away, and they'd decided to call it quits at three. Then they'd agreed for a fourth, hoping it would be a boy, but regardless, a fourth child was the limit. They had enough love and money for four, but part of him couldn't help remembering how he'd grown up. The hardship. Mentally, the cost felt high, especially with all the activities in their children's futures and the rising cost of college educations.

The decision not to have any more kids had been one they'd both been okay with. For him her unexpected pregnancy was a game changer. Maybe it should not have been, but it was. At least for him, and he felt bad that she couldn't see that.

What if he'd come home two weeks from now instead of two days ago? She would have had the surgery by then. And what bothered him more than anything was that she felt that was what he would have expected. He wished he could claim that she didn't know him at all, if she believed that, but all he could say was that she thought it because she *did* know him.

When Mac returned with the last load of hay, he glanced over at Teri and saw what she'd done. She had separated the hay into two stacks to make separate beds for them. That was quite obvious now that she'd spread the blankets over the hay. Did she honestly think they wouldn't be sleeping together?

"What are you doing, Teri?"

Without looking up she said, loud enough for him to hear, "What does it look like I'm doing?"

Mac rubbed a hand down his face in frustration. "We aren't going to have separate beds. It's going to get cold tonight."

She looked up at him. "It won't be the first time I've had to keep myself warm, Mac."

That was a low blow, he thought. Was she itching for a fight? If so, one quick way to do it was to start complaining about the time he was gone from home as a SEAL. She'd known the score when she married him.

"Fine. Suit yourself."

She would discover soon enough just how cold it got in here at night. It didn't matter one iota what season it was—autumn, winter, spring or summer—since they were practically buried beneath the earth.

"I'm turning out the light now," he said, just seconds before he did it.

"Why did you do that?" she asked and he could hear the near hysteria in her voice.

"To save the battery," he said. He figured the answer was obvious.

"I haven't gotten ready for bed."

What was there to get ready for? It wasn't as if they were at some hotel. They would be sleeping in their clothes. Tomorrow, when he hoped there would be more light, he would move around and explore. If there was another opening out of this place, he intended to find it.

He had dropped down to the bed of hay and covered up with the blanket. He could hear movement where Teri was and wondered what she was doing but decided not to ask. He was following the advice of the marriage counselor they had gone to that time. He'd said, *When you feel yourself getting angry, allow yourself time to calm down and reflect and remember. Definitely re-*

*member. You have to force your mind to recall what
drew the two of you together in the first place.*

His answer to that question was simple. It had been
Teri's smile. It didn't just touch her lips but extended
to her eyes, as well. Then it had been her body. It was
definitely a body any man would love looking at. Then
it had been her warm sense of humor.

It suddenly occurred to him that he saw less and less
of that sense of humor each time he returned home.
Why? Was any of that his fault? Probably. Just like it
was his fault that she believed she had to have that surgical procedure done despite her unexpected pregnancy.
He shifted in bed, thinking it was a damn shame he and
Teri were doing something tonight they'd never done
in the years they'd been married, which was to sleep in
separate beds while he was home.

He figured she had a lot to think about and so did
he. Tomorrow they would talk. When he heard the even
sound of her breathing, he knew she'd drifted off to
sleep and he allowed his eyes to drift closed to do the
same. And he dreamed about how he'd made love to her
that morning before she'd left to go riding.

How he'd kissed her awake with a desperation he
wasn't aware he could experience. And how she had reciprocated, letting her tongue duel with his. He'd pulled
her closer to him, not only needing to taste her but
needing to feel her all over. His hands ran all over her
naked body, down her back, before cupping her backside. He'd always loved the feel of her in his arms and
this morning hadn't been an exception. He'd been gone
for long periods of time before, but this had been one of
the longest in years. He hadn't realized just how much
he'd missed her until he'd begun making love to her.

And when he'd straddled her, the moan she'd emitted when his hard erection had slid inside of her, pressing her into the mattress, spurred him to go deeper. The moment he was buried inside her he went still, savoring the feel of his engorged flesh held tight in her warm, wet body.

It took everything he had within, his total control as a SEAL, every ounce of restraint he possessed, not to explode inside of her at that moment. He'd fought the urge to do so. It had been the questioning look in her eyes, and then her question of, "What are you waiting for?" that had made him start moving. Made him thrust hard and then harder. It was that question that had made him tip his head back and growl while appreciating how it felt to sink deeper still into her body.

More than once he had to make sure she was right there with him, especially those times when he was a mere heartbeat away from climaxing. The room had been filled with her moans as he continued to stroke nonstop inside of her. Those moans of pleasure had driven him to kiss her harder and longer, and to thrust repeatedly inside her body.

As he drifted deeper and deeper into sleep in the recesses of his dreams, he could still hear those moans.

Teri woke up. No matter how much she tried, she couldn't get warm. She shifted her position again and had a feeling her toes were frozen. She needed Mac's body heat. Point-blank, she needed Mac. Besides, she owed him an apology.

She should not have made that wisecrack about being used to keeping herself warm. That hadn't been fair to him. She'd known what he did for a living when she married him but she couldn't imagine living without him. He couldn't keep her warm when he was gone and that wasn't his fault. And whenever he was home, he not only kept her warm on cold nights, but he also made her feel loved and protected. So why was he over there and she over here?

Because they'd had one of their disagreements, the ones that were happening way too often. But this time it was serious—it had included another life, one they'd shared in making. And she knew that, like always, any decisions on how they moved forward would be shared by them, as well.

Not able to stop shivering, she stood and grabbed her cover and moved over to where Mac lay. As if he'd been expecting her, Mac pulled himself up in a sitting position and reached out a hand to her. She grasped it and he drew her close to ease down beside him. He didn't say anything. Not even "I told you so." But then, that was Mac's way whenever he was proven right. He wouldn't dig it in. He probably figured swallowing her pride was enough humiliation.

When he practically wrapped his body into hers, she immediately felt warm and couldn't help sighing. "Thanks, Mac."

"Don't ever thank me for taking care of what's mine, Teri," he whispered close to her ear, causing her body to shiver again. However, this time it was for a different reason.

Teri knew that to anyone else, his words would sound too possessive, as if she was an object he owned. She knew that wasn't the case. He was merely stating what was the truth. She was his—heart, body and soul—like he was hers. But still, that made her wonder how two people so into each other the way they were could be at odds with each other as much as they were.

They had different personalities. She got that. The

marriage counselor they'd met with for an entire three months had made sure they understood that. They'd been backsliding and now it was up to the both of them to get back on track. But the issues they were dealing with now were pretty major and he didn't know the half of it.

"Mac?"

"Yes."

"I'm sorry about what I said about you not being home to keep me warm on cold nights. I didn't mean it the way it sounded."

"No harm done."

She had found a comfortable position and was about to drift off when Mac's voice stopped her. "Teri?"

He shifted his body around to face her and automatically, she threw her leg over his thigh. Too late she realized that wasn't a good move. "Yes?"

"I'm sorry you thought I would not have understood or supported your decision to delay having the surgery. I would have."

She didn't say anything for a minute. "Dr. Gleason told me I could reschedule the surgery a month ago but emotionally, I couldn't do it. I just wasn't ready. That's why it's scheduled for next week. At least it *was*."

There was no reason to tell him that it wouldn't be happening for a couple of reasons. First of all, even if they were rescued, there was no way she would feel up to having any type of surgery done. But the most important reason was that when they'd made love they hadn't used protection. That meant there was a possibility she could be pregnant now. Why didn't the thought of that bother her? In fact, the thought of having another baby lifted her spirits.

"And now you could be pregnant again."

His words had her looking over at him. So that possibility did occur to him. "Yes. How do you feel about that, Mac?"

"How would any man feel when the woman he loves carries his child? I just worry about your burden while I'm away. And I don't want our children to want for anything."

"You have always provided for us. The girls and I have never wanted for anything."

"But I want to give you more."

She wondered if he would ever realize that "more" wasn't everything and having each other was enough. "You can only do so much, Mac."

"How do you feel about us having another child, Teri?"

"Do you want me to be truthful?"

"No, Teri. I *expect* you to be truthful."

Yes, he would. "Then my answer is that I love the idea, Mac. Tasha is getting more independent and she doesn't want to be thought of as a baby anymore. She wants to be a big girl like Tatum and Tempest. I hate seeing my babies grow up."

"But they do," he said, being the voice of reason as usual.

"Yes, they do, and I know I can't replace one baby with another when that happens, Mac."

He didn't say anything for a minute. "I just worry about you, when I'm away. And I still think about how hard I had it growing up. I know that although we agreed not to have any more kids, deep down you would have been happy having a houseful."

He was right about that. She would love to have a houseful. Being the only child had been the pits.

"Yes, but I understood, Mac."

She loved her husband and knew carefully watching their finances was something he felt responsible for doing because of his background. Even though they had plenty. That made telling him about her purchase of the ranch that much harder.

"You said you have something else to tell me. What is it?"

Since they were talking, this would be the perfect opportunity to come clean and tell him everything. But she couldn't. It was lousy timing and she wasn't ready. However, she would be ready in the morning. She promised herself.

"Let's talk tomorrow, okay? I'm feeling sleepy, Mac."

He was quiet for a long moment and then he said, "All right, we'll talk tomorrow. Go to sleep."

Teri closed her eyes, appreciating her husband's body keeping her warm.

Eight

Mac woke up the next morning and immediately noticed two things. First and foremost, his wife was sleeping soundly in his arms and her too-tempting body was pressed close to him. Second, the level of oxygen in the air had changed. He didn't need a barometer to detect that. The pressure wasn't at an alarming level; it was even one he'd expected, but he was fully aware of the change. In fact, he had even predicted the level to be lower than what it was. That meant air was seeping into the mine from somewhere, and he was determined to find where.

He figured his teammates had heard he was missing about now and would be looking for them. He believed that. He had to believe that.

He glanced down at Teri. Why did he have a feeling there was something she wasn't telling him, something she was stalling? He wouldn't bring it up again but would let her decide when the best time would be.

Hopefully, they would talk this morning as she'd said they would do. But now, while she slept, he would explore the mine without her. When he'd walked yesterday to where all that straw had been, he had felt moisture in the air. Today he would investigate where it was coming from.

Untangling their limbs, he eased from Teri's side, immediately missing the feel of her body. But separating himself from her was a good idea, especially since he'd maintained an erection all night. It wouldn't have taken much for him to break down and try coaxing her into making love with him. They'd taken a few chances already and she could very well be carrying his child.

Stretching the kinks out of his body he glanced back down at Teri again before moving away to explore the mine without her. It didn't take long for him to come to the area where they'd found all that hay. He kept moving. The deeper he went into the mineshaft, the more the air changed, and he could feel moisture, to the degree that the rock walls around him were damp in some places.

He smiled when he came across the small pool of crystal clear water. Nature never ceased to amaze him. He figured the water was a spill-off from that lake a few miles back. From the steam it generated he knew it was connected to some kind of underground heated spring.

He couldn't wait to bring Teri here. With that thought in mind, he headed back.

Laramie Cooper observed from beneath hooded lashes the man, a first responder, who was talking to Bane, Viper and Flipper. Coop had decided to hang back and check out their surroundings. He was certain that before the tornado had hit, this had been a pretty nice area. It reminded him of his spread in Texas. Now all he saw was devastation for miles. The majority of the trees were down and those left standing were barely doing so.

He suddenly turned his full concentration to the man because he'd offered his condolences, saying there was a chance Mac and Teri had not survived. The cabin where they'd been staying, as well as many others in the vicinity, had been flattened. A number of bodies had already been recovered, but not the McRoys'.

"And you won't recover them," Coop decided to say. "Thurston McRoy isn't dead."

The first responder, with an overly tired look, was about to reply to what Coop said when an approaching voice stopped the man. "I'll take over here, Floyd."

The man glanced over his shoulder, and then nodded. "Okay, Sheriff." He then walked off, his exhaustion apparent. The newcomer, who looked a little older but just as tired, faced them now and Coop quickly assessed him and concluded he was ex-military. It was his stance even under extreme fatigue. Before the man began speaking, Coop asked, "What branch of the military?"

The man turned his gaze to Coop, who'd moved to stand beside Bane, Viper and Flipper. As if he'd sized them up, he said, "I'm Sheriff Derwin Corilla, former marine." He then asked, "And you guys?"

It was Flipper who answered. "SEALs."

The man nodded, smiling. "I should have figured as much."

No one asked why. There had always been this rivalry between the navy and the marines but when it came to a mission and they were called to work together, they did. Most military men respected anyone who was willing to serve their country, no matter the branch.

Introductions were made, and Viper spoke up. "We share Coop's sentiments, Sheriff Corilla. Mac isn't dead."

Coop expected the man to ask why they were so certain. Instead he said, "I'm not going to go so far and say he isn't dead, but I don't think he or his wife were in that cabin when it came down."

"And why do you think that?" Bane asked.

Sheriff Corilla shifted his gaze to Bane. "Because we used the dogs and they didn't sniff out any bodies at the cabin. Then yesterday the two horses assigned to them to ride while they were here were found wandering the range, after having found refuge somewhere during the storm."

"They were saddled?" Viper asked.

"No, but one of my men, who is a trained horseman, checked them over and it looked as if they'd been ridden. I believe the McRoys had been out riding somewhere when the tornado hit. They must've set the horses free and hopefully found cover somewhere."

He paused and then said, "That tornado hit a vast area and we're still looking for survivors. I'm not giving up on anyone."

Coop nodded. "Not enough manpower." It was a statement and not a question.

Sheriff Corilla shook his head. "Is there ever? Right now, we're forming a search party to look for a seven-year-old kid who survived but somehow got away from his parents. So far we haven't found him."

"We're here to find Mac, but we'll be glad to help your guys out any way we can."

The man lifted a brow. "All four of you?"

Flipper grinned. "For now. To help find Mac we've called in the cavalry. A former teammate who now works for Homeland Security is on his way here, and then my four brothers who are SEALs are coming, as well. Mac's kind of special to all of us."

"Even when we have to do our best to tolerate him," Viper added, grinning, as well.

"We'll be glad to help look for that kid," Bane offered.

Corilla looked at Bane oddly, but he didn't question what he said, evidently accepting the SEALs had the rescue of the McRoys well under control. "In that case, thanks for the offer and I'll take any extra help we can get."

Viper nodded. "Then you got it."

Sheriff Corilla walked off.

Coop, Bane, Viper and Flipper glanced at each other. From their last phone conversation with Mac, they concluded that as usual, he was in need of an attitude adjustment when it came to Teri. Maybe with them stranded together they could use that time to hash out a few issues plaguing their marriage.

Nick had been monitoring Mac's brain waves via the tracker and at present, there was no reason to think he was in immediate danger. When Nick arrived later that day, he would be able to pinpoint Mac and Teri's exact location.

In the meantime, they would join that search party.

Teri woke up to the sounds of Mac and glanced around to focus directly on him. The flashlight from his cell phone illuminated the area. He was shirtless, down to his briefs and exercising. Running in place. As she watched him her blood began running in place, as well, rushing like crazy through her veins.

Although the air was cool, he'd worked himself into a hefty amount of sweat. It covered his chest and drenched his hair. She had a workout routine, as well, but her regimen was definitely not as intense as his. She would join him sometimes when he was home and knew to stick to her own pace and not try to keep up with him. That attempt would be impossible.

As she lay there, she recalled she had slept in his arms and they hadn't made love. That was a miracle in itself since she and Mac were two people with high sexual energy. But that meant he'd accepted what she'd told him. Not only did they have issues to resolve, there was a chance those issues were now compounded by a possible pregnancy.

Mac finished his sets of running in place and bent over to draw in deep breaths. She loved watching him do that, as well. She pulled herself up. "Good morning, Mac."

He glanced over at her and when he did so, those dark, piercing eyes captivated her. As usual. "Good morning, Mrs. McRoy."

Teri smiled at him. She loved it when he called her that. It was a reminder that he'd chosen her, had given her that name to wear proudly and that made her his to claim. And she liked whenever he claimed her.

"Isn't exercising wasting air that we need?"

"Air has the ability to get in and out of places where people can't. I've noticed a fluctuation in oxygen levels in here, but never anything to be concerned about. It appears higher now than when I woke this morning, so I decided to take advantage of it and work out."

"I would join you, but I don't want to get all sweaty."

He chuckled. "A little sweat never hurt anyone."

"In my case it wouldn't be a little sweat. Whenever I work out with you, I tend to sweat a lot."

He chuckled. "That's what you get for trying to keep up with me."

"Trust me, Mac. I don't try keeping up with you. I'd be crazy to try, believe me. I work at my own pace."

He gave her an admiring nod and a sensuous smile that caught her low in her stomach. "In that case, you do a pretty good job of holding your own."

"I try."

"Then come try with me. You'll be glad to know you don't have to worry about the sweat. I'll wash it off you."

She lifted a brow. "Do we have that much water to waste?"

"Yes. I found a pool of clear water on the west end of this mineshaft."

Excitement filled her. "You did?"

The corners of his mouth lifted in another smile. "I did. Come join me."

She hesitated for a minute, remembering other times they'd exercised together and how they would shower together afterward. That always led to other things. Things they were better off not doing. He knew that, yet he was inviting her to work out with him anyway, with the promise of a shower afterward. He evidently had more willpower than she did. But then, she knew he honestly did.

"Okay. My muscles are kind of sore after a few days of riding Amsterdam."

He crossed the floor and offered her his hand to help her up from the bed of hay. "You sure it's Amsterdam that has you sore and not me?"

She couldn't help the blush that spread across her features. She'd been married to this man for over ten years, yet he could still do this to her. "Now that you mention it…"

He pulled her to him when she was on her feet and wrapped his arms around her waist. Her chest was pressed against his solid one, which was drenched in perspiration. "I hope you weren't teasing about finding that pool of water."

He held her gaze. "I kid you not. When was the last time we went swimming together alone?"

"In case you've forgotten, I believe that's how I got pregnant with Tatum." She studied his features to see if her reminder would squash the desire she saw in his eyes. It didn't. In fact, she could feel the lower part of his body harden.

To further confuse her, he smiled. "I remember now. The folks kept Tia so you could join me that time in Germany."

So, he had remembered his R and R time, when he'd rented a house with a pool. She had stayed two weeks. When she'd left, she was pregnant. They had hoped for that, thinking it was time for Tia to have a sibling.

"Now we work out," she said, trying to ease from his arms.

"Not yet. I haven't kissed you good-morning yet. Do you have any idea how often I wake up whenever I'm on an operation, wishing it was your face I was waking up to see, and not my teammates'. I would give anything to be able to kiss you when it's a real kiss and not a dream. So, Teri McRoy, I hope you don't mind indulging me right now."

She swallowed while gazing up at him. They were supposed to talk this morning. She knew that. But a kiss, exercise and a swim sounded a whole lot better.

For now.

"Not at all, Mac, as long as you promise that's all it will be, a kiss."

As he lowered his head to her lips, he whispered, "I promise."

Nine

Mac was convinced he could stand there and kiss his wife forever since he enjoyed doing it just that much. He intended to make sure she enjoyed it, as well, and from the way she was kissing him back, she was.

It was times like these when he missed her the most. Times like these when he regretted being away from her and the girls as much and as often as he was. Losing the baby had been hard on her, and he of all people knew it. A part of him knew she was still going through a grieving period, a period he'd yet to share with her.

Yet, he grieved regardless. For the son he'd lost and for the wife a part of him felt he was losing.

His concentration was pulled back to her when she began wiggling her tongue all around in his mouth, something he had taught her to do years ago. It was during those times when pleasuring him was the only thing she wanted to do, and he'd been all in.

But not now. Although it might kill him, he would keep his promise. If nothing else, he now understood what she needed and he knew what he needed. There were a number of issues on the table. First and foremost, he needed to prove to his wife that she mattered. If he had made the mistake of taking her for granted, taking their marriage for granted, it was time he shaped up or shipped out. Mac had no intentions of calling it quits where his wife and family were concerned. He needed them as much as he wanted them to need him.

He reluctantly broke off the kiss and pulled his mouth back. He had to take control, both mentally and physically...especially physically. He couldn't take care of the latter until they wrapped themselves around the problems that could eventually destroy their marriage if they went unchecked.

His wife could be pregnant. He knew how she felt about that possibility because he'd asked, and she'd had no problem telling him. The one thing she hadn't asked was how he felt about it. Why? Did she think he wouldn't feel the same way?

He knew they had a lot of emotions to deal with. They were emotions he had conditioned himself not to feel.

But not anymore.

"Come on, time to join me and work out."

"You did good, kiddo."

Totally out of breath and bending over with hands resting on her knees, Teri glanced up at Mac. "Thanks. Glad you approve." She'd worked out in moderation. It was too early to tell if she was pregnant but just in case, she'd decided not to overdo anything. "I'm ready for my swim now."

"Then come with me." He took her hand in his and she tried not to think about how good it felt whenever he did that.

They didn't say anything and she wondered what he was thinking. He hadn't put his jeans and shirt back on but seemed perfectly at ease to walk through the mine-shaft in just his briefs and carrying his clothes in one hand while holding her hand with the other.

Glancing down, he asked, "How did you sleep last night?"

She smiled up at him. "Great. You kept me warm and I appreciated that. You took good care of me, Mac."

"And I always will."

For some reason his words touched her. Now if she could only get him to believe in her. But then, was she being fair wanting him to do that when she hadn't been totally forthcoming with him about what she'd done? She still had the issue of her buying the ranch between them. She still intended to tell him about it today like she had promised. But she wanted to find the right time to do so.

"So what do you think?"

She glanced up and saw the inlet, a small pool of crystal clear water. This was better than she expected. "How is this possible?" she turned to asked him.

"I figure it's part of that lake we saw a mile or so back and is a spill-off running underground. Because the water is warm, it must be connected to a hot spring, as well. I checked it out to make sure it's not a whirlpool. It doesn't look deep. You can swim, so you'll be fine."

Yes, she could swim. There had been a number of swimming holes on her grandparents' ranch. "Are you swimming, as well?" she asked, unbuttoning her shirt. She paused and glanced over at him upon realizing what she was doing. She was about to strip in front of him. He was her husband, so honestly, there shouldn't be an issue in her doing that. But there was. Could she honestly expect him not to touch her if he saw her naked? She'd never placed restrictions or limitations on their lovemaking before.

She looked over at him. "Mac?"

"Go ahead and take off your clothes, Teri. I understood what you said about us not making love until we get some issues in our marriage resolved. I won't touch you, no matter what. I do have control, you know."

Yes, she knew about his control, but he'd never had to exercise restraint when it came to her. She nodded and then, while he watched, she stripped down to her bra and panties.

She glanced over at him, saw the heat in his gaze. He gave her one of his sexy smiles and said, "Maybe I shouldn't have encouraged you to remove your clothes after all."

She returned his smile. "Too late to call it back now."

He shrugged massive shoulders before shoving away from the wall to move toward her. "I guess so. Come on, let's swim."

When they got close to the water, they dived in.

As Mac watched Teri glide through the water, he realized he had forgotten just what a skilled swimmer she was. She looked good and he was fighting every part of his desirous body. He'd done several laps and now just preferred hanging back while she did hers.

Her body was perfectly arched as she progressed through the water, moving her head from side to side as she concentrated on her strokes.

It dawned on him then how relaxed she appeared,

so carefree. Today she didn't have to be the mommy in control or the wife in demand. She could be Teri. It had been years since he'd seen her this…at peace. It was then he blamed himself for a lot of things. For not recognizing that she needed downtime. As her husband he should have taken her away somewhere, and often. Just the two of them.

They could have not only stimulated their minds but talked about a lot of things that bothered them. Parents needed "me" time, and he could see that now. She'd held a part-time job at a library for a couple of years now and he'd never even asked how she liked it. Mainly because he hadn't wanted her to work. He now saw just how unfair that was to her.

"I enjoyed that, Mac."

He blinked, realizing Teri had swum over to him. He'd been so caught up in his thoughts that he hadn't noticed her approach. "I'm glad you did." He pulled himself up over the edge and then reached his hand to help her out, as well.

"Thanks."

"You're welcome." He stepped back since standing too close to her could affect his self-control. "No towels, so we'll have to air our bodies dry."

"And risk catching pneumonia?" she asked, ringing the water out of her hair. "Do this."

He lifted a brow. "Do what?"

"This." She then demonstrated using her hands to wipe off excess water from her body and doing it in such a way that her palms appeared to act as a sponge.

Mac doubted Teri had any idea how turned on he was getting just watching her rub her hands all over herself. It was a definite turn-on, which was something he could do without right now. Not to call attention to his growing erection, he followed her lead and saw her technique was working. "How do you know about this?"

She chuckled. "Nothing top secret here. Just one of those 'mommy knows it all' things."

"I see." And in a way, he was at least beginning to see. It wasn't that he hadn't appreciated her role as the mother of his kids before because he had. However, he would admit he'd never been privy to those 'mommy things' and just how good she was at them before now.

He didn't say anything as they put their clothes back on and he didn't try to be discreet in watching her.

He'd said he wouldn't touch her; he hadn't promised he wouldn't get his fill of admiring how her body looked.

"I'm hungry now."

He smiled. "Tuna and water again. This time with peaches."

"I'll take it. My grandparents used to say beggars can't be choosers."

He laughed. "That's funny. My parents would often say the same thing. Come on, let's eat."

Sheriff Corilla smiled appreciatively. "I can't thank you men enough for what you did. I doubt little Larry Johnson will be wandering off again anytime soon."

"We were glad to help, Sheriff," Bane said. The little boy had been found alive and well, although hungry, and had been returned to his parents. "Now we could use your help."

"Certainly. What can I do?"

"This is our former SEAL team member, Nick Stover. He was able to pinpoint Mac's location."

Sheriff Corilla lifted a brow. "You did?" he asked, shaking Nick's hand.

Nick nodded. "Yes, and that's where I need your help," he said, clicking on his laptop, which immediately flared to life. Within seconds an aerial view came on the screen. "Based on the latitude, longitude and altitude I've documented, Mac's location has been pinpointed to this area."

"Information you've documented?" Corilla asked, rubbing his chin. It was obvious he was trying to figure out just how Nick had managed that. But they figured he knew it was something for which he wouldn't be getting answers, so he turned his attention to the laptop screen.

"That's Martinsville," he said. "It's a mining site that's been deserted for over five years now. I had my men check out the area and they said the tornado ripped through there pretty bad. Since the place has been deserted we had no reason to hang around."

"Evidently Mac and Teri were in the area and sought refuge in one of those mineshafts. That's where we're headed," Coop said.

"We figure there's a lot of debris in the area, so my four brothers are on their way with heavy equipment and machinery to help plow our way through," Flipper added.

Sheriff Corilla nodded. "You're going to need it. There are three shafts there, within several feet of each other. And according to my men, the windmill came down in that area and several trees were uprooted and landed on them, as well. I don't know which one your friend and his wife might be holed up inside, but I'm hoping it's not this one," he said, pointing at the mineshaft on the right.

"Why?" Viper asked.

Sheriff Corilla glanced over at him. "It contains a pool of water, a hot spring, so to speak."

Bane lifted a brow. "We have several of those on my property in Denver. Why would that pose a threat?"

"Because it's a spill-off from McKevor Lake and I understand that the runoff from the lake is blocked with fallen trees and limbs acting like a dam, impeding natural flow. That means the water has nowhere to go."

Nick stared at the sheriff. "You believe there will be flooding in the area?"

"Yes, and it's already started. But what causes grave concern with this particular mineshaft is that because of the spring inside, it will start flooding when the spring overflows, with no warning. Unfortunately, there is no high section within the mineshaft to escape the rising water. It's happened before, and a couple of unsuspecting miners lost their lives. If you honestly think this is where the McRoys are, then I suggest you get them out as soon as possible."

Ten

"Tell me about your job at that library, Teri."

She glanced over at Mac, wondering why he wanted to know more about it when her working there had been a sore point with him. Besides, he'd never before asked her about what she did at the library. Was this his lead-in question before they argued about her keeping her job?

"What do you want to know about it?"

"Anything you want to tell me."

Honestly? Did he? There was only one way to find out. "I only work three days a week, four hours a day, but I love what I do."

"Which is?"

"I'm in charge of the history section. That's great for me because of my degree in history. I get to suggest good books to the people who come to the library, about whatever part of history they are interested in. You won't believe the number of young people who come to the library wanting books on the World Wars, specifically World War II."

"Why do you think that is?"

"Not sure, but I'm just glad they are interested in it. I believe you can't fully appreciate your present until you know your past. At least that's what's my grand-dad used to say."

"I wish I could have met your grandparents. They sound like swell people."

He'd told her that several times before, when she'd told him something her grandparents had passed on to her. "And there's no doubt they would have wanted to meet you." Sadly, her mother had died when she'd been two and her father before her tenth birthday, leaving her to be raised by her grandparents.

They had been the best and when they'd died not long after she'd finished college, within the same year, it had been hard for her. Selling the ranch they'd loved had been even harder and a part of her felt she'd let them down by doing so. Now she owned it again. Would Mac understand her need to atone for those feelings of guilt? Would he understand that was one of her reasons for doing what she'd done?

"I'm glad you're doing something that you enjoy, Teri."

She looked over at him. Did he really? If he did, then that was a switch. "Why, Mac? Why are you glad now when you've always been resentful?"

"I've never been resentful, not really. I just never understood your need to work outside the home."

"And you do now?" she asked, staring at him.

He nodded. "Yes, I'm beginning to. In a way, it's no different than my need to do something I love. I wanted to be a SEAL since listening to my maternal grandfather tell me of all the things he did as one. I wanted that kind of life. The adventure. The need to protect my country. Mom and Dad didn't understand why I would pass on a football scholarship to apply to the naval academy instead."

He didn't say anything for a minute and then added, "The only other thing I needed to make my life complete was something I thought I'd never find, and that was a mate who was willing to put up with it. But then I found you. However, in creating the life I wanted, I failed to realize something."

"What?"

He studied her for a moment. "That you had dreams of your own. Dreams I expected you to forgo for mine."

Teri didn't say anything, realizing this was the first time they'd had a heart-to-heart talk on things that bothered her and that had affected their marriage. Yes, they'd sought counseling, but even then she'd felt Mac had never given those sessions his absolute all. He'd merely been placating her at the time.

"And do you know what's obvious to me now, Teri?"

"No, what?"

"That you did forgo them. And instead of appreciating your sacrifice, I scorned you every time I returned from a mission for decisions you made in my absence."

Teri couldn't let him take full blame. There were some decisions she could have given more in-depth thought to before making them. But then there were some decisions, like the purchase of the ranch, that, although made on the spur of the moment, had been a dream come true for her.

"It wasn't always that way, Mac. Even I admit there were some things I could have done differently." She paused. It was time to tell him about the ranch. She'd withheld it from him long enough. "Mac, I—"

"Wait," he said, holding up his hand. She saw his body go on full alert as he glanced around.

She glanced around, as well, wondering what had drawn his attention but knew now was not the time to ask. He was in his "ready to act" mode.

"You hear that?" he suddenly asked, quickly coming to his feet and placing his tuna can aside.

She strained her ears. "No, I don't hear anything. What do you hear?"

He looked at her. "Rushing water. Stay here." He quickly walked off.

Rushing water?

She didn't like the sound of that. Suddenly an eerie feeling passed through her. No, she wouldn't stay here. She stood, put her own tuna can aside and went after Mac.

Bane Westmoreland glanced around at what used to be a mining site. It had taken a full two hours to cut through downed trees and plow through all kinds of debris to get there. He appreciated one of Flipper's brothers for having the mind to bring several bulldozers. If it hadn't been for that equipment, they would still be miles away from here.

That tornado had done more damage than they'd thought. Since this was uninhabited land, the devastation in this section of Torchlight hadn't made the news. Nick had decisively pinpointed the mineshaft that Mac was holed up in as the one with the spill-off. Even though they didn't have concrete proof, they figured he and Teri were together. Getting them out safely from among all this rubble would be a challenge but they intended to do it.

According to Nick, who was monitoring Mac's tracker, he'd been pretty active this morning. From the timing and frequency of Mac's movements they'd concluded he'd been working out. Not surprising, since Mac could be anal when it came to fitness.

"I checked on him twenty minutes ago and he was in a relax mode," Nick was saying to them now.

"That means he hadn't detected anything," Coop surmised.

"That was twenty minutes ago, and he might have figured it out by now," Viper chimed in to say. "We need to get them out. We've seen that lake and the water has to go somewhere. Since it's not flooding aboveground, that means it will be flooding connecting outlets below. Mac has no idea that's going to happen."

"Or no way to stop it when it does," Flipper added.

Bane, like the others, knew the seriousness of what was about to happen. He was about to say something when Nick interrupted. "Hey, guys, I just got a new reading on Mac. He's on the move and his brain waves are signaling trouble."

Bane nodded, his expression serious. "Okay, guys, let's get Mac and Teri out of there and send them home to their girls."

Mac rushed quickly to where the pool was located and got halfway when the sound of rushing water increased. When he got to where the troughs of hay had been, he stopped. There was standing water in that area. "What the hell!"

He quickly moved past the troughs and when he stepped on what had been a solid floor, suddenly the board beneath him collapsed. He broke the fall by grabbing hold of a boulder, the same one he'd sat on that morning. Gripping tightly, he barely held on. There was no doubt in his mind that if he fell he would get swept away in the rushing water below.

"Mac!"

He snatched his head upward and saw Teri coming toward him. Hadn't he told her to stay put?

"Go back, Teri. There's a chance the floor might collapse under you. Water is flooding the mineshaft. You need to go back and find a high place and stay there."

"And leave you here?"

"Yes."

She frowned at him. "Not on your life, Thurston McRoy!"

"Teri..." he said in a warning tone. "Please do as I say."

"Save your breath," she said, glancing around. "Hold on, Mac. I've got an idea."

She had an idea? What kind of idea could she have? Teri needed to get her butt out of there and try to find higher ground, although he didn't recall there being any higher ground. The thought of anything happening to her had him—

Suddenly Mac felt a rope tossed around him. He glanced up and watched Teri reviving her role as a cowgirl. Twirling the rope around the air in perfect precision, she then lassoed him in with a second rope that went around his body perfectly.

Ropes? What in the world? Where did those ropes come from?

"Pull yourself out now, Mac!"

He tugged upward and found it was tight. Where had she tied the end of the rope for it to be as sturdy as it was? Knowing the answer would come soon enough, he used the rope to hoist himself back up on solid ground.

"Mac!" Teri threw herself into his arms and he held on to her tight. "I thought I was going to lose you."

He then pulled back but kept his arms around her waist. "Thanks, but I told you to stay back."

She lifted her chin. "And I disobeyed. Good thing I did."

"Where did the ropes come from?"

"Some troughs are built with a compartment underneath to hold a rope. I checked and they were there. I hadn't lassoed in a while but knew I had to do it. I tied the ends around the trough to take your weight when you pulled yourself up." She glanced around and saw the flooding waters. "What is going on?"

"Looks like the lake is flooding with the spill-off, which means we need to find higher ground."

"Is there higher ground in here?"

He had been afraid she would ask that. He took her hand when more water began flowing in around them at a high rate of speed. "Come on. If there is, we need to find it."

They were trying to outrun the water and Teri saw they couldn't. Already the water was waist-deep and just as she'd feared, there was no higher ground. She wouldn't get hysterical, but they were going to die.

At least the girls were in good hands and she and Mac were together.

He'd stopped and was looking around and she knew without him saying that there was nowhere else to go. They were back where they started, which was at the entrance, but nothing had changed and it was still blocked.

He was still holding her hand and she tightened her

hold on his. "Mac, I love you and you've been a good husband, and—"

"We will be rescued, Teri," he interrupted her to say.

She lifted a brow. "By who?"

"The guys."

She knew what guys he was talking about. His teammates. Did he really believe that? Or in their last moments of life was he trying to give her hope? "How will they rescue us, Mac?"

He shrugged as he looked at the blocked opening. "Not sure how, but they will get it done. In the meantime, I need you to stand on my shoulders."

"What? Why?"

"Because that will keep the water from getting to you until they do."

She frowned, knowing that meant the water would get to him first. "And what about you?"

"Don't worry about me. Timing is important. We could tread water, but not for long. If the guys can't save us both, at least they will have more time to save you. Now, let me hoist you up on my shoulders."

She shook her head, imagining the weight of her on his shoulders with water steadily surrounding them. "No, I won't do it."

"Don't argue with me," he said, trying to lift her up.

She pushed his hands away, although already the water was nearly up to her breasts. However, she didn't care. She would not have him risk his life to save hers. "Mac, please don't ask me to do that. What will I tell the girls?"

He reached out and caressed her cheek. "The same thing we agreed long ago to tell them if I never returned home. That I love them and will always love them. Just so you know, the same applies to their mother, as well. I love you."

Mac leaned down to kiss her. She knew it was supposed to be a brush of his lips against hers but the moment their lips touched, their passions were inflamed. It didn't matter that water was still increasing around them. Nothing mattered but this kiss and she refused to believe this was their last.

Mac finally broke off the kiss and whispered against moist lips, "And if you are pregnant, Teri, please let our son or daughter know I would have welcomed them into our world with all the love a father could give."

She fought back her tears. "Don't do this to me, Mac. You just said that your teammates are coming. Are you now doubting their abilities?"

"No. They are SEALs. They just might not have enough time to save us both and you are more important."

"Says who?"

"Says me." Then, in an unexpected move, he quickly pulled her up to sit upon his shoulders. She tried struggling free and he said, "Stay put or you'll knock me off-balance and we'll both drown."

"Don't do this, Mac. Let me down."

"No."

Mac was six-foot-three and water had already reached the upper part of his chest. Had she remained standing beside him, it would be up to her neck now.

It seemed the water was coming in faster and when she felt her backside get wet she knew the water was up to Mac's shoulders. Tears she couldn't hold back anymore began to flow.

Then suddenly, when she knew the water was close to Mac's neck, she heard him laugh out loud and say, "About time."

She glanced down from her place perched on Mac's shoulders to see one of his teammates. Flipper. Where had he come from?

"Whatever," Flipper said. "Stop being an unappreciative ass." He then glanced up at her and smiled. "Hi, Teri," he greeted, like it was a normal thing to find them trapped in a mineshaft that was quickly filling with water.

"How did you get in here?" she asked, needing to know. Mac had said they would be coming, but honestly, she truly hadn't believed him.

"We figured it would take longer to remove all the debris from the entrance, so they made an opening large enough for me to swim through," Flipper explained. "We need to hurry up and leave out the same way. Here," he said, handing her a snorkel mask and then giving Mac one, as well.

"Where is yours?" she asked him.

He gave her an arrogant smile, his blue eyes flashing. "I don't need one. Now quickly put it on."

Teri did as he said, remembering Mac's claim that Flipper, master diver, could hold his breath underwater longer than any human he knew.

"You can release Teri off your shoulders now, Mac, to put on your mask." The water was close to Mac's face and he reluctantly released her to Flipper so he could put on his mask.

"I will lead you guys out. Follow me. We need to be careful. Some of the pieces of debris floating around in the water have jagged edges."

Flipper dived into the water, and Mac motioned for Teri to follow. She dived in behind Flipper, knowing Mac was bringing up the rear.

Eleven

"**I** am so glad to see you guys," Mac said to his friends. He was surprised to see Nick as well as Flipper's four SEAL brothers. "I had no idea that the mine would flood."

"We didn't, either," Bane said, grateful their mission had been accomplished and Mac and Teri were safe.

"Had we known we would have rescued you sooner. We've been here for two days," Coop added.

Mac lifted a brow. "Two days? Then what took you guys so long?" he asked.

Viper's shoulder lifted in a careless shrug. "We assisted the sheriff in finding a little boy. That took an entire day. Besides, your brain waves were signaling you were in a pretty calm state, so we figured you and Teri could use that time to work out a few issues."

"Oh, you did, did you?" Mac said, frowning deeply.

"Yes, we did," Bane replied. "When we talked to you

the day you got here you were in a foul mood, already eating nails, shooting fire and ready to give your wife hell. We were hoping the time alone would help. Did it?"

Mac glanced over at his wife, who was being checked by one of the first responders. Damn, he loved that woman. She'd been a real trouper and he could credit her with saving his life. He looked back at his friends. "Yes, but it will be an ongoing process, guys. I admit I'm seeing things in a different light, but..."

"You'll still resort to being an ass when the mood suits you," Viper said, frowning.

Mac gave Viper a daggered look. "You act like I enjoy being difficult."

"Don't you?" Coop asked. "You've had plenty of time to clean up your act and accept Teri as your equal."

"I do accept her as my equal. Damn it, she saved my life in that mine," he snapped out.

Surprise and shock appeared on his friends' faces. "She did?"

"Yes." He then told them what happened.

"Wow," Flipper said. "It's a good thing you married a cowgirl with smarts. Some people would have freaked out."

Mac nodded. "Teri has a level head on her shoulders."

"She just doesn't know how to spend your money, right?"

Instead of waiting for his answer, his friends walked off.

Out of the corner of her eye, Teri had watched Mac talk to his friends. Even across the distance, she could feel the closeness he had with them was unlike what he had with her. Of course, it would be different since they were his friends and she was his wife, but he trusted them unequivocally. He trusted her but with conditions.

She appreciated their time together in the mineshaft. They'd ironed out a number of things that had been eroding their marriage. But they still had work to do. She still had confessions to make. And she believed they would do that work because they loved each other and neither of them wanted what they had to end.

Teri knew she still had to tell him about the ranch. She had been about to tell him when he'd detected something was wrong. Now she had to find time to discuss it with him. Right now, she was just glad they'd been rescued. She was ready to go home to their girls.

First thing she wanted to do was check into a hotel and take a good bath and wash her hair. They'd been told the cabin had been destroyed and they would be allowed to go look through the rubble to recover any of their belongings. Then there was the issue of more clothes, which meant she and Mac needed to go shopping.

For now, she didn't want her husband out of her sight. She'd come close to losing him. They'd come close to losing each other and she was still having a hard time getting beyond that fact.

"You're free to go now, Ms. McRoy."

She glanced up at the first responder, who'd been treating the minor cuts on her arm from a piece of debris. "Thanks."

She stood and glanced back over at Mac. He was now standing alone and looking at her and doing so in such a way she could feel heat stir in the bottom of her stomach. No matter what, they had shared an experience in that mineshaft that would always be there, unifying them, bonding them.

She broke eye contact with him and looked down at herself. She'd been given a blanket. His clothes were still wet and so were hers. They'd also been told the vehicles they'd driven to the ranch had been totaled. More bad news. The main ranch house had sustained a lot of damage and was now uninhabitable. But the good news was that Amsterdam and the other horse had survived the tornado. She'd been glad to hear that.

"Ready to go to the hotel?"

She looked at the man with the deep, husky voice. Her husband. "How will we leave?"

He held up a key fob. "Bane left us his rental. I figured we could go get cleaned up, buy new clothes and then return to the cabin to see what we can recover. However, I have a feeling a lot of the stuff is lost."

She had a similar feeling about that. Luckily, she'd only brought a few things with her. "What about your things?"

He shrugged. "All replaceable. Ready?"

She nodded. "Yes, I'm ready." She had already thanked Mac's teammates but wanted to thank them again. She looked round and didn't see them anywhere. "Where did the guys go?"

"They're on their way back home."

She could understand that. Like Mac they'd returned to their homes only a few days ago from their last operation. Yet they'd left their families to come here to save her and Mac. And they *had* saved them. She and Mac had been just minutes away from drowning.

"I really appreciated what they did, Mac. You are part of a wonderful team." Teri figured he already knew that but wanted to speak the obvious anyway.

"Yes, I am."

From Mac's expression Teri could tell he, too, was

filled with deep gratitude. They knew what the outcome would have been if Mac's SEAL team hadn't arrived when they had. And then for Nick Stovers and Flipper's brothers to be included in the mix was super special. She truly appreciated everyone's help.

"Yes, I'm ready to leave. I need a bath and my hair needs washing."

"I'll take care of both for you. Come on." He took her hand and headed toward the waiting SUV.

Mac glanced over at his wife as he backed the vehicle out of the parking lot. Her eyes were closed and he figured it wouldn't be long before she was asleep. She deserved to rest and he would be the first to say she'd been more than a great trouper. She'd been a real lifesaver. It was something he would never forget. His gut tightened at the thought of how she'd put her own life on the line. She had kept a level head and done what she needed to do.

His friends had given him food for thought. But he'd been doing a lot of thinking long before they'd fed him any words. The problems in his marriage wouldn't disappear with just a few days holed up in a mineshaft. It would take continuous work on their part. Especially on his.

"Mac…"

He glanced over at Teri when she said his name. She'd fallen asleep, so in sleep she was thinking about him. Such a thing touched him deeply. While at the hotel he intended to pamper her. What he hadn't told her was that thanks to the wives of his teammates, certain arrangements had already been made.

A smile touched his lips. He needed more time with

his wife and intended to get all the time he could. They would be returning home to Virginia soon.

When he stopped at a traffic light, he turned to look at her and saw how her head was resting against the back of the seat. Hair had fallen in her face and he couldn't resist the temptation to reach out and brush a few dark curls back from her forehead. He didn't stop there. The pad of his finger gently rubbed against her cheek. His action didn't wake her, didn't even make her stir. Instead she continued to sleep.

He had a stop or two to make before they got to the hotel, one place in particular.

"We're here, Teri."

Teri slowly opened her eyes. Yawning, she pulled up in her seat and looked through the car's window. "Where are we?"

"At a hotel in Cheyenne. All the ones in Torchlight were filled to capacity with so many first responders arriving. They still have a lot of people unaccounted for."

"I hope they find them. That first responder who treated me told me how your teammates helped find a little boy. That was special." Easing her seat belt from around her waist, she asked, "Are you sure we can get a room here? The place looks full, if the parking lot is any indication."

"Don't worry, we have a room."

Teri glanced over at him. Something about his words sent heat flowing through her. They had a room? It wasn't what he'd said but how he'd said it that made certain areas within her stir. "Good."

"Stay put. I'll be around to open the door for you, Teri."

Last time he'd given her such an order she'd defied

him, but not this time. She was too tired to move just yet. Swimming out of that mine hadn't been easy and she had been grateful for Flipper being in front of her and Mac at the rear. Paramedics had been there to check them over the moment they'd reached solid ground. In less than five minutes after they'd gotten out, the sheriff announced the mineshaft was filled with water from top to bottom and she'd known there was no way she and Mac would have survived.

"Do you need me to carry you inside?"

She glanced up at Mac. He'd come around the side of the car and opened the door for her. He had a store bag in his hand. "No, I can walk. You made a stop somewhere?" she asked. He reached out and circled her wrist with his long fingers. He was wearing another Stetson and she wondered where he'd gotten it when the one he'd purchased the day he'd arrived had been destroyed in the flood.

Mac smiled. "Yes, I made a couple of stops. You slept through them."

"Oh. I guess I was more exhausted than I thought."

"You've been through a lot, Teri."

She glanced over at him as they walked inside the hotel. "We both have."

Teri noted that instead of checking in at the front desk, Mac led her over to the bank of elevators. It was a beautiful hotel, one of the well-known chains. The lobby was filled with a lot of fresh flowers. She didn't know how long they'd driven to get here. This hotel wasn't located in downtown Cheyenne but on the outskirts of town.

"We don't have to check in?"

He looked down at her when they stepped inside the elevator. "No. The guys took care of it."

She wondered what else the guys had taken care of and found out when they reached their hotel room. A bottle of champagne was on ice with a card that said Compliments of Team Six. There was also a huge bag from the hotel's gift shop and another bag from a well-known clothing store in the middle of the king-size bed.

"What's this?" she asked, moving toward the bed. Although the hotel room wasn't a suite, she thought it was larger than most. It even had a small balcony instead of just a window. They were on the tenth floor and the balcony overlooked some of the most beautiful valleys and meadows she'd ever seen.

"Clothes that my teammates' wives ordered for you from a clothing store downtown. I told them what we needed and the sizes. The guys ordered clothes for me from one of those western outfitters in town. They picked everything up and delivered it here before heading out to the airport."

"Who? Your teammates?"

"Yes, thank God for online shopping."

Teri was touched by what everyone had done. His teammates and their wives. Women she'd gotten to know. "That was truly nice of them, Mac."

"Yes, it was." He tossed the bags he was carrying on the bed to join the others. "Now for your bath. You prefer the tub or a shower?"

"The shower will be fine. That way I can wash my hair." She went through one of the bags and pulled out a pair of jeans and a Western shirt. There were also underthings—bra and panties. She also had more boots and another hat. She looked at the tags on the clothing. Of course they were her size. When it came to her, Mac knew every single physical detail.

She glanced over at him. "You did good in telling them what I needed."

"I try. Now go ahead and get started on your shower. I have an important call to make and I'll be in there in a minute."

He would be in there in a minute? Did that mean he planned to join her in her shower? It wouldn't be the first time if he did, so why did the thought of him doing such a thing arouse her with anticipation?

"Oh, okay." She grabbed the underthings from the bag and quickly headed for the bathroom.

Twelve

Mac hung up the phone after ordering room service from the hotel's restaurant to be delivered in a few hours. He and Teri needed to go back to the cabin, search through the rubble to see if they could recover any of their belongings. But not today. They had more urgent and pressing business to attend to.

Going over to the nightstand, he pulled open the drawer to retrieve the bag he'd kept separate from the others. Pulling out one of several condom packets, he headed for the bathroom.

The room was steamy and although he couldn't see her, he knew Teri was somewhere behind the opaque glass wall. He placed the condom on the vanity before stripping off his clothes. Reclaiming the packet, he moved toward the shower door. All he could think of was a naked Teri, that fine body of hers and how much he needed to sink into it.

When he opened the door, she had her back to him

with her head under the sprayer as she washed her hair. But the swoosh of air as the door opened must've alerted her that she was no longer alone. He saw her body tense and go still.

"Mac?"

"Who else would it be?" he asked, placing the condom packet in the soap compartment before easing up behind her.

She relaxed her body against his. "Can't ever be too sure. I've watched enough *NCIS* to reach that conclusion."

He started to tell her that was television fabricated for her enjoyment and then decided not to bother. If watching those shows kept her cautious whenever he was gone, then so be it. "Then rest assured it's me, baby," he said, bringing her body back against him and leaning close to whisper in her ear.

"Okay, it's you. I thought we decided we wouldn't do this."

"Because you're not on any birth control," he said, using the tip of his tongue to lick against the side of her ear.

"Yes, and we need to reach an understanding in our marriage."

He pushed the wet hair from her face after he turned her around to look at him. "Taking you or our marriage for granted is something I've never wanted to do, Teri, and if I did do that, then I'm sorry. I do understand your feelings, trust your decisions, respect what you do while I'm gone. I will get better but don't expect me to change overnight. Please accept me as 'work in progress.' I promise to do better but I'm human, I might make mistakes along the way."

"I'm human, too, and I might make mistakes, as well, Mac."

"Good, now we understand each other and agree to work together to improve our marriage."

"Yes, but I need to tell you what I bought while you were gone. You're not going to like it."

"It doesn't matter this time. Considering what you've gone through, what we've both gone through, it doesn't matter to me now. Whatever it is you bought without talking it over with me, I'll forgive you for it this time. Consider it a pardon."

She raised a brow. "A pardon?"

"Yes. Everyone is entitled to at least one during their lifetime."

"But you don't know what I bought or the cost."

He shrugged as he reached above her head for the shampoo. "Doesn't matter. We still have a roof over our head and food to eat, right?"

"Yes."

"Then whatever you bought didn't put us in the poor-house."

"You sure, Mac?"

"Positive. And you can tell me all about it later. Better yet, surprise me."

"Surprise you?"

"Yes. Surprise me. Right now, the only thing I want to think about is doing other things."

"Other things like what?"

"Making love to my wife. And don't worry. I stopped by a store to grab a few condoms." There was no need to tell her he'd gotten the economy pack of a dozen.

She smiled up at him. "Why aren't I surprised?"

"Not sure. Why aren't you?"

Instead of answering him she raised up on tiptoe, wrapped her arms around his neck and pressed her mouth against his.

* * *

Joy filled Teri.

Mac was giving her a pardon. That meant even if he hadn't agreed with her purchase of the ranch, this time he wouldn't make a big deal out of it. But still, she knew moving forward he had to agree to trust her more to handle things when he was gone. They would both be works in progress and she didn't have a problem with that.

He broke off the kiss and reached up to fill his hands with shampoo from the dispenser. "Turn around. I know you've already lathered your hair but I want to do it again. I love washing your hair."

She turned her back to him and sighed deeply at the feel of his fingers working lather into her scalp. That, coupled with her backside resting against his groin, sent a multitude of sensations all through her.

Teri was convinced nobody could wash her hair the way Mac did. He had the best fingers…for everything. She recalled those same fingers touching every part of her body, especially when he worked those same fingers inside her, making her reach an orgasm of gigantic proportions.

"You like the way that feels, baby?"

"Hmm," she said, not able to say the words, yet knowing he knew what she meant.

"Now for the rinse-out."

He tilted her head back under the spray and she felt warm water rushing through her hair and down her back. After squeezing excess water from her head, he said, "Now to clean the rest of you."

Then, filling his hands with soap, he used his hands to lather her body. The feel of his hands on her body made her moan because he knew exactly what areas to touch.

"You shouldn't stir me this way, Mac," she said, when he turned her around to face him.

"Why not?"

Did he really have to ask her that? "I can't think straight when you do."

He began lathering her front and said, "It wouldn't bother me in the least if you were to stop thinking at all. Or if you think only about me."

Little did he know she did that anyway. He didn't know how lonely her nights were without him in bed with her. "How can you be so sexy and so annoying at the same time?"

"It's a gift, babe," he leaned in and whispered before placing a kiss across her lips.

Then, using the sprayer, he washed the suds from her body and then ran his hands all over her. "You're squeaky-clean now."

She believed him. He had washed her hair and her body. "Now for me to wash you."

Lathering her hands with soap, she began rubbing them all over his body. Her husband was well-endowed and his erection was showing her how loaded he was. Touching him made sensations flood her insides, made a tingling sensation settle between her thighs. No part of his body missed her care and attention.

When she heard him moan, she glanced up and met his gaze. Held it and felt desire and love in the very depths of her soul. Holding him in her hand always did this to her, empowered her as a woman.

His woman.

"You're killing me, you know."

She shook her head and smiled. "You're a SEAL.

I heard they don't die easily. They're too rough and tough."

"Then why do I feel like putty in your hands?"

Teri threw her head back and laughed as she continued to hold him. "Trust me, this does not feel like putty. Not one single inch of it."

After figuring she'd tortured him enough, she used the sprayer to wash all the suds from his body. No sooner had she done that than he suddenly backed her against the shower stall. "Now I'm going to take care of you, Teri Anne."

"You always take care of me, Thurston."

He smiled and she watched him retrieve the condom packet from where he'd placed it earlier. He made quick work of sheathing himself. Returning to her, he asked, "Now, where was I?"

"If you have to ask, then maybe we—"

He didn't give her a chance to finish. Mac lifted her onto him at the same time he captured her mouth in his. And when he began thrusting hard into her, Teri was convinced that, considering his ferocious sexual appetite, he intended to make up for lost time.

Thirteen

Mac opened his eyes to find Teri sitting cross-legged in the middle of the bed, staring at him. Seeing her flooded his mind with memories of how they'd spent the last few hours. They had made love in the shower, dried off and made love again in the bed. Dinner had arrived in their room and afterward they'd taken a walk outside only to return to their hotel room to make love again. All night long.

It was morning and the sun was shining brightly through the window shades. It was a beautiful day and he had awakened to the face of an even more beautiful woman. A woman sitting in the middle of the bed with a huge grin on her face. A stunning smile. It was even a mischievous smile. For a minute, she looked like the cat that ate the canary.

"Good morning, Mac."

Instead of responding, he reached out and cupped his hands behind her head to bring her face closer to his. And then he did something that he'd done a lot of lately. He kissed her, getting the feel of her that he definitely needed.

It was strange how things worked out. He'd left Virginia to come after his wife. There began an adventure, one he could certainly have done without, but possibly one that was needed. He couldn't recall when the two of them had spent so much "us" time together. They missed their girls, he knew that, but they were enjoying the time they were spending here with each other. He and Teri would return to the cabin to go through the rubble and sometime later today they would be returning home.

By the time the kiss ended, he was ready to pull her deeper into his arms for another kiss, but she pulled back and said, still smiling brightly, "Today you get your surprise."

He lifted a brow as he reached out and gently rubbed up and down her arm, needing the contact and loving the feel of her smooth skin. "My surprise?"

Her smile got even brighter. "Yes. I've made all the arrangements."

He was trying to keep up with her but failing. "What arrangements, sweetheart?"

"To take you to see your surprise. Mac, please keep up," she said jokingly.

He was trying. He leaned up and kissed her again, this one just as thorough but not as long. "I'm trying. How about you start from the beginning since I'm sure there is something I missed."

She didn't say anything at first. It looked as if his kiss had left her dazed. He wanted to take advantage of that look and tumble her back into bed with him and make love to her all over again. He was about to do just that when her next words stopped him.

"Your parents have agreed to watch the kids, which works out since they hadn't expected us back until Sunday anyway. I've called the airlines and booked the flight. We leave this evening."

Whoa, things were now moving so fast his head was spinning. He pulled himself up in bed. "Where exactly are we going?"

"Texas."

"Texas?"

"Yes."

He ran a hand down his beard. "Why?"

"To show you what I bought and that's all I'm saying about it. The rest is a surprise. And when you see it, you'll be okay with me buying it because it was a pardon, remember?" she said grinning. "Now I'm going into the bathroom to get ready for our day. We've got a lot to do." Before he could say anything, she'd slid off the bed and rushed into the bathroom.

As soon as the door closed behind Teri, Mac eased to sit on the side of the bed. Damn, he needed a cup of coffee. Black. A little gin in it wouldn't hurt, either.

What on earth had his wife bought in Texas? A purchase he'd pardoned. Had he spoken too soon?

He remembered the smile on her face and how excited she was to share this surprise with him. He wanted to share her happiness, but that feeling of doom wouldn't go away.

Getting out of bed, he went to the coffeepot in the room and got it started. By the time he was sipping his first cup he'd figured it out. Teri had bought Tia a horse. That had to be it. He recalled her bringing up the subject of doing that last year, saying how well Tia was doing with her riding lessons.

Mac had squashed that idea when he'd made Teri

see that not only did they not need a horse but they
had no place to keep one. She'd come back to say the
stables where Tia's lessons were held kept horses for
other owners and for Tia to have her own personal
horse to ride would be wonderful and a great ninth
birthday present. He hadn't agreed and he had pretty
much told her he hadn't wanted to discuss it any further. And they hadn't.

Had she gone behind his back and purchased the
horse anyway? Knowing how he'd felt about it? Tia's
tenth birthday was coming up in a few months and usually whatever gift they gave their daughter was a joint
decision. Had Teri made that decision without him?

Mac pushed back the anger he felt, remembering he'd
decided that when it came to Teri and any decisions she
made without him, he wouldn't sweat the small stuff.
But there was nothing small about owning a horse. Not
the boarding of it or the cost of shipping it from Texas
to Virginia.

"I'm back."

He turned around. An ache slipped through him and
the lower part of his body hardened. She was standing there after having showered, a towel covering her
middle. Barely. His wife was definitely acting the part
of a seductress this morning. A very happy and elated
seductress.

Had buying a horse for their oldest daughter and now
knowing he wouldn't be blowing a gasket about it put
her in such a happy mood? At that moment he knew if
that was the case, then he would let her play out her surprise. Just seeing that huge smile on her face, something
he hadn't seen in a long time, was worth it.

Placing his coffee cup down he slowly crossed the
room to her and drew her into his arms. "Had I known

you were taking another shower I would have taken it with you."

She laughed. "That shower gets us in trouble, Mac."

"But it's trouble we can handle."

She didn't look too convinced but eased closer to him anyway. "Did you forget we're supposed to go to the cabin today and look around?"

"No, I didn't forget," he said, pulling her closer to his naked body. "We have time and we will still make the flight to Texas."

"In that case…"

She reached up and cupped his face in her hand, leaned up and kissed him. He decided to let her do her thing before taking over. Mac liked the way she was using her tongue to entice him and when he was certain he couldn't handle it any longer, he swept her up into his arms and headed back toward the bed.

Teri squeezed Mac's hand as they stepped off the plane in Dallas, Texas. She glanced over at him. He'd slept on the plane during most of the fight and a part of her wanted to believe she'd worn him out that morning. If so, it would have been a first during the ten-plus years of their marriage.

After making love, they'd dressed and breakfasted downstairs in the hotel restaurant before leaving for the cabin. Seeing the wreckage had nearly broken her heart since she'd liked the cabin and enjoyed the days she'd spent there.

The tornado had flattened it, but Mac's duffel bag was located practically intact in a tree not far away. Most of Teri's stuff had been destroyed but she was happy when Mac had come across her driver's license and her house keys.

They had gone back to the hotel, packed and headed for the airport. Instead of heading for home they had caught a flight to Dallas. It was late and she'd booked reservations at a hotel. It would take an hour to drive to Terrell in the morning.

She still hadn't told Mac where they were going and he seemed okay not to ask questions. He was going to accept the surprise she had in store for him. Now, as they drove to the hotel in the car they'd rented at the airport, she glanced over at him to ask, "You okay?"

"I'm fine. How long will we be in Dallas?"

She chuckled, wondering if he was trying to get her to spill her surprise. "Not long. You'll get your surprise tomorrow, after we get a good night's sleep."

She could tell from the look on his face that a good night's sleep wasn't something either of them would be getting.

"I miss the girls," he then added.

She missed them, too, but she knew what she had to show him and share with him would change their lives forever. And regardless of his so-called "pardon," she wanted to believe that after analyzing the benefits of owning a ranch he would see it was a win-win situation for them.

Once the pressure of having to tell him about the purchase had been lifted from her shoulders, she'd been able to closely examine the advantages of moving the kids from Virginia to Texas. And with Mac retiring in a couple of years, she could see him becoming a rancher. He could handle a horse just as well as she could and he would be his own boss. She couldn't help getting excited at the prospect, and a part of her felt she was insuring their future and their kids' futures.

They arrived at the hotel in Dallas, where she'd been

able to get a suite, unlike the one they'd stayed at in Cheyenne. The moment the door closed behind them, he pulled her into his arms. The move surprised her. She had figured that, pardon or no pardon, he would be asking her questions by now, but he hadn't. It seemed as if it was her rodeo and he intended to let her ride it like she wanted.

And speaking of riding...

She liked riding horses but she liked riding her husband even more. Deciding to let him take control for a while, she accepted his kiss with the same hunger that he was showing. And when he broke off the kiss moments later to lift her into his arms and head for the bedroom, she wrapped her arms around his neck and buried her head into his chest. His masculine scent aroused her, made her want him in a way that had all kinds of sensations sweeping through her, rushing through her bloodstream.

And then every so often, he would lean down and devour her mouth with those barely-touch-your-lips kisses that literally curled her toes. When they reached the bedroom, he stood her on her feet and plowed her mouth with another kiss that made the earth feel like it was tilting on its axis.

"Mac..."

"What do you want, baby?"

She wrapped her arms around his neck. "I want to show you what I can do."

He smiled at her. "Then do it."

Having him give her the word emboldened her and she stripped off her clothes while he watched. She wanted him to watch. When she was totally naked, he began removing his own clothes.

"So tell me, Teri. Do you have a plan?"

Oh, boy, did she. Now if she could stop staring at his body long enough to regain her senses and put her plan into action. She followed the movement of his hands as they went to the zipper of his pants. She continued to watch as he removed his jeans to expose a pair of sexy black briefs. It was then that she saw he was every bit as aroused as she was. When he had completely stripped, she drew in a deep breath. Regaining her senses, she pushed him down on the bed on his back. Then she quickly straddled him.

"I'm about to put my plan in action, Mac."

"Baby, go for it."

She did.

Lifting her body, she eased down on his shaft, loving the way it felt inside of her. As soon as he was snugly there, to the hilt, she smiled down at him. She began moving, up and down, withdrawing in a way to set a rhythm that had him moaning, growling her name, as she rocked down on him with an intensity that drove her deeper and deeper with each downward plunge.

She'd become an expert horsewoman at sixteen and she was showing him just how well she could ride. It wasn't the first time she'd done so and it wouldn't be the last. She loved when she was in control like this, with him beneath her, taking her body while she took his. Just the way she liked and the way he wanted.

She felt so much love and desire. So much need.

From the first, when he'd introduced her to lovemaking for the very first time, she'd never wanted a man the way she did him. That thought rang through her mind every time her body lowered down on him and then lifted up. Her knees ground into his side and it seemed instead of reining him in, it spurred him to lift up the lower part of his body to meet hers.

Her fingers gripped his shoulders and his hands were wrapped around her waist. Suddenly, his hands moved up to the back of her neck to maneuver her head down to capture her lips. His tongue took control of hers and she could feel his heat, every ounce of strength within him and the full throttle of his masculinity.

Suddenly, a bolt of sensation struck her. She pulled her mouth from his to scream as an orgasm tore through her and she could feel the same rip through him. He quickly reclaimed her mouth and switched their positions where she was now beneath him, their limbs entwined, their bodies plastered together.

Moments later, when he broke off the kiss, she slowly opened her eyes and smiled at him. In a voice filled with sexual exhaustion, she said, "Plan accomplished, Mr. McRoy."

Mac woke the next morning to glance down at the beautiful woman in his arms. Their second round of lovemaking had completely worn out his wife—to the point where she'd immediately drifted off to sleep.

Easing out of the bed, he closed the door behind him and went into the sitting area to call his teammates. If he didn't, they would wonder why he hadn't returned home by now.

He told them about his surprise and what he'd guessed it was. Of course, Bane, Viper and Coop were excited at the prospect of Tia getting a horse. They would be, since they owned plenty of horses and the animals had been part of their lives for years. All three owned ranches and Bane had family members—a brother and several cousins—who raised and trained horses for a living. Mac admitted that after thinking about it, he'd decided Tia having a horse wouldn't be so bad. Especially since she did enjoy her riding lessons. Coop, who had a ranch in Laredo, even explained to Mac the best way to ship the horse to Virginia.

Mac recalled the horse that had been kept for him at his grandparents' ranch in Florida. Riding that horse had been the highlight of his summers each year, when he and his sister would leave the city to enjoy their time with their grandparents.

From the bright light coming in through the window, he figured it was about eight, and a glance at the clock on the nightstand confirmed it. He would let Teri sleep. Once she awakened, their day would get started. He figured, at least he hoped, she would take him to see the "surprise" so they could get back home to the girls.

"I love Dallas," Teri said, looking around after the waitress had taken their order.

They had decided to get out of the hotel to dine at a small café within walking distance. What Mac liked about this particular café was that it was one of those mom-and-pop establishments and wasn't crowded. Only a few of the tables were taken.

He leaned back in his chair while sipping on his coffee as he gazed over at her. He'd drifted back to sleep after his phone call to his teammates and he and Teri had awakened just before noon. Hungry. He hadn't asked her anything other than how soon they could eat since they'd skipped breakfast.

"Do you?" he asked her.

"Yes. Have you forgotten I used to live not far from here?"

She was right. He had forgotten.

He'd never visited her in Terrell, where her grandparents' ranch had been located. But he did recall how hard the decision had been for her to sell it. "Yes, I had forgotten," he admitted. "I guess a lot of things bring back memories for you here."

"Yes," she said wistfully.

He reached across the table and took her hand into his. "I don't have a problem with that, just as long as they don't include an old boyfriend."

She chuckled. "They don't. If you recall, I was too busy trying to juggle both school and the rodeo to have a steady beau."

He did recall her telling him that one of her grand-parents' stipulations about her involvement with the rodeo meant she had to also do well in school and col-lege. Since education was important to him, he could see him making a similar stipulation with Tia if she ever decided she wanted to one day compete on the rodeo circuit like her mother had done. He'd long accepted the rodeo might be in his oldest daughter's blood and he was preparing for that day.

"I find that odd," she said suddenly.

He lifted a brow and looked at Teri. "You find what odd?"

"That man and his daughter. Their behavior."

He glanced across the room. The little girl who sat across the man appeared to be about eight. The two were eating breakfast and he didn't see anything the least bit strange about them. They were just two people eating breakfast.

"What's so odd about them?" he asked, looking back at his wife.

"She seems petrified of him."

Mac again glanced at the two. Again, he saw noth-ing amiss. The man seemed to be enjoying breakfast and the kid was not eating anything. In his opinion, the little girl appeared defiant, not afraid. "He probably laid down the law about something she didn't like. It happens, Teri."

"How would you know?" she asked, grinning.

"What do you mean how would I know?"

"That's what I'm asking. When have you ever laid down the law to your girls?"

He grinned back when he actually couldn't think of one single time. "I have good girls. I don't have to lay down the law. I lay it down to their mother, who I'm sure passes that law on to them when needed."

Teri rolled her eyes. "You come home after I've established the law and let them break it."

"No, I don't."

"Yes, you do."

Mac smiled. Okay, maybe he did. "So, I spoil them a little whenever I'm home. Is there anything wrong with that?"

"Yes, a lot."

He didn't want to argue with her about it right now and was glad when the waitress delivered their meal.

Teri clicked off her cell phone after talking with Mac's parents to check on the girls. According to them, everything was fine. Mac had gone to the men's room and she was slipping her phone back into her purse when her eyes fell on the table where the man and girl still sat.

She had tried not to stare, but more than once her gaze had been drawn to the two. Regardless of what Mac said, Teri was convinced something wasn't right. She was about to take another sip of her tea when the girl caught her eye while the man talked on the phone. There was a look in the little girl's gaze as they stared at each other. The man noticed the exchange and frowned at Teri, quickly clicking off the phone and saying something to the girl, who looked at him with what Teri felt was fear in her eyes.

Then, as she continued to watch them, the girl intentionally swept her plate and eating utensils to the floor. The man stood and grabbed the girl, nearly snatching her off her feet.

Teri was out of her seat in a flash and had crossed the room. "Turn her loose," she told the man.

He pulled the child behind him. "Do you dare to interrupt me chastising my child?"

"Yes, because if she was yours, you wouldn't handle her that way."

"Get out of my way, lady."

"No, I won't. Prove she's yours." Teri knew they were drawing stares and she didn't care.

"You either get out of my face so I can get my child out of here or I will—"

"You will what?"

Before he could respond the little girl said, "He's not my daddy!"

When the man turned as if he was going to give the child a slap, Teri pushed him and grabbed the child. Now it was the man hollering. "She took my child."

"What the hell is going on here?"

Teri immediately recognized Mac's booming voice. When the man tried to push Teri aside to reclaim the child, Mac intervened to protect her and shoved the man back instead, nearly knocking him to the floor.

"I asked, what the hell is going on?" Mac roared again.

"This woman took my child," the man snapped, straightening on his feet.

Mac looked at his wife, who had a furious expression on her face. There was no doubt in his mind she was ready to fight to shield the child if she had to. Teri Anne McRoy, the mother, was showing her protective colors.

Mac then looked at the little girl hiding behind Teri, who seemed to be holding on to his wife for dear life. He saw the fear in her small eyes. His gaze shifted back to Teri and before he could ask her anything, she got back in the man's face and said, "This child isn't yours. She gave me the signs."

"What signs?" Mac asked, trying to figure out why his wife thought this girl was not the man's child.

Teri glanced at her husband. "The same ones I've told our daughters to make if they were ever taken against their will."

"She's crazy!" the man shouted. "That is my child."

"Prove it!" Teri snapped at the man.

Mac noticed the man had yet to ask anyone to call for the police. Leaning down to the child, who was still clutching Teri, he asked, "Is he your father?"

The little girl shook her head. "No. He took me from Mommy."

"She lies! She is my daughter!" the man shouted.

"Then prove it," Mac said, backing up Teri by making the same demand she had earlier. He noticed the other customers in the restaurant were evidently suspicious of the man's relationship with the little girl and were taking out their cell phones.

The man reached into his jacket as if he was going to pull out his wallet. Instead he pulled out a revolver and pointed it at them. "Give me the girl!"

Teri knew from the growl she heard from Mac that all hell was about to break loose. Mac could handle himself and would protect her. Teri's main concern was the child. When the man repeated his words, someone in the restaurant shouted, "The police are on their way."

That announcement angered the man. He tried reaching for the girl and Teri snatched back at the same time Mac moved forward, knocking the gun out of the man's hand before giving him a hard blow to the gut, sending him sprawling to the floor. When he made an attempt to get back up, Mac knocked him out cold.

"Teri, you could have gotten killed," Mac said. She heard the anger in his voice.

She smiled up at him before leaning up on tiptoe and kissing him on the cheek. "Not with my husband standing here protecting me. You're my hero."

She then looked down at the little girl and asked softly, "Are you okay?"

Instead of answering, the little girl threw herself into Teri's arms and cried. Moments later, the police burst into the restaurant.

Fourteen

Mac sat beside Teri at police headquarters while she gave a statement regarding what had happened in the restaurant.

The little girl had been reported missing that morning, snatched from her mother in broad daylight at a shopping mall. Instead of taking her immediately into hiding, the man had probably figured he had time to enjoy a meal first with her in plain sight. As Teri spoke to the police, explaining why she'd decided to come to the girl's aid, he could see obvious admiration and respect in the officers' eyes.

"His name is Leonard Caper and he has a rap sheet a mile long. This was the first time he tried snatching a child. He's confessed to some guy paying him to do it, pick up any little girl. He's singing like a canary and we're following up all leads," a police detective was saying.

"Well. I'm glad he's off the street and I hope you get everybody who's involved."

"Yes, ma'am, we intend to."

Mac and Teri had met the little girl's parents. They hadn't wasted any time arriving at the police station to get their daughter. He doubted he'd ever met two more thankful individuals. The girl's mother had thrown her arms around Teri and cried profusely. Teri had cried, too. As the father of four girls he understood the father's need to get a piece of the guy, and more than one officer had to hold the man back from doing just that.

"If there's a trial, ma'am, you might be called back to testify," the detective added.

"I don't have a problem doing that if needed."

"Thanks, we appreciate it. And there is a ten-thousand-dollar reward for you, Mrs. McRoy. It was set up by the Dallas Fire Department, where the little girl's father is employed."

Teri shook her head. "I don't want it. Give it to the parents to go toward the little girl's college education."

Even more admiration shone in the officers' eyes. "You will have to sign papers for that to be done."

"Sure, I can do that," Teri said.

Mac raised a brow when Teri turned to him with a worried look on her face.

"What's wrong?" he asked her.

"I hope not keeping that money is fine with you. We didn't discuss it."

"And there's no need. I agree with what you've decided to do. Besides, it was your money to do whatever you want with."

Teri shook her head. "No, it's our money. That's the way it is between us, Mac."

He knew that to be true. That was the way it was

between them. Mac sighed deeply. They still had a lot of talking to do, things he needed to find out that he still didn't know. Namely, what she had bought that had her anxious.

One thing he'd discovered today was that his wife was capable of holding her own, even without him.

"Man, do us a favor," Bane said, as he and his teammates talked to Mac on the phone later that day. "You and Teri need to go home as soon as a flight can get you there. Instead of spending quality time together, the two of you are doing nothing but finding trouble to get into."

Mac couldn't help laughing at that, since it certainly seemed that way. They had finished giving their statements to the police but not before the news reporters had gotten there. "I'm just glad Teri picked up on the fact that little girl was in trouble. I hadn't suspected a thing."

"That just goes to show that she has certain skills you don't have, Mac. When will you realize you have a special woman on your hands?" Coop asked. "It's all over the news how she faced that man and took that girl from him."

That part angered Mac. "She could have gotten hurt. That bastard had a gun." Mac didn't think he would ever forget the moment when that man had pulled his weapon out and pointed it at them. Namely, at Teri.

"And you got back in time to take care of business like you were supposed to do," Viper said.

"I'm going to make sure my daughter knows the signs when she grows up. People are messed up these days," Coop tacked on.

"Just the thought of that bastard assuming he could snatch somebody's kid like that," Flipper said. "It was a good thing you and Teri were there."

Mac nodded. "Well, it was almost too much action for me," he said. "I expect it as a SEAL but as a civilian? What's wrong with coming home to peace and quiet?"

"Nothing is wrong with it, unless you're married to Teri," Bane said, laughing.

Mac chuckled, knowing he wouldn't have it any other way. Moments later, after ending the call with his friends, he left the sitting area to go into the bedroom, where Teri was just clicking off her own phone.

She glanced up at him. "That was the folks. They saw us on television. The girls saw us, as well. They think their parents are heroes."

Mac smiled. "You mean they think their mom is a hero. You're the one who figured the kid was kidnapped. You want to tell me about these signs?"

She smiled over at him. "Keep your fingers on one hand crossed, and when you can, get someone's attention."

"And the kid did that?"

"Yes. She was sitting with her fingers crossed, and after you left, she knocked her dishes off the table, hoping to get someone's attention. But I was already on it."

"Apparently." He had walked out of the restroom to return to his table, only to find Teri confronting the kidnapper, with the child cowering behind her. He was certain that had he not knocked the man out then Teri would have done so herself. After ten years of marriage, he was surprised to be seeing his wife in a new light.

"Her parents told her what to do and she did it. Like I told the police, she was a real trouper. If anyone was a hero, that little girl was."

"Well, more than ever I'm ready to go home," Mac said. "When are we going to see the horse?"

She lifted a brow. "What horse?"

"I figured that was the surprise. Am I right?"

She shook her head. "No, you aren't right."

He didn't say anything for a minute and then he asked, "Then what kind of surprise is there here in Dallas? What on earth could you have bought here?"

"Nothing in Dallas."

He lifted his own brow. "Then where, Teri?"

"In Terrell. I was able to buy back my ranch. So I did."

Mac stared at her, certain he'd heard her wrong. "Could you say that again?"

She nodded. "I got a chance to buy back my grandparents' ranch due to a 'first right of refusal' clause I had included in the contract when I sold it. That meant the current owners had to offer it to me first before they put it on the market."

"And you bought it?" he asked, incredulously.

"Yes."

He stared at her for a minute. "And how did you pay for it?"

She nervously licked her lips and he immediately knew that he wouldn't like her answer. Because he could think of only one way she could have paid for it. "Teri, how did you pay for it?" he repeated.

"I used some of our savings."

"Some of it?"

She shrugged lightly. "A big chunk of it."

He stared at her. "How much, Teri?"

"Not as much as you think."

"How much, Teri?"

"Remember your pardon, Mac."

"How much, Teri?"

She then gave him a figure that made him see red after his head began swimming. He knew how much they'd had in their savings and he now knew how much was left.

He thought about how long and hard he'd saved. How carefully he'd guarded each purchase. Yes, they had enough, but that money belonged to both of them and she hadn't consulted him at all. That money was for their future, for their girls. Generational wealth.

He didn't want them to worry the way he'd had to worry growing up.

He drew in a deep breath and then said, "The pardon is off."

She frowned. "You can't do that."

"I just did." He then walked out of the hotel room.

Teri froze the moment she heard the door slam shut behind Mac. He was mad. Furious was more like it. She had expected his anger days ago but when he'd said he would give her a pardon, she had believed him. He'd said it extended to her last purchase, no matter what she'd bought. Granted, a horse was definitely not as expensive as a ranch, but still...

And now he had left.

His usual mode of operation whenever he came home and discovered she'd purchased something he thought was outrageous would be to put distance between them to cool off. Then he would return in an hour or so but ignore her for a day or two. Next would be the lectures, where he would do all the talking and like a disobedient child she was supposed to listen. Hadn't expressing how she felt over the past few days gotten her anywhere other than back to square one with him?

Okay, she would admit using so much of their savings was something she should have consulted him about since it had been funds set aside not only for emergencies but for the kids' education. Maybe wanting to buy back the ranch had been selfish of her. Had she put her wants ahead of her family's needs? It had been her decision not to keep the ranch years ago and it was a decision she should have accepted. She had for years, but then lately she'd begun regretting that decision, wishing she could offer their kids the same lifestyle that she'd had growing up. And she knew that moving to the ranch would be the right thing for all of them.

Granted, she should have consulted Mac, but he hadn't been available for her to do that. So she'd made the decision for them. He hadn't bothered to find out why. She would have gladly laid out the advantages if he'd given her a chance, but he hadn't. Now they had a ranch house that she wanted but he didn't. And she and the kids wouldn't live there without him. Was it wrong to want it all? The Ranch. Mac. She and the girls there with them. A happy family. A marriage that was not filled with arguments. Teri knew she would do whatever it took to keep them together. She would put him and their marriage first.

Getting up off the bed, she knew what she had to do. She grabbed her purse and reached inside for the business card of Jack Polluck, the man who'd handled the sale for her years ago and her recent purchase. Within minutes she was placing a call to him.

"Yes, Mr. Polluck, this is Teri Cantor McRoy. I want to put my ranch up for sale." She paused and then said, fighting back her tears, "Yes, I'm sure."

Mac tried to cool his anger by walking around a nearby park. He still couldn't wrap his head around the fact that his wife had bought not appliances, a new television or a horse. But a ranch. And she had used most of their savings to do so. What in the world had she been thinking?

And he hadn't bothered to ask her that?

He rubbed a hand down his face in frustration, realizing he was acting just like he usually did whenever he returned home from being gone for a long period of time to find the balance of their savings account less than what it had been when he'd left. He hadn't given her a chance to explain her actions.

He dropped down on a park bench. How could she explain buying a ranch in a state where he'd never lived? But then, she had lived here and evidently liked it enough to want to move back. However, after this morning, would he move to an area where kids could easily be snatched from their parents?

Mac was fully aware that he needed to be fair. He had to admit such a thing could have happened in any city in the United States. Even in Virginia. It was up to parents to prepare their kids and it seemed like Teri had prepared theirs. They knew how to give out signs. Hell, he hadn't even been aware of that. But Teri had.

What was it going to take for him to realize and accept that Teri had never bought anything foolishly? Whatever she did, whatever she bought, was something that would eventually benefit the family. He wasn't sure how a ranch in Texas would benefit them, but he was certain she would have laid it out for him if he had given her the chance.

And hadn't he pretty much acknowledged days ago that the recent problems in their marriage were more than her buying stuff? They included his habit of taking her and what she brought to their marriage for granted. He realized that, yet he was again doing that very thing.

He stood up and began heading back toward the hotel. Determined that this time they would handle the situation differently.

When he got back to the hotel it was to find it empty with a note left in the middle of the bed.

> *Mac,*
> *Sorry. Once again, I blew things. Even though I'd imagined we could all be happy there at the ranch, I thought more of my happiness than that of you and the kids and that wasn't fair. I've called the real estate agent to put the ranch house back up for sale and he feels certain he will be able to sell it for what I paid for it within a month or so. I'm heading back home to the kids.*
> *Teri*

He crumpled the paper up after hearing the defeat in her words. He glanced around. She was gone. For the second time in less than a week his wife had left him.

The key to the car was on the nightstand, which meant she'd taken a cab. He grabbed the key and headed for the door, knowing he was the one who was sorry.

Teri flipped through a magazine. She was on standby but she didn't mind waiting. She would rather sit here than be at the hotel with Mac giving her the silent treatment. There was nothing left to be said. She hoped the note she'd left him explained it all.

Time passed. She was reading an interesting article and barely noticed the person sliding into the seat beside her until he said, "Aren't you tired of running away, Teri?"

She jerked her head up and stared into Mac's face.

He wasn't smiling but then neither was she. "Why did you come here?"

He shrugged. "My wife is here and whenever I'm in the States, I like being with my wife."

"The same wife who likes spending your money?"

He chuckled. "Yes, that one. But then, my money is her money."

She rolled her eyes. "Yes, until she buys something. Why did you come here, Mac? I left a note."

"That note wasn't good enough."

"Well, it was for me." She then checked her watch. "Are you on standby, as well?"

"No. I came to get you. Our flight leaves out tomorrow and not today. You were supposed to show me my surprise."

She jutted out her chin. "You said my pardon is over. So is the surprise."

He didn't say anything for a minute. "I want to see it."

"See what?"

"This ranch you bought."

"The same one that is now up for sale? Well, I have no desire to show it to you now. It doesn't matter."

He reached out and took her hand in his. "Maybe I need to explain something to you, Teri. Everything you do matters because *you* matter. I'm the one who owes you an apology. I know there're reasons for you to have bought the ranch and I need for you to tell me what they are."

"Why? The reasons won't change anything."

He shrugged. "Maybe not. But this time I'm willing to hear you out before passing judgment."

She lifted a brow. "Why? You've never done that before."

"I know. I'm honestly trying to do better. I told you I was one of those works in progress. Why didn't you take me at my word? Why were you so quick to walk out on me?"

She looked away for a minute and then back at him. "Because I'm tired of fighting."

"We don't fight, Teri. We disagree. All couples do it from time to time. We shouldn't be any different."

"But we are," she implored.

"Then it's definitely something we should be working on correcting." He stood. "Come on. I want to see the place."

She looked up at him. "Do you really?"

"Yes. On the way there you can tell me why buying it was so important to you and how you believe it will benefit us and the girls. That's what's it's about, Teri. That's what it's always about with you. What's always in the forefront of your mind. I know that and truly believe you wouldn't do anything that wouldn't be for our best interest."

She fought back her tears. "I want to believe that, Mac. All I'm asking is for you to hear me out. And if you don't agree with my assessment after seeing it, then so be it—we will sell it."

He nodded. "Fair enough."

She then took his hand and stood. He gave her a wry smile and said, "I have a feeling I'm going to like it."

She lifted a brow. "Why do you think that?"

"I just do."

Fifteen

Mac did like it.

The moment he drove down the long driveway, he knew he was a goner. Probably before that, when she'd persuaded him to take the scenic route lined with large magnolia and oak trees and a number of bluebonnets. Then there were the lush meadows and valleys and the numerous lakes.

At one point he'd pulled to the side of the road, a part that had a beautiful view of the lake. He could see himself riding bicycles with the girls around here or having a picnic with Teri. He had visited Bane's, Viper's and Coop's spreads and he thought this place rivaled theirs in size and could be just as productive.

During the drive, Teri had made her pitch, and a pretty damn good one, too. She told him of the improvements the family that had last owned the ranch had made. They'd been improvements that had been needed but that she hadn't been able to afford, which was one of the reasons she had sold.

There was a spanking new barn and several small outbuildings that could be used as guest cottages whenever anyone visited. Another thing that impressed Mac was the size and style of the ranch house. Each of his daughters could have their own room with no problem. It was spacious and built in the ranch style he preferred.

He'd met the previous owners, who would remain in the house for the next couple of months. He'd done the figures in his head and would admit Teri had been able to buy back her home at a fair price, which showed just what a good negotiator she'd been in making the deal.

And this had been her home. The glow in her voice and the smile on her lips when she talked about it was a strong indicator of just what this home had meant to her. He hadn't known. After she'd sold the place, he had assumed she had walked away without looking back. Although that might have been true, losing her home had been a pain she'd refused to let surface. But it had been there.

She'd never admitted such to him, but it had been revealed in her voice when she'd told him of all the fond memories she had shared here with her grandparents.

Another plus that he hadn't yet shared with her was that his investment in Bane's family land management company, as well as their horse business, had showed a damn good profit last year and that had been passed on to the shareholders. That, along with his bonuses over the last two years, would be enough to replace the money from the girls' college fund, and they'd still have more than enough left over to start a business here. Already he could envision him going into the horse business with Bane's relatives, like Coop had done.

Even though they owned huge spreads, Viper and Coop had hired capable men to run things whenever they were gone. He could see himself doing the same thing.

"So, what do you think?" Teri asked, when they returned to the hotel hours later.

Closing his fingers around her wrists, he reached out and drew her to him. "Do you want me to be truthful?"

She ran a hand through her hair and sighed. "Not want, Mac. I *expect* you to be truthful."

He smiled, remembering when he'd made the same stipulation of her. "I will always be truthful with you."

Pausing a moment, he pulled her over to sit on the sofa. "You did good for your family, Teri. You might have thought of your wants with the purchase of the ranch, but you still considered the needs of your family, as well."

His eyes held hers. "I can see future growth here and generational wealth we can pass on to the girls. That's something I've always worked hard to do. It's why I took it so hard when you made purchases. Well, I can see it now. I can see this being a working ranch, one we can make profitable to pass on to the girls. I'm sure one of the four, maybe all four, would want to continue it like you wanted to do."

He reached out and took her hand in his. "Spending this week with you has opened my eyes to a lot of things, Teri."

She lifted her brow. "Such as?"

"What a lucky man I am. Hell, you saved my life in that mineshaft. I hadn't known a rope was under that trough or about any signs kids are taught in case they're ever snatched. In addition, you're pretty damn smart. I admit there was nothing you've ever bought while I was away that did not benefit us. I know you don't think I trust your judgment, but I do and I intend to do a better job proving it."

He decided to add, "That doesn't mean I won't ever question you about anything, because I might. When I do, please take it as my need to have more clarification versus questioning your judgment."

She nodded. "Thank you."

"No, I want to thank you. You're my wife, my partner, my soul mate and the mother of my kids. I love you, Teri. Don't ever forget that. Although I was upset about how you placed yourself in danger with that guy to get that little girl away from him, for you to have the guts and courage to even do such a thing showed just what a strong, capable woman you are. I am so proud to be your husband."

"Oh, Mac," she said, reaching out and cupping his beard, running her fingers through it.

He reached out and lifted her up to place her into his lap, wrapping his arms tight around her. "And another thing, I do want another baby, Teri. Like you, I didn't know how much I did until you told me about the son we lost. It doesn't matter whether we have a girl or a boy—I want to be a father again."

"Oh, Mac, I do want another baby, too, but what about all your concerns?"

"I believe in you. I know you will always do your best for all our kids."

"Thank you."

He'd entertained the thought of retiring in a few more years. Now that there was a ranch to run, they would run the ranch and raise their kids together.

"I don't think you know how happy I am right now, Mac. I was so scared and worried. What I haven't told you is that I blamed myself for losing the baby."

"Why?"

"Because I lost the baby two days after I returned home from Terrell. I thought the flight had something to do with it, although the doctor said it didn't."

"And you should believe the doctor and not blame yourself for anything. I don't."

"You don't?"

"No, and you shouldn't, either."

"I love you so much," she said, before burying her face in his chest.

"And I love you." He stood with her in his arms. "And I intend to show you just how much."

He carried her into the bedroom knowing there would always be days when they didn't see eye to eye on everything, but at least they would agree on this one thing. They were a team.

And his wife would always be his to claim, just like he would be hers.

When they reached the bedroom, he placed her on her feet. She reached up and wrapped her arms around his neck and pulled his mouth back down to hers. He had no problem giving her what she undoubtedly wanted. Namely, appeasing the hunger taking control of both of them.

He knew what she wanted and he was right there with her. Stripping his wife out of her clothes, he proceeded to do just that. His hands were busy, unbuttoning her shirt, then taking it off, unsnapping her jeans and letting her lean on him while he slid them down her hips. Her bra and panties followed and before removing his own clothes, he straightened and stared at the beautiful body before him. Her breasts were absolutely gorgeous and her waist small, even after four children.

He recalled that after Tia had been born, Teri had

hated the stretch marks left from her pregnancy, but he had convinced her that any marks from giving birth to a child of theirs would be her badge of honor. A badge he appreciated her wearing and one he wanted her to do so proudly. After that, she never mentioned the stretch marks again.

"You know what I think?" he said, still staring at her. He was ready to do more than just look. He was ready to touch.

She smiled up at him. "No, what do you think?"

"That you're the most beautiful woman I know."

His words made Teri smile.

She was fully aware that other women found her husband sexy and could understand them doing so. She was cognizant of walking into rooms where women nearly drooled when they saw him. And she could honestly say she had never felt threatened. Mac made it a point to assure her how much he loved her and how beautiful he thought was. He said he didn't mind if his compliments ever went to her head.

He leaned down close to her ear and whispered, "And you know what else I think?"

"Um, you're on a roll, so you might as well confess all."

He leaned closer. "I think you would look even more beautiful pregnant again."

She fought back tears. For him to say that meant he wanted to see her pregnant again. They had been using a condom for all their sexual encounters after being rescued. Was he hinting that he wanted to have unprotected sex with her again? That he was willing to not only risk her getting pregnant but also was hoping that she would be?

"I'm on board if you are, Mac. It will take two for that to happen."

He cupped her face in his hands. "Then let's get it on, Ms. McRoy."

He leaned down and kissed her breasts and when he did so, she closed her eyes and drew in a deep breath. When he sucked a hardened nipple between his lips she felt her breasts swelling in his mouth, making her moan.

When he pulled his mouth away, he said, "Not sure I'm ready to compete with my baby for these breasts, Teri."

Since she breastfed all her babies, she knew what he was referring to. "Poor baby."

He chuckled. "For some reason I don't think your sympathy is sincere. That means I'm going to have to torture you for a while."

Teri knew all about Thurston McRoy's type of torture. She didn't want to admit it, but she loved it.

"Please don't." Inwardly she hoped that he would.

He bent down and licked his tongue across her stomach. When he did so, every cell inside her body flared to life. And when the tip of his tongue began swirling around her navel, she felt every nerve ending in her stomach flare to life. This was torment, and with every flick of his tongue she felt a pull, a tingling sensation between her legs.

As if he sensed her predicament, he glanced up at her and smiled. "You haven't felt anything yet, baby. Get ready. Here I come."

Getting down on his knees he stared down at the juncture of her thighs, and at that moment her legs began to quiver with the intensity of his gaze. He uttered a growl before leaning in and burying his mouth there.

* * *

Mac intended to show no mercy. Just pleasure. With that goal in mind, he used the tip of his tongue to stir a fervor within Teri, widening her thighs to capture the bud of her womanhood.

He took his time and showed no signs of letting up, intending to pleasure her. Even if it took all night. Already she was rocking her body against his mouth. He had no problem with her doing that since the more she rocked, the deeper his tongue intended to go.

Then he felt it, the first sign that she was about to come. Her thighs were quivering around him and when she suddenly threw her head back and screamed his name, he knew a maelstrom of pleasure was engulfing her. He could taste it.

When her trembling ceased, he stood and pulled her into his arms, capturing her at the same time his hand settled right between those legs.

"Now for something else going in here," he said, after breaking off the kiss. Using his fingers, he began stroking her there.

"You're torturing me again, Mac," she accused breathlessly.

"Guilty as charged," he whispered in her ear.

And then he edged her closer to the bed and eased her down on her back and joined her there, sliding on top of her. Teri lifted her hips and Mac knew why and what she wanted.

Deciding he'd teased her enough, he eased inside of her, and instinctively, she opened her legs. Then he began thrusting in and out, back and forth. She moaned his name when he increased his strokes and he felt her body shudder again beneath him.

A growl escaped Mac's throat when he became

caught up in the same pleasure he was giving his wife. Over and over, their bodies worked in unison as her hips rose off the bed at the same time his came down on hers.

"Mac!" She screamed his name when they both exploded in an earth-shattering climax that seemed never-ending.

He kissed her, slowly recovering from the effects of one hell of an orgasm and knew that before the night ended, there would be more, and all just as powerful.

Sixteen

Teri glanced across the table at Mac as they enjoyed breakfast at the hotel's restaurant. "What do you mean we aren't going home today?"

Mac smiled. "That's what I mean. Do you know that of all the days we've spent together this week, not a single one has been relaxing?"

She raised a brow, remembering all the hours spent in his arms making love. "So, you don't consider any of our time together relaxing?"

"I'm not talking about the lovemaking, Teri. I'm talking about just normal, uneventful time with you where we aren't trapped in mineshafts or you're not risking your life saving little girls or you're not showing me our future on the ranch. I want to go out and do something. Together. You like this area? Then show me why. The only time I've been to Dallas is when we came for Flipper's mom's birthday celebration. I didn't get to see much of it then."

Teri smiled, glad Mac was truly interested in the area she called home. "There's really a lot to do here. I can show you all my favorite places."

"Then let's spend the day together. When we go back up to our room, you can map out places for us to visit."

Teri appreciated Mac's thoughtfulness. Although he'd told her that he was looking forward to moving to Terrell, what he'd just said meant that he truly was. She would include getting together with Flipper and Swan in their plans since they were still in Dallas visiting Flipper's family.

After changing into more comfortable clothes and shoes, they hit the streets. They walked and checked out the Sixth Floor Museum at Dealey Plaza, a museum dedicated to the life and death of President John F. Kennedy. Since she was a history major, she was able to tell Mac a lot of things she figured he hadn't known.

They went to several other museums and the botanical gardens, as well. Holding hands, they walked through the gardens with rows and rows of both flowering and nonflowering plants.

"Do you think the girls will have a problem leaving their friends?" he asked her when they left the gardens to head out to the Reunion Tower.

She was excited about taking him on the high-speed elevator ride that went to the top in sixty-eight seconds. It had always been a fun place for her while growing up.

"I think they will at first, but I also think they'll love it here and make new friends. I can't wait for them to see it," she said.

"Neither can I."

After visiting a number of other sights, they drove into Terrell, and she took him around town. News had traveled fast about her buying back her family farm and everywhere they went people told her how glad they were that she'd decided to move back home. They visited her old high school and she even took him to the rodeo school where she'd learned to rope her first calf.

She knew Mac had an ulterior motive for wanting to meet some of the people in Terrell. He would be gone for long periods of time during covert operations and needed the peace of mind that she would have a similar network of friends in Terrell like she had in Virginia. He soon saw that this was home for her and everyone in the area around the ranch knew her and looked forward to her return. He mentioned that he was glad Flipper's parents lived close by, too, in Dallas.

Teri was happy, too. She was excited to meet Flipper and Swan for lunch. The couple were thrilled to hear that Teri and Mac had bought back the ranch that had been in Teri's family for years. Flipper and Swan had their own good news to share. They were expecting their first child. Teri was happy for them. She would never forget how Flipper had risked his life by swimming into that flooded mineshaft to save them.

Later, on the drive back to the hotel that evening from Terrell, she tried calling Mac's parents to check on the kids. When she didn't get an answer, she turned to Mac. "That's odd."

He looked over at her when he brought the car to a traffic light. "What is?"

"I can't reach the folks."

"What's odd about that? This isn't a school night so they probably took the kids out for pizza or something. You know how the girls wrap them around their fingers."

Teri chuckled. "If anybody knows about their ability to wrap someone around their fingers it would be you. The girls have you wrapped so tight it isn't funny."

"Whatever. And about it being not funny, you don't hear me laughing, do you?"

Teri smiled. "Although I totally enjoyed our time together today, I really miss the kids."

"I do, too, and I enjoyed our time together, as well. We need to do it more often. How does the idea of date night sound?"

"It sounds great and the Wilkersons' daughter turns seventeen this year, and old enough to babysit for us. She's smart and levelheaded."

Once they got back to the hotel, they stopped at the ice-cream shop and enjoyed a bowl of ice cream together. When they reached their hotel room, Mac opened the door and then stepped aside for Teri to walk in ahead of him.

"Mommy! Daddy!"

A surprised Teri shrieked upon seeing the girls and raced across the room to give them hugs. She gave her in-laws hugs, as well. She then turned to Mac. "You arranged this?"

He grinned as he walked across the room to give her a hug, since she was obviously in a huggy mood. "Yes. I knew that although you were enjoying my company, you were missing the girls as much as I was. I called Mom and Dad after you went to sleep last night and made arrangements to get them here."

"That's why you kept me away all day?" she asked, grinning back at him.

"No, I kept you away because I wanted to spend time with you," he said, leaning in and kissing her across the lips.

"Do we really have a ranch, Mommy?"

"Will we have horses?"

"And plant our own food to eat?"

"And make new friends?"

All the questions came at them from the girls seemingly at once. Together Mac and Teri answered each and every one of them to the best of their ability, although the reply to a number of them was "We'll just have to wait and see." It was important to them that their girls looked forward to making the move as much as they did.

"So when can we see this ranch?" Mac's father asked, and Teri could hear the excitement in his voice.

"Tomorrow," Mac said, wrapping his arm around Teri's waist. "I talked to the owners and they are looking forward to showing you around."

"And it's the house where you lived as a little girl, Mommy?" Tia asked her.

Teri smiled down at her daughter. "Yes." She wished she could tell Tia about her and Mac's plan to get her a horse, but she knew it would be a surprise. Tia had a birthday coming up and that would be soon enough to share the news.

School would be out for the summer in three weeks and they intended to put their current home up for sale and begin packing. They hoped to be settled in at the ranch before school started in the fall.

That night when they went to bed, Mac held her in his arms. He had arranged for the girls and his folks to have a hotel room next door with a connecting door. It was hard to deny Tasha when she wanted to stay and sleep with them, and Teri was surprised Mac couldn't be charmed by their youngest daughter. Usually he would give in to her, but this time he didn't. He told Tasha that she needed to stay with her grandparents because Mommy and Daddy needed time by themselves together. Teri could tell Tasha didn't agree, but she left with her grandparents anyway.

"Thanks for bringing them here," she said to Mac when they were alone in bed. She wasn't dumb. At some point during the night Tasha would get out of bed and knock on the connecting door. And when she did, Mac would get out of bed, open the door and let their daughter into their bed to sleep with them.

"You were missing them and so was I. Besides, the folks wanted to see the ranch. It was the perfect time."

"And your parents are perfect with them."

"I have to agree with that," he said. "I have a feeling we'll be seeing a lot of them once we move to the ranch."

"I hope we do. We'll have plenty of space at the house, or they might prefer one of the cabins for privacy. One thing is for certain, we'll have plenty of room."

"We will definitely have that." He then pulled her deeper into his arms.

When he leaned down and kissed her, every part of her yearned for him, aching in a way that had the area between her legs throbbing unmercifully. "I hope you know sooner or later we're going to get a little knock on that door. Tasha never takes 'no' as an answer, especially when it comes from her daddy. You know what that means, right?" she asked Mac.

He grinned. "Yes, I know what that means. We don't have any time to waste."

Mac pulled her to him and kissed her, and she nearly drowned in the masculine essence of him. Something he always said rang through her mind.

She was his to claim. Now. Forever. Always.

Epilogue

Five months later

Bane Westmoreland opened the door and smiled at the couple standing on his doorstep. With the arrival of Mac and Teri, all his team members were accounted for.

"About time you guys got here," Bane said, leaning over to give a very pregnant Teri a kiss.

"Stop complaining," Mac said. "Teri doesn't move as fast these days as she used to."

Teri glanced over at her husband and frowned. "Don't you dare blame me for us being late, Mac, when you refused to move from in front of the television until that football game was over. I tried to get you to leave the hotel an hour ago."

Bane shook his head since it was obvious Teri was in a tiff about it. "I see it's business as usual with you two."

"Not exactly," Mac said, grinning and wrapping an arm around his wife's protruding stomach. "We found out yesterday before leaving home that we're having twins. Both boys."

"Congratulations!" Bane said, happy for his friends. "Now, get inside so everyone can congratulate you two, as well. Six kids. Wow!"

Mac grinned proudly. "Yeah, that's what I say. Wow! The good thing is my folks love the ranch and are crazy about the cabin we're giving them. They will move in soon. Mom's going to be a big help to Teri and our six kids while I'm away."

Bane nodded, smiling. "Sounds like you two have things worked out. After having only three kids I understand how important extra help is."

Mac, Teri and the girls had moved to their ranch in Texas a couple of months ago. Of course the SEAL team members had been there to help. Their ranch would be a horse ranch, and thanks to Bane's family, who owned a horse breeding and training company, already several horses had been added. Like Coop's ranch, Mac's would also serve as a horse depot that housed the animals before they were shipped off to be trained. There was even some discussion about later making Mac's ranch an official horse training site. The partnership was proving to be a financial incentive for Mac and Teri.

Since Mac was still on active duty, one of the Westmorelands' foremen, who wanted to move closer to his son, daughter-in-law and grandkids in Dallas, had accepted the job as Mac's foreman. The McRoys' ranch had been named Timberlake, a joint effort by their daughters.

Mac had surprised his wife last month. On her birthday, he had given Teri a special gift. A horse. Namely, Amsterdam. Upon discovering how much the horse had meant to Teri, Mac had bought it from the owners of the

Torchlight Dude Ranch. Mac had also bought horses for each of his daughters.

Tonight they were all gathered to help Bane and Crystal celebrate their move to their new home on "Bane's Ponderosa," his stretch of land in Westmoreland country. Once Mac and Teri were inside, no introductions had to be made. Bane's teammates knew all of his family members, those living in Denver, Atlanta, Texas and Montana. They also knew the Westmorelands from Alaska—who went by the last name of Outlaw.

Also present tonight was the newly elected local sheriff, Peterson Higgins, better known to everyone as Pete. Pete had been best friend to Bane's brother Riley and Bane's cousin Derringer since grade school and was like a member of the Westmoreland family.

Bane and Crystal circulated around the room and Bane couldn't help noticing that the two senators in the family, Reggie Westmoreland and Jess Outlaw, had their heads together discussing a piece of legislation they intended to pass with the help of their colleagues.

A couple of other Outlaws—Garth and Cash—were talking with Bane's brothers Dillon and Canyon and his cousin Riley, hashing out how their two companies, the Outlaw Shipping Company and the Westmoreland Land Management Company, could benefit each other.

In another corner of the room, Teri was getting tips about what to expect with the birth of her multiples from Bane's wife, Crystal, and Nick's wife, Natalie, both mothers of triplets, and Bane's brother Jason's wife, Bella, who had twins.

Bane was happy for Mac and Teri. Mac would be retiring as a SEAL in a couple of years to become a full-time rancher and Bane knew his friend was looking forward to it. With Teri and six kids, Mac would certainly have a lot of help.

The doorbell sounded and Bane wondered who the latecomer could be. With the arrival of Mac and Teri, he'd figured everyone on his and Crystal's guest list had already shown up. Giving Crystal a sign that he would get it, he moved to the door and opened it to find an older couple, who appeared to be in their late sixties or early seventies, standing there with a baby in their arms.

Bane was certain he did not know the couple. "Yes, may I help you?"

The man spoke. "We hate to impose but we were told Peterson Higgins was here tonight. We are the Glosters, his deceased brother's in-laws."

Bane nodded. "Yes, Pete is here. Please come in."

The man shook his head. "We prefer not to, but we would appreciate it if you could tell Peterson we're here. We would like to speak with him. We will wait out here."

Bane nodded again. "Okay, just a minute." He circled around the room before finally finding Pete in a group in the family room, discussing motorcycles with Bane's cousins Thorn, Zane, Derringer and one of the Alaska Westmorelands—Maverick Outlaw.

"Excuse me, guys, but I need to borrow Pete for a minute," Bane said to those in the group. Once he got Pete aside, he told him about the older couple waiting outside. Pete placed his cup of punch aside and quickly moved toward the front door.

Bane wasn't sure how long Pete had been gone, but when he returned he was carrying a baby in one hand and a diaper bag in the other. Everyone's attention was drawn to Pete when the baby released a huge wail.

It seemed all the mothers in the room hurried toward Pete. "Whose baby?" Bane's cousin Gemma was the first to ask, taking the baby from a flustered-looking Pete.

"This is my nine-month-old niece, Ciara," he said, noticing how quickly the baby girl quieted once Gemma held her. "As most of you know, my brother, Matthew, and his wife, Sherry, were killed in that car crash six months ago. This is their daughter. Sherry's parents were given custody of Ciara when Matt and Sherry died. But they just gave me full custody of her, citing health issues that are preventing them from taking proper care of her. That means I'm now Ciara's legal guardian."

Pete looked around the room at the group he considered family and asked the one question none of them could answer.

"I'm a bachelor, for heaven's sake! What on earth am I going to do with a baby?"

* * * * *

Note from the Author

I want to take this opportunity to thank Kim James for sharing her experiences and challenges as a military wife with me in order to give greater depth to my heroine, Teri McRoy.

And to all military wives everywhere, you are deeply appreciated for serving your country right along with your enlisted spouses. We honor you. Thank you so much!

RANCHER IN HER BED

JOANNE ROCK

One

Frankie Walsh understood that her generation had killed romance.

Sure, some people said that dating apps were responsible. And it was true the swipe-left mentality definitely smothered every last hope of spontaneity and excitement. But whether the blame rested with millennials or apps or the parenting that had let a crop of kids grow up thinking they were the center of the universe, Frankie agreed with the consensus among her girlfriends that romance was a thing of the past.

Which begged the question, why was she lingering outside the main house at Currin Ranch, heart fluttering wildly while she hoped for a sighting of her boss, Xander Currin?

Because she was ten kinds of foolish, that's why.

She'd already accomplished her errand here—a two-second task of retrieving the keys to the barn where the haying equipment was stored. Xander had kindly left them outside the back entrance on a huge wooden patio table, right where the maintenance manager had told her they'd be. One of the other hands who'd helped with the haying equipment yesterday was out sick today, and he'd accidentally taken the other set.

Frankie had volunteered for the errand so fast the other ranch hands had all looked at her sideways. If she wasn't careful, her ill-advised crush on Xander would become a running joke all over Currin Ranch. She valued this job too much to make her workplace uncomfortable that way, and she'd strived for too long to prove she could hold her own with the physical demands of the job.

With the fear of being laughed at spurring her boots, she jammed the keys into the back pocket of her jeans and turned away from the massive log mansion overlooking a creek bed. She kept to the stone path that wound past the pool house and through a low shrubbery hedge, returning to the edge of the lawn where she'd left the energetic young mare, Carmen, she'd ridden over. Her time spent with the animals was the best reward of the job and a necessary part of the requirements for veterinary school. If she could ever make enough money to pay for it.

Yet another reason why this job was so crucial for her. Her other gigs were of the volunteer variety—shadowing a local vet on his calls during her off days and helping out at a local animal shelter. Currin Ranch was the only job she had that came with a paycheck.

Stroking the mare's flank, she was just about to mount up when she heard laughter and voices in the backyard. Male. And female.

A warning prickled along the back of her neck, urging her to go. Or maybe calling her to stay? Because she recognized the deep tone of the man, a warm and sexy chuckle pitched low in a way that made Frankie's skin heat. The object of her silly crush.

But a fluffy feminine giggle smothered any wayward thoughts Frankie might have been entertaining about Xander. Frozen in place, she watched as the couple emerged from the shrubbery together. Xander escorted a strawberry blonde in a bright yellow sundress that accentuated considerable curves. The woman's glossy waves bounced along with everything else as she tapped her way down the path in kitten heels. Reaching the driveway less than ten yards from where Frankie stood, the woman didn't so much as glance her way as she lifted a hand to wave goodbye to Xander. She slid into an ice-blue convertible that looked like it cost more than veterinary school.

Had she been an overnight guest?

Jealousy flared. Feeling every inch the ranch hand she was, Frankie fought an urge to at least swipe a dusty streak off the front of her jeans. Instead, she hauled herself up on the mare's back even as the horse startled sideways away from the convertible's racing engine.

It was all Frankie could do not to glare at the woman

for punching the accelerator while the vehicle was still in Park. Blondie squealed the tires on her way out.

Soothing the mare with a reassuring hold on the reins and a squeeze against her flanks, Frankie was about to turn tail and ride for the barn when she noticed Xander charging her way. Tall and muscular, he wore his jeans and fitted tee with the ease of any other ranch foreman, but as the heir to the Currin family fortune, there was something commanding about his presence. Right now, with his blue eyes fixed on the horse and his stubble-shadowed dark jaw flexing, he had an air of restrained danger. The allure of a man who could hold his own with a surly beast without breaking a sweat.

"Whoa. Easy, Carmen," he called to the anxious palomino, his stance the same one the ranch trainer used when breaking a new mount, positioned just outside the reach of her dancing forefeet. "Easy."

"She's okay," Frankie assured him, leaning back slightly in the saddle to cue the mare. "I've got her."

Her heart sped faster, more from her boss's sudden appearance at her side than the mild scare with Carmen. Frankie wouldn't have taken her if she'd felt the least bit uneasy with the spirited youngster. Besides, keeping her seat on Carmen was a cakewalk compared to bronc riding, the rodeo event Frankie had recently taken up. She'd tried it on a dare from one of the other ranch hands and discovered she wasn't too bad at it. And considering how badly she could use the extra money, she couldn't deny the appeal of the cash prizes.

Xander peered up at her with narrowed eyes.

"I didn't think the trainer had cleared this one for

work." Shifting closer, his gaze darted from the horse to her and back again. "Carmen hasn't been with us long."

Her boss reached to stroke the palomino's muzzle, his dark hair a stark contrast to the horse's golden coat and white mane. She was used to seeing him in his black Stetson around the ranch in his work as the foreman.

Much to his father's frustration.

Everyone involved with Currin Ranch knew that Ryder Currin wanted his only son in the family's oil business and not overseeing the ranching operation. But for the eleven months that Frankie had been on staff, Xander had been personally involved with everything from the herd to the haying, making sure the collective efforts ran smoothly. He was good at his job, but even she knew the foreman's role wasn't where the heir apparent belonged.

"I'm not using her for work today," she explained, forcing herself to relax, if only for Carmen's sake. She hadn't meant to rile the boss. "I rode her over to pick up the barn key because she seemed restless. I thought she could use an outing."

Why couldn't Xander's blue eyes be focused on her for positive reasons and not because he thought she'd screwed up? So many times, she'd hoped to snag his attention, and now, when she'd finally accomplished it, he seemed on edge. Irritated, even.

"Not cleared for work means no riding." His jaw flexed as he moved closer, stroking down Carmen's neck to her shoulder, quieting the animal. By now, his shoulder neared Frankie's calf, his body in tantalizing proximity. "A good ranch horse doesn't spook at engine noises. No sense putting her in a position to fail when she isn't ready yet."

Frankie bit down on the inside of her lip to keep from pointing out that an over-revved Italian luxury car wasn't the kind of "engine noise" horses heard in the normal course of ranch work. Neither was screechy bubblegum pop dialed up to full blast on a convertible stereo as his guest peeled out of the driveway.

Then again, she didn't think she could muster an impartial "yes sir" when he was dead wrong about Carmen. Carefully, she quit gnawing on the inside of her lip so she could speak.

"Then I guess I'd better get her back to the barn." Frankie managed a tight smile. "I'll let the trainer know Carmen needs to broaden her musical tolerance."

Xander's head snapped up to look at her, his dark brows angling down with his frown.

Had that slipped out?

Her fake smile froze in place.

In the silent moment that followed, she became aware of the soft buzz of electric hedge trimmers as a gardener worked nearby. The scent of cut grass hung in the Texas June air, growing more sweltering with each breath.

"What's your name again?" he asked, a warning note in his voice.

Was he going to write her up? He couldn't fire her for being a smart-ass, could he? She really needed this job and the hundred hours of animal care that would help her get an interview for vet school. She might have been on staff for almost a year, but she'd only just started working more directly with the horses.

For the first six months she'd done only the worst of the grunt work, no doubt why the boss hadn't recalled her name.

"Frankie Walsh," she said quickly, kicking herself for spouting off and tugging her hat just a little lower on her forehead. Wishing she could hide. "Thanks for the key."

He gave her a nod but didn't step back, a barrier of impressive muscle and denim. "The rules are in place for a reason. Not just to keep Carmen safe, but the ranch staff, as well."

That caught her off guard.

"Meaning me?" She shook her head, her ponytail swiping across her back as she thought about all the times she'd landed on her butt in local rodeo competitions. Bronc riding wasn't for the faint of heart. "No need to worry about my safety. I'm tougher than I look."

Turning to go, she hoped Xander would forget about the embarrassing encounter.

Her ego was the only thing bruised, after all. His safety concerns were misplaced. Clearly, he favored a softer kind of woman than Frankie would ever be, which was just as well since she should be concentrating on earning enough money to live her dreams instead of mooning over her off-limits boss. There was an open rodeo at a local county fair next weekend, and she needed to be focused if she was going to enter the saddle bronc competition, a sport attracting more women in recent years. She could ride better than most of the other hands at Currin Ranch, and it wasn't like the small rodeo would attract many female competitors.

She hoped.

She had an outside chance of walking away with the prize—enough money to buy herself a coveted ticket to the Texas Cattleman's Club Flood Relief Gala. The swanky event would be a great place to see the other side of the ranching world and meet the wealthy ranch owners she hoped to one day serve with her veterinary practice.

Better to scuttle back to the barns and forget about Xander. Romance was dead anyhow, right?

Even so, she could almost feel the foreman's gaze following her as she rode away. And she'd be lying if she said it didn't give her a Texas-sized thrill.

A battle of the bands was in full progress when Xander parked his truck outside the fairgrounds for a Friday night rodeo. Because Currin Ranch was a major sponsor of the event, he'd been allowed to park right near the barbecue cook-off pavilion where he was meeting his father for their weekly dinner together.

Normally, dinner with Ryder Currin was a long, drawn-out affair since his father appreciated five-star dining, an attentive waitstaff and the best vintages a wine cellar had to offer. But since Xander would take barbecue from a Texas grill master over a four-course meal any day of the week, tonight's supper promised to be a whole lot more fun.

Besides, a shorter dinner meant less time for his dad to quiz him about when he was going to return to the front office of the family's oil business.

Dropping his Stetson on his head, he stepped out of the pickup and into the hubbub of a rodeo night. Boots crunching on dry gravel, he walked through the VIP gate as the growing crowd broke into enthusiastic applause for the country band sweating under the gazebo's canopy of decorative lights. The sawdust-covered dance floor was almost full even though it was early. The rodeo wouldn't start for another hour, and the carnival rides were in full swing despite the heat. The scent of slow-roasted brisket hung heavy in the air, grills smoking around the perimeter of the pavilion where chefs from all over the state prepped their best ribs and pulled pork.

"Xander," a familiar deep voice called from inside the covered dining area. "Over here."

Spotting his dad, he edged past a family maneuvering a stroller through the crowd, then joined Ryder at one of the few private tables in the reserved section up front.

His father never wore a suit but somehow, even in jeans and a button-down shirt, he still carried himself with considerable authority. With his boots and his dark brown Stetson, Ryder wore much the same outfit as the rest of the rodeo-goers, yet looked like a man in charge.

"Hope you don't mind, but I took the liberty of ordering a little of everything." Ryder leaned back in his chair as a curvy redhead in a fringed shirt and denim miniskirt delivered a tray full of barbecue steaming from at least ten different plates. Two beer bottles reigned over the center of the tray.

While the server set out a basket of biscuits, the beers and food, Xander steeled himself for the weekly interrogation about his life, his career plans and how soon he'd be ready to give up his "wild hair" of working the land. The dinners were Ryder's thinly veiled way of delivering regular guilt trips about not fulfilling his family obligations.

Xander might still live in a private wing of his father's home, but they rarely saw each other around the ranch. Ryder Currin kept his personal affairs closely guarded. Rumors had been flying around the Texas Cattleman's Club recently that Ryder was seeing Angela Perry, the daughter of his bitter business rival, Sterling. But Xander wasn't about to ask his dad about that.

"I happen to know she's single," Ryder observed as the server walked away from their table. He tipped his head in the departing woman's direction. "In case you're interested."

Xander's thoughts were so far from women it took him a moment to realize what his dad was talking about. Strangely, the only female who'd been circling his thoughts lately was a fierce brunette named Frankie, of all people.

The willowy ranch hand with the big green eyes and dust-smeared jeans wasn't Xander's type, but something about her prickly attitude and challenging stare had gotten under his skin.

"Definitely not interested," he told his father honestly, taking his hat off and settling it on the empty chair beside him. "And I'm pretty sure I passed the stage where I needed your help closing the deal with a woman at least a decade ago."

He plucked one of the longnecks from the center of the table and took a sip.

Ryder chuckled. "I suppose that's fair. Are you still dating Kenzie then?" he pressed, lifting his own beer for a swig. "I thought I saw her car parked outside the house last week."

A loudspeaker announcement called the contestants for the mutton-busting event into the arena, and a handful of families with kids hurried out of the dining pavilion. The band kept playing, their amps only muted periodically for the PA system. Behind them, the big Ferris wheel turned slowly, the neon lights flashing on the spokes even though it wasn't dark out yet.

"No. She only dropped in that morning to ask me to judge the rodeo queen competition with her." Xander had escorted her back to her car as fast as possible, knowing she'd only inquired about the rodeo queen pageant as an excuse to stop by. To see why he hadn't called. "But I'm not ready for a relationship with her or anyone else. Not after—"

The stab of pain over losing his fiancée in a tragic horse fall had eased in the last two years, but he felt as certain as ever that he wouldn't tread down that path to love and happily-ever-after again. That relationship had been complicated, with unhappy layers he hadn't ever understood. And in the end, it had gutted him. So working the land had been the only thing that offered any healing, and Xander wasn't willing to give that up anytime soon.

"I understand." Leaning forward in his chair, Ryder turned serious. "Better than you think. When I lost Elinah—" His lips compressed into a flat line at the mention of his second wife, who'd died of cancer thirteen years ago. "I know it's not easy to love again after losing someone."

Xander had only been twelve at the time, and he hadn't been living with his father then, spending most of his time with his mother, Penny, Ryder's first wife. But even as a kid, Xander had seen how his father retreated into himself for years afterward. Elinah had been the love of his life.

Now he appreciated his father's understanding.

"To be honest, I've got zero interest in the whole idea of love." Drawing one of the plates of ribs closer, he took a big bite.

"No need to rule it out altogether," his father cautioned, ignoring his vibrating phone next to him on the table. "Maybe you'll meet someone at the Texas Cattleman's Club Flood Relief Gala tomorrow night." He gave Xander a level stare. "You *are* attending, I trust?"

Ryder had already insisted on it, since he was hosting the event himself. Xander had no desire to spend the evening at a black-tie shindig, but he planned to support his father in his ongoing war with Sterling Perry for control of the Houston branch of the Texas Cattleman's Club.

While Sterling might be a wealthy businessman with a vast company that dealt in real estate, construction and property management, Xander didn't trust the guy. Part of that was because Sterling hated and resented Xander's father, of course. But Xander found it tough to respect a ranch owner who never spent any time on the land, and that was Sterling to a T. He might own the prosperous Perry Ranch, but that didn't mean its success had anything to do with his ranching IQ.

"I'm going stag." Xander had a spare ticket, but his awkward meeting with Kenzie had reinforced his decision to engage in only the most superficial kinds of affairs. She'd clearly been upset with him when she'd squealed her tires on her way out of the driveway.

If Frankie Walsh hadn't been such an accomplished horsewoman, Kenzie's childish act could have seriously endangered the ranch hand. Frankie had really handled herself well, especially on an excitable young mare.

"There will be plenty of single women there, anyway." His father wiped his hands on a paper napkin as their server appeared to clear a few of the plates. He waited until she retreated to finish his thought. "Just keep an open mind where romance is concerned."

Not going to happen, Dad. But as soon as he thought that, Frankie's long legs and sexy smile smoked through his thoughts. He willed away her image and took another swig of his beer. The sound of cowbells and cheering erupted from the nearby arena, and he guessed the children's rodeo event had started, a precursor to the adult competitions that would start soon.

"Most of the women I meet are more interested in the Currin name. Or the fortune. Or—" he'd been about to say *my sexual prowess*, but that hardly seemed like a topic to share "—who knows what. But regardless, I'll be there tomorrow."

Another announcement came over the loudspeaker for the barrel-racing contestants. Showtime must be soon. Xander gladly used it as an excuse to finish his meal.

"I'd better get into the arena." He'd asked his father to meet him here for their weekly meal since several employees were competing in tonight's events. "I want to wish the guys good luck before things get under way."

And yes, a part of him wondered if he'd see Frankie. She might attend to support the other hands. Or hell, maybe she'd be competing in the barrel race or one of the other women's events. He really didn't know much about her, which was unlike him.

Truth was, he'd avoided her the few times their paths had come close to crossing around Currin Ranch. He'd felt the pull toward her before and had always tamped it down deep, unwilling to get drawn into that kind of affair with someone who worked for him. He only knew she had the least seniority around the ranch up until a few months ago, when they'd brought on a new kid, which meant Frankie often got stuck with some of the worst jobs.

"Sure." Ryder lifted his beer. "If I don't see you inside, I'll definitely catch up with you at the gala, son."

Nodding, Xander scooped up his hat and replaced it on his head before leaving the dining pavilion.

Outside the arena, he could see the flag bearer lining up on horseback with her attendants. A few rodeo clowns waited with them, part of the processional that would kick things off soon. Inside the open arena with its high metal roof and dirt floor, Xander could see a couple of kids in cowboy hats riding the sheep used for the mutton-busting competition. The crowd was cheering, cowbells rang and the event announcer narrated the action.

He'd been to plenty of rodeos, from the big Houston Livestock Show to the local Friday night events like this one, and he enjoyed the small-town, grassroots competitions far more. While he appreciated the national spotlight that the multibillion-dollar rodeo industry brought to ranching, he had more fun at the community affairs that celebrated the hardworking men and women who made their living off the land.

Ranching was tough, but there was something cathartic about putting in the hard manual labor day after day and seeing the results firsthand.

"Hey, boss!" someone shouted from behind the chutes.

Peering over that way, Xander spotted a throng of soon-to-be competitors congregating, black-and-white numbers pinned to their Western shirts. A bowlegged cowboy was flagging him down, waving the end of his lasso.

Xander recognized Reggie Malloy, a longtime member of the Currin Ranch team. He headed that way, side-stepping a few families retrieving their kids after the mutton-busting event.

"Good to see you, Reggie." He clapped the senior-most herdsman on the shoulder. "Just came down to wish everyone well before the competitions start."

They moved out of the way of the stock contractors bringing in the calves for the first round of roping events. Out in the arena, the procession to kick off the rodeo began. Purple spotlights circled the venue, casting streaks across Reggie's face as they spoke.

"We're all fired up down here," Reggie told him with a wide grin, his cheeks red from the heat. He wore a championship buckle that broadcast his experience in roping. "My money's on the new kid, Wyatt, to do the ranch proud tonight. I've been working with him off and on since Christmas, and he's come a long way."

"That's good of you, Reg. The young guys all look up to you." He lowered his voice as the crowd quieted for the national anthem.

Even the people backstage went still. Only the calves shuffled their feet while a local high school girl dressed in red, white and blue belted out the song. When she finished, the crowd cheered and the announcer started to rev things up.

Reggie tucked his rope under one arm and started to head back toward the other competitors in the first go-round. "Boss, you might want to stick around for the lady bronc riders later."

"Lady bronc riders?" He'd been to plenty of rodeos before, and it wasn't often that he'd seen women competing in rough stock events, especially at the smaller venues like this one.

"There are more and more of them," Reggie assured him while the rodeo clowns performed a few tricks to warm up the crowd. "There are only a few signed up tonight, but our own Frankie Walsh is one of them. I've seen her ride and she's not bad."

Frankie?

A vision of the ranch hand on the back of a bucking bronc flashed through his mind. Followed by memories of Rena's fall. He hadn't been there the day his fiancée had been thrown, but that had never stopped his brain from imagining it thousands of times.

His gut balled up in a cold knot.

"Where is she?" Clammy sweat popped out along his brow. "Where's Frankie?"

He needed to talk her out of it. No, he needed to lay down the law and tell her she couldn't compete. What in the hell was she thinking to tempt fate like that? Bronc riding was a dangerous sport for anyone—man or woman.

"You okay?" Reggie's blond brows knit. Frowning, the wrangler reached for a bottled water resting on an empty bleacher off to one side. "Have a drink. You don't look so good."

Swiping a hand along his forehead, he tried to shut off the images flashing through his mind.

"I'm fine. Just—" He was already scouring the arena for any sign of the saucy brunette with killer legs. "Where's Frankie?"

Reggie pointed outside the arena. "Last I saw her, she was heading outside to give herself a pep talk. Looked to me like she was walking in the direction of the Ferris wheel."

Xander's boots were already in motion.

Two

Frankie paced quick circles around a broken passenger cart tucked behind the Ferris wheel, out of the way of the kids and couples in line for their turn on the carnival attraction.

Nerves always set in before an event like this. She'd only done half a dozen rodeos, but she recognized the mixture of butterflies and doubt that came before the exhilaration of her moment in the arena. This part—the waiting—was far more of a challenge than the eight seconds she needed to last on the back of a bucking horse.

Rock music blared from the ride's sound system, competing with a local country band playing nearby, the pings and whistles of various skills competitions along the carnival main strip, and the shouts of carnies urging on the guests to play longer. Spend more.

Every now and then, an announcement over the loud-speaker reminded the fair attendees who needed to report to the arena next for their event in the rodeo. Barrel racers, calf ropers and wranglers of all sorts took their turn.

Pacing faster as she let herself get keyed up, Frankie knew tonight would be tough. There were only a handful of lady competitors in the saddle bronc event. But she'd seen the list and recognized the names of two top-notch riders from an all-women's tour that had made its way around Texas the year before. She'd seen those ladies live and guessed she didn't have much of a shot against them tonight.

Then again…who knew?

The broncs could surprise anyone. And Frankie had never walked away from a challenge. Her mother had told her more than once it was her worst failing.

Not that she was going to think about her adoptive mom. Or dad. Or the home she'd run from the moment she'd turned eighteen. She'd save those worries for another night, when she wasn't about to risk her neck.

"Frankie."

A man's voice cut clean through her tumultuous thoughts. Her head snapped up to see Xander Currin striding toward her.

Purposefully.

A thrill shot through her at the sight of him in his dark jeans and a fitted black button-down. His Stetson was the same one he usually wore, but his boots were an upgrade from the ones he wore for work. His blue eyes zeroed in on her face, stirring more butterflies.

"Yes?" Puzzled that he would seek her out, she listened hard to hear over her galloping heartbeat.

He didn't look pleased. He couldn't possibly still be mad about her taking Carmen out the other day, could he?

"I just saw Reggie." Her boss stopped a few feet away from her, closer than he'd ever stood before. "He told me you're entering the saddle bronc event."

"That's right." Relief seeped through the awareness of him. He wasn't here to give her a hard time about riding Carmen. "There's a ladies' competition tonight."

"Do you have any idea how dangerous rough stock events can be?" His voice was all sharp edges and accusation, just like the last time they'd spoken.

Defensiveness flared. How was it she could irritate this man just by existing?

"I work with horses and cattle every day, the same as you do. I suppose I know a thing or two about them." She folded her arms, refusing to let him intimidate her here, off the Currin Ranch.

She'd worked too hard in life to be steamrollered by people who thought they knew what was best for her.

"That doesn't mean you're ready to ride a surly, pissed-off beast trained to buck." His jaw clenched. "Do you know how hard riders prepare for this event?"

A burst of applause broke out at a nearby midway game while she reeled from Xander's sexist audacity.

"Did you give Reggie the same speech you're giving me?" She felt a flash of impatience that bordered on anger. "Or Wyatt, the greenest of your employees entering a competition tonight?"

Xander's lips flattened into a thin line. "No. But—"

"Then don't you think you're being a chauvinist to call me out for doing an event that I have spent time preparing for and that I'm actually good at?"

His expression shifted slightly, some of the tension around his eyes easing a fraction. He seemed to force in a deep breath before responding.

"You have a reputation as a very hard worker around the ranch, but if you've been training for this, it's the first I've heard," he acknowledged, dialing back the confrontational tone.

And taking a bit of the wind from her sails along with it.

"Well, I don't have much spare time to train given my schedule." Some days she ached so much from the physical grind of the labor she did, she could barely force her arms to shovel food in her mouth before showering and heading to bed. "I take as many hours as I can to make ends meet."

She lifted her chin, daring him to find fault in that. There was no shame in hard work.

The country band playing nearby launched into a crowd-pleasing favorite, eliciting whistles and shouts from the dancers on the other side of the Ferris wheel. Neon lights blinked in varying shades as the spokes of the ride spun past them.

"I don't want you in that arena tonight," Xander informed her, his eyes utterly serious.

She reminded herself she worked for him. That she

didn't want to land on the wrong side of the powerful Currin family. But damn it, who did he think he was to call the shots for her tonight?

"That's too bad," she found herself saying anyhow, "because I'm not on the clock now, which means you can't order me around."

Xander glanced away from her and then back again. More gently, he asked, "Can you tell me why it's so important to you to enter an event so fundamentally dangerous?"

Something in his voice compelled her. So she decided to be honest.

"I'm working hard all the time trying to earn enough money to put myself through veterinary school, and I don't get many breaks." She forced herself to unclasp her folded arms. To stand up straighter and own her thoughts and feelings. "And when I heard about the Texas Cattleman's Club Flood Relief Gala, I thought *that* was the kind of break I'd love—something fun and different that would let me have a glimpse of the life I'm working toward. A chance to see the reward with my own eyes to keep me on the path. You know?"

Xander cocked his head like he didn't quite understand.

"You want to go to the Flood Relief Gala," he said slowly.

"I do. It's healthy to give yourself some tangible rewards in the process of working toward a big goal," she explained, sharing an insight gleaned from a college counselor who'd helped her figure out how to start on a path toward achieving her big dreams. "And the prize money tonight will give me enough to afford a ticket to the gala."

The loudspeaker blared a call for the competitors in her event. Nerves fluttered in her stomach.

Because of the upcoming ride or the man?

"I've got to go." She took a step forward, but he stepped in front of her.

"You can't enter, Frankie. I mean it."

How had she missed all the signs that her boss was this bullheaded? "You can't fire me for being in the rodeo when you've got five other employees entering."

Eyes on the arena, she didn't want to lose her spot. She started forward again.

"Then I'll make you a deal," Xander offered, his voice deep. "If you don't set foot in that arena tonight, I'll take you to the gala as my guest."

She stopped. Turned back to look at him. Gauged his expression.

"Since you can't fire me, you'll take me to the gala as your...guest?" She found that hard to believe. Xander Currin could have his pick of beautiful, accomplished women. "Why would you do that?"

Her heartbeat sped in a way that didn't have a damned thing to do with nerves or the competition about to begin. Her racing pulse had everything to do with Xander's blue eyes on her. And the potential of what he offered.

"You said you wanted a ticket. I'm offering you one." He sidestepped her question neatly. "Be my date tomorrow night."

"What's in it for you?" She knew better than to think her boss wanted to date her.

"I've got two tickets." He spoke clearly enough, but sure didn't explain. "Would you like one or not?"

She couldn't argue. Not when she knew her chance of nabbing that prize money was small with the level of competition here. Furthermore, how many times had she indulged fantasies about this man? An evening with him would be…exciting. To say the least.

"Very well." She swallowed back the surge of feminine awareness. She couldn't believe she was going to be her boss's date at such a huge, important event. "I will go to the gala with you."

"Good." He didn't look happy so much as relieved. "Now let's get out of here. I'll take you back to the ranch."

Disappointment stung a bit, but she told herself to be happy for the unexpected opportunity she'd just won.

"You don't want to see how the guys do tonight?" she asked, hating to leave and not support the rest of the ranch team. The guys at Currin Ranch were her only family now.

Living on-site at the ranch made the group close-knit.

"I'm not taking any chances you'll change your mind." Xander palmed her back, briefly, steering her toward the exit. "My truck is right through this gate."

The one marked VIP. Of course.

His touch stirred her senses. She tried to hold on to her frustration with him, but it was tougher to do with the memory of that brief caress between her shoulder blades still warming her through her shirt.

"You don't have to take me home. I can catch a ride with the guys." She didn't want them to worry about her. "Reggie will wonder what happened to me—"

"I'll text him." He withdrew a phone while they walked out of the fairgrounds into the parking area. He made a few taps on the screen and then shoved it back in his pocket. "There. Done."

She wondered what it must be like to be a Currin and have the world ordered to your personal preference at all times. She'd fallen right in line, too, unable to argue with someone who could fulfill her wish for a ticket as easily as he had.

All her life she'd struggled. Hard work and grit were her keys to making things happen and getting ahead in life. She didn't regret that, either.

Still, she wondered how the other half lived.

"I can't believe you don't already have a date for the gala." An awful thought occurred to her. "You're not canceling on the blonde just to keep me out of the rodeo, are you?"

Although, remembering the way the woman had peeled out of the driveway with no regard to poor Carmen, Frankie found it hard to empathize with her.

"Blonde?" He sounded genuinely perplexed as he gestured toward his big black pickup.

"The one who startled my horse," she reminded him as he opened the passenger-side door for her. "Not that it's any of my business."

She waited to step inside the truck, more curious than she had a right to be about his answer. Surprised he didn't know who she meant.

"Her name is Kenzie, and no, she was never my date for the gala." He still held the door for her.

How very interesting. Did that mean he was currently unattached? Not that he ever seemed to date anyone for long. She'd seen a lot of women come and go in Xander's life in the months that she'd had a crush on him.

"Don't you think it will be awkward for you to take me? Since I'm—you know—a ranch hand?" A trace of misgiving crept through her.

"Not at all." He offered her his hand to help her up, clearly impatient to be under way. "There's enough drama brewing in the Texas Cattleman's Club without anyone worrying about who I bring to the party."

Ignoring his hand to pull herself up into the truck cab—mostly because she was extremely aware of the effect his touch had on her—Frankie mulled over his words. She hoped he was right. And yet another tiny piece of her wished that it wasn't easy for him to brush aside their evening together so casually.

What would it be like to attend the party with him? she wondered. Would it be like a real date? Or would she simply be circulating through the party on her own once he got her through the door?

It was one thing to be brave about riding a bucking bronc. At least then, you knew what you were getting. Facing Xander's peers at a fancy party had the potential to be more humiliating than landing on her butt in the dirt. What did she really know about him other than his reputation for never staying with any woman for long?

Stealing a sideways glance at him as he got behind

the wheel of the truck, Frankie promised herself to keep a rein on her attraction to him tomorrow night. To simply enjoy the event she'd been wanting to attend so badly.

Because letting herself think for a moment that Xander Currin noticed her as anything more than a troublesome employee would only lead to heartache and disappointment. Now that she knew he was prone to chauvinism and arrogance, it ought to be easy to quit crushing on him.

Except the truck hadn't even pulled out onto the main road before she was already imagining what it might feel like to be in his arms for a dance.

Crisis averted.

Xander tried to tell himself he'd done the right thing as he steered his pickup onto the highway back to Currin Ranch. He'd ensured Frankie wasn't competing in a dangerous event, and now he was delivering her safely to her cabin on his family land.

But while the country love song crooning on the radio filled the truck cab, he couldn't deny that in dodging one disaster, he may have set himself up for another. Because no matter that he'd told her it wasn't a big deal to take her to the Texas Cattleman's Club Flood Relief Gala tomorrow night, he knew plenty of people would talk. Not that he gave a rat's ass about his own reputation, but he didn't like the idea of anyone giving Frankie a hard time. Rumors spread fast in the tight-knit ranching community.

He wasn't sure how to address that, so he tried to

focus on the positive of what he'd accomplished. He kept his eyes on the road, knowing it was better to concentrate on that and the drive home than let himself think about the undeniably appealing cowgirl in the passenger seat.

"Do you mind if I change the station?" Her voice slid through his thoughts, her hand hovering over the radio dial.

His gaze flickered briefly from her fingers to her profile silhouetted by a streetlamp.

"Suit yourself." Damn, but she was pretty. Even after he'd returned his attention to the view in front of the headlights, he could still see her dark braid resting on her shoulder and tied with a blue ribbon.

She wore a bright blue Stetson he'd never seen before, and a brown suede vest over her turquoise-and-yellow-plaid Western shirt. The feminine touches didn't quite soften the proud tilt of her chin or the stubborn set to her jaw, but the contradictory side of her claimed his interest just the same. A ranch hand willing to risk her neck in the arena for the sake of a gala ticket.

"Thanks." Spinning the radio dial, she found a more fast-paced, rock-inspired country song and turned up the volume.

To avoid conversation? Fine by him. He didn't want to think too long about what he was getting into by accompanying her tomorrow night. And he sure as hell didn't want to contemplate the attraction he felt for her. She worked for him and that made her off-limits. End of story.

But she broke the silence between them just a moment later, turning down the volume again as he pulled off the interstate onto the dark county route that would lead back home.

"You mentioned there was a lot of drama in the Texas Cattleman's Club." She shifted in her seat to turn slightly toward him, her elbow resting on the console between them.

Close to his.

"Did I?" He'd never had any use for gossip, so he hadn't paid much attention to the rumors. But his father had been so involved with opening a branch of the TCC in Houston, it was impossible not to overhear things.

"You said no one would think twice about you bringing a ranch hand for a date tomorrow night because there was a lot of other drama brewing." Her voice had a soft huskiness that made him think of morning-after pillow talk and shared confidences. "What's that about? Anything I need to be aware of?"

He glanced her way again, her green eyes fixed on him with a warmth he couldn't ignore.

Better to talk about the TCC than dwell on the spark of awareness growing between them. Besides, he had to admire her quick mind and her willingness to prepare for the social outing.

"I'm sure you've read about the badly decomposed body found at the construction site where the Houston branch is being renovated." He straightened in his seat, putting some more distance between him and the intriguing woman beside him. "Having a murder victim linked to the TCC has everyone…anxious."

His father hadn't said much about it, but Xander guessed his dad must have some suspicions. Ryder Currin knew everyone involved in getting the Texas Cattleman's Club Houston branch off the ground.

"I read all the articles about that," Frankie mused, her finger tracing the leather stitching along the side of the console. "It seems like they're not speculating much while they try to identify the body."

"No one is speculating in an official capacity, but believe me, there's plenty of talk. Some people think the victim could be Vincent Hamm, an assistant on the executive floor at Perry Holdings, who vanished into thin air right before the flood."

"Has anyone tried to locate him?" She went still, a note of alarm in her voice.

"Apparently his family told police he's always been a loner. He hated his job and often spoke of disappearing to a Caribbean island to be a surfer." He hadn't meant to worry her. "Maybe he finally did just that."

She fell quiet again, peering out her window as he passed a slow-moving farm vehicle.

"I did something like that once," she said after a long moment.

She surprised the hell out of him with the turn in conversation. He needed to stay on his toes around this woman.

"I can't picture you leaving it all behind to take up surfing." Although then again, she seemed to have a daring streak.

"Definitely not." She laughed, the sound bringing a rush of pleasure that made him want to hear it again.

"I meant that I took off from home a long time ago and never looked back."

A chill went through him and he glanced over at her again. "I hope no one hurt you back home."

"No. Nothing like that." She brushed aside the worry quickly, and she sounded sincere. "My parents treated me well enough, but they weren't my real parents, and I always felt like they'd hidden something from me about the day they found me."

She went on to explain how her parents had found her as a toddler, abandoned on a highway outside Laredo. They'd raised her as their own but had always been cagey about the circumstances of her arrival into their lives and what steps they'd taken—if any—to find her real parents.

"They were kind to me, but something always felt off about it." She lifted one shoulder in a shrug that looked more pained than casual. "Anyway, your mentioning Vincent Hamm's possible decision to leave everything behind made me think of my hometown. I wonder what my friends and parents thought happened to me after I took off."

"I don't know, but I'm sorry you went through that." He wondered what had made this driven, fierce woman decide to turn her back on the people who raised her. There was probably more to that story, and he was curious, but he refused to pry when he was only just starting to know her. "I wish you could meet my sister, Maya. My father adopted her when she was a baby, and as far as I know, he's never told anyone how she came into his life."

"Seriously? How old is she?" Frankie steadied herself as the truck bounced over a pothole near the turnoff for the main house.

"She's eighteen and away at college. My dad was supposed to tell her the whole story once she reached adulthood, and Maya is more than a little upset he hasn't done that yet."

Xander clicked on his high beams as the truck reached the wooden archway bearing the Currin Ranch sign.

"I hate secrets." The passion behind her words was obvious.

"That makes two of us." He'd had his own issues with secrets and surprises, and he sure as hell didn't plan to tread down that path again. He steered past the bunkhouse where a lot of the younger guys slept and headed toward the cabins. "But I'm guessing my dad has good reasons for keeping his. Maybe your parents are trying to protect you somehow."

"Maybe." She didn't sound convinced. "Anyway, thanks for the ride home."

She was tugging at her seat belt before he even had the truck parked. Because she wanted to escape his company? Or was she trying to ignore the same spark that kept drawing his gaze over her way?

"You don't have to thank me. I know this wasn't the ending you wanted for your evening." He switched off the truck to walk her to her door.

"It's fine," she rushed to say, already opening the truck door. "I can see myself inside."

He reached across the cab to put a hand on her forearm. "Frankie, wait."

Touching her had been a mistake—he knew it as
soon as soon as his fingers landed on her sleeve. They
wanted to linger there, to glide up her arm and around
her shoulder to draw her closer. But he could hardly
yank his hand back like he'd gotten scalded without revealing just how damned much she affected him.

So he let his fingers rest lightly where they were.

"I was hard on you tonight. Let me at least walk you
to your door so I can tell myself I made an attempt to
be a gentleman."

"You're my boss, not a gentleman," she argued, then
frowned. "That came out wrong. What I mean is—"

"But as you pointed out earlier, we're not on the clock
tonight." His fingers grazed her bare skin on the underside of her wrist, a surprisingly tender spot where
he could feel her pulse thrum fast.

Her green eyes were wide in the glow of the dome
light.

"Right." Her voice was all rasp and no substance.
She cleared her throat. "Okay."

He slid his hand away and stepped out of the truck,
walking around to her side.

He reached up to help her down, but she hopped out
on her own. Wary of his touch? Or stubbornly proud?

Maybe a little of both. She was an intriguing woman.

"Thank you." She chewed her lower lip and peered
up at him in the moonlight. "What time will I see you
tomorrow?"

His gaze zeroed in on her mouth, his own suddenly dry as dust.

"I'll pick you up at seven." He was already questioning the wisdom of this bargain he'd made with her.

If she was affecting him this much now, what would it be like tomorrow night when they had a whole evening together? Already, the memory of the feel of her made his hands itch to touch her again. He hadn't thought this through well at all.

She nodded, her dark braid sliding down her shoulder. "And just so I'm clear, will we be off the clock tomorrow, too?"

Was she flirting with him? Or was he reading too much into it because he wanted her?

The tension of holding himself back was quickly knotting his shoulders, and they'd been together less than an hour.

"I'm going to let you make that call. You can tell me how much of the evening you want to be business and how much should be—" he couldn't think of any way to say it that didn't sound like a come-on "—pleasure."

She must have heard it, too, because her lips parted in soft surprise.

"Good night, Frankie." He was already imagining her in an evening gown and liking what he saw.

He played a dangerous game letting his thoughts wander there, but he'd be damned if he could stop himself.

And with a silent nod, she pivoted on her boot heel and disappeared inside her cabin.

Three

Frankie finished her work as fast as possible on the afternoon of the gala, knowing she'd need extra time to get ready. She'd worked on the irrigation system most of the day, and had the dirty boots, jeans and face to prove it.

No doubt her hair was a hot mess under her hat, too.

Anticipation fired her movements as she returned one of the ranch's all-terrain vehicles to an overflow bay in the mansion's garage. She left the keys in the ignition, noticing that Xander's pickup was there, but his sports car wasn't. She hadn't seen him at all around the ranch during the day, but he'd told her he'd pick her up at the cabin at seven.

Which left her less than two hours to get ready.

At least she didn't have to spend any time choosing

a dress, since she had only one possibility in her closet. Her lone black cocktail dress seemed like a boring option for an event like the gala, but it would have to suffice. Striding across the big horseshoe driveway toward her cabin, she noticed a sleek white Mercedes coupe parked in front of the main entrance of the Currin home.

As she neared the vehicle, the tall oak door of the house opened and Annabel Currin, Xander's half sister, stepped out onto the porch. She carried an armful of dresses—turquoise silk and emerald satin hems peeking from beneath the plastic bags with the name of a pricey local boutique.

"Those look like some gorgeous gowns," she called to her. She didn't know Xander's sister well, but Annabel had always been nice to her.

Tall and willowy, Annabel had been doubly blessed in the beauty department thanks to her Kenyan mother, Elinah, and movie-star handsome father, Ryder Currin. Frankie had seen photos of the couple before Elinah's passing, and Xander's stepmother had been stunning. Annabel favored her mom, with high cheekbones and dark brown eyes.

"Don't make me second-guess myself!" Annabel warned her with a laugh as she rushed down the steps toward her car. "I decided to keep the yellow one for the gala tonight, but it was a tough call because I love them all. I was just loading these up to donate tomorrow."

Frankie knew that Annabel was a local fashion and style blogger and often received samples from designers.

"Do you mean to tell me these are the rejects?"

Frankie slowed her step as she neared Annabel's car. A fresh pang of worry about the dress code hit her. "Do you think a cocktail dress will be okay for tonight, or will I feel really underdressed if I don't have a gown?"

"You need a gown?" Annabel's eyes widened. "You're going to the gala?"

Frankie nodded, her anxiety doubling. "A cocktail dress is the wrong choice, isn't it?"

"You can wear one of these! No need to return it, even. I'll bet you are exactly my size." Annabel looked her over.

She felt self-conscious, knowing that she'd never worn an article of clothing as fine as the dresses in Annabel's arms.

"That's far too generous," she demurred. "I couldn't possibly—"

"Nonsense." Annabel clamped a hand on her wrist and tugged her toward the steps. "Cowgirl makeovers are my specialty."

Was she serious? Frankie had seen a few makeovers on the successful blog.

"Annabel, I'm a mess." Trepidation growing, she followed her onto the porch and through the front door, into the Currin family's home, which was more like a palatial Western retreat.

"That's why you'll make such a rewarding subject." Annabel headed straight for the grand staircase. "It will be fun."

"But you need to get ready, too." Frankie paused. "I don't want to be in your way."

"You won't be. I can get myself ready in ten minutes

flat, if necessary." She shot her a level look. "Trust me, I timed myself and made a video for my beauty blog about paring down a routine when you're in a hurry."

Frankie laughed. "That's impressive. Okay, I'm game if you are. But I should take my boots off."

A few minutes later, they were in Annabel's huge suite. Frankie had stepped inside the Currin home before, but she'd never been past the foyer. Now she peered around Annabel's massive room in dove gray and off-white, the muted color scheme relaxing and peaceful. She listened to Annabel hum softly to herself while she hung the spare dresses on a narrow wall full of antique hooks near an old-fashioned changing screen. Then she reached into a shelf just inside the walk-in closet and emerged with a pink silk drawstring bag.

"Come with me." Annabel waved her toward an open door to the en suite bath. "There's an extra robe on the back of the bathroom door." She peeked behind the door to be certain. "And toiletries in here." She set down the pink silk bag on the marble vanity top. "While you shower, I'll think about what we can do with your hair. Sound good?"

Touched at the thought of Annabel opening her home to her, sharing an expensive gown with her and walking her through getting ready for such a special night, Frankie found herself at a loss for words. She feared if she tried saying thank you she would embarrass herself by bursting into grateful tears.

Nodding, she took refuge in the giant bathroom, surrounded by sleek white marble and pale gray tile accents. A bouquet of gardenias and white clematis spilled over a pewter vase, filling the air with fragrant notes. She washed up as fast as possible, making sure to remove all traces of Texas dust. When she was certain she was spotless, she toweled off with one of the fluffy bath sheets that Annabel had set out for her. Beside the towels, she saw the pink silk drawstring bag. Inside, she found pretty, barely-there underthings with tags still attached, along with a spare toothbrush and sample-sized toiletries. After brushing her teeth, she slid into the spare white robe.

When she opened the door to Annabel's suite, the space had been transformed. The recessed lights were on a dimmer, so that the bed and living area were now darkened. The brightest area of the room was now the corner that had been behind the changing screen. The painted screen had been folded aside to reveal an old-fashioned dressing table. The whitewashed French country piece had yellow and blue stenciled flowers on the drawers, and a round mirror was illuminated by wall sconces on either side. A small leather stool sat in front of the vanity.

"Are you ready for your makeover?" Annabel waved her deeper into the suite and Frankie noticed her hostess had applied her own makeup in the interim. "I've got your seat ready for you."

"I can't believe you're doing all this for me." As she dropped down onto the leather stool, she tried to articulate the gratitude that had seized her before the shower. "You're like a fairy godmother."

"This is fun for me," Annabel assured her. "I never

really found my place on the ranch, but the style business suits me."

She talked a little more about her work in fashion and beauty blogging, then chatted about her fiancé, Mason Harrison, an executive at Currin Oil. Frankie found herself relaxing while she let Annabel dry her hair and set it in hot rollers, something Frankie had seen but never used.

"So who are you going to the gala with tonight?" Annabel asked once she'd moved on to makeup.

She tipped Frankie's face this way and that, studying it in the light before reaching for a palette of colors in shades of cream to dark brown.

"Xander, actually." She explained about the rodeo and the deal they'd made. "So it's not like a date or anything. Just his way of making sure I didn't break my neck, I guess."

Annabel stiffened, dropping the compact she'd been holding.

"Annabel?" Frankie leaned forward to pick up the pretty red case with all the powders. "Are you okay?"

Had she said something wrong?

"I'm fine." The other woman seemed to force a smile. "Sorry about that, I just got distracted for a moment. You know, we should choose the gown before we do any more. So I can use the right colors for your face."

Was it Frankie's imagination, or had Annabel been in a hurry to change the subject? But since she didn't want to make her hostess uncomfortable, she hopped out of the chair to try on dresses. While she was in the huge closet—really like a room of its own, with a chandelier and padded window seat—trying on the first one, she could hear Annabel talking in the other room. When she emerged in the turquoise silk, however, Annabel was alone, texting on her phone.

She glanced up and gasped. "Oh, Frankie, that one is going to be the winner."

"Really?" She couldn't help a pleased smile. "I tried it on first because it was my favorite."

"It's a perfect color on you. I love the way it makes your eyes even greener." Annabel steered her in front of an antique cheval mirror. "What size are your feet?"

"Nine." She hadn't thought about shoes.

"That's Maya's size. She'll have something in her room to go with the dress, but I really think this one is the winner." She smoothed the hem and frowned down at Frankie's toes. "We'd better hustle if we want to get those toenails painted. Oh!" She gripped Frankie's forearm. "I almost forgot. Xander texted me about something else and when I mentioned you were here, he asked me to tell you that he's sending a car for you. His meeting ran late, but he'll have your ticket hand-delivered for you, and then Xander will meet you at the gala."

Frankie hadn't realized how much she was looking forward to seeing Xander tonight until that bit of news burst a hopeful bubble inside her. It was just as well that she keep in mind her Cinderella moment ended with her fairy godmother makeover. Xander wasn't really her date tonight, so she needed to focus on making contacts at the gala and enjoying just being there.

Romance wasn't on the agenda and the sooner she got it through her head, the better.

* * *

Xander waited for the meeting to end inside the specialty golf suite that his father had booked for the Texas Cattleman's Club VIPs to gather before the gala. He wanted to get out of here and find his date. He was looking forward to the night more than he ought to be, given that it was supposed to be an opportunity for Frankie to network. She had been in his thoughts far too often today.

For now, he was stuck in the golf suite. The Four Seasons in Houston had ballrooms to host the gala downstairs, but Ryder Currin had gathered his powerful friends ahead of time to discuss TCC business. The sports-themed suite upstairs contained a golf simulator like the pros used, and guests who weren't taking swings could relax on the leather couches or at a small bar. Normally, Xander didn't care much about golf, but he picked up a club now to try his luck at the simulator while his father continued to discuss last-minute details for the gala. He was restless and wanted to work out the edginess.

Lining up a shot on the green, Xander resented being here and dealing with local politics instead of escorting Frankie to what was most likely the first gala she'd ever attended.

Damn it, he hadn't wanted to meet her at the event, but he couldn't very well walk out of a meeting his father had asked him personally to attend. Ryder wanted Xander there in case his archrival, Sterling Perry, crashed the meeting.

The tension in his shoulders made him slice right,

the ball bouncing into a water feature on the simulator's huge video screen. Continuing to play while the meeting got tense behind him, Xander heard his father arguing with someone about Sterling Perry. The two men had a history of enmity that started before Xander was born, so he didn't pretend to know all the nuances. There'd been rumors that Ryder had had an affair with Sterling's then-wife, Tamara. But Xander had never bought that. He figured Sterling just hated his dad because Ryder had once worked as a ranch hand for Tamara Perry's wealthy father, Harrington York, and inherited a small piece of property in that man's will. The property proved to be rich in oil and made Ryder a very wealthy man.

Sterling had resented the hell out of Xander's dad ever since, and the feud seemed to have taken on new life with the Texas Cattleman's Club opening a Houston branch. Both men wanted control, and Ryder's play to host the fund-raising gala tonight was probably a point in his favor.

Xander took a couple more swings, perfecting the shot he'd messed up the first time. But as he checked his watch and saw the time, he decided enough was enough for playing politics.

He was about to tell his father he was going downstairs to find his date when a woman entered the golf suite.

All of his father's cronies—eight men and a couple of women including his assistant, Liane Parker—stared as Angela Perry, Sterling's daughter, strode deeper into the room. Angela wore her long blond hair in a simple knot, her red dress simple and understated. Xander guessed she was under forty, though not by much, and she was already the executive vice president of Perry Holdings.

What the hell was she doing here?

He only had a moment to wonder about it when his father broke away from the rest of the group to stride toward her. He slid an arm around her waist and greeted her with a kiss on the cheek.

Well, holy hell.

"You look stunning," he overheard his father say.

Xander damn near swallowed his tongue, and he guessed the rest of the room did the same. Ryder Currin was dating Angela Perry, daughter of Sterling, the man he hated most in the world? Apparently his dad didn't practice what he preached about loyalty to blood and putting the family business first.

Returning his golf club to the rack near the simulator, Xander left the room to find his own date. Tonight was already getting off to a rocky start. But he still had something to look forward to this evening. Because he couldn't wait to see Frankie. He hadn't felt this pumped about a date since—

His heart hitched at the thought of Rena.

He pushed the thought aside. This didn't have to be complicated. He could just enjoy the moment. The date.

The woman.

Ten minutes later, entering the gala space glowing with candlelight from standing wrought iron fixtures, Xander searched the room for Frankie. He scanned past some of the Perry Holdings bigwigs, including Tatiana

Havery and her brother laughing together, and a few ranchers he recognized at the bar.

Xander had almost given up finding her when... He did a double take.

Frankie?

Frankie.

She stood out in her turquoise gown all the more since she lingered with her back to a wall of bright fuchsia orchids. The Flood Relief Gala theme was "Blooming through Adversity," so flowers of all kinds filled the Four Seasons ballroom, but she outshone them all. Frankie's dark hair curled in soft waves around her face, so different from the functional ponytail she wore every day for work. Faceted crystals dangled from her ears, almost skimming her bare shoulders. Two delicate straps held up her close-fitting silk gown adorned with sequins, the shape fitted until it flared around her knees, mermaid style.

More beautiful than any woman in the room, she turned heads all around her as the orchestra launched into a slow song. The lights dimmed, and in his peripheral vision, he noticed couples take to the dance floor. But Xander couldn't take his eyes off Frankie as she clutched a tiny silver bag between both hands. She peered about the gala, as if looking for someone.

Him, no doubt.

He kicked himself for not getting down here sooner.

Pulled to her, he wished he'd brought her flowers. Done anything to make this evening more romantic and memorable for her. Because he couldn't deny it any longer. He wanted Frankie Walsh, and pretending otherwise wasn't going to make this keen need to have her disappear.

He snapped off an orchid bloom from a display spilling out of a silver urn near an ice sculpture of the new TCC building. He carried it over to her, his eyes holding hers every step of the way until he reached her.

"You look…incredible." He lifted her hand and brought it to his lips, lingering while her startled gaze collided with his.

Her eyes were deep green, like a lush field of spring grass. Her mouth was painted a bright shade of rosy pink, making him crave a taste of her. The scent of her skin—peaches and roses—stirred a deeper hunger.

"May I have this dance?" He tucked the bloom behind her ear, wondering how she'd managed the transformation from muddy cowgirl to exotic society beauty. He'd always found her attractive, but that attraction had been one-dimensional. Seeing this side of her, too, made her come to life in a multifaceted way that rivaled the earrings grazing her shoulders.

No one would ever guess she'd spent half the day digging out a leaking irrigation system for repairs. Or that he'd had to stop her from entering a bronc riding event just the night before.

How many more hidden depths did this woman have?

"Yes, I'd love to dance." Her quick agreement, softly spoken, gave no hint of the strong, stubborn will that lurked beneath this delicate feminine guise.

Gratefully, he led her to the dance floor, wrapping her hand in his, stroking his thumb lightly over the center of her palm while they walked. He set her purse on their reserved table along the way.

When he reached an empty corner of the hardwood floor, he took his time skimming his hand down her back until it rested in the center. The back of her gown was low-cut enough that his palm grazed bare skin above the zipper, the tantalizing feel of her filling his senses.

Her fingers rested on his shoulder and she looked him in the eye as he swept them into the dance, moving with her easily. He wasn't letting her go tonight if he could help it. Frankie Walsh had become too much of a distraction for him to pretend otherwise.

But first, he couldn't resist teasing her while they swayed together.

"I've never seen you here before. May I ask your name?"

Four

Seriously?

Frankie's step faltered.

She knew that Annabel had transformed her. From the magic of makeup that gave her smoky cat's eyes complete with winged eyeliner, to the elegant dress and jewelry, the makeover was complete. But she wouldn't have guessed she'd be unrecognizable. She felt a flare of irritation that Xander would dance with another woman when—as far as he knew—he hadn't even taken the time to find his date yet.

"Francesca," she answered coolly, giving him her full name, a pretty, feminine moniker she'd never believed suited her.

But if there had ever been a time when she felt like a Francesca, it was right now, wrapped in a handsome man's strong arms as he whisked her around the dance floor in this fairy-tale setting full of flowers. She wouldn't have guessed a big, muscular cowboy like him would be so effortless on his feet, but he was such a sure, commanding partner, she didn't even have to think about following him. Her feet moved with his, her body in tantalizing proximity to him at all times, as she was swept away by the music, the moment…the man.

The custom-fitted tux couldn't hide the lean muscle of his shoulders, arms and chest. She felt his strength as they swayed together. Her body hummed with awareness.

"And what do you think of the gala so far, Francesca?" Her name was a seductive sound on his lips, his head inclined toward her ear so she could hear the softly spoken words over the orchestra's lilting strings.

"It's beautiful," she admitted, grateful to be here even if her date didn't recognize her. "I've never seen anything so lovely."

Bright fuchsia flowers spilled from centerpieces and twined around the tall columns framing the orchestra box. Tiny white lights threaded through greenery-laden tables. Added candlelight from tall sconces gave everything a warm, dreamy glow. The fragrance of roses, hyacinths and orchids was a heady aroma.

"I have." He slowed his steps as the music came to an end. The rest of the dancers applauded the musicians while Xander tipped her chin up to see her better. "You are the loveliest woman here, Frankie."

Her breath caught and she couldn't deny the delight. "You did recognize me."

"Of course." A smile pulled at the corner of his lips. "I asked your name as a way to start the night fresh. I thought if we were strangers meeting for the first time, we could enjoy our evening together without worrying about what it means for our working relationship."

She took his hand as he led her from the dance floor, a bolt of pleasure tickling its way up her arm. "It would definitely be easier for me if I wasn't your employee for a few hours."

"And yet I know you wanted to be here in order to network." He paused near the massive ice sculpture of the TCC Houston building, a historic former luxury boutique hotel that fell into disrepair and was now being renovated for the clubhouse.

Frankie had been following all the news about it, intrigued by the power struggle between Ryder Currin and Sterling Perry, two of the wealthiest men in town.

"It will be a while before I have my veterinary degree since I haven't even started a program yet," she said wryly, plucking a strawberry from a nearby table of desserts. "So I don't necessarily *need* to network. I just wanted to see the Houston branch of the Texas Cattleman's Club come together since I hope to serve these people with my practice one day."

"Nevertheless, I will introduce you to some of the club's key members. Would you like to eat first?" Xander gestured to the buffet full of desserts. "Our table is over there, where I left your purse before the dance. If you want to have a seat, I can bring us both plates."

"I'd like that. Thank you."

Moments later, they were seated at their reserved

table with Ryder Currin and—Frankie couldn't believe her eyes—Angela Perry. Together. They barely had time for introductions, however, when Ryder asked his date for a dance.

Excusing themselves, the surprise couple moved toward the dance floor. Heads turned as they went, which told Frankie she wasn't the only one shocked to see them together.

She turned back to ask Xander about it, but she caught him staring at her in a way that scrambled her thoughts. Self-consciously, she patted her hair.

"I'm not falling apart, am I?" She hated to reveal her nervousness, but she didn't want to mess up all Annabel's hard work. "I'm having visions of my makeup smearing or my hair rebelling and standing on end—"

"No. I'm sorry." Xander shook his head. "I didn't mean to stare." His hand came up to her hair, pushing a few waves behind her shoulder. "I thought for a moment it was a tattoo on your neck."

She felt her cheeks heat. "It's a birthmark."

She wasn't embarrassed about it or anything. It was visible all the time at work when she had her hair up. But Xander's close regard made her far too aware of herself. Of him.

Of the heat that simmered between them.

"It's such a perfect crescent moon." He skimmed a knuckle along the spot below her right ear, his fingers brushing her dangling earrings. "But I will confess, it wasn't just the birthmark. I was also trying to reconcile the elegant woman I'm seeing with the hard-nosed wrangler who was ready to bronc ride her way to a ticket last night."

"I thought I was going to be Francesca tonight and not Frankie?" she teased, stirring her spoon through a crème brûlée in a tiny ceramic dish.

"I'm intrigued by both of you." His blue eyes held hers, and she felt desire smoke through her.

Her mouth felt too dry to answer.

She'd had a crush on Xander Currin for as long as she'd worked at his ranch. So no matter how much she told herself that romance was dead and that he wasn't the kind of man who wanted romance anyhow, she still hungered for his touch. His attention.

And yes, his kiss.

Surely she wasn't alone in feeling that attraction now? His touches lingered, as did his stare. She might work for him, and she might be just a ranch hand in his big, wealthy world, but she could read the signs of male interest well enough.

"That's good," she told him, gathering up her courage. Or her foolishness. She didn't know exactly which it was that made her say, "Because we're both fascinated by you, too, Xander."

Something stirred in his gaze. Interest. Arousal. Whatever it was made an answering flame leap inside her. He had a way of looking at her that made her feel like the only woman in the room. A unique experience for her. Was it only because of the magic that Annabel had wrought?

He leaned close to her as the number of partygoers grew. He slid his arm along the back of her chair at their private table, now empty except for them. His fingertips rested lightly along her shoulder, a touch that made a pleasurable shiver tremble along her nerve endings.

"I've avoided you around the ranch because of this." He pointed vaguely back and forth between them. "This awareness. I noticed you long ago and have tried to make sure that our paths didn't cross more than necessary."

"You noticed me?" She sounded too eager. Too breathless. But she was genuinely surprised. Her appetite for the rich desserts vanished as a new hunger took its place. "I had no idea."

"I try to put forward my professional best at work. So having my attention linger on a beautiful woman on my team would be a bad idea." His voice rumbled, low and gravelly, the admission sending a thrill through her. "But I don't think there's any sidestepping it tonight."

He looked into her eyes, a current of understanding passing between them. Her gaze dipped to his mouth and she found herself thinking about what it would be like to kiss him. A flush crept up her face, heat flaring over her skin.

Startled by the vividness of the things she imagined, she sucked in a breath while Xander traced one thin strap of her gown. The pads of his fingertips glided up the silk, leaving chill bumps in their wake.

"Definitely no sidestepping it tonight," he mused, seeming to answer his own unspoken question. "Why don't I introduce you around the room so we can take care of business before we continue this far more interesting line of discussion?"

"Thank you." She nodded, pushing aside the china plate of decadent desserts he'd brought her. "I'd like that."

It would buy her time to think about what to do next. With her pulse racing and her thoughts full of Xander Currin, she needed a mental time-out to be sure of her next move.

As she took his hand and let him lead her toward an elegant-looking older couple taking a breather from the dance floor, Frankie went on social autopilot for the introductions. While she smiled and asked questions about their animals, Frankie was thinking about Xander all the while. Should she take the leap and give herself over to the attraction? Or keep fighting it for the sake of...what? Her job?

She wasn't worried about that. Xander was too honorable a man to make things awkward for her at work in the aftermath of whatever happened tonight. He'd avoided her before; he could avoid her again.

Her heart? She couldn't pretend she didn't have feelings for Xander. But she knew all too well from her close observation of him over the last year that he wasn't the kind to get attached. Surely she was smart enough to recognize that a love-'em-and-leave-'em guy wouldn't suddenly become a one-woman man after one night.

But as Xander slid an arm around her waist and introduced her to a rancher from the original TCC in Royal, Texas, who'd made the trip to Houston to support the new branch, Frankie knew she'd be hard-pressed to walk away from the temptation of even just one night with her sexy boss.

The attraction was so intense it was distracting when she needed to be focused on making enough money to afford veterinary school. On remembering the people here tonight so she could foster those connections down the road. She really did hope to have a mixed animal practice in the area. Or maybe a large-animal specialty. Yet she found it impossible to stay focused with Xander's touch making her so aware of him. Maybe indulging one fantasy evening in Xander's bed would finally excise him from her thoughts, freeing her to focus on her dreams?

Possibly she was simply rationalizing what she really wanted to do. But tonight, with the charismatic rancher beside her and the magic of her Cinderella transformation at work, Frankie couldn't deny herself the chance to follow the attraction wherever it might lead.

Xander knew he couldn't just tuck her under his arm and flee the gala with Frankie Walsh. But two hours after her revealing admission that she was "fascinated" by him, he still couldn't will away the desire for her that plagued his every move.

Now he pulled her onto the dance floor once more, wanting to be sure she enjoyed herself. She'd been willing to risk her beautiful neck for a ticket to this party, so he wasn't going to deprive her of the full gala experience just to indulge his personal desires. He'd introduced her to all the most prominent ranchers, giving her time to voice her goals of opening a veterinary practice in town once she completed her schooling. She'd received two offers to spend time in the barns if she

needed more hours of animal time for her admission—
something he hadn't known was required for her program.

He'd also learned that she volunteered most of her
free time to shadow a local vet or to work at an animal shelter.

"Frankie, I hope you know you can ask for more
hours in the barns at Currin Ranch." He hadn't meant
to talk business with her when they were alone, but
he didn't like the idea of other ranchers trying to lure
her away with better positions. "I hate thinking you
spent the day on that irrigation system when you need
hours with animals in order to be admitted to veterinary school."

She was already shaking her head, a few dark ten-
drils of hair twining around her dangling earrings as
she moved.

"I'm not the kind of worker who requests special
treatment," she insisted. "I have low seniority right now,
so I'm willing to take the work that comes with that."

He wanted to know more about her. Where she got
her work ethic, what inspired her to be a vet and why
she would take foolish chances bronc riding when she
had a bright future ahead of her. His gut knotted at the
memory of how it had made him feel when he was trying to talk her out of it. His fiancée had been wearing
a riding helmet when she fell during a jump, but that
hadn't prevented her from hitting a fence post awk-
wardly.

"But you've been with us for nearly a year. It's not
special treatment to share your work goals with your

direct supervisor." He would make sure she was more involved in the barns. "We want you to remember us well when you've got your degree."

"I will." Her feet followed his, the hem of her gown sliding against his pant leg as he twirled her. A seductive whisper of touch. "I'll never forget what you did for me tonight, Xander. Meeting so many successful ranchers, getting to see the new Texas Cattleman's Club forming, I can't tell you how much that means to me."

One of her hands rested on his shoulder; the other was folded inside his. She wasn't nearly close enough to him. It was all he could do to keep his own palm steady on her back when what he really wanted was to skim a touch down the curve of her hips and pull her to him.

"Does that mean you've enjoyed your evening?" He liked seeing the way the candlelight brought a warm, burnished glow to her dark hair.

As for the pink in her cheeks, he'd like to think he put that there.

"It's even more beautiful than I imagined a fancy gala would be." She peered around the ballroom still packed with men in tuxes and women in gowns of every shade. "Seeing the world of the Texas Cattleman's Club is going to motivate me even more."

"What made you want to be a vet?"

"I think I first fell in love with animals when I saved a baby bird from a neighbor's cat." She smiled at the memory. "My parents homeschooled me and wouldn't allow me to join any local sports teams or—" she shook her head, the smile vanishing "—or any kind of club, really. I didn't have a lot of human companionship, but they were good about letting me keep strays. I survived some lonely years because of my animal friends."

"Like what?" he pressed, wanting to see her talk about happy memories. "I assume you kept the bird, for starters?"

"Not for long." Her smile returned. "I only kept the bird until he was strong enough to fly again."

"So what other strays did you take in?"

"Cats were a constant." Her voice was more enticing than the music, and he found himself wanting to listen to her talk at length about most anything. "I always fed at least ten cats every day, and considering the price of cat food, that necessitated a paper route."

"Industrious of you."

"Thank you. Over the years there were a handful of snakes and lizards, a very big iguana, assorted squirrels and chipmunks, two deer—"

"You had deer?" He'd underestimated her passion for the local wildlife.

"One was a doe that had a near miss with a hunter. The other was an abandoned fawn that I only kept until I was sure how to release her successfully back into a herd."

He was enjoying her story of rehabilitating a bat when the music came to an end, shifting to a more up-tempo song. Xander drew her to a quieter corner of the room.

Or it was until a woman's voice rose in volume at the table behind them. He turned in time to see Angela Perry glaring at her twin sister, Melinda. With blond hair and blue eyes like Angela, the two definitely resembled each other even though they weren't identical. Right now, however, they appeared unhappy with each other.

Angry, even.

"Seriously?" Angela clenched her fists, not even bothering to lower her voice. "How dare you question my romantic choices when you're dating a *mobster*!"

Melinda paled.

Xander searched the crowd for his father and didn't see him. He guessed Angela's first public appearance with Ryder Currin wasn't making her family happy.

"He's not a mobster!" Melinda shot back, her eyes blazing. "For your information, he just has mob *ties*." She snatched up her beaded handbag from the table and stormed off, leaving Angela alone.

Looking devastated.

Xander hated to pretend he hadn't overheard them, but wouldn't that be the most polite thing to do?

Frankie appeared ready to offer some words of comfort to Angela, taking a step in that direction. But at the same time, Ryder came striding through the crowd toward his date, two champagne glasses in hand and a concerned expression on his face.

No doubt his father would remedy the situation. Or try to.

"Let's go," Xander urged Frankie, wrapping his arm more securely around her waist. He noticed several people turning to stare at Angela as Melinda left the event in a huff.

Or were they turning to look at someone else? There was a lot of movement in the crowd suddenly.

"Out of my way," a man shouted right before Xander spotted Sterling Perry hurtling through the partygoers in the direction of Ryder and Angela.

"Damn," Xander muttered under his breath, regretting the turn of events on a night that he wanted to make special for Frankie. He'd been enjoying his time with her. "As much as I'd like to whisk you away from here right now, I need to make sure there's no bloodshed. Or arrests."

He didn't trust Sterling one bit, and the man looked ready to spit nails despite his polished boots and the heavy silver bolo tie he wore with his flashy tux. He stopped a few feet from his daughter, where she stood beside Ryder.

For his part, Ryder looked unflustered, his expression patient. Xander guessed his father had faced down Sterling this way plenty of times over the years.

"I wouldn't believe it if I didn't see it with my own eyes," Sterling shouted at them while half of the party turned to see what was going on. "Bad enough this rat bastard undermines me by throwing a gala on behalf of a club he isn't even in charge of, but now my own daughter betrays me by—"

He halted midsentence, as if he was too angry to think of what he wanted to say. A hush fell over the gala guests nearby, everyone waiting to hear and making no secret of it.

"I've done nothing of the sort," Angela told her father in a more subdued voice. She sounded composed, but Xander noticed the white-knuckled hold she had on her champagne glass.

"If you don't stop seeing this upstart ingrate Currin, I'll cut you out of the company," Sterling threatened his daughter, leaning forward with his big shoulders. "Just see if I won't."

Xander was ready to jump in if needed, his muscles tense. This wasn't turning out to be the fun evening out he'd hoped to offer Frankie. The whole Perry family seemed to be angry with one another. And Sterling was angriest of all.

Ryder put a hand on Angela's back and spoke softly to her alone. Angela shook her head sadly. At least twenty people nearby strained harder to listen.

"I'm sorry, Ryder," she told him, setting down the crystal champagne flute right before she retrieved her small purse. "But I think it's best if I leave."

"Just like that?" Ryder's gravelly voice was pitched low, but Xander still heard him. "You're going to let him dictate what you do?"

His father was angry. Xander could see it in the way he held himself, even though to the rest of the world he might appear composed. No doubt, he'd put himself on the line to bring Angela with him here tonight. To have her walk away so publicly had to upset him.

But that's just what Angela did, taking Sterling's arm as the two of them left the gala together.

Xander could have sworn the musicians played louder, as if the whole place conspired to be more festive so the party could continue. He empathized with his father, knowing the pain of having a woman surprise him that way. Rena's shocking news before her riding accident had haunted him long afterward.

Old regrets of his own churned.

"Should you talk to your father?" Frankie asked, laying a gentle hand on Xander's tux sleeve while they watched Ryder disappear into a private room in the back. "He looks upset."

Xander forced himself to let go of his own demons, knowing this wasn't the time for bad memories.

"I think he'd prefer to be by himself." Xander recognized that set to his dad's shoulders, the stress of the night weighing on him. "I'll check in with him tomorrow. Right now, I'm more concerned about you. This isn't how I wanted to end the evening. It's your call if we stay longer or call it a night."

For his part, he knew what he preferred.

He'd wanted Frankie alone ever since he'd first spotted her in front of that wall of flowers.

"As much as I hate for the night to end, I guess I'm ready to leave." She took a party favor—a silver horseshoe charm—from one of the tables near the door. "I'm going to take this as a memento, though. It's so pretty."

Her quick smile at the gift charmed him.

For that matter, her simple appreciation of the token made him feel jaded to think how many functions like this he'd attended over the years, how many party favors he'd walked right past without even noticing them. Frankie looked at the evening in a much different way. Was it selfish of him to want to keep her with him longer, to see the world through her eyes for a little while?

And yes, he wanted her close in every other way, too.

So he wrapped his arms around her, drew her near to tell her what he'd been wanting to say all evening long.

"Keep in mind, just because we leave the party doesn't mean the night has to end."

I sip my whiskey slowly, savoring the taste. The hundred-year-old brew is smooth, mellow and delicious, but it can't compare to the thrill of another satisfying night's work. Standing at the back of the Flood Relief Gala, I can't help but savor how well things went tonight in my plan for revenge. I hate Sterling Perry and Ryder Currin for what they've done to me. For everything they've stolen and ruined in my life. But things are starting to turn in my favor. Every day, I get closer to bringing them down and making them feel my pain. Tonight, Sterling Perry was so angry he was breathing fire when he saw his daughter with Ryder Currin. I thought he might keel over from the fury!

And Ryder didn't fare much better in all the drama. His date walked out on him in front of the whole Texas Cattleman's Club. The man hides his emotions a whole lot better than his rival, but of course he felt humiliated. Who wouldn't have been?

So much success to savor, and I hardly had to lift a finger.

Now, I just have to keep my eye on the prize. Once Angela Perry discovers the information I planted about Ryder, she's sure to cut him out of her life forever.

As for Sterling? His good reputation is about to crash and burn.

Five

Frankie had driven through the front gate to Currin Ranch many times. But when Xander slowed his luxury coupe in front of the six-foot stone pedestals that held the wooden arches for the ranch's welcome sign, the electronic sensor swinging the gates open, she acknowledged that her arrival felt very different this time as a guest.

Xander's guest.

Back at the gala, he'd made it clear the night didn't have to end when they left the party. She'd understood that the invitation meant they might well end the night in bed. Now, as he steered the vehicle through the gate and down the main drive toward the mansion, she knew it was up to her to make it clear what she would like to happen next.

She knew what she *wanted*. She just didn't know if

indulging her desires was wise. It had been fun learning a little more about her sexy boss and his world, even though he'd been very skilled at getting her to talk about herself more than the other way around. She didn't usually share details about her past like that— the way she'd grown to love the company of animals, or how she'd felt lonely as a kid because of her parents' isolating lifestyle.

But somehow, she'd shared all those things with him.

"Do you want me to take you to your cabin?" He glanced over at her, his face illuminated by the amber glow of dashboard lights. "Or stop at the ranch house for a drink?"

What she preferred was a kiss. And everything that went with it. But did she dare act on that inclination?

She hadn't come this far in life by backing down from what she wanted.

"My place is a bit of a disaster," she admitted. It was also very small and humbly furnished. "So if yours is an option, that might be better."

This was happening.

"Definitely." He pulled into the driveway and hit the button for one of the garage bays, the door yawning open at his approach. "The pool house is all lit up," he observed before driving inside the mammoth structure. "It's not too hot out tonight, if you want to sit outside for a little while."

"That sounds nice." And romantic. Tempting. She waited in the passenger seat after they parked, and he came around to help her out of the vehicle. "I wouldn't mind some fresh air."

She took his hand, unaccustomed to managing a gown and heels in a ballroom, let alone getting in and out of a low-slung sports car. Straightening, she followed him through a side door out onto the stone deck and around to the back of the pool house. The building had the same Western log style as the main house, one side full of floor-to-ceiling windows and a pair of French doors. Outside them, a patio table and cushioned loungers were half hidden by bright bougainvillea draped down from the red cedar pergola. Landscaping lights hidden in the surrounding trees and bushes made the pool area look like a nighttime oasis.

"I'll get us some drinks," he offered, releasing her hand to open the door.

"I'll help." She darted through ahead of him as he held the door for her. "Plus, I'm curious to see what a pool house looks like inside."

The Currin family's lifestyle intrigued her. She was happy with the cabin she lived in that was part of her compensation as a ranch hand, but walking into the Currin world was like opening a glossy magazine about the rich and famous. She didn't need that life, but it was beautiful to see.

Her childhood home had been tiny, an out-of-way converted barn with no neighbors for miles.

"My father isn't much for decor," Xander explained, gesturing to the huge open living space flanked by a bar on one side and a small kitchen on the other. "He's definitely from the 'less is more' school of thought."

"Annabel's suite wasn't like that. But I'm guessing she decorated that herself." She spun around in a circle as she strode deeper into the room. The natural stone floor was a nod to wet bathers, but other than that, it was graciously appointed. A leather sectional couch sat in front of a fireplace on the opposite wall.

While the space was furnished simply, everything was high-end and luxurious, from the silent spinning ceiling fans overhead to the heavy bronze accents around the fireplace and pendant lights over the gray quartz bar. The pendants were dimmed to a low setting, casting a muted golden glow in the room. It was brighter outside by the pool, but the tall windows let in some of that light, too.

"Annabel definitely put her personal stamp on her rooms. But the rest of the house is more stripped down. Have you ever seen the Perry place?" Xander asked as he poured two glasses of sparkling water. He returned the bottle to the refrigerator in the kitchen and then brought her a glass. "His ranch house looks more like a castle, so I guess I think of Dad's taste as fairly subdued."

"I've seen photos of Perry Ranch in the news, so I know what you mean. But this is beautiful in a different way. Understated can be lovely, too."

Standing near a sofa table, she peered around the room, admiring it a little longer, until her gaze collided with Xander's. Her skin heated.

He raised his glass, his eyes still locked on her. "Cheers to making it through your first gala."

Her heartbeat sped faster as she lifted her glass. "Cheers to seeing the world I've been dreaming about with my own eyes. Thank you taking me tonight."

She took a slow sip, letting the cool water quench some of the fire rolling through her at the realization they were more alone than they'd ever been. The only sound was her breathing and the clink of ice cubes in their glasses.

"The pleasure was all mine." He set his drink aside on the sofa table. Then he took hers from her as she lowered it, and set that one down, too, balancing each one on a marble coaster. "I don't usually care about glitzy events like that, but I enjoyed being with you tonight."

Her throat felt dry already, even though she'd just had a drink. She stared up at him, mesmerized, aching for his touch.

"I've wanted to kiss you from the first moment I saw you tonight," he confided. Reaching toward her hair, he plucked the orchid bloom from behind her ear. She'd forgotten that he'd placed it there when he first walked up to her at the gala. Now he laid the delicate petals on the table, too, while her heart kicked harder against the inside of her chest.

She'd dreamed of him too many times in the months that she'd crushed on him. It hardly seemed possible she'd fantasized this moment into reality.

"You have?" Her voice was a breathless squeak of sound, but she was determined to claim this one night with him. Or however many nights he was prepared to give her. So she forced herself to make her feelings more plain. "Then what are you waiting for?"

He stared down at her for an interminable moment before one knuckle brushed the underside of her chin, tipping her face toward his. Anticipation tingled over her skin. He angled closer and she breathed him in for an instant before his lips met hers. A tender brush of his mouth.

Sweet. Sensual. Tempting.

She went still under the onslaught of sensations. The scents of cedar and musk. The warmth of his hand sliding around her waist. She all but melted against him, craving the feel of all that delicious male muscle. The silk of her dress slid between them in a teasing glide of fabric.

The kiss tantalized her, reminding her of all the times she'd imagined this moment, and all the ways her imagination hadn't done it justice. The reality of Xander was hotter. Harder. Hungrier.

Or maybe that last part was her.

Because when he deepened the kiss, she thought she might spontaneously combust. The press of his lips sent ribbons of pleasure through her. Her fingers were raking off his tuxedo jacket and wrestling with the buttons on his shirt, a feverish desire for more of him making her ache.

He broke away suddenly, his breath ragged as if he'd been running. "Hold that thought."

Pulling his hands from her waist, he moved toward the door and locked it. The bolt slid home in a welcome, satisfying sound. When he turned toward her again, she took in his shadowed jaw and newly rumpled silk bow tie thanks to her questing hands. Two buttons on his pleated tuxedo shirt were unfastened, giving her a tantalizing glimpse of his chest.

Her heartbeat echoed his footsteps, getting faster as he neared.

"Come with me." He took her hand and led her deeper into the pool house.

She hadn't noticed the archway off the kitchen earlier, but he led her through a nook where a coffee bar lined one wall and a wine cabinet the other. Then he opened a door to a guest bedroom. The white walls were offset by the gray stone fireplace at the foot of the bed and a gray planked ceiling that sloped under an exterior gambrel. A bed was tucked into the corner, the white comforter and gray leather headboard as understated as the rest of the room.

Behind her, Xander closed the door. Blinds covered the windows, and it was dark for a moment before he hit a switch to light a wrought iron lamp on the mantel. She slid out of her shoes while he disappeared into the bathroom, emerging a moment later with a foil packet that he placed on the cedar chest beside the bed.

He met her gaze. Waiting.

She recognized the moment for what it was—a chance for her to be certain this was what she wanted. The condom was a clear indication of his desires. Now it was her turn. And she didn't think twice.

With a roll of her shoulder, she shrugged off one strap of her gown. Then she slid a finger under the other strap and skimmed it down. Turning her back on him, she put the zipper in easy reach before she swiveled a look over one shoulder.

"A little help, please?" she asked, although she was

so ready to be naked with him, she would have wriggled her way out of the dress if necessary.

He shifted closer behind her, his knee grazing her. He pushed aside the luxurious waves Annabel had created with her hair, baring her spine before he placed a kiss there. The shiver that tripped through her was pure pleasure.

Then he inched the zipper down. Silk fell in a sensual flow down her skin, the tissue-thin gown pooling at her hips. From behind her, Xander snaked one arm around her waist, nudging the fabric the rest of the way off.

"Wow." The soft word, reverently spoken, made her suddenly self-conscious.

She'd never been a woman who inspired that kind of reaction in men. Spinning in his arms, she faced him.

"Now I get to see you." She unfastened the next button on his shirt, pressing a kiss to his heated skin as she worked one after the other. Losing herself in the feel of him, the rapid tattoo of his heartbeat under her lips, the taut muscle of his abs as she neared his waist.

When she flicked open the hook on his trousers, he returned the favor by undoing her bra clasp. And while she still didn't trust her wow-factor, she enjoyed the gleam of appreciation in his eyes before he cupped a breast in his hand, thoroughly distracting her from undressing him.

She swayed on her feet, bracing herself by gripping his shoulders. Naked, hot, strong shoulders. Her knees wobbled even more until he walked her backward toward the bed, lowered her onto the downy comforter, then joined her there. The press of his hips against hers reminded her that the night was going to get so much better.

Desire fluttered along her feminine muscles, like a butterfly kiss, and they hadn't even gotten all their clothes off yet. Arching harder against him, she wanted more.

Now.

He obliged with a kiss to her breast, drawing on the nipple until the peak pebbled impossibly tighter. She tunneled her hands through his dark hair while he kissed and laved the other breast, and tension coiled tighter inside her.

"I'm so close. Please." She stroked her palm down his back, fingers combing aside the waistband of the tuxedo pants.

"You are?" He reared back to look down at her, his blue eyes a shade darker, the black centers wide. "You don't need to wait for me."

He reached between her thighs, cupping her through the tiny scrap of silk she still wore.

All that delicious tension stirred. She gasped from the pleasure of it.

"I can wait. I just—" She reached for the condom, but the nightstand was too far. "It just feels—"

He slid aside the silk and stroked circles right *there*, where she needed him most.

"I can't wait to make you feel good," he whispered in her ear, his lips brushing her cheek while he spoke, one of his legs pinning hers in the most pleasant way imaginable.

More than pleasant. It was sexy as hell.

And whatever he was doing with his hand felt so—

The building tension burst, her release hitting her hard and fast, the waves of oh-so-amazing fulfillment racking her body. Again. And again. He seemed to know exactly how to make it last, touching her in ways that elicited every ounce of bliss from an orgasm unlike anything she'd ever achieved on her own or with help.

None of which she could articulate, since sparks still shimmered behind her eyes. Vaguely, she knew he'd stood up long enough to undress and retrieve the condom. By the time he dragged her panties off and stretched out over her, she was recovered enough to kiss him. To wrap her arms around his neck and stroke a caress up the hard, hot length of him.

To look in his eyes as he eased his way inside her, inch by delectable inch, filling her.

She wrapped her legs around him, holding him there while her body adjusted to him, and she tried to catch a breath. But looking up into the blue eyes she'd dreamed about too many times, she knew that probably wasn't going to happen. She was in bed with someone she'd fantasized about. Someone she'd never hold on to.

It was okay if she just sank into the moment. Closing her eyes, she gave herself over to the feelings and met his hips thrust for thrust, finding her own rhythm.

When he rolled her on top of him, she moved with abandon, letting her body take the lead, feeling the delicious heat build again. She staved it off by focusing on him. On kissing his neck. Nipping his jaw. Tipping her head to one side to drape her hair along his chest and drag it upward like a silken touch.

She knew he was close when he gripped her hips. Holding her where he wanted her. Guiding her. Only then did she give herself over to everything she was feeling. For the second time. When his muscles tensed everywhere, hers did, too. She flew apart a moment before him, his shout drowning out her soft cries as pleasure tumbled through her until she was wrung out from it.

She slumped to his side, holding him tight. Wanting to curl up against him and stay there forever.

Dangerous thoughts.

But she was too damned fulfilled to push the notion away. The aftershocks still trembled through her as their heartbeats slowed, their breathing synched.

While the spinning ceiling fan cooled her skin, she did exactly as she pleased and laid her head on his chest. If she only had one night with Xander Currin, she was going to make the most of every moment.

Xander knew he'd stepped over a line by sleeping with someone he employed. It had been unethical. Selfish. Shortsighted.

And he still couldn't scavenge up even the slightest regret about it.

Frankie had brought him something more valuable than physical pleasure tonight, although the sex alone had floored him. She'd also somehow given him a night of peace from his personal demons, and that was a surprise he wasn't ready to analyze. He combed his fingers through her hair in the quiet aftermath of lovemaking, savoring the stillness in his brain. The lack of guilt and grief that had dogged him after nights with other women.

How had she done that?

Or was it simply time for him to turn the page on his past for good? He tamped down those questions to focus on the woman beside him.

"Can I get you anything?" He twined a lock of dark hair around his finger, wanting to be thoughtful. Considerate.

Wanting her to stay longer.

"Clean skin." Glancing up at him, she grinned. "I've never worn makeup like this before and I'm scared I'll leave half my face on the pillow."

Gently, he traced one of the wings on her eyeliner where it slanted toward her temple.

"It still looks perfect." Her skin was so soft. "But if you come in the shower with me, I can promise you'll end up with a clean face. Eventually."

He could read the desire in her eyes as she followed his thinking. Her fingers flexed against his chest.

"That sounds…ambitious of you." She walked her fingers down his abs. Lingered there.

Hunger for her stirred. Already.

"I aim to please." He slid off the bed and tugged her to her feet. "Besides, I already know what it's like to be with your exotic alter ego, Francesca. But I've got a serious thing for Frankie."

He pushed open the door to the guest bedroom's en suite bath and reached into the shower stall to flick on the water. Eight jets turned on at once, but he dialed off four of them to give them more options.

"I might need a putty knife," Frankie observed as she rubbed at a streak of gold-flecked shadow on her brow bone. "Your sister used something called makeup setting spray on my face. I didn't even know there was such a thing."

"Annabel is a beauty artist." He grabbed two washcloths, a condom and a bar of scented soap from the cabinet and set them on the teak shelf in the shower. "But in my opinion, you're even prettier without the wizardry."

Frankie turned away from the mirror, her eyebrows raised in surprise for a moment, before she shook her head. "Thank you. But Annabel made me feel worthy of the dress and the event, you know? Like my face was dressed up, too."

"Well, we're undressing you now. And I have to say, I've thoroughly enjoyed unveiling you tonight." He pulled her into the shower with him and she tipped her head back into the spray.

He took his time washing her—massaging shampoo into her scalp until her head tipped back against his shoulder. After rinsing out all the lather, he went to work with the washcloth, lingering in some areas. Behind her neck where she was exquisitely sensitive, and at the small of her back where touches made her shiver with pleasure.

Xander would have gladly denied himself longer, enjoying the discovery of what she liked best. But when he teased the cloth just inside her hip bone one time too many, she reached for the other cloth and began her own sensual journey around his body. She used her lips, too, arousing him with hot, wet kisses while she massaged his skin with her fingers. Driving him to the brink with no more than that.

When he didn't want to deny either of them another minute, he tugged the terry cloth from her hands and tossed it on the tile floor along with his. Sheathing himself with the condom, he shielded them from the spray with his back. Her breath came in fast pants, her green eyes unfocused and desire-dazed. He parted her thighs and entered her in one stroke.

He lifted her higher until she wrapped her legs around his waist. Water sluiced over her while she arched into him, her hands splayed on his shoulders to steady herself, her head tipped back in abandon. There was something so uninhibited about her. So damned sexy.

He wanted to delay his release, but seeing her like this was more than his senses could take. He reached between them, trying to throttle back his needs for the sake of hers, stroking the sweetest center of her that elicited soft cries from her throat. Tiny moans. He felt the tension in her, too. Her back bowed harder, her ankles locking him in place.

The rapid pulse of her feminine muscles against him was the last straw, drawing him deeper. Finishing him. He gripped the partial wall of the shower to steady himself while pleasure pummeled him.

He didn't move for long moments afterward, not trusting his legs if he shifted his feet. Finally, she unwound herself from him with his help, until she stood on her own feet again. He'd never felt so damned good.

And with that thought, the guilt came crashing back over knowing he had nothing left inside him to offer a woman after losing Rena.

Fighting through it, he turned off the water and passed Frankie a towel, then grabbed one for himself. As they dried off together, he acknowledged that the bout of grief felt further away than normal. He might not have even experienced it this time if he hadn't thought about how damned amazing it felt to be with Frankie.

The best, a contrary part of his brain insisted.

All the while, he somehow carried on a conversation. He helped Frankie find a comb so she could untangle her hair. He urged her to lie down with him afterward, assured her that she didn't need to leave yet.

But he knew he'd checked out on her. The same way he had with other women ever since his fiancée died. What disturbed him was that this time, he hadn't simply enjoyed the sex for a temporary escape.

Tonight was different because he didn't want their time together to end. And considering that he had no plans to enter a real relationship again, Xander could tell things were about to get complicated.

Six

Back in bed an hour later, Frankie wouldn't let herself fall asleep.

Lying beside Xander under the covers, she listened to the sound of his breathing slow as she tried to figure out what had happened tonight. Something had shifted between them after the shower. Or rather, something had shifted for Xander afterward. She could practically feel him pull away from her in the moments after the incredible release. A tension had crept into his whole body. Whereas after the first time, he'd been just as relaxed as she in the aftermath.

Had she reached the time limit Xander seemed to put on all his relationships? It was like a stopwatch had gone off in his head telling him that he'd spent long enough with her. And that stung—hard—even though she'd known going into this that it would happen.

He'd continued to be kind to her, saying the right things, massaging her shoulders and finding a clean T-shirt and shorts for her to wear. But she could tell he'd checked out on her. Emotionally. Mentally.

So when his breathing grew deep and even, she slid from the bed and retrieved the beautiful gown and shoes Annabel had let her borrow. Her cabin was close, but the barn with the vehicles was even closer, so she borrowed a ranch pickup truck to drive herself home. She'd return it early in the morning anyway, because she didn't expect to sleep much after everything that had happened.

Her brain would be busy churning through all the details and trying to figure out what would happen next. She wasn't worried about her job, per se, because Xander was too honorable to make her work difficult for her. But she did worry how the rest of the ranch workers would treat her once word got around that she'd dated the boss. It would be awkward.

But somehow, she had to move forward now that she'd slept with a man she'd crushed on for the better part of a year. He shouldn't have the power to distract her from her future anymore.

Except she had the sinking feeling she was fooling herself about that. Because even now that the mansion lights were well behind her, she still caught herself looking back in the rearview mirror, thinking about what might have been if she could have spent the night.

* * *

The morning after the disastrous Texas Cattleman's Club Flood Relief Gala, Angela Perry woke to the sound of text messages on her phone. One chime after the other—all notifications from Ryder Currin.

Closing her eyes against the cheerful sound that she'd assigned to his messages, Angela burrowed deeper in the pillow of the guest suite at Perry Ranch—formerly her childhood bedroom. She'd ridden home with her father after the gala in an attempt to calm him down. He was so upset with her for daring to date Ryder that smoothing things over had taken the better part of the night. Instead of calling for a car to drive her back to her condo, she'd retreated to one of many vacant bedrooms at the ranch, gravitating toward the one that used to belong to her back when she, Melinda, Esme and Roarke had been raised here.

The house echoed now, with everyone gone but her father. Roarke had moved all the way to Dallas to escape the family. Esme and Melinda both lived downtown, like she did. Their mother had been gone for ten years now, and Angela missed her every day.

Being here wasn't the same anymore, but Angela had been too tired to argue with her dad last night. Besides, she had an ulterior motive by staying here.

Levering up on one elbow, she checked her phone and saw three texts from Ryder.

Does Sterling dictate who you date?

Last night didn't end the way I had hoped.

I'd like to speak to you in person.

Tension balled in her gut. She felt guilty about leaving the party without him last night, but she wasn't ready to face Ryder yet.

Not until she spoke to a neutral third party to learn whatever she could about Ryder's past with her mother. She'd heard the gossip that he'd had an affair with her mom, Tamara, back when Ryder had worked at Tamara's father's Ranch. There were rumors that Ryder had blackmailed her mother into convincing her own father to will Ryder the land that had made the Currin family wealthy.

Angela didn't buy it—not any of it. But her closest friend and a fellow Perry Holdings vice president, Tatiana Havery, had convinced her to ask around the ranch and speak with employees who'd lived here back when Ryder worked for Angela's maternal grandfather—Harrington York. To find out if any of them remembered seeing her mother and Ryder together in a way that seemed suspicious. In those days, the place hadn't been called Perry Ranch. Angela's father had changed the name from York Ranch after Harrington died.

Tatiana's advice had seemed wise, but then, it was no surprise Tatiana would look out for her since they'd been friends as far back as boarding school days. When they'd first met, the Havery family had been even more influential than the Perrys, and Angela had always appreciated Tatiana's blunt honesty. Now, taking her friend's advice, Angela would simply learn whatever she could for herself about Ryder's old friendship with her mother, and then she could move on.

Once she'd done that, then she'd answer Ryder's texts. Because if it was true that he'd had a secret affair with her mother long ago… Angela couldn't even contemplate that. Especially not now that she'd kissed him and the chemistry between them had been amazing.

Clutching her phone tighter, she forced herself out of bed because she knew whom she needed to seek out. One of the older ranch hands who'd been on staff forever and Carla, the maid who'd worked in the house the longest. Angela just needed to be discreet about questioning them because she couldn't afford to give her father any more reason to get riled about her relationship with Ryder.

There was no question Sterling Perry hated Ryder. But was it simple resentment that Ryder had made a fortune from land that Sterling had coveted for himself? Or did her father know firsthand that Ryder had had an affair with Angela's mother?

The sickening feeling in her belly grew worse. She couldn't imagine her mother having an affair, no matter how much Sterling ignored her. Tamara hadn't been that kind of woman, had she?

Angela believed her mother would have gotten out of her marriage before she did something like that. But then again, those rumors persisted.

One thing was certain, however.

She wasn't leaving Perry Ranch until she got some answers.

* * *

By noontime, Frankie hadn't seen any sign of Xander, but she told herself that was only because she'd been in the far west pasture all morning, checking and mending fence before they moved half the herd there next week.

As sundown approached and she still hadn't seen him around the barns, however, she guessed he was avoiding her.

Because he was angry with her for leaving while he slept?

Or would he simply behave as though last night had never happened—and go back to his old pattern of avoiding her?

She was repairing a gate to prevent one of the escape artist goats from opening the latch when Xander entered the paddock area. He'd always snagged her eye in the past with his lean, muscular build, his long-legged stride and those blue eyes clear as a Texas summer sky. But now that they'd been together and she knew what it felt like to be at the center of that azure gaze, the draw of his presence was almost impossible to resist. Could it have been any more obvious to her that spending one night with Xander hadn't cured her crush on him? It took a supreme act of will to straighten up from her work with a casual air.

"The gate is fixed." She demonstrated the new double-latching mechanism because she was nervous and didn't know what else to say to the man who was her boss but also her temporary lover. "No more late-night roaming for the goats."

"Thistle is getting ready to have her foal," Xander told her as he stalked past her, heading into the barn without slowing his step or giving more than a passing glance to the gate latch. "I told Len to schedule you in the barn tonight, and let him know you need more hours with the animals."

She tucked her screwdriver into a side pocket on her work cargoes and hurried after him. She didn't know what she was more excited about—being with the mare who was going through her first delivery, or having Xander's approval to log more time with the ranch's livestock.

Did that mean he wasn't upset with her? Or had he simply given her this boon because he was going to drop her like a hot potato after last night? She tried to steel herself for either scenario.

"Really?" She sidestepped a couple of barn cats asleep on the walkway. Apparently they were taking the afternoon off from hunting mice. "Thank you so much."

Once they neared the birthing stall, Xander toed the barn door shut behind them. No doubt to help keep Thistle isolated and calm for her first birth. Frankie had been around the barn for births of calves and kids, but never for one of the foals. And never for the whole delivery.

She'd assisted in plenty of other births while shadowing a local vet, but this was different. Special, somehow, because she knew these animals. She might just work here, but that connection sort of made them "hers," too. In her mind, anyway.

"You left last night." He faced her head-on, a stubborn set to his jaw as he stood in the shadows cast by the huge post beams holding up the roof. "Care to explain that?"

His eyes found hers even as she tried to adjust to the dimness. She could see the disappointment in his face. Hear it in his voice. Confusion knotted inside her. Had she misinterpreted his signals? She was so sure he'd pulled away from her.

"I didn't want to overstay my welcome," she told him carefully, surprised he was willing to bring up the private subject while they were working.

She wandered closer to Thistle, a pretty buckskin quarter horse with sooty shading on her back.

The mare didn't seem agitated yet, nickering softly as Frankie rubbed her muzzle. The scent of fresh hay drifted up from the horse's hooves as the mare shifted her weight.

"Did I make you feel unwelcome?" Xander asked, keeping his voice low, probably out of deference to the soon-to-be mother.

Even so, the deep rumble sent an answering shiver through her as he ran a hand along Thistle's flank, most likely assessing the position of the foal.

"No." She'd felt very welcome. Also, she'd felt more sensually fulfilled than she'd known a woman could be. But she wasn't sharing that. "Maybe I just didn't want to face morning-after awkwardness."

How could she tell him she was scared he'd ditch her the way he did every other woman?

If he knew how closely she'd watched ladies come and go over the last eleven months, he'd realize that she'd been having feelings for him for a long time. Too long.

It was embarrassing and sort of cliché to have a crush on the boss, wasn't it?

"Right. Because this isn't awkward at all." Sarcasm laid heavy on the words, even though his gentle tone never changed as he straightened up.

"Do you honestly think me staying longer would have made today any different? It was going to be tense no matter what."

For her, anyway.

Maybe for him, working with someone he slept with wouldn't have been a big deal. But how long could she pretend to be the kind of woman he preferred—someone who was okay with a casual hookup? Then again, maybe she should try to become that woman. She needed her mind focused on getting into school, not mooning over a man.

When he didn't reply right away, she glanced over at him across Thistle's muzzle and realized he was studying her a bit too thoughtfully.

"I don't want to make things difficult for you here," he said finally. "Did anyone say anything to you to make today uncomfortable?" He took her hand to draw her out of the birthing area.

Her boots crunched over clean straw until they were back on the concrete floor outside the foaling stall. Xander pulled the door shut to help Thistle relax.

"No. I don't think word has gotten around that we attended the gala together." The whole night seemed like something she'd dreamed.

Except that she was standing in the barn with Xander today, and he'd given her new responsibilities that would help her on her path to vet school. She appreciated that he took her dreams seriously. That he would try to help her achieve her goals.

"Even if gossip does spread, why should it matter? It's no one's business but ours." He checked his wristwatch and then glanced back at her. "I can have someone else keep an eye on Thistle for an hour or so to give you time to wash up and get something to eat. It's going to be a long night and Len told me you were here at dawn."

"Are you sure?" Frankie peered back into the stall where the horse paced. "I don't want to miss anything."

This was the whole reason she'd become a ranch hand. Not to fix drainage ditches or mend fences, although she'd understood that was part of the job description. She'd always been in it for the chance to work with animals.

"She's a first-timer. We've got a lot of hours before she foals."

"In that case, I'll be back in an hour or less. And thank you for giving me the chance to be here." She felt a pinch of guilt that he'd only extended the opportunity to her because he'd overheard her mentioning her need for hours in the barn to other ranchers at the gala.

Had she taken unfair advantage of their date?

"You've more than earned it," he told her easily, not sounding at all taken advantage of as he stepped closer to her. "But I'll give you fair warning that it's not just because I want to help you get into veterinary school that I'm inviting you back here tonight."

Something about the look in his eyes made her throat dry up. Gave her visions of the two of them twined around each other, peeling clothes off while they kissed. Touched. And more.

"You have an ulterior motive?" She shook off her imaginings, reminding herself she was still on the clock.

"I do." He leaned against the wooden framing of a vacant horse stall, his head inclined toward hers. "Because you might run from me, but I know you won't leave Thistle's side tonight. And I'm going to use that time to get to know you better, Frankie. Without the distraction of—" his gaze roamed over her in a way that set her on fire "—everything that distracted us last night."

"Then I'll consider myself warned." She tried for what she hoped was a playful tone, needing to keep things light.

With another man, she might be flattered. But Xander wasn't the type of guy who invested in romantic relationships. She'd been here long enough to take note of that. And she couldn't afford to get attached. Didn't dare give him a piece of herself that she wouldn't be able to get back when he walked away.

Xander's whole world had been tilted sideways since he'd woken up alone this morning, Frankie's peaches and roses scent still lingering in his sheets.

Now, as the clock neared midnight and Thistle's labor progressed in the birthing stall, he had to admit Frankie was still keeping him off-kilter. She was obviously excited to be in the barn for the delivery, a fact made evident by how many times she hopped up from the portable camp chair he'd moved into the barn for the night. They could both see into the stall from where he'd set up the chairs, a couple of yards away from the foaling area to help Thistle relax as much as possible. The mare's tail was wrapped and the foaling kit was handy.

Yet Frankie got out of her seat time after time to take a closer look, especially when the mare's back was to them or when she lay down in the straw.

"You must have assisted at plenty of animal births by now, I'll bet," he said, honest about wanting to get to know her better.

Tipping back in his chair, he watched as she settled in beside him again, the scent of hay and horses heavy in the air while fans moved some of the night air through the building.

"I have. I've been shadowing Doc Macallan for almost two years." She referenced a rural animal practice about ten miles west of Currin Ranch.

"He fills in here sometimes when our regular vet is away." Xander remembered him from when he was a kid; the guy was older than his dad.

"He helped me get hired on here, actually, so I could have a paying job that was close to his practice." She tightened the band around her ponytail, the crescent moon birthmark on her neck visible as she moved. "And he tries to schedule fieldwork on the days I'm around to shadow him, so I've gotten some cool experiences that way—from treating small wounds to emergency surgeries."

"And that's how you spend your days off from the ranch?"

"Most of them. Sometimes I squeeze in some time volunteering at an animal shelter, too. Because even though Doc Macallan has enough work to keep me busy, it can help my application to have multiple animal experiences."

"That's ambitious." He'd gotten his MBA in a condensed amount of time, but he hadn't needed to worry about the cost of the degree. "Will you be able to focus full time on your studies if you get accepted?"

"*When* I get accepted," she said immediately. Then she bit her lip and looked embarrassed. "Sorry. Positive thinking about that is a habit of mine, but I absolutely didn't mean to put words in your mouth."

He chuckled. "It's fine. Good for you."

"But to answer your question, I don't think I could manage the course load and working full time, too, so I'd definitely have to scale back my hours."

He asked her more about the animals she liked working with—dogs and horses were some of her favorites—and those that presented the biggest challenges. Cats could be fractious, she admitted, but apparently her vet had a recovering ostrich at his small farm and the bird had been a bit of a terror.

But what threw Xander was her caginess about her family and friends. She would discuss animals and her dreams for as long as he wanted, but she didn't seem inclined to share any more about her unusual upbringing or the fact that she'd left home at eighteen and hadn't looked back. He hadn't pushed, but he wondered how tough it must be for her to be without a family.

He mulled that over while she got up to check on

Thistle for the fifth time in the last half hour. She was nothing if not devoted to the dam.

"Oh!" she called out softly from where she stood at the entrance to the birthing stall, her green eyes bright. "Xander, it's time. I see the hooves."

He bolted from his seat, cursing himself for not focusing on the mare. Thistle was lying down, and appeared as comfortable as a first-time mother could be during strong contractions. She was agitated and sweating, but she didn't seem to be fighting the labor. The mare blew hard.

"We'll monitor her over the next half hour." He wouldn't interfere unless Thistle stopped making progress.

The horse whinnied and tossed her head, nudging her side with her nose. The next contraction broke the water sac, and Frankie brought fresh straw while Xander kept his eye on the mother.

Half an hour later, a perfect black foal emerged.

It was a nice moment to share with Frankie, and they worked in tandem to clean up the stall and give the new mother room to recover. Once Thistle was on her feet again, they left the stall, taking turns washing up in the utility sink. Then, finally, they had time to watch the foal.

"She's so beautiful!" Frankie exclaimed as she returned to the bars of the stall, her voice full of awe. She reached for his arm and squeezed, as if to share her excitement. "Isn't she most precious thing?"

Her touch reminded him how amazing their night together had been. How much he wanted to be with her again. He wrapped an arm around her waist, holding her close to his side while they watched the baby's attempts to stand.

"She's a beauty, no doubt." His gaze slid to Frankie's profile while she watched the foal navigate her wobbly legs. "Let's give them some room to bond."

Her dark hair was in a ponytail, the end draped over her bare shoulder since she wore a black tank top that said Keep Calm and Cowgirl On.

"Of course." She nodded, misty-eyed as she turned toward him. "We don't want Thistle to reject her own baby."

Something about the way she said it—a hint of wryness creeping into her tone—let him know she was thinking about something else. Her own parents? The night he'd driven her home from the rodeo she'd told him that her adoptive family found her wandering a road outside Laredo.

"It's very rare for that to happen." Xander rubbed her shoulder as they turned to sit in the seats outside the stall.

He flipped off a spotlight in the birthing stall now that the dam had safely delivered her foal. They could still see the animals in the glow of a lower-wattage lantern hanging overhead.

"Among horses, maybe." She dropped into the canvas folding chair and crossed one denim-clad leg over the other. "Humans are another story."

He reached over to take her hand, thinking how very different it was to sit beside her in a barn tonight after dancing her around a gala the evening before. At the gala, he'd been pursuing her, no question. Tonight, he saw her pain and couldn't help but feel protective.

"Do you have any reason to believe your birth parents abandoned you?" he asked gently.

"No. But I have no reason to believe they wanted me, either." She lifted her shoulder, as if to shrug it off, and the gesture looked as pained as the words sounded. "Who lets their two-year-old wander the streets?"

He could see her point. He stroked his thumb along the backs of her knuckles, wishing he could soothe away the hurt she felt. "I told you that my sister Maya was adopted, and I really do think my father's never told her—or any of us—how she came to be in our family because in his mind, he's protecting her in some way."

"Where is she now? I'm just surprised I've never seen her in all the time I've worked here." She peered over at him briefly before turning back to watch the foal nose around the stall in search of her dam.

"Maya has been away at college. She was supposed to come home this summer but she hasn't shown up yet. I'm hoping we'll see her soon, though. I miss her."

He'd ask Annabel if she'd heard from her. It seemed strange that she hadn't flown home for the summer yet.

"I don't know if I buy into the whole idea of protecting a child after she's reached adulthood. Whatever the truth is, it has to be better than not knowing," she told him with a fierceness in her voice, emotion in her gaze that was visible even in the dim lighting. "You can't properly process sorrow unless you understand it in the first place."

The mare nickered at her foal, encouraging her. Xander watched the baby try again to get on her feet while Frankie's words chased around his head.

"I'm not sure there's a right or wrong way to process sorrow." The words surprised him. He hadn't meant to share anything about Rena.

As much as he wished he could call them back, however, he knew that Frankie deserved to know the truth about him. About his own sense of loss.

She shifted to face him, her green eyes full of empathy as her fingers flexed around his hand. "I'm sorry, Xander. You lost your mother when you were young—"

"I did." He nodded, remembering those dark years when Annabel's mother had died and then his own mother passed away three years later. His father had barely finished grieving for his wife when Xander came to live with them. "I was fifteen when she died. But I was thinking of my fiancée."

She blinked. Twice.

"I'm so very sorry." She shook her head, her ponytail sweeping back and forth against her arm. "I didn't know you'd been engaged."

He nodded. "For six months. We were two months away from our wedding date when she died in a riding accident."

Even two years after the fact, the words still felt strange to say. Wooden and awkward. He'd never shared anything about Rena with any other woman he'd dated. He wasn't sure why it had come tumbling out tonight, but with an ache opening up in his chest, he realized now he wasn't ready to share any more about his convoluted relationship with Rena before her death.

"That must have been devastating." Frankie bit her lip. "I didn't mean to sound insensitive about grieving when I said what I did about sorrow—"

"You could never sound insensitive." He squeezed her hand, understanding all at once that the ache in his chest was only going to go away once he had Frankie with him again. He needed her tonight. "I only told you because I wanted you to…" To understand that he could never be that kind of man again? That he didn't have the emotional resources to be in a relationship like that again? "To know," he finished lamely.

He'd shared as much as he could about that. The deeper hurt of his past with his fiancée wasn't something he was willing to trot out tonight.

Inside the birthing stall, Thistle's foal found her mother's udder and began to nurse. His work here for the night was done. Frankie's lips curved in a small smile at the sight, a happy note in a conversation that had hit too close to home.

"Thistle's a good mama," Frankie observed deftly, turning the topic away from Rena. "I'm glad I got to be with you tonight for this."

He knew she was talking about more than the delivery. And he was so damned grateful she hadn't pressed to learn more about his past. The relationship that had gutted him.

"I am, too," he admitted, needing her in his arms as fast as possible. To forget everything else but her. He tugged her to her feet, pulling her close, all the emotions beneath the surface finding the most appealing outlet.

"And I'll walk you back to your cabin, no expectations, if you're ready for the night to end."

He didn't want to hurt her. She deserved better than what he could offer her.

"What's the alternative?" she asked breathlessly, her green eyes searching his. "Say, for example, I have some expectations about what happens afterward?"

An answering hunger surged. His fingers flexed on her hips as he restrained himself from kissing her here. Now.

"In that case, I come home with you, and I don't leave until the sun comes up."

Seven

Unlocking the door to her cabin half an hour later, Frankie knew she took a dangerous risk with her heart.

Xander's sorrow for his fiancée was tangible; she understood that now. She also recognized that he'd buried it in meaningless relationships. It hurt to know she was just another way to forget about the woman he'd loved.

And yet, as he followed her inside the cabin, Frankie's heart whispered that maybe she was different from his other affairs. Hadn't he confided in her something significant tonight? Hadn't he told her he was disappointed when he woke up alone this morning?

What if there was a chance that they could have something more? She understood that he wanted to lose himself in their sizzling chemistry for the night. And since she needed that, too, she couldn't deny them both.

As long as she remembered that this was only temporary, she would be okay.

She couldn't let herself forget that Xander had been clear about not wanting more.

Now, full of emotions from all they'd shared tonight, she hung her keys on a metal hook by the front door and turned into Xander. He was right there, a foot behind her, bolting the door behind them. He didn't hesitate. Twining his arms around her waist, he drew her more fully against him.

The scent of hay and antibacterial soap rose from their clothes, the warmth of his body intensifying the last hint of spicy aftershave under his neck as she rose on her toes to kiss him there. Her eyes drifted closed, the feel of him somehow already familiar, but different and exciting at the same time. She tunneled her fingers into his short hair, tilting his mouth down over hers.

The kiss fired through all her nerve endings, desire spiraling out from that point of contact. Xander's hands splayed along her back, pressing her to him tighter. Her breasts molded to the wall of muscle that was his chest, the feel of him making her knees weak, her limbs liquid. She made tiny, hungry sounds in the back of her throat as she tried tugging his T-shirt up and off, getting hung up on his wide shoulders until he helped her.

For a moment, she took in the sight of him, bare-chested and breathtaking, still just a step over the threshold of the cabin. The dim light from a nearby lamp burnished his skin with a golden glow.

"Come upstairs." Taking his hand, she pulled him

with her to the steps that led to the loft of her small cabin, the area she'd made into her bedroom.

The smooth-planed log stairs led them up over the kitchen to the nook where she'd tucked a full-size bed and a nightstand. There wasn't room for much else. The scent of pine hung heavy in the air, even with the overhead fan spinning on low.

It was a far cry from the luxurious pool house where he'd taken her the night before. But they stood under the skylight, the white glow of the moon spilling over them. She'd always liked looking up at the stars before she fell asleep at night.

Reaching to pull Xander toward the bed, she noticed him frowning down at the living room from his stance near the heavy wood banister.

"We have bigger cabins around the ranch that are sitting vacant," he told her as he turned to face her. "I'll find you one with more room."

The different worlds that divided them felt very far apart.

"I'm happy here. It's more than I need." Living rent-free had helped nudge her closer to her goal of being able to pay for veterinary school.

"You should have a bedroom with four walls." He looped his arms around her neck, tipping his forehead to hers. "I'll make sure of it."

"I don't need help," she bristled, tensing. "I prefer to take responsibility for myself."

His jaw flexed. She could see the shift of shadows on his face, despite the dim lighting. He remained silent.

"Besides," she continued, needing to be very clear

about this, "upgrading my accommodations on-site is the surest way to get everyone gossiping about us. People will say I'm getting preferential treatment, and that wouldn't be fair."

Waiting for his answer almost killed her. She didn't want to argue. Didn't want to think about all the things that divided them. They were better when they were working together—whether it was to deliver a foal or to make small talk with local ranchers like they did at the gala.

Xander nodded, some of the tension leaving his shoulders.

"All right. We'll leave it for now," he conceded, stroking a stray hair from her temple and smoothing it back as they stepped away from the banister and closer to the bed. "I just want you to be comfortable. Happy."

His touch stirred her, the heat that had been simmering earlier returning quickly. He bent to drop a kiss on her jaw, nibbling his way down her neck in a way that made quivers race up and down her spine. His hands slid beneath the hem of her tank, skimming up her ribs to stroke the undersides of her breasts through the lace of her bra. Desire unfurled and she sucked in a gasp.

"*This* makes me happy," she murmured, arching closer. "Your touch."

He studied her through heavy-lidded eyes, his thumbs stroking back and forth over the taut peaks pebbling against his hand. "In that case, I'll make sure to provide all the touching you want."

His voice smoked over her, the promise teasing a shiver from her as they stood together in the white spill of moonlight. Her calves nudged the footboard of her bed as she shifted on her feet.

"I'd like that." She ran her hands over his shoulders, his skin hot to the touch, the muscles shifting and tensing under her hands, his sensitivity as heightened as her own. "But getting naked will make all this more fun."

"Is that so?" He lowered one hand to flick open the button on her jeans, his fingers lingering in the square inch of skin he'd uncovered. "It could be rewarding to take our time."

Pleasure vibrated through her, the heady buzz of it thrumming along her nerve endings.

"No," she told him firmly, pressing her hips closer, her belly resting against the hard ridge behind his fly. "The best reward is putting an end to this hunger fast. To take the edge off. Afterward, we can discuss the merits of teasing touches."

"No one said anything about teasing," he clarified as he peeled her tank top up and off. His gaze roamed over her. "You're so damned beautiful."

His words moved her, especially since she knew she was a wreck after their work in the stables. She didn't have a chance to reply, however, as Xander moved to free the clasp on her bra and tug down the zipper on her jeans. The promise of being naked with him distracted her from everything else. Wriggling her way out of her clothes, she stripped off the rest of her garments while he discarded his denim and boots.

He flipped a foil packet on the pillow before drawing her onto the mattress with him in a tangle of limbs.

She slid her arms around his neck, absorbing the sensation of having him next to her. The bristle of his jaw and the texture of the hair on his chest. The impressive muscle underneath it. His lean hips pinning hers while he stroked his way up her thigh.

Their gazes collided and she melted inside at the intensity of his expression. The heat in his gaze. She hooked her calf around his, wanting more. He shifted, his knee pressing hers wider. Her pulse raced.

When he kissed his way down her body, her breath caught. Each twitch of his lips turned her to liquid. She thought she might die of pleasure when, at last, he kissed her intimately. Her senses swam. She gripped the duvet beneath her, a fistful in each hand, as she braced herself for the completion shimmering so very close now.

Then it hit her and she cried out, the rush of fulfillment so strong that it broke over her again and again. Xander coaxed every last spasm from her before he stretched out above her, covering her. He retrieved the condom and rolled it into place while she tried to find her breath again.

She skimmed her hands over his arms and his chest, finally clutching his shoulders while he edged his way inside her. When they were fully joined, she kissed him deeply, her emotions winding around him along with her arms.

She wanted this moment to last, relishing the feel of him inside her, the tension threading through his muscles as he moved, the way the moonlight played off his skin, casting them in alternating shadows as they moved together in sync. Each thrust stoked the passion higher. Hotter.

He stole her breath away.

And possibly her heart.

She couldn't gather either of them as the fluttering sensation started in her womb. By the time it burst through her in another delicious spasm, she held him tight.

His shout resonated through her body along with the lush sensations. Once her senses returned and she became aware of her own breathing again, she knew something momentous had happened. Maybe not for Xander. But for her.

She'd known it was a risk to be with him like this again, but she hadn't realized how quickly she might lose her heart to him. With tenderness welling up in her chest, she feared that was exactly what was happening. She was developing feelings for Xander Currin, a man who refused to fall for anyone since his true love had died.

But then, maybe that shouldn't come as a surprise when she'd swooned over him for months. Was it any wonder that this kind of time with him would make her want him in her life for more than just one night?

Breathe.

Just breathe.

Frankie staved off the chance of hyperventilating, knowing that wouldn't be a good way to end their night together. Instead, she kissed his bare shoulder and hoped for the best.

"Stay," she whispered in his ear, not ready for a conversation that might reveal some of what she was feeling. "Sleep."

She tugged the tangled duvet from where it lay half on the floor, covering their cooling bodies.

Xander kissed her forehead, stroking aside her tumbleweed hair.

"Good night, Frankie." He tucked her against him, her ear pressed to the steady thrum of his heart.

She wondered, right before she fell asleep, was he truly saying good-night?

Or had he really meant goodbye?

Xander had every intention of spending what little remained of the night with Frankie. She didn't need to work in the morning since she'd spent long hours in the barns while the rest of the ranch slept. He'd thought he would make her breakfast, show her that she didn't need to worry about morning-after awkwardness between them. He felt certain they could just enjoy what was happening between them without having to look at more than one day at a time.

But his father had texted him in the predawn hours to ask a question about Thistle, the message leading Xander to believe Ryder was wandering around the barns by himself. That alone would have been rare enough. Combined with the fact that he'd reached out to his son, and Xander knew something must be wrong. His father might ask Xander for help with the oil business, but he never inquired much about the ranch. Did his father find the same solace in the barns that Xander did? Concern about his dad was the only reason he left Frankie's side before the sun rose. It didn't have a damned thing to do with the heightened intimacy of their night together.

Dressing quietly so as not to wake her, he jammed his phone in his back pocket and left the cabin, heading toward the barns. It was a short walk, and he couldn't help but think there had to be better accommodations for her on the ranch. He respected her grit and her work ethic for taking on the ranch hand job in the first place, but she'd been on the team for almost a year so she deserved some consideration for her contributions. There were vacant cabins farther from the barns, with more room, but maybe she appreciated the proximity for the extra hours she put in.

He entered the horse barn in the gray light of pre-dawn and found his father sprawled in one of the camp chairs outside the birthing stall.

"Xander." His father speared his fingers through his hair. "I didn't expect you to come down here at this hour."

He sounded surprised.

"And I didn't expect to hear from you," Xander returned, stroking the nose of his favorite work horse as he lingered by her stall. "You don't usually take a personal interest in the livestock."

His father had worked out of an office for years, more focused on oil than cattle.

"I needed to think about something else for a few days." Ryder tipped back in the chair, his boots crossed on the hay-strewn floor in front of him. "I figured I'd check on Thistle."

"She did well, and the foal nursed soon afterward. I told Len to check on them when he gets in." Still stroking Domino's nose, Xander didn't see a need to mention Frankie, not ready to share whatever was happening between them with anyone else.

Just taking her to the gala had been more of a commitment than he'd made to any woman in the last year. Certainly, it was a more public statement than he'd made about anyone else. He guessed she wouldn't be impressed if he told her that, however.

"The last couple of days have been…frustrating, to say the least." Ryder shrugged, his wrinkled tee suggesting he'd never gone to sleep the night before. "It's not every day that a woman walks out on me in public."

Angela Perry, Xander realized. He'd shoved the incident at the Flood Relief Gala to the back of his mind, but it was clear his father hadn't. "Have you spoken to her since she left the gala with Sterling?"

"She hasn't answered my calls or texts." His father leaned forward again, leaving the camp chair to pace the barn between stalls.

The horses, picking up on his restlessness, stamped their hooves or tossed their heads. Ryder didn't seem to notice, though, a dark scowl etched in his features. The hint of frustration was unusual for him, since he was far more even-keeled than his longtime enemy, Sterling Perry.

"Her father has a lot of leverage over her," Xander pointed out, hoping to calm him down. "Not just because she holds the VP job with Perry Holdings. The emotional aspect has to weigh on her, too. Her dad was furious."

"He's always been a hothead. With too much damned pride." Ryder quit pacing to lean against a stall, frowning.

Xander didn't say anything, hoping his father might reveal something about his long enmity with Sterling. Had Ryder made overtures toward Sterling's young wife long ago?

But his father pulled his Stetson off a hook near the tack room and set it on his head.

"I should go see Angela in person," he announced, striding toward the exit.

"The sun isn't even up yet." Xander walked outside with him, breathing in the June air that was marginally cooler at this hour. "Are you sure that's wise?"

"Son…" His father stopped, his voice even more gravelly than normal from lack of sleep. "If I've learned one thing about relationships over the years, it's that you don't wait for them to fall apart before you pull your head out of the sand."

Did that mean a man should run headlong into trouble because a woman retreated for a day or two? Perhaps his skepticism showed in his expression, because his father shook his head.

"When it comes to relationship problems, a man's natural inclination might be to wait and hope things get better. But the women I've known tend to view that as a lack of caring." His father straightened, pulling his truck keys from his pocket. "So if a woman is unhappy with you, you're better off facing it head-on than finding out afterward that you lost out on something that could have been special."

Xander mulled that over while the first hints of purple lit the sky in the east. Would Frankie be unhappy with him that he'd left her side? Or would she be relieved that he hadn't made it awkward for her, something she'd been worried about after their first night together? He honestly didn't know.

"I still say she's not going to be thrilled when you knock on her door at dawn."

"Maybe not." Ryder tossed his Stetson on the passenger seat before he slid behind the wheel. "But I guarantee you she'll be glad I cared enough to show up. To try."

With that, he fired up the engine and took off in a plume of dust, taillights glowing red.

Xander stood in front of the horse barn, halfway between the main ranch house and Frankie's cabin. The pull of her was so damned strong. He wanted to be with her again. And again. He also wanted to help her get into vet school. Move her into a more comfortable cabin. Keep introducing her to prominent members of the Texas Cattleman's Club so she had a ready clientele for her practice.

But he knew in his heart that she deserved more than that. She had focused all her love and affection on animals as a kid because her parents hadn't given her any other viable outlets for friends. Didn't that say something about her? She'd resented them enough to leave home at eighteen and not look back, so chances were good she was a tough judge of character when someone didn't live up to her expectations.

Hell yes, she deserved better than what Xander had to give.

In theory, he *could* go back to her place right now, and maybe she'd never be the wiser that he left. After all, his father certainly had a point that it carried weight in a relationship to show up and make that effort.

But as much as Xander wanted Frankie, he still couldn't risk the heartbreak that came with a relationship.

Not now. Not ever.

He pivoted toward the main house and headed home.

Ryder arrived at Angela's downtown condo after sunrise, the pink-and-orange sky warming the limestone building with the same colors. He parked his truck and took the elevator up to the fifteenth floor after giving his name to the security guard.

He hadn't warned her he was on the way. No sense giving her a chance to bail. At least she hadn't refused to see him.

Knocking on her door, he waited for her to answer. A moment later the door swung wide, and Angela greeted him in a fitted navy blue dress with silver buttons up the front. Her hair was still damp from her shower, her face free of any makeup. She looked beautiful, and he wished like hell their evening together had ended differently two nights ago.

The scent of her soap mingled with fragrant coffee brewing from somewhere in her apartment.

"Ryder." She hesitated only a moment before stepping back and opening the door wide for him. "Come in."

"I know it's early." He stepped inside, wondering if he should have brought something. Flowers, maybe. "But I really wanted to see you."

He'd never visited her apartment before, but she'd been easy enough to find. She'd referenced her downtown apartment building when she'd been discussing local real estate before she closed the deal for the Houston property that had become the location for the new Texas Cattleman's Club. He recalled her saying that her twin sister, Melinda, lived in the same condominiums.

"It's fine." Angela closed the door behind him and waved him toward the kitchen. "Can I get you some coffee?"

"Sure. Thank you." He followed her into the open-concept kitchen and living area, where the expansive views of downtown were visible from the huge windows out to the terrace.

"I was going to call you today anyhow." Barefoot, she padded silently over the hardwood floors to take a second mug from a cupboard. "I just needed a little time yesterday to sort through things in my mind."

He heard the stilted tone in her voice and knew it didn't bode well for them. Whatever she needed to "sort through" couldn't be good. He watched as she poured him a cup of coffee from the elaborate stainless steel machine before topping off her own. She slid the mug and a spoon across the counter toward him as he settled into a spot at the breakfast bar.

"I'm sorry that you were put in an awkward position at the gala." He peered around her living space, which was as tastefully appointed and restrained as the woman herself.

The gray couches and white accents were broken up by an occasional splash of yellow. There weren't many photos anywhere, but one silver framed picture held an image of her and Melinda flanking their father.

Another one—from when she was much younger—showed her and her youngest sister, Esme, with their mother, Tamara. Memories swamped him. Tamara Perry had been a rich man's daughter who married for duty and power but wanted love. Her husband had always paid more attention to business than his wife, and Ryder had always thought that was damned foolish of Sterling. Of course, Ryder had made the same mistake with his first wife, Penny, and regretted it.

All the more reason to ensure he didn't make those kinds of mistakes again. He refocused his attention back on Angela, where it belonged.

"Are you?" she asked him, passing the sugar bowl his way before he waved it off. "Sorry, that is? I wondered afterward if your invitation to the gala was just another way to continue your rivalry with my father. Maybe it was the perfect opportunity to get under his skin?"

The suggestion rankled.

"Absolutely not." He waited until she sat beside him at the breakfast bar, giving her 100 percent of his focus. "Angela, I tried like hell to ignore this attraction because I knew it would make things difficult for you."

"Until I kissed you." Her expression softened at the memory of that shared kiss. "I surprised myself that day."

"You surprised me, too, but I'm glad you did." He wanted to take her hand. To touch her, and convince her that he didn't have anything but good intentions where she was concerned. But this conversation was too important for them to get sidetracked by attraction. "I couldn't exactly pretend I didn't feel something for you once that kiss happened."

A sad smile curved her lips before she took a sip of her coffee from a bright red cup that said "girl boss" in white script. His mug, on the other hand, was plain white. He'd bet hers had been a gift.

"The real question is are *you* sorry that we kissed?" Ryder continued, watching her pretty profile while she sipped her drink. "Is the pressure from your father too much? Are we going to throw in the towel on this already?"

He didn't realize how much he wanted to keep seeing her until he'd voiced the question. But now, with their fledgling relationship hanging in the balance, he knew that he wanted Angela in his life.

A memory of Xander's expression this morning crossed his mind, reminding Ryder how far away his son was from realizing that living without love was a lonely way to move through the world. Xander still thought he was protecting his heart by keeping the pretty ranch hand at arm's length. When really, he was only hurting himself. And her.

Damned foolish, but he couldn't tell Xander that in so many words or his son would only dig his heels in deeper.

Ryder didn't want that for him and Angela.

"I'm not sure." She set her mug on the granite counter and swiveled toward him on the leather padded bar stool. "I spent yesterday at Perry Ranch, and I spoke to one of the maids who remembered you from the time you worked there. She made it sound like there might have been more to your relationship with my mother than just friendship."

The hurt in her voice cut right through him. How could they be back to this? He'd thought those blasted rumors had finally died when Tamara passed, but apparently someone was giving the story new life. He clenched his fist, wishing he could make those ugly accusations disappear.

"Angela." This time, he did touch her, covering her hand with his. "I cared deeply for your mother, but I never had romantic feelings toward her." He'd never worried about what the rest of the world thought about his relationship with Tamara, but he damned well cared what Angela thought. "I swear to you, I never so much as kissed her, let alone anything more."

She was quiet so long he feared he'd already lost her faith in him. But then she gave a small nod.

"Thank you for sharing that. I—" She closed her eyes for a moment and then opened them again. "I have a lot to think about."

Disappointment landed heavy on his shoulders. Sliding his hand away from hers, he told himself not to push her. He didn't blame her for being confused. Her father had hated him all her life, so it had come as a surprise that she'd even considered being with him in the first place.

Maybe he just needed to give her time.

"We shared a beautiful friendship," he said finally, wanting to put what he'd had with Tamara into some kind of context for her. "A friendship that your grandfather recognized. That's the only reason he gave me that land. Because I'd been a friend to your mother when she needed one."

There wasn't anything more to say about that. Angela would have to either believe him or not, because there wasn't a soul on earth who knew what had happened between him and Tamara the few times they were alone besides Tamara and him. And her mother had died in a car accident the same year that Xander had lost his mother.

Three years after Ryder had lost Elinah.

The hits had kept coming during those years. Losing Elinah had devastated him, so Ryder could understand why it was tough for Xander now, when his son was learning to move on without the woman he'd planned to marry. Xander had all but retreated from the world after Rena died, immersing himself in the foreman job at Currin Ranch, the only work he'd cared about. And Ryder had understood the pain all too well, which was why he'd allowed Xander to stay in a job that didn't utilize his brilliant business mind. He believed his son would come around one day and want to learn the business. To embrace the CEO job at Currin Oil.

The toughest truth Ryder had ever faced was that life continued to go on, even after the people he loved most in the world had died.

The loss of Elinah had almost killed him. But here

he was, putting one foot in front of the other. Trying to find happiness. And the woman next to him was the best chance he'd had since then.

Beautiful Angela Perry, his enemy's daughter.

But Ryder wasn't willing to let rumors and old gossip cost him this shot at something deeper with this rare and lovely woman who still looked at him like he meant something. Like he could make her happy. If there was even the slightest chance that he could find love again with Angela, he was sure as hell going to try.

Eight

In the morning, after a quick stop in the barn to check on Thistle and the new foal, Frankie tried to decide how to spend her unexpected time off. She lingered with the horses, scratching one of the older mares on the muzzle, wondering if she should take her out for a ride as a way to ease the ache in her chest that felt dangerously close to heartbreak.

Waking up alone this morning, when she'd been fully expecting to see Xander in bed beside her, had hurt. Hours later, she still couldn't shake the sense that the night together that had been so significant to her hadn't meant anything to him.

She'd known better than to let herself get attached to a man who never stayed with one woman for long. She was supposed to be in it strictly for fun. For the toe-curling kisses, the off-the-charts sex, the physical release that was so good it was practically transcendent.

Except her emotions couldn't seem to resist getting involved, no matter how many times she reviewed the ground rules.

Stepping out of the barn, she decided to walk instead of ride this afternoon. There was a shady path around one of the irrigation ponds that would keep her out of the sun. Normally, she spent all her downtime volunteering with the animal shelter or shadowing Doc Macallan on his rounds. And she loved that work. But today, she was glad to have a few hours to herself to get her head on straight.

She hurried her pace as she passed the main house, but she stopped when she heard a woman's raised voice.

"Frankie!"

Annabel Currin waved to her from the driveway near the side yard where she walked from the garage with her keys in her hand.

"Hello," Frankie called, returning the wave and hoping Xander wasn't around.

She wasn't ready to see him yet.

Already, Annabel was hurrying toward her, tucking her keys in a yellow leather handbag as she went. She wore a white sundress with a bright turquoise necklace. Beaded blue-and-yellow sandals glinted in the bright sun. No surprise the style blogger looked beautiful and fashionable.

"Do you have a minute? I've got lunch waiting for me in the pool house, and I'm sure there's plenty for two." She gestured toward the building where Xander had taken Frankie after the gala. "There's an outdoor table under the overhang, so it's cool enough to sit there and still feel like we're getting a little fresh air."

A landscaping service truck was just pulling out of the driveway. The scent of freshly cut grass hung in the air, all the flowers and trees manicured to perfection.

Frankie hesitated, mostly because she didn't want to run into Xander when she hadn't figured out a game plan yet. "That's kind of you, but I was just heading to the pond for a walk."

"You'll melt in this heat," Annabel declared, gesturing toward the pool area. "Sit with me for a few minutes so I can at least get the scoop on how things went at the gala."

Annabel was too warmhearted to deny. Besides that, it felt nice to have someone *want* to spend time with her. As an only child, with parents who'd kept her isolated, Frankie really hadn't made friends until she'd left home. Even then, she'd moved around so much, trying to find a place that felt "right," she hadn't grown close to many people.

"If you're sure." She might as well enjoy the fact that she didn't have any plans for the day. "But you don't need to feed me."

"Trust me, there will be plenty. Our cook still prepares food for me like I'm getting ready for a growth spurt." Annabel laughed as she opened the gate to let them inside the pool area. "I don't think she realizes I'm no longer twelve."

Frankie's gaze went straight to the pool house, memories of her night with Xander swamping her. The whole

evening had been magical, from her Cinderella makeover and beautiful dress to the way Xander had made
her feel.

She didn't realize she'd stopped on the deck to stare
at the doors until Annabel said her name. From the
puzzled expression on her friend's face, she guessed it
wasn't the first time she'd called to her.

"Hmm? I'm sorry, I was thinking what a pretty spot
this would be to read a book." Distractedly, she followed Annabel to the wrought iron patio table tucked
under the pergola covered with vines and greenery. A
misting hose sprayed the finest cloud of cooling water
while an overhead fan kept the temperature to a bear-
able level.

"I love coming out here to work on my blogs. But I
want to know all about your evening at the gala. Did
you have a good time?" Annabel dropped her purse into
one of the patio chairs before tucking into a seat herself.

"It was amazing," she told her honestly, sliding into
the chair opposite Annabel, already feeling cooler as
they sat in the shade. "I'd never been to the Four Seasons, and I couldn't believe how stunning it looked with
all the flowers."

She'd pressed the orchid Xander had given her between sheets of wax paper to preserve it. Not to overly
romanticize him or the date. But her parents had been
adamantly opposed to big populated venues, ensuring
she hadn't gone to public school or experienced a prom
night. So in a weird way, the Flood Relief Gala had been
her first formal.

Maybe she had totally romanticized it. But in an era

where romance was dead, who could blame her for holding tight to a few girlish traditions?

"It was beautiful," Annabel agreed as she slid an extra plate and crisp linen napkin toward Frankie. Her smile faded. "We didn't stay for long, but we did make a brief appearance."

Something seemed off about that, making her wonder if Annabel had a falling-out with her fiancé.

"Is everything okay?" she asked, laying the napkin over her lap.

"Fine. It's fine." Annabel brushed aside the concern with an airy wave of her hand, her smile returning as she pulled off the cover on a chilled plate of finger sandwiches. Her diamond engagement ring still glittered on her hand. "So what did Xander think of your gala look?"

Frankie wondered about friend etiquette in a situation like that where she suspected something had upset Annabel. Would it help to talk about it? Then again, she didn't know Annabel all that well, so she hated to press her.

"He seemed to like it." Frankie couldn't help the smile that came with the memory of their first dance.

"I'll bet he did. That dress was fantastic on you." Annabel passed the plate of finger sandwiches toward her while she poured two glasses of water from a pewter pitcher.

"That's a ton of sandwiches," Frankie offered as an aside, taking one after all.

Although they were tiny—just a couple of bites each—they were piled in a neat stack of circles, each layer a little smaller than the last.

"I know," Annabel exclaimed, sliding two onto her own plate. "We could invite all our friends and still have enough. But back to your date." She slanted a more side-long glance her way. "I feel like it must have gone well because I made a trip out to the barn last night to check on Thistle, and I heard both of your voices."

"You were there?" She tried to remember what they'd talked about last night when they weren't focused on helping the mare.

Xander had asked her a lot about her plans for vet school, and the preparations she was making to be accepted into a program.

Things hadn't heated up until later.

"Just long enough to realize that Thistle was already well tended." She peered over her shoulder, as if checking to be sure they were alone. Then she leaned forward to confide, "And to be honest, it was nice to hear my brother sound…happy. So I decided not to interrupt."

"You don't think he's been happy these last months?" Surprised to hear Annabel's view of her brother, Frankie wondered if she'd missed the signs that Xander was still grieving his fiancée during the time she'd worked here.

"He puts on a good front, but he's not the same man he was before Rena's death."

It stung to realize she'd never really known the version of Xander that Annabel talked about. Perhaps some of the hurt showed on her face, because Annabel clapped a hand on her wrist.

"But you're good for him, Frankie. There was a tone in his voice last night that I haven't heard in a very long time."

Could that be true? Or was Annabel just hearing evidence that her brother was healing simply because she loved him and wanted to believe that?

"I'm not so sure." Setting aside the remainder of the egg salad sandwich she'd sampled, Frankie leaned back in her chair, tension balling in her stomach. "He left in the middle of the night without telling me. I thought we—" She forced herself to stop, to button down the notion that she had hoped they were growing closer. She was unaccustomed to sharing her personal life. "I just don't want you to get your hopes up, because I don't have any reason to believe we'll ever have another date."

She'd tried so hard to tell herself she was just having fun. But waking up alone had been far from it.

"That must have been hurtful." Annabel frowned, her eyes full of empathy. "I'm sorry he treated you that way, Frankie, but for what it's worth, he's loved in the past. I believe he can be persuaded to love again."

Frankie appreciated the thought. But she knew it was also heavily slanted toward what Annabel wanted to believe. Of course she hoped that Xander would find love again.

That didn't mean he was capable of giving his heart to someone. Rena was gone. And Frankie was just... Frankie.

She knew she wasn't anything like the women he normally dated.

"It's okay," Frankie reassured her, unwilling to accept any more of Annabel's kindness when she'd been convincing herself to stay away from Xander anyhow. "I knew when I accepted his offer to go with him to the Flood Relief Gala that he's…not looking for anything serious."

She pasted a smile on her face. Because she'd been fine with that. She'd even assured herself that she wanted that, too. To put an end to her distracting crush and get him out of her system before she went to veterinary school.

"What about you?" Annabel's dark eyes seemed to see straight through her. "Are you okay with that?"

She was terrified that she wouldn't be.

But she had no choice.

"Of course." She nodded, hearing the false note in her voice.

And knowing that Annabel couldn't miss it.

"Okaaay," Annabel said slowly enough to acknowledge that she wasn't buying it. "But Xander is a good man. And if it was up to me, you wouldn't give up on him yet."

Frankie nodded, unable to speak, let alone commit to what she suggested. But she enjoyed the other woman's friendship. The moment to share some of what she was going through.

Instead, she sipped her water, wishing it would cool the new emotion simmering inside her. Because the little flicker of hope she felt at Annabel's words was bound to burn her if she couldn't keep her emotions on lockdown.

Thankfully, Annabel steered their conversation toward lighter topics, topping off their drinks. Lemon, lime and orange wedges mixed with the ice.

"There's a Texas Cattleman's Club planning meeting

next week, by the way." Annabel checked her phone as she spoke and then settled the device back on the table. "Even if you don't want to move forward with Xander romantically, you would benefit from getting to know the most influential ranchers in the area."

"A meeting?" Curious, she tried to shove aside her thoughts about Xander to focus on her career dream.

"It won't be as stuffy as it sounds. The TCC movers and shakers will all be there, so they're holding it in a conference suite at a local historic inn called the Haciendas. There will be a cocktail meet and greet afterward. I'm sure I can get you an invitation."

"Will you be there?" Frankie asked, thinking it would be more fun with Annabel in attendance. Besides, she'd need a barrier if Xander was there.

"Maybe." She checked her phone again, her brow furrowing as she squinted to see it despite the sunlight. "I've been messaging Maya to convince her to come home for the summer and attend some of the TCC events, but I haven't heard back from her yet."

"I'd like to meet her," Frankie murmured, remembering the story Xander had told her about Maya not knowing the identity of her birth parents. She definitely had that in common with Xander's adopted youngest sibling.

When they finished their visit a little while later, Frankie thanked her and tucked away the idea of asking Xander about the meet and greet after the TCC meeting. Checking with him about that sounded easier than Annabel's other suggestion—that she give romance a chance with Xander.

That sounded risky. Dicey.

And it had the potential to hurt her badly.

Yet in the past, she'd prided herself on never giving up without a fight. Not her dream of breaking free from her family's constraints. Not her hope of attending college. She'd even tried bronc riding.

Was she going to start running from a challenge now? Frankie ground her teeth together, not ready to be the kind of woman who turned tail and ran at the first bumpy patch in the road. Ever since she'd left home, she'd told herself she was going to embrace every possible new experience to make up for the suffocating world of her childhood.

Maybe she wasn't ready to give up on Xander yet.

Maya Currin stared at the fifth text from her sister, Annabel, and huffed a sigh.

She loved Annabel and missed her sister more than anyone else back home. But no matter how many sweet notes she got from her, Maya wasn't going back to Houston this summer.

No way. No how.

Stabbing the phone icon on her screen, she called her sister to tell her as much so she could move on with her day. Sitting by herself at a picnic table under the pine trees while four hundred tween-aged campers finished their lunches, Maya waited for Annabel to pick up.

"Maya!" Annabel squealed with the soft Texas drawl that Maya missed in this corner of the world. "Where in the world are you, and why haven't you come home yet? I haven't heard from you in ages."

"No guilt-tripping allowed," Maya snapped, more

sharply than she'd intended. Then, softening her tone, she said, "I miss you too much already."

"Sorry, sweetie. Is everything okay? Are you still at school?"

Maya had just finished her freshman year at Boston College, but she was too mad at her father to return home this summer. Not that she needed to share that part with Annabel and drag her into that drama.

A few campers ran past her toward their next activity, shoving each other and laughing, their footsteps pounding the packed dirt under the pines.

"Everything's fine. I just decided to take a summer job at a sleepaway camp on Cape Cod." She'd applied to as many jobs as she could think of to justify the time away from home.

She'd turned eighteen this year, and her father *still* hadn't told her the story of her birth and how he came to adopt her. Even though he'd promised. Why was he hiding the real story? What was he so afraid of her finding out?

"A job?" Annabel sounded deflated. "Do you get any time off? I wanted you to go to some of the fancy Texas Cattleman's Club events for the opening of the Houston chapter."

"Really?" She asked only because she was hungry for news of home. Even though she was mad at her dad. Even though she wouldn't go home until he told her the truth.

For now, she just missed Annabel. The sleepaway camp was okay, but it wasn't home. She even missed the Houston heat, since Cape Cod was having a cool spell. She wore a hoodie in the middle of the day.

"Yes! It's the summer of galas and parties. I thought maybe you could be a guest on my blog and I could make you over."

It meant a lot to her that Annabel wanted to hang out. That she mattered to someone back home, even if her father thought she was still a kid who couldn't be trusted with the most basic information.

Like the name of her birth parents.

"That sounds fun," she admitted, her chest hurting while a long line of junior campers walked past with their counselor toward the archery field. "I'm sorry I can't be there. I'll be working all summer."

Annabel made idle chitchat a while longer, until Maya heard the bell that precipitated the next activity change.

"I'm sorry to cut you short, but I have to get back to the stables," she told her older sister as she hurried to her feet. "We'll catch up soon, okay?"

She disconnected fast, before the mixture of homesickness and anger at her father became apparent in her voice. No need to upset Annabel.

Maya would figure out how to get back at her father soon enough. For starters, she was certain it would get his attention if she didn't return to school in the fall.

He wouldn't be able to ignore her then.

Finishing up a few phone calls on the private flight home from Amarillo, Xander tipped his head back in the leather seat and wondered about his next call.

To Frankie.

He had missed her during this unexpected trip. He

hadn't seen her for three days, since he'd been called away on Currin Ranch business with zero warning.

He didn't appreciate his father orchestrating the trip that had ended up being more executive-level than Xander had been led to believe. Attending stock sales was part of the job as foreman, but Ryder had asked him to meet with several ranch owners in Amarillo while he was there.

Was that his father's way of coercing Xander into taking a more active role in the business? By doubling up his work responsibilities?

With the TCC planning committee meeting just two days away, Xander knew tensions were ratcheting up in the group since Sterling and Ryder were locked in a power struggle. Whereas even a month ago he hadn't really cared about the new Texas Cattleman's Club branch, Xander found himself wanting more buy-in now. Was that because he was starting to put his grief to rest for good? Or was it because Frankie had taken an interest in the TCC and he wanted the group to be a warm, welcoming place for her?

Possibly a little of both.

Either way, he couldn't deny that knowing her had brought him back to life in a lot of ways. He hadn't completely balked at the Amarillo venture, for one thing. And even though he hadn't appreciated not being consulted about the added meetings, he hadn't found them as tedious as he might have in the past months.

His brain was kicking back to life to the point where he wondered about the possibility of stepping into the role that awaited him at Currin Oil—the CEO position once his father stepped down.

Maybe he was even ready for more with Frankie. At the very least, he wanted to see her again. That in itself was a huge step forward for him.

Dialing her number, he stared out the plane's window as the flight neared Houston. The light on the wing blinked back at him in the dark.

"Hello?" Her voice, soft and sexy, triggered a wave of longing and lust.

Damn, but he'd missed her.

"It's Xander." He regretted not calling her before now, since he'd been the one to walk away last time. He'd messaged her that he was going out of town, but she hadn't replied. "I'm going to be back home in about an hour."

"You'll be pleased to know the ranch is still standing." Her voice struck him as carefully neutral.

He hoped that didn't mean she was upset with him. Because he'd been looking forward to seeing her all day. He hadn't expected to miss her as much as he had.

"I'm more interested in how you're doing." He gripped one of the armrests as the jet hit a pocket of turbulence. "I've missed you."

The silence on the other end lingered a beat too long.

"I assumed you'd moved on," she finally replied. "When I woke up without you, I figured maybe that was your way of letting me know things had cooled off."

He closed his eyes, regretting that he'd hurt her. She'd probably observed more of his bachelor ways than he'd realized over the last year.

"Not even close." Thinking about that night together

in her cabin revved him up even now. "I wanted to talk to you, but when my dad asked me to take the Amarillo trip for the stock sale, I couldn't say no. His plate's full with Texas Cattleman's Club responsibilities and the ongoing battle with Sterling."

"How'd the sale go?" she asked, drawing him into a conversation that lasted straight through the landing and well into his ride home.

She'd seemed interested in every aspect of the sale, from the business side to questions about the trends in breeds he was seeing. She knew a surprising amount about cattle, but she also had questions about the possibility of sheep and goats at Currin Ranch, ventures that had been discussed as ways to diversify and grow the business.

It wasn't until he steered the truck under the ranch's welcome sign that he realized how long they'd talked.

"How do you feel about company when I get home?" he asked, wanting to see her.

Touch her. Talk to her more.

"I'm not really dressed for company. Maybe tomorrow?"

Disappointment stung. Right up until a wicked laugh floated through the phone.

"Unless you don't mind seeing me in my night-clothes," she added, a sly note in her voice.

Desire for her surged and he tapped the gas harder.

"I'll be at your door in five minutes."

Nine

Xander wanted to romance her.

He'd missed her, and tonight, he planned to show her how much.

But when Frankie answered the door of her cabin in a sleep T-shirt and nothing else, any words he'd been going to say dried right up and vanished. With no makeup and her dark hair tousled, she robbed the rest of his reason when she slid her arms around his neck and kissed him.

She was warm and soft, every delectable nuance of her body apparent through the well-washed fabric of the tee. He coiled his arms around her waist and hoisted her against him. He toed the cabin door closed behind them with his boot and carried her deeper into the cabin, every step causing sweet friction, making him burn hotter. Harder.

Her lips were perfect, molding to his one moment, sliding down to the hollow of his throat the next. She was as hungry for this as he was, as restless for what they'd found the other times they'd been together.

When he started up the stairs to the loft, she locked her ankles around his waist, anchoring them together. Every step tantalized him, the movement eliciting a throaty moan from her in a way that only compounded the teeth-grinding need he felt.

Reaching the bed, he deposited her in the middle of the comforter, the scent of lavender and warm woman rising from the linens while he wrenched off his shirt and unfastened his belt. Her green eyes tracked his actions, lingering on his chest before dipping lower.

Without taking her gaze off him, she reached for a condom on the bed and shifted to her knees while he removed the last of his clothes.

"May I?" she asked.

"Hell, yes." He couldn't have been more eloquent, his whole world narrowed to the all-consuming need.

She tore open the package with zero finesse, but her hands were careful—oh, so damned careful—as she rolled the condom in place. He nearly didn't survive the process, especially when she stroked her hand from base to tip, as if to test her handiwork. The touch wrenched a groan from him, desire for her so intense it ached.

He skimmed off her T-shirt and tipped her back against the comforter, positioning himself over her. Locking eyes with her, he slid inside her, joining them. Her breasts pushed against his chest and he claimed her mouth, kissing her over and over, letting the heat build as he rocked his hips.

Her nails raked his back, her teeth sinking into his shoulder. He appreciated the sting when he was so damned close to losing it. Forcing himself to slow down, he listened to her breathing, taking her where she needed to go.

She was close, too, and it wasn't long before her back arched hard, her release coming in one sweet wave after another. He didn't have a prayer of lasting after that, so he let himself follow her, the pleasure so perfect he couldn't remember ever feeling this close to anyone.

And this time, he wasn't going anywhere.

When their breathing finally slowed, he hauled her back against him to keep her close to him, making sure she knew how much he wanted her right there.

All night long.

Frankie slid from her bed before dawn.

Not to leave. Just to put on the coffee and revel in the most perfect night ever.

As the pink fingers of sunrise crept toward the horizon, she leaned on the kitchen countertop and stared out over the hayfields behind her cabin, thinking she could get used to this. She had succeeded in turning her crush on Xander into something more—something tangible—and it had led to the best sex of her life. She understood now why it had to be temporary. That Xander couldn't give more than this because he'd lost the love of his life.

The reality of it had settled in after her talk with Annabel, when she'd realized that she wasn't ready to give up whatever it was that they shared. Temporary or not, she wanted him in her life. And maybe—just maybe—it would be okay this way. Because Frankie had to focus on getting into vet school anyhow. There could still be a middle ground where they simply enjoyed the here and now without worrying about when it ended. Yet, as much as she reassured herself of that, something still felt…off about her thoughts. Maybe she was just over-thinking things. They barely knew each other, after all.

Things had progressed so fast between them, but she was only just beginning to get to know him.

The scent of coffee filled the kitchen, the sound of the machine percolating punctuated by a chime that let her know the brew was set.

"Good morning." Xander's voice was a welcome, deep hum across her senses as she straightened from the countertop.

Bare-chested and sporting a pair of half-buttoned jeans, he was absurdly handsome in her kitchen as he leaned a hip against the stove. His dark hair looked like a wild woman had raked her fingers through it over and over during the night.

Which, of course, she had.

"I must have been lost in thought." Pleasure smoked through her at the memory of how thoroughly she'd lost herself in being with him. "I didn't even hear you come down the stairs."

"You were probably too busy fantasizing about what we could be doing right now if you'd stayed in bed with me."

How could he turn her on so thoroughly when they'd just been together hours before? Her belly flipped at the idea of being with him again.

"Maybe I was." Happiness curled around her at having him here with her. She pulled mugs down from a cupboard. "Or maybe I was just surprised we made it through a night together with no one running out the door."

She didn't mean to break the mood, but that's exactly what her comment had done. She could see it in the way his smile faded.

"I regret leaving that night. I'm so sorry if I upset you." He slid onto one of the counter stools at the narrow breakfast bar that took the place of a table in her small cabin.

Carrying the two mugs over to him, she sat on the stool next to his. "I don't know why I brought that up—"

"It's fine. I knew my dad was wrestling with some problems that night and went outside to talk to him. I should have left you a note."

"Xander, I know you're not ready for anything more. I'm fine with that." She'd been bracing herself for him to walk away since that first night.

"I didn't leave because I wanted to break things off. But you deserve to know the truth about why I've been so hell-bent not to repeat what happened with Rena."

"Anyone would have been heartbroken to lose their fiancée," she assured him, her hand covering his forearm.

"She ended our engagement right before the accident."

Frankie's coffee cup froze on the way to her lips. Her

gaze flew to Xander's. The stark truth of the words was reflected there.

"I've never told anyone," he continued, taking a sip from his steaming cup. "Not a single soul. We'd argued the night before she went on the trip with her girlfriends. I told her she was overreacting when she said she wanted to call off the wedding. That she was just having jitters and it would be fine when she got back home."

She slid her palm under his and squeezed it, not wanting to interrupt when the memory was clearly painful to him.

Setting his mug back on the white tile counter, he stared down at their clasped hands.

"After she'd fallen, when I drove like a madman to get there, hoping somehow I'd reach her bedside before she died, I was too upset to figure out whether her parents or her friends knew that she'd called it off." He shook his head before he peered up at her again. "I'm still not sure if they knew she was ready to start a new life without me."

"I'm so sorry." Frankie's heart ached for how much he'd had to grieve for at once. "That had to have made losing her all the more difficult and stressful. You had to deal with navigating what people did or didn't know, and at a time you were devastated and could have used their support."

"It's in the past. It took me some time, but I've moved on." He slid his hand from hers to take another sip from his mug.

To keep her at arm's length? Or because he needed more coffee? She told herself not to overthink things. To just be in the moment.

"I'm glad." She bit her lip, wondering if he really had moved on considering his refusal to be in a serious relationship. But that wasn't her business, since "serious" wasn't what they were about. "And I appreciate knowing what was going through your head that night when you took off."

Xander's phone vibrated, but he ignored it, focused on her.

"It took me some time to put Rena in the past because I wasn't just dealing with losing her. I was trying to figure out how I could have missed the signs that she wanted out." He rolled his shoulders, as if shrugging away a weight.

"Did she say why?"

"Not anything that made sense to me. She said something about needing more time to find ourselves. As if I didn't know exactly who I am and what matters to me already." His jaw flexed just remembering the conversation. "But I don't think that was the real reason. And I know she didn't just make a snap decision about it. It was building for a while and I didn't see it. Or I did, but I chose to ignore it. Hell, I don't know."

She couldn't imagine how he'd worked through those things after her sudden death. No wonder it had taken him time to move on. While she searched for the right words to offer what comfort she could, he continued speaking.

"I immersed myself in work on the ranch for a long time, but this trip to Amarillo made me realize I'm ready to get back to my future with Currin Oil."

Surprised, she tried to imagine working here every

day without seeing Xander. The vision of Currin Ranch without her favorite Currin left her feeling hollow. She barely fit into his world when she was a ranch hand and he was the foreman. How much greater would the divide be when he took over a multibillion-dollar corporation?

"Really? That's wonderful. Your father must be thrilled." She tried to hide her mixed emotions, knowing she should be happy for him. Knowing it shouldn't matter. She had her own dreams she was excited to follow, after all, and he'd been supportive of them.

Yet their worlds would be so very different.

"I haven't told him yet. I only just figured it out last night on the flight home." He stroked a hand over her knee, his palm a warm weight even through the denim of her work clothes. "I also wanted to see if you'd attend the next Texas Cattleman's Club planning meeting with me. There's a meet and greet afterward and I could introduce you around."

Touched that she didn't even have to ask him about the party, she tried to focus on the positives. Xander might be leaving his work on the ranch, but at least he was still thinking of her. Helping her to achieve her dreams. Maybe that boded well for them to enjoy their affair a little while longer, until the flame burned out.

She wasn't sure what to think about his revelation about Rena, let alone how it affected them. She needed time to think about that, too. At times like this, her lack of experience with people felt all the more frustrating. If she hadn't been raised in a vacuum, might she understand Xander better?

"Annabel mentioned the meet and greet. I'd be glad to go with you." That much, she was sure of.

"Then it's a date." He finished his coffee before standing. "I'll let you get to work and I'll tell Len you'll need the day off for the meeting. Can you be ready to leave by noon?"

"For sure." She put a lock on her runaway emotions, struggling to understand where she would fit in his new life now that he'd made a significant career decision. "We can celebrate your future as an oil executive."

It sounded a world away from ranch foreman, a job that had defined the Xander she knew.

Still, she couldn't deny that he seemed happier. Freer. As if he'd made peace with his past and was ready to move on. Frankie felt glad if she'd played a small role in helping him get there. Glad for his sake, anyway.

For her own, she was already feeling him pulling away to embrace the life he was meant to lead. One that didn't include an orphaned, runaway cowgirl with big dreams and an uncertain future.

Frankie had barely made it to the mall before closing after her volunteer shift at the animal shelter, but she'd been determined to buy an outfit worthy of another glitzy Texas Cattleman's Club function.

But the rush to shop—and the sting of parting with the extra cash for an outfit—paid off when she walked into the fancy Haciendas meeting space the next day in her sleek white sheath dress and matching short-sleeved jacket. While she knew without question that Annabel would have helped her in the wardrobe department, it seemed good to have chosen her own clothes. Today, she wasn't the Cinderella beauty she'd been at the gala—a look that wasn't really *her*. In today's smart peep-toe pumps and fitted dress, she felt like the business professional she one day hoped to be.

She'd put her hair in a low ponytail, neat and simple. With a gold bangle on her wrist, she was done accessorizing. And as she glanced around at the other women who attended the meeting and cocktail hour that followed it, Frankie felt she'd done a good job of choosing her outfit. Angela Perry was pretty and understated in a dark-cherry-colored skirt with a lightweight black blouse that had sheer sleeves. Her twin, Melinda, wore a more sophisticated suit that could have come straight off a Paris runway, but it wasn't anything Frankie would have been comfortable wearing.

"You look incredible," Xander whispered in her ear as the formal meeting broke up and the social networking began.

The Haciendas historic property was made up of four buildings just outside downtown. The largest of them served as today's venue. The high cathedral ceilings were made of rich, dark wood, the oiled bronze fans spinning silently overhead. Whitewashed stucco walls and dark wood floors gave the place a Spanish feel echoed in the simple, heavy furnishings. Red hibiscus arrangements were the only pops of color.

"Thank you," Frankie murmured as she helped herself to a glass of seltzer water from a passing waiter while the staff steered the guests onto a large patio addition. Bamboo plants and potted palms lined the walls.

"It's unlike me to splurge on clothes, but if this is my last chance to spend time with the Texas Cattleman's Club for a while—"

"Why would it be the last chance?" Xander asked, his hand briefly touching the small of her back.

He stopped off to the side of the room while the rest of the Texas Cattleman's Club organizing members moved onto the patio that extended outdoors. A bar was set up on the far end of an outdoor garden, and a lone classical guitar player strummed a tune near a wall of live plants. The volume of the party turned up a notch, everyone relieved to have the business part of the day behind them.

Even Sterling Perry seemed content to stay on the opposite side of the room from his rival, Ryder Currin.

Frankie wished she could simply focus on the party and regretted her verbal misstep, since Xander hadn't officially told her that things were over between them. But she wanted to make things easier for him.

For both of them.

"I just mean—I know you're taking the job with Currin Oil, so we won't be seeing each other as much."

His head tipped to one side as he studied her. "Why would you think that?"

She was saved from answering the question when Xander's father, Ryder, appeared over Xander's shoulder.

"Hello, Frankie. I'm sorry to interrupt, but, Xander, I wonder if you would consider keeping an eye on things for a few minutes while I step out to speak to Angela?" Ryder glanced over his shoulder toward where Sterling held court near the bar. "We don't need a repeat of what happened at the Flood Relief Gala."

"Of course." Xander nodded, but he kept his focus on Frankie.

Her belly knotted from nerves. She really didn't want to upset Xander, especially when she'd hoped to use the meet and greet as a chance to network.

"You should introduce Frankie around." Ryder smiled down at her, his blue eyes so like his son's. "I'm sure she'd like the chance to speak to Zane Daughtry. His son is a veterinarian in Galveston, you know."

"I'll do that," Xander assured him, his hand curving possessively around her hip as he shifted closer. "Thanks, Dad."

When Ryder moved away, Frankie peered around the room. "Which one is Zane Daughtry?" she asked, hoping to distract Xander from the conversation they'd been having.

But before Xander could answer, an auburn-haired beauty stopped in front of them, gasping audibly as her eyes met Frankie's.

Noticing the other woman, Xander pasted on his social smile. He greeted the newcomer kindly enough, but his cadence sounded stilted as he spoke. "Good to see you, Abby." He followed the woman's gaze to Frankie, clearly recognizing that Abby stared at her openly. "Have you met Frankie Walsh? Frankie, meet Abigail Langley."

Frankie had the strangest sensation looking at the woman. Abby Langley was probably in her mid-to late-thirties, with long red waves. But the most striking thing about her was that she gaped at Frankie as if she'd seen a ghost.

"How do you do, Ms. Langley?" Frankie said politely, offering her hand.

"Pardon me for staring." The woman's voice was whisper thin before she blinked and continued, louder this time. "That mark on your neck, my dear. I'd swear it's the Langley birthmark."

The floor felt like it opened up beneath Frankie as she absorbed those words. Her hand went to her neck.

"My birthmark?" she repeated, not understanding.

"Most of the women in my family are born with it," Abigail informed her. "And you'd be just the right age. How old are you?"

"I'm sorry. I'm confused." She gripped Xander's free hand, needing it to ward off the faintness she felt as a buzzing started in her ears.

Xander intervened, his tone concerned. "Abby, what are you talking about?"

"Your eyes are just the right shade of green." Abigail still stared at Frankie, to the point their conversation was attracting attention from the rest of the party. "My cousin, Josie Langley, lost her little girl twenty-three years ago in a flood like the one that rocked Houston this spring. And I can't help but notice you bear more than a passing resemblance to Josie. That's why I gasped when I saw you."

Abby Langley pulled her phone from her leather clutch and flipped through screens while Frankie tried to get her head around what she was suggesting.

The room started to spin. The math added up, since

Frankie was indeed twenty-five years old. And her parents had claimed to have found her when she was two.

"You think that I could be—"

Abby flipped her phone around to show Frankie a photo of an attractive woman with dark hair and green eyes. The expression on the brunette's face was familiar because it was the same one Frankie glimpsed in the mirror every day.

The woman in the photograph bore her an uncanny resemblance. An older version of Frankie herself.

"Even without the birthmark, I would have been stunned at your resemblance," Abby said, her hand trembling as she shared the picture. "But considering that distinctive crescent moon on your neck, my dear, I'd say there's an excellent chance that you're the lost Langley heiress."

Ten

An hour later, Xander sat beside Frankie in one of the historic inn's private rooms close to the Texas Cattleman's Club meet and greet. He hadn't known where else to go with her to have an uninterrupted conversation, so he'd flagged down one of the event organizers and requested accommodations.

Frankie had been so pale after the intense encounter with Abigail Langley that he'd been worried about her. Now, they sat in a glassed-in sunroom off the back of a secluded hacienda on the ground floor. They could look out over the meet and greet spilling out onto the inn's private grounds in the larger hacienda nearby, but he didn't think anyone could see into their suite with the way the windows were tinted.

He'd ordered a tray of food from catering, but so

far Frankie hadn't shown any interest in the five-star offerings. She sat on a leather upholstered chair at a heavy hardwood table, her fingers clamped around a mug of tea that she'd accepted from him even though she hadn't taken a single sip. She stared out at the cocktail party going on without them, but her green eyes were unfocused.

"Should we call someone? Your parents, perhaps?" he suggested gently, not wanting to upset her. "If you shared what Abigail told you, maybe they could offer more answers for you. One way or another."

He wasn't sure what he believed about Abby's shocking revelation. While he couldn't deny Frankie bore a resemblance to the Langley relative whose picture he saw on the phone, he also didn't want to get her hopes up. What if Abby's insistence that Frankie was heir to the Langley fortune was born out of the woman's own desire for family? It sounded far-fetched to find a long-lost relative in a crowded cocktail party.

After her pronouncement, Abigail had been ready to arrange for Frankie to have DNA testing, but Xander had asked for some time to digest the news since he'd seen how upset Frankie was. He'd then promptly spirited her away. He would have left the party altogether but that would have necessitated walking through the crowd. The deserted side room offered a speedier, more private respite.

"Why would my adoptive parents start telling me the truth now?" She lifted the mug toward her lips and then hesitated, setting it back on the table, her hands trembling, her voice tight, angry. "I asked them for answers my whole life, and all that ever accomplished was a greater commitment to keeping me isolated from the rest of the world."

Isolated because they were protective? Or because they'd kidnapped her? She had to be wondering the same thing.

"But if they knew about this—about Abby Langley's insistence you're a relative—maybe they could at least give you enough details to explain why that couldn't be true."

If they weren't kidnappers. Although there were other options, like a sketchy adoption with someone else at fault.

"You don't think it's true?" She peered across the table at him where he sat diagonally from her. Her gaze was focused now. Intent. "That I'm this long-lost heiress?"

A candle in the table's centerpiece flickered in the breeze from an overhead fan, the surrounding fresh sunflower blooms rustling slightly.

"That's not what I'm saying. I just meant that your parents might share enough facts to quickly disprove it, and save you from the angst of waiting for DNA test results."

He couldn't help but feel protective of her. Her pain reached out to him, drawing him in and making him hurt for her.

"Or they could hedge, the way they always have, and make me all the more resentful that I lost out on a normal childhood because they were continually worried someone would show up with a better claim to me." She set aside the tea and stood, pacing over to the wall of windows looking out on the cocktail party.

The blue glow of the lighted swimming pool illuminated the garden as the sun set, the landscape spotlights flickering on automatically.

Not sure how to comfort her when he had the same concerns, Xander followed her to stare out over the festivities. He slid an arm around her waist, drawing her against him. She fit there perfectly, her head tucked under his chin. He tipped his cheek against the silky strands of her hair.

"No one can claim you now, though, Frankie," he reassured her. "You are your own woman. Everything you've achieved, you've accomplished on your own. And that's a lot to be proud of."

"But how much easier might it have been with the help of a family?" She edged back a step to look at him. "I've tried to cram a lifetime worth of experiences in the last seven years since I left home, desperate to make up for the way I couldn't do anything as a kid. The ranch work, bronc riding, straight As in school, volunteering my free time at the shelter—I was starving for a taste of the world."

Had their affair been another facet of her attempt to taste the world? The realization stung. He hadn't guessed that about her, although perhaps he should have made the connection. He admired how high-achieving she was, but had her need for experiences come at a price? To both of them?

"No one can take away what you've accomplished," he insisted, wondering if she understood how impressive it was to be on the verge of veterinary school when she'd done it all on her own. "No one can say you got where you are because of your family."

"Maybe I wouldn't have minded some help." Folding her arms, she glared out at the party continuing without them. "The Perrys and the Currins might vie for an advantage over each other, but they're both very sure of their place in the world. Just the name—either name—gives you power."

"You want it to be true." He hadn't been sure of that until now, hearing the edge in her voice. "You *want* to be the Langley heiress, don't you?"

She turned back to him. This time, the pain in her green eyes was startlingly clear.

"Who in their right mind would choose to be an orphan over a woman with family and connections? A family whose powerful name could have given me the kinds of advantages you've had?"

Intellectually, he could see her point. Of course he could.

That didn't mean he was as ready to embrace her future as a Langley. Everything between them would change. Both of their families would take an interest in their relationship. The Langleys and the Currins— two well-known Texas families—would each have a stake in their dating lives. There would be more pressure. More scrutiny.

More of the suffocating atmosphere that had made Rena want to escape from their engagement.

Then again, would a Langley heiress even want to date the Currin who'd been working as a ranch foreman? He hadn't stepped into the Currin Oil CEO role yet. Things were already shifting between them faster than he could keep up.

"My family may have given me advantages," he acknowledged carefully, returning to the catering tray left on the sideboard to escape the naked anguish in her expression. Or was it so that she didn't see his? He wanted to pour himself a drink, but there was nothing but sparkling water and an unopened bottle of champagne on the tray. And this hardly felt like a celebration. He took a deep breath before continuing, "But like you, I've worked hard to get where I am. And you can't deny that you've enjoyed the privileges that come with the Currin name. The access to the Texas Cattleman's Club, for example. The networking for your future."

Giving up on the drink he wanted, Xander pivoted back toward Frankie. She was staring at him as though she was seeing him for the first time, her expression puzzled.

"I have appreciated that, Xander." Her reasonable tone didn't do anything to soothe his sense of things falling apart.

He could feel the thin foundation of their affair crumbling beneath his feet.

"But you won't need my help any longer once you're a Langley, will you?" he pressed, seeing the truth of what being an heiress meant for her. "With your inheritance, you certainly won't need to work on the ranch. You'll have all the backing you'd need for membership in the Texas Cattleman's Club. Hell, Abby's a past president of the Royal branch, so you're in good hands there. She's surely better connected than I am."

He wanted to stop the flow of words, to shut down the certainty that this was the end of them. He knew he was being unfair to her. They didn't even know for sure that she was a Langley. But the thought of losing her like this was tearing him apart. More than it should. And that had him itching to run, far and fast.

"I didn't enter this relationship for the help," she shot back with a fierceness in her tone, revealing that he'd touched a nerve. "If you'll recall, I was ready to buy my own ticket to the gala."

Damn it.

This was not the conversation he should be having with her right now. Especially here, with partyers only a stone's throw away. But right or wrong, they were stuck with this conversation. Consequences be what they may.

"By risking your neck," he reminded her wryly. "I remember. You were prepared to succeed without me then. But now we've shared something, even if it was a fling. I think you owe me at least a goodbye if you're intending to walk away."

"I never said I wanted to end…this." She hugged herself tighter, more beautiful in her simple white dress than any of the socialites draped in jewels and designer outfits mingling at the party that played out through the glass behind her.

"You didn't have to." His chest ached to look at her, so delicate and strong at the same time. "You've been preparing for the end of this affair ever since the first night we spent together. You left that time, Frankie. Not me." The sense of loss closed over him like a dark cloud. Smothering him. He needed to get away from here.

"That's not fair," she told him softly, her green eyes wounded, yet she didn't draw near him.

None of it was fair. That didn't make the hurt any less real.

He backed up a step to retrieve his truck keys from the table. "I'm going to get some fresh air. The room is all yours for the night if you want it."

"I don't." She lobbed the retort his way as he headed for the door.

Of course she didn't want the room. He shouldn't be surprised. Xander didn't have one damned thing left to offer her anymore.

Frankie stared out the sunroom windows of the private hacienda, watching the beautiful party going on without her or Xander.

The sun had fully set since he stormed out of the private lodging, the quiet descending on her like a shroud after their heated exchange. It hadn't been an argument, really. But the darker emotions it had churned in her were volatile enough.

And she knew it had done the same for him. She'd heard it clearly enough in his voice right before he'd walked away.

Not in a million years would she have guessed she could wield the power to hurt Xander Currin, a man she'd viewed as invincible to softer emotions, judging by the revolving door of women he'd dated. But that hadn't been fair of her. She'd assumed that he lacked deeper feelings, when he'd simply locked them away as effectively as she had.

He had been protecting himself after the loss of his fiancée. She'd been protecting herself against the abandonment that had been burned into her nature at a young age. Maybe she should have recognized his kindred spirit, but she'd been so busy worrying about the risk to her own heart she hadn't given enough thought to his.

Now Frankie took in the lush garden setting just outside the window, seeing it without being a part of it. What a perfect metaphor for her whole life. Always on the outside looking in. She'd never had a deep sense of family from the couple who'd raised her. Never had a sense of belonging until she'd come to Currin Ranch, where her "family" was made up of grizzled wranglers and herdsmen. Even there, she'd had different dreams than them, wanting to work with the animals more than the people.

The shock of Abigail Langley's revelation was making her feel even more untethered than usual. Every abandoned child dreamed of unlikely scenarios like this one—a stranger sees beyond the surface to the person she was born to be. But Frankie had outgrown dreams like that long ago, so she wasn't going to get suckered into some fanciful vision of her future.

An heiress.

She couldn't even imagine how radically that would change her life. She wouldn't have to scrimp every cent for veterinary school and for a place of her own one day. Even more importantly, she would be able to afford to focus all her time on her studies instead of working to support herself. That would be…too incredible.

Aside from the obvious benefits of money, Frankie would belong. Xander had a point about not needing him—she would have her own place in the Texas Cattleman's Club. A privileged family who would help her secure that spot.

Yet just because she didn't need Xander didn't mean she wouldn't want him. She feared she would always want him, whether he wanted her or not.

She didn't know how much time she passed staring out at the party, picking through her feelings, but a swish of blond hair outside drew her attention to where Angela Perry and her father were having an intense private conversation beneath a sprawling old live oak tree, hidden from view of the rest of the party. Father and daughter. Family.

As much as Sterling seemed overbearing and far too intrusive in his daughter's life, at least Angela had the certainty that she was deeply loved. The longing for family intensified the ache in Frankie's heart.

Did she want to rejoin the glittering party on the other side of the windows? This time, she would be all alone. No Xander to smooth her way or make introductions.

Should she hold her head up high and force herself into the future? Go back to the party and tell Abigail Langley she'd take the DNA test, even if she didn't understand how she could possibly be a Langley?

It would be easier to hide in the private room Xander had reserved for them, nursing the ache in her chest that burned ever since his parting words. But that had never been in her nature. Xander had been correct about that much. Even if it meant risking her neck, she would forge ahead.

In this case, maybe what she really needed to risk was the piece of her she'd guarded so carefully. The heart that she'd wanted to keep safe from Xander at all costs.

But first, she needed to get some answers about who she was, even if meant going back to Laredo and facing the home she'd run from the moment she'd turned eighteen.

Angela Perry hadn't wanted to confront her father here—at the cocktail reception following the Texas Cattleman's Club planning meeting. But her dad had a way of forcing his own agenda, demanding to speak with her privately unless she wanted another very public showdown.

As if *she'd* been the one to initiate their argument at the Flood Relief Gala.

"I thought I made myself very clear regarding that bastard Ryder Currin," her father fumed, his eyes narrowing. His Stetson and boots were both brand-new, and diamond cufflinks in the shape of horseshoes glittered at his wrists.

Her father was a very different man from Ryder.

Angela clutched her purse tighter, mindful of eyes all around them, even if they were tucked behind the trunk of an old live oak. The landscape lighting kept the garden area in a golden glow as the temperature dropped enough for more people to venture outside in the June heat. Strategically placed outdoor fans kept air circulating.

"You made it clear you'd rather be unreasonable than listen to what I have to say." Angela's eyes found Ryder on the other side of the party, his dark Stetson a perfect complement to his jeans and jacket.

His ease in his own skin had always attracted her. He'd never needed anything flashy for himself, and she liked that about him. She wasn't going to pretend otherwise for her father's sake.

"Are you aware of the rumors?" Sterling demanded, the cords in his neck standing out visibly as his anger ratcheted up.

"I am," she told him defiantly, shifting position on her heels so they didn't sink into the soft earth. "I know about the alleged affair with Mom, and I don't believe it for a minute. I know you don't, either, or you would have settled that with Mom long ago."

Sterling wasn't the kind of man who would take that offense lying down. Angela's mother must have been able to prove her innocence. Or else Sterling had never had a shred of evidence to begin with. Angela wasn't going to let a whisper campaign prevent her from finding happiness with Ryder.

"Ryder Currin has tried to undermine me my whole life." He pointed at her with the tip of his longneck bottle. "Do you really think you mean anything more to him than as a tool to weaken Perry Holdings?"

Angela tried to ignore the hurt that came with the words—the implication that she meant nothing to Ryder.

"I believe I have more appeal than that, Dad. And I also believe I'm too important to Perry Holdings for you to dismiss me just because you don't want me to have a relationship with Ryder. My personal life is my business. Not yours."

Her father looked ready to explode with anger. Angela debated walking away before he could respond, but she knew that would only delay the inevitable confrontation. Besides, there were two men in poorly fitting suits headed their way. Something about them appeared off, alerting her they didn't belong here. One of them was gray-haired and grizzled. The other tall, thin, with a clean-shaven face that made him look like he was barely out of college.

A handful of party guests turned to watch their progress through the crowd toward Angela and her father. As they neared, one of them pulled out a badge.

The police.

"Dad," she said, keeping her voice low. "We have company." Then, to the closest police officer, she asked, "What's going on?"

Sterling turned to see the men, then stepped closer to Angela. "I'm sure it's just about the body at the TCC renovation site," he reassured her.

A bad feeling made her stomach sink. The officers didn't look friendly. And their attention was fixed firmly on her father.

"Sterling Perry?" the gray-haired shorter of the pair asked, shoving his badge back inside his jacket pocket.

"Yes," her father answered.

A glint of metal distracted her and she realized in

slow-motion horror that the younger officer withdrew a pair of handcuffs.

"Sterling Perry, you're under arrest for conspiracy to commit fraud. You have the right to remain silent—"

The rest of the words were lost on Angela in her shock. Stunned, she struggled to take in the pandemonium around her. Her father began shouting that he was innocent even as the handcuffs went around his wrists. Angela's knees turned to liquid under her. Stumbling forward, she felt blindsided as the arresting officer continued to read a laundry list of charges that made it sound like her father had masterminded a Ponzi-style scheme.

What the hell? She hadn't even known he was under criminal investigation. All her anger at him from earlier in the evening evaporated as she saw him in handcuffs. He was her father and this couldn't be true.

Beside her, her twin sister, Melinda, suddenly appeared, linking hands with her and squeezing so tightly her fingers went numb.

"Why is this happening?" She glanced over at Melinda. Her twin was usually so unflappable, but her viselike grip relayed her own disconcerted feelings.

"I don't know, but I'm afraid it's going to get worse before it gets better," she said softly, careful not to be overheard. "Once investors get wind of this, they will start to panic, wanting to sell their shares."

Melinda didn't have to spell out what that meant. Widespread fear for their finances would result in too many shareholders trying to cash in at once. Which meant a whole lot of good people could go broke, even if her father wasn't guilty.

* * *

I staked out an excellent view of Sterling Perry's dramatic exit. Of course, it was easy to put myself in a good position since I may have leaked a few things to the police. When Ryder and Angela didn't have quite the splashy public breakup I was hoping for, I will admit I began getting antsy for things to start happening.

Having Sterling behind bars will do wonders for my plan. Public opinion will shift quickly now. People who held Sterling in such high regard are sure to turn on him overnight. What perfect punishment for him, considering how quickly my life went up in flames because of Sterling Perry and Ryder Currin.

I remember all too well how that felt. How it still feels. My lost family. My lost wealth and privilege. Sure, I'd salvaged the pretense of reasonable success, but it was nothing compared to my old life.

Seeing Angela and Melinda now, holding hands while they worry about their precious father, reminds me how I have no children in my life to worry about me. I hate that Sterling has that kind of support. Even as I celebrate seeing him taken away by the police, I regret that I can't yank everything out from under him all at once.

Patience.

Strolling out of the gardens, I step inside the main building into the cool air-conditioning. It's better not to get overheated or overzealous about the revenge scheme. One thing at a time, and I need to be satisfied with the progress I make each day toward my re-

*venge. Because rushing the agenda only adds a risk to
getting caught.*

And I refuse to let that happen.

From the opposite side of the garden, Xander saw
Sterling being taken away in handcuffs.

He'd lingered outside the suite he'd obtained for
Frankie, knowing he should figure out a way through
their problems. Yet before he could come up with the
right words to say to her that might smooth things over,
the police had arrived to cart Sterling off the property.
An absolute disaster of an evening from start to finish.

Even now from his vantage point near the outdoor
bar, Xander could see Frankie silhouetted in the sunroom window by the candlelight behind her, the white
dress making her easier to see. Then again, his eyes
would be drawn to her anywhere, anytime.

His lungs constricted around a breath while the Texas
Cattleman's Club party dissolved into tense conversations, panicked phone calls and a sea of gossip. The
anxiety of seeing Sterling being taken away was affecting everyone—friend and foe alike. Xander knew
he should check in with his father, who might have his
hands full comforting Angela in the aftermath of this
latest adversity. But he couldn't quite tear his gaze from
Frankie when he knew she must be in shock over Abigail Langley's revelations.

Whether or not she was the missing heiress, Frankie
deserved his support. Yet he couldn't forget how completely she'd withdrawn from him afterward. Just like
Rena had.

It would haunt him forever that he hadn't seen the signs of his fiancée's unhappiness before her untimely death. He'd never had the chance to find out why she'd broken things off so suddenly, and he had been completely unaware that she'd wanted to end it. Now, in the first significant relationship he'd had since then—the first relationship that really meant something to him—he'd missed the bigger picture once again.

Wrestling with his conscience about walking away, he knew he needed to talk to Frankie. When his cell phone vibrated in his jacket pocket, he felt a moment's hope that she'd reached out to him. Checking the screen, however, he saw a text from his father.

We need to meet. Now.

Damn it. The whole Texas Cattleman's Club community would feel the reverberations of Sterling's arrest. Xander understood he needed to help his father put out fires.

Maybe it was best that he and Frankie take time to think through things after their exchange anyhow. For tempers to calm. He'd talk to her once cooler heads prevailed.

And even as he told himself that, Xander suspected he was just avoiding the truth of what his gut was telling him—that he'd already fallen in love with Frankie and he was scared as hell she would never love him back.

Eleven

Four days after the party, Xander still hadn't seen Frankie. He'd left her a message that he hoped to see her, but didn't want to pressure her. Especially since he'd been the one to walk out on a night that must have been devastating for her.

He regretted that deeply, even as he knew he would while it was all unfolding. But he hadn't been ready for Abby Langley's surprise announcement, let alone what it meant for his future with Frankie.

If there was such a thing. He might have destroyed any chance he had for a future with her by not putting her first when she needed him most.

Giving in and rapping on the door to her cabin, he figured she must be avoiding him. He'd been working almost nonstop since the Texas Cattleman's Club planning meeting, the fallout from Sterling's arrest spilling over into the new Houston branch as members questioned whether Sterling belonged in the club.

That work had taken up much of Ryder's time, giving Xander more work with Currin Oil. His father was thrilled to have him in the office, and Xander was glad he was finally stepping into the role he'd always planned to have with the company. Especially since he knew his second-in-command on the ranch would finally have a chance to test out the foreman role. But it meant he hadn't been on the ranch to see Frankie.

"Frankie," he called as he knocked a second time.

The only sound he heard in response was a raven cawing at him from her porch rail. Overhead, the late-afternoon sun beat down with an oppressive heat.

"She's out of town, boss," a man's voice called to him from the grassy ranch road.

Xander turned to see Reggie Malloy, the longtime member of the Currin Ranch team who'd been there the night of the rodeo when Xander had talked Frankie out of competing.

"Out of town?" Xander stepped off the small porch of the cabin, heading down the path toward the dirt road where Reggie sat on a spotted Appaloosa.

"She asked Len for a couple of personal days. Said something about going to see her folks in Laredo, I heard." Reggie tipped his hat up, mopping his forehead with the sleeve of his work shirt.

No surprise that Reggie knew about the trip, since word spread fast in a small community like theirs. Len, Xander's second-in-command, oversaw more of the personnel concerns. What bugged Xander was that he hadn't heard a thing about it. Why would she risk a confrontation with her parents by herself? Damn it, he knew he should have checked on her sooner. In giving her time to cool off, had he pushed her away completely?

He hated the idea that she would see her parents alone after all this time.

But he'd lost the right to weigh in on those decisions when he'd walked away from her after the meet and greet. The need to be with her, to lend whatever support he could, was so strong he wanted to get in his truck now and start driving. Lost in his own thoughts, he was surprised when Reggie spoke up again.

"Do you think it's true she's going to turn out to be the lost Langley heiress?" The saddle creaked under Reggie as he shifted his weight. "We heard what happened at the Texas Cattleman's Club meeting—about Abigail Langley recognizing that birthmark."

"I'm not sure what to believe." Xander's gut told him it was probably true; however, he didn't want to speculate about her when she wasn't involved in the conversation.

He knew she'd probably already made her decision about whether or not to submit a DNA test, but he hoped to at least speak to her before she got the results back, if that was the route she'd chosen. He needed to assure her it didn't matter to him what the results said—that he wanted her in his life no matter what.

Reggie grinned from atop the Appaloosa. "Hard to imagine that one of the toughest hands on the payroll might turn out to be as good as Texas royalty. But we told her she's got a place with us forever either way."

Clicking softly to his horse, the herd driver set the Appaloosa in motion, leaving Xander there alone with his thoughts.

It didn't speak well of him that the staff of Currin Ranch all knew exactly what to say to Frankie when she'd been confronted with a dramatic revelation about her birth, whereas Xander had put his foot in his mouth and left her to face the consequences alone.

But he intended to fix that. Right now.

Tossing her rubber apron in a bin outside the back door of a local veterinary practice, Frankie went inside to scrub off the day of volunteer work in the field. She'd put in almost eight hours with Doc Macallan in the mobile veterinary van, visiting sick calves, a wounded horse and one very unhappy pig with an infected hoof. The vet lived on the property, in a farmhouse nearby, and had already retreated to his home for the evening, hoping to leave for a fishing trip as soon as he cleaned up.

She was on her second round of antibacterial soap up to her elbows when her phone chimed with a text message. She glanced over at the counter above the sink, where she could see the sender's name.

Xander.

Her chest ached and she found her eyes reading the text before she could debate the wisdom of it.

Flying to Laredo ASAP. Please wait to speak to your parents until I can be there.

Surprised, she dried her hands quickly.

The parting with Xander might have hurt, but that didn't mean she wanted him to waste a flight. Two of the other clinic staffers had left for the day, leaving her alone at the practice with the vet's niece, who was playing with a kitten one of their clients had found abandoned by the highway and decided to keep.

Just like me, Frankie thought wryly. She'd been adopted into a strange home, too. Except the family who'd found her hadn't wanted to look too closely at the truth of where she'd come from. They'd hidden her away from the world on purpose, to prevent her real family from finding her.

And now she had the DNA test results back that proved in no uncertain terms she was a Langley. The confidential letter from the laboratory had been waiting for her when she'd returned from Laredo. Abigail Langley had paid extra to rush the results, but she'd been kind enough to have the correspondence shipped solely to Frankie so she could have time to think about how she wanted to handle the information.

She still hadn't decided.

Settling into one of the break room chairs near the coffeepot, Frankie typed a response to Xander while the weariness of the day caught up with her. Ranch hand work took a physical toll, but her efforts with the animals took an emotional one. Even the victories in the field could be tiring, as frantic owners worried about their pets and distressed animals needed soothing. As she let the exhaustion roll over her, she tried to contain the spark of hopefulness she felt at hearing from Xander.

Not in Laredo anymore. Finishing shift at Macallan Clinic.

She guessed he must have learned her whereabouts from one of the guys at Currin Ranch, since the other ranch hands were the only people who'd known she'd wanted to go home this week. She hadn't wanted to hear the DNA test results until she'd given her parents an opportunity to tell her the truth.

Not that she'd had any luck.

The next text was almost immediate.

Please don't leave. I'd like to speak to you.

To call it quits for good? To tell her he'd had time to think it over and he was more certain than ever that they weren't a good match? Those were her fears. But her hopes were quite different. She'd missed him these last several days while she'd been finding the courage to speak to him.

Okay.

She hit Send on the message, unable to say more than that when her feelings were in knots. She'd been so busy indulging her crush on Xander—so determined to squeeze all the pleasure out of a relationship with him— that she'd missed the chance to really get to know him.

To understand him.

To find common ground.

So now that their relationship was falling apart, she didn't have a clear idea how to talk to him about the things that mattered. About those hopes and fears of hers.

She guessed he had plenty of his own, too. Maybe she'd be able to see them now that she'd stopped viewing him as an unattainable hottie and started looking at him as a man.

A smart, caring, generous man, who'd extended himself to help her even when she hadn't been able to give him anything in return. No matter what else came of their relationship, she owed him a debt of gratitude for the connections she'd made within the Texas Cattleman's Club. The access to more potential references for veterinary school. The possibility of new volunteering opportunities that would give her the hours she needed to work with animals.

But what she still craved was *him*.

The anguish in her heart this week hadn't really been rooted in the DNA test results or her choices about her future with her family or career. All the pain had been over losing Xander. She had the courage to face a lot of challenges, it seemed, but the thought of life without Xander had the power to bring her to her knees.

When the knock sounded on the back door of the clinic, Frankie felt an answering thump of her heartbeat. Spearing to her feet, she hurried out of the break room to open the door.

Xander stood on the top step, wearing jeans and a

gray jacket, his dark Stetson shielding his face from
the late-afternoon sun. The frisson of awareness that
jolted her was familiar by now, but it amazed her that it
never seemed to fade. She realized that she'd been kid-
ding herself to think an affair might quench her thirst
for this man. The more time she spent with him, the
more she wanted him.

The deeper she fell in love with him.

She understood that now.

Behind him, the vet's rural practice had an almost-
empty parking area except for his truck and the vet's
mobile treatment van. Nearby pens held some of the
large animals that were recovering from surgery. A couple of older horses munched their hay while a solitary
ostrich squawked unhappily in an enclosure of her own.

"Hi." Frankie stood on the threshold, her gaze greed-
ily soaking Xander in after the days spent apart. Longing pierced her heart. "You got here fast."

She wondered what he was thinking behind those
very blue eyes. She'd always known that he wouldn't
stay in her life, but she hadn't recognized how much it
would devastate her when he left. Thinking about the
mystery of her birth these last few days had been—for
once in her life—a welcome distraction from thinking
about Xander.

From wishing she knew how to fix things between
them.

"I was halfway to the private airstrip to take a flight
to Laredo," he admitted. He turned to look out over
the vet's small farm. "Is there anywhere we can speak
privately?"

"Sure." She waved goodbye to the vet's niece before she closed and locked the door behind them, nervous and agitated. Scared, even, that she'd screwed things up irreparably. "There's a spot back here if you don't mind walking for a few minutes."

It was still hot outside, but Xander had spent long hours on the ranch in the Texas summer. She led them past the hog pen and donkey barn where Doc Macallan kept his own collection of animals. A rural windmill turned overhead, aerating a pond kept stocked with fish.

A few moments later, Xander must have caught sight of their destination—a round tent permanently erected on a wooden platform among the pine trees. A small deck extended from the front entrance, where a pair of Adirondack chairs sat side by side.

"A yurt?" Xander glanced from the tent to her. It was a fleeting moment of shared amusement that made her wonder if she'd ever feel this connection to any human being again.

The amusement vanished.

"The vet calls it his retreat space." She'd visited the spot to have her lunch sometimes when the weather was cooler. "He left town for a long weekend, though, so it's all ours."

Xander followed her up the narrow steps to the deck under the shade of dense pine trees. She took a seat in one of the Adirondack chairs and Xander lowered himself into the other. He sat forward, though, on the edge of the chair, looking at her intently. He removed his hat and slid it on the wood railing along one side of the deck.

"First of all, I'm sorry you made that trip back home by yourself." The sincerity in his voice was unmistakable, but then, he was a kind, thoughtful person. "How did it go?"

Birds argued in the trees overhead, shaking a few needles down onto the soft earth. And Frankie was only too glad to talk about something besides the ashes of their relationship.

She seized on the topic gladly.

"I didn't learn anything." She'd made the decision to go impulsively, not wanting to call ahead to alert them to her arrival. "At least, not about my past. When I arrived at the home where I grew up, someone else was living there. Turns out my parents put that place on the market two months after I left home."

It had hurt to know they'd pulled up stakes so quickly. Not that they could have gotten in touch with her to tell her anyhow, since she'd changed her number deliberately to give herself space from their controlling ways. But their quick departure had told her they hadn't been concerned about keeping the house in case she wanted to return one day.

"You didn't get to see them?"

"No." She'd felt foolish when she got there. "I couldn't decide if I was relieved or disappointed that I drove five hours for nothing. I'm still not sure how I feel about that, but the fact is, I have no idea where to find them."

"A private investigator could track them quickly enough," he volunteered, shrugging out of the suit jacket and laying it over the arm of the chair.

She followed his movements, watching the play of muscle through the white cotton shirt. Wishing she still had the right to take shelter in his strong arms. But they'd lost themselves in physical attraction too many times, failing to build the deeper connection that might have helped them weather the last tumultuous week.

Had she lost that right forever?

Tension and wariness strung her nerves tight.

"I'm not sure that I want to contact them." She'd had a long time to think about it on the drive back to Houston and still wasn't sure of her next step where her adoptive parents were concerned. But she would phone the authorities and give a statement about what had happened so there was an official record of it. "I only made the trip because I thought it would be wise to give my parents an opportunity to come clean before I found out the results of the DNA test."

His mouth compressed into a flat line. Because he disagreed with her decision not to track her adoptive family? Or because he didn't think she should take the DNA test?

"Has Abigail Langley been in contact with you?" he asked, the question not revealing his thoughts.

"I spoke to her the night of the party—after Sterling's arrest—and agreed to go through with the test." Frankie had known she'd never get any sleep until she addressed the problem, and that meant finding out the truth one way or another. "I've asked her not to share the results with anyone for a few more days, even though she generously paid an exorbitant fee for rushed results."

Xander went still. Only the sound of a distant tractor and a few chirping birds broke the silence.

"You already know the results?" His dark eyebrows lifted.

"I do." She was still struggling to come to terms with the fact that she had parents out there she'd never met. A sister, too. Would her return to their family cause them upheaval or happiness? "You're the first person I've told. The first to know besides Abby and me that I'm a Langley."

She'd called Abigail after opening the letter to inform her, feeling that she deserved to know firsthand.

His hand clamped hers tightly, squeezing. "Frankie, I couldn't be happier for you."

The warmth of the words and the sentiment behind them were a welcome relief. She hadn't realized she'd been holding her breath until it huffed out in a sigh.

"Really? I wasn't sure how you'd react." Her gaze darted to where their hands remained clasped.

A friendly, empathetic gesture? Or could it mean more than that? Her nerves were stretched thin. The thought of losing him for good was killing her inside.

"I know I didn't express myself well the other night when we talked about it." He shook his head, regret tingeing his words. "What I was trying to say—while doing a poor job of it—was that you are an incredible person no matter your name. But knowing how difficult your childhood must have been, I'm happy that you will be surrounded by a very worthy family from now on. I've never met Abigail's cousin, but if Abby is any indication of the kind of family you come from, rest assured, you'll be very loved."

His words cheered her. Made her hopeful that he wouldn't turn his back on their friendship even if he wasn't ready to embrace a deeper relationship.

But she wanted it all. His heart. His love.

Xander.

"Thank you." The restraint of not talking about them was starting to wear on her, her control fracturing as her voice caught. "That means a lot to me."

Nodding, she cleared her throat. Tried to get a hold of herself so she didn't fall apart in front of him.

Was she just delaying the inevitable?

"I'm surprised you aren't more eager to share the news with the world, though." He released his hold on her, making her very aware of the absence of his touch. "Is there any reason you don't want to tell people yet?"

"I'm still navigating what it means for me, so I'm not sure I'm ready to field the questions about what I'll do next." Tucking her feet under her seat, she looked out over the animal pens and picturesque old farm where she'd been volunteering for months, unwilling to think about what a life without Xander would look like. "Do I want to build a mixed practice like Doc Macallan? Specialize in large-animal medicine? Or forsake it all and go into a life of philanthropy now that I'm the heir to a fortune? What kind of obligation do I have to a family who mourned a lost child for twenty-three years?"

Of course, none of those worries mattered half as much as the one she didn't speak. The one she couldn't speak.

Sliding his chair closer, he draped an arm around her, squeezing her shoulder.

"Frankie, your first obligation is to yourself." He comforted her with his physical presence, and with his words even more so. "I know the Langley family, and they would be saddened to think they caused you a moment's unhappiness after all you've been through."

"I'm not unhappy." She didn't want to sound ungrateful. Part of her whole decision to wait with the news was so that she could avoid revealing the confusing mix of emotions. "The news is better than I ever could have hoped for. But after spending a lifetime feeling like I didn't fit in with my adoptive parents, I just don't want to be a disappointment to a new family."

"You could never be a disappointment." His assurance warmed her, soothing the mix of fears that had been dogging her ever since she learned the good news. "More than anything, I wish I could have articulated that at the party the other night instead of letting my own concerns get in the way."

Bracing herself, she straightened, needing to be alert for this part of the conversation. She didn't want to misunderstand him or what was happening between them.

She also wanted to be very, very clear about what she hoped for. What she wanted.

"I think I was in a state of shock at the party," she admitted, remembering feeling distant from everything going on around her that night. "I didn't express myself well, either."

He let out a gusty sigh that she hoped was relief. If

so, it could be a sign that he cared about saving this relationship, too.

"Do you mind if we have a rewind then? Go back and fix some of the things that didn't come out the right way?" He studied her, his arm sliding away again.

"I'd like that." She needed this second chance. She was determined not to waste it.

"When Rena broke off our engagement, I never found out why—not really. And I've avoided relationships since then because it made me wary that I couldn't see the signs when things were falling apart."

The simple truth made sense in retrospect. It certainly explained the endless parade of women before her. But at the time, it had felt like he'd been pulling away. As she stared down at her feet, trying to collect her thoughts, a chipmunk dived headfirst into a hole in the wooden decking.

"I didn't want to end things between us," she told Xander honestly, remembering the hurt and confusion of that conversation. "You were right that I've been bracing myself for the end, but only because I assumed you'd move on eventually and I didn't want you to take my heart with you when that happened."

This time, she gathered her courage and reached out to him. Taking his hand between both of hers, she held it tight, wishing she could impress upon him how much she still wanted things to work out.

"Xander," she continued, wanting to get it all out on the table before she lost her nerve. "All that time, I'd been thinking my heart was this tangible thing I could decide to give you or not. But I realized this week that

I've had absolutely no control over it—no matter what I told myself. And as it turns out, I gave it to you that first night in the pool house."

The risk of revealing herself to him was the scariest thing she'd ever done. Bronc riding hadn't even been a close second. She held her breath, waiting for him to say something.

"You're telling me that I already have your heart?" His fingers flexed beneath hers, squeezing against her palm.

"I am." She nodded, nervous and anxious, but knowing that Xander deserved to hear those words from her.

Even if he didn't return the feeling.

"In that case…" He rose out of his chair and pulled her to her feet. Before she knew it, his arms were around her waist while they stood toe to toe. "I'm going to promise to take the best care of it." He kissed her cheek with a whisper-soft brush of his lips. "And I'm going to give you my heart in return, along with all my love."

Her lips parted in surprise, her heart pounding wildly.

But before she could ask for clarification on those points, his mouth was on hers, kissing her as if they had all the time in the world. As if this kiss was the most important thing that Xander Currin had to think about.

For a moment, she lost herself in that sweet dance of tongues and lips, the sensual draw pulling her in deeper. Making her hungry for more.

Then she recalled they'd gotten in trouble in the past from letting desire carry them away. Edging back, she tipped her face up to his.

"Can you repeat that last part, please?" Blinking away some of the dizzying chemistry, she focused on his eyes.

A warm, wicked laugh escaped him.

"Gladly." His words were a warm rumble against her skin, reverberating in his chest where the sound originated. "I said I love you, Frankie Walsh. Or Francesca Langley. No matter what name you go by, no matter your past. I love you when you're a muddy cowgirl, a studious vet school candidate or a breathtaking society beauty. Every facet of you mesmerizes me."

There was no answer for how deeply his words touched her. How very loved he made her feel by caring about those different aspects of her world.

So she kissed him again, with all the hope and longing in her soul. She kissed him until her knees were weak and she felt light-headed from the sweetness and sultriness of their bodies pressed together.

"Is it crazy to fall in love so fast?" she asked, even though she knew she'd been falling for him all year long. Her eyes had followed him everywhere, observing him every day, and she'd fantasized about him every night.

She might have started out with a crush, dreaming of an idealized version of Xander. But she knew him now. And loved him even more.

"Other people only dream of finding a love that feels like this," he said against the top of her head, kissing her hair. "So I'm not going to call it crazy. I'm going to say we're very, very lucky."

"Me, too." Her heart smiled, the knowledge that

he was right filling her up inside. Making her happier than she'd ever been before. "Can we go home together now?"

She wanted this man all to herself for days on end.

"We can go anywhere you want," he promised, retrieving his Stetson and his jacket before he drew her forward into their future. "We've got a lot to talk about."

Her feet hurried on the path that led to his truck and, eventually, back to Currin Ranch.

"We do." She wrapped her arm around his waist, tucking her hand into his back pocket. "But I think we should ease into all that conversation. Intersperse it with a lot of kissing…and things."

His hand squeezed her hip, a warm, delectable weight against her. "I can only drive so fast to get us home," he reminded her as they strode past the donkeys, pigs and goats.

"Right. We'd better stick to just talking until then." She tipped her head against his shoulder, full of hope and perfect contentment. "You can tell me what animals you like best since I'm envisioning a life surrounded by them."

She liked the vet's rural practice where he saw every kind of animal imaginable.

"As long as I get you in the bargain, it doesn't matter." Xander held open the passenger-side door for her and she climbed inside the big pickup truck.

"So you're saying you're open to an ostrich?" The exotic bird was still squawking loudly, driving the older horses to the far side of their pen to keep space between them.

"For you, I'd consider it." Xander leaned over in the truck to kiss her again, making her forget what they'd been talking about. "But maybe let's start with a dog and see what happens."

Buckling in, Frankie couldn't stop smiling. She had the man she loved by her side and a future sparkling with possibilities. It seemed romance was very much alive and well after all.

And she planned to do everything in her power to make sure it stayed that way.

* * * * *

COMING SOON!

We really hope you enjoyed reading this book. If you're looking for more romance, be sure to head to the shops when new books are available on

Thursday 13th June

To see which titles are coming soon, please visit

millsandboon.co.uk/nextmonth

LET'S TALK
Romance

For exclusive extracts, competitions
and special offers, find us online:

[f] facebook.com/millsandboon

[twitter] @MillsandBoon

[instagram] @MillsandBoonUK

Get in touch on 01413 063232

For all the latest titles coming soon, visit
millsandboon.co.uk/nextmonth

JOIN THE
MILLS & BOON
BOOKCLUB

* **FREE** delivery direct to your door

* **EXCLUSIVE** offers every month

* **EXCITING** rewards programme

50% OFF
YOUR FIRST
PARCEL

ANNIE BURROWS

The Marquess
TAMES
His Bride

MILLS & BOON
HISTORICAL

Alison Roberts
The Doctor's Wife
FOR KEEPS

Best Surprise for the
ITALIAN DOC

MILLS & BOON
MEDICAL

Tara Pammi
BOUGHT
with the
ITALIAN'S RING

MILLS & BOON

Join today at
Millsandboon.co.uk/Bookclub